GOODE TO BE BAD

GOODE GIRLS

Jasinda Wilder

ONE

———— ❧❧❧ ————

Lexie

LISTENING TO SOMEONE TALK ON THE PHONE IS JUST plain annoying, especially when you're out shopping or in a restaurant, but I had to admit that even my short attention span was pretty engaged with the one-sided conversation I could hear from my spot on the sofa. Apart from being impossible to ignore, it was not your everyday exchange. How often do you hear your boyfriend talk about buying a jet?

"No, Mick, listen, I don't want a stupid Learjet. I don't fly anywhere near enough for it to be worth shelling out twenty-some million. I ain't that fuckin' flush yet, my man." Myles was on the phone with his manager and his money guy. "Yeah, I get that I can take out a loan, but I'm not throwing that kinda money around for fucking shits and giggles. And Tony—you're my money manager. I figured you'da been on the other side of this argument...a *what?* Cirrus? Show me." He pulled the phone away from his ear, put it on speaker, and flicked through photos. "Fuck that. It's goofy looking. I'm not cheap, you know that. If I'm gonna spend money on something, I'm gonna do it right. I'm just saying I'm not sold on the need for a private jumbo jet or whatever the fuck you're pitching. I want to get to Alaska without flying commercial. That's it. Why not charter something?" He winced. "I don't know what I'm doing long term, guys. I don't. I'm sorry. I'm not planning beyond the overseas leg of this tour...because, Mick, I got a feeling shit is changing for me. Not going into details because I ain't got details. But yes, I do imagine it will entail more time here in Texas."

I was on his couch—our couch—in his...our... condo in Dallas. How complicated. It was his—I owned nothing. But I had a key, half his closet, and the place felt like mine. Which was the scary fucking part.

I waved my arms to get his attention and said, "Let's just fly commercial, Myles."

He shook his head, not even looking at me. "No, babe. You don't get it. I can't."

"You're too famous, huh?" I knew I sounded snarky, but I was feeling irritated. "We can just skip the trip."

He glared at me. "We're going to Alaska. I'm meeting your mom and sister, and you're spilling your guts. It's happening."

"There's no reason for you to spend millions of dollars on this dumb trip."

He muted the phone and came over and sat beside me. "Mick and Tony have been after me to get a plane for a while now. The crew and equipment drive around like usual, but the band and I travel separately in the tour bus. I've been resisting the whole flying bit. I like being on the road. I like the bus. I like being with the crew, hanging out, partying with them. Also, I'm kinda cheap, and jets are big money."

"I know you're, like, doing really well, but can you really afford a twenty-million-dollar jet?" I wasn't sure I wanted to know the answer.

He shrugged. "I could get…well, Tony, my wealth manager, says I could get an essentially unlimited line of credit. He's got fancy ways of talking about finances and finagling things. I don't like thinking about money, honestly. I'm like Crow in that regard—I don't think that putz has a clue how much he's worth—how much I've paid him over the years, or how well his wealth manager has done for him.

I've always had Tony look over Crow's finances once a year, just to be sure things are on the up-and-up. I still do, even though he's out on his own now—best thing he ever did was leaving the band."

"How well off is he?" I ask.

"He's a New York real estate tycoon and he don't even know it, or at least not the extent of his holdings or how much they're netting him." He snorts. "Plus he's pulling in thirty-five percent of the royalties my songs earn. *Our* songs, I should say. I get thirty, fifteen goes to the other guys in the band, and the rest goes back into our company. I was with a big-name label for the first few years, but they wanted to push me more commercial, more pop-flavored and we weren't fuckin' having *any* of that, so we started our own label. I've got all of Dad and Grampa's music, meaning I own the rights to their entire combined estates and everything, and someday I'm going to remaster and rerelease their stuff. Do some covers of it, shit like that."

He glanced down at his phone.

"Oh shit, I forgot I had them on mute." He unmuted the phone. "Sorry, fellas."

"I got other clients, Myles," Tony said, his voice deep and gruff and Brooklyn-accented. "I don't have time to sit around on hold."

"Sorry, sorry." Myles sighed. "Okay. I'll give you five million to play with. Whether you buy something outright or use it as down payment on something fancy, I don't care. But don't pauper me on this, yeah? I don't need a twenty-passenger fuckin' airliner. I ain't Kanye or Jay-Z. Small, luxurious, fast. Nice. But not ostentatious and glitzy."

Tony sighed. "Fine, sounds good. When do you need it by?"

"Yesterday, I guess. I want to be up in Alaska by Wednesday, I might as well get it sooner than later since I gotta be in Japan by the end of the week after, and then we've got the international tour after that. Might as well travel in style."

"It's a short order, but I got it." Tony tapped away at a keyboard on his end of the line. "I'll have something for you in a day or two. I'll send you a package to look over." A pause. "You want a full crew?"

"Like flight attendants?" Myles said. "Nah. Just stocked with the same kind of stuff my bus would have. I can take care of myself, and so can the guys. I do want a full cockpit crew, though, and the best available. I ain't crashing because a half-rate pilot got tired and had no backup."

"Smart. Heard some stories, I'll tell ya."

Myles snorted. "Yeah, me too. Scared me shitless. Make sure the pilots are vetted ten ways to Sunday. Perfect records, lots of flight time. I want Jesus himself flying that jet, yeah?"

"I got you, Myles. Flying out of Dallas?"

"For now, yeah. I'll let you know if and when that changes. First flight will be Dallas to Ketchikan as soon as it can be arranged, so make sure that gets filed and we're ready to go the second the jet and the pilots are ready."

"Will do. Okay, boss, I'll talk to you in Tokyo, if not before."

I waited for Myles to end the call, and then he turned to me and I said, "So. You bought a jet?"

He laughed. "Not quite yet. Knowing Tony, he's gonna ignore me and get me something stupid. As long as I can afford it, I guess it's fine. He knows I don't like debt, so he won't go too bonkers. Hopefully."

I laughed. "You just gave him five million dollars to spend. That's bonkers."

"Nah, jets are stupid expensive. Especially if you want to fly international, which I do. But I only need it big enough for the band, and maybe a few extras. Ten-person max, I'd say. Tony ain't stupid, and he knows my taste."

I sighed. "Five million dollars."

He shook his head. "Don't wig out about it, Lex. It's just money. I'd be doing this gig if I was still in a beat-up old church van hauling my gear in a trailer. I don't mind admitting I like the fame most of the time, and the money all the time, but I ain't fixated on it. I'm just me."

"How much *are* you worth?" I asked out of curiosity. Getting to know Myles over the past couple of months, I never saw him be stupid with money, nor flaunt it in gaudy or ostentatious ways.

He shrugged. "Ten? Fifteen? I don't know. I had Tony take a big percentage of my income and invest it from the very beginning, so that if this gig ever fizzles out, or some sort of crazy shit happens, I'll be okay. He's a wizard with money, so he's done really well by me. I still give him at least fifty percent of my total net income after taxes to invest, and I try to live off of twenty-five percent or less, putting the rest into savings. So I've banked a lot, and invested a lot, in diverse areas—real estate, stocks, shit like that. I'm part owner of a minor league baseball club here in Dallas, and I've got a few used car lots, a handful of strip malls, some condo buildings. Lots of business, lots of diversity, lots of various streams of income, so if my music stops earning, I'll have income."

"Smart." I gestured at the building. "So what about this condo building?"

He grinned. "I own it. Actually, I bought the land it's on, and invested in the builder who built it, and funded the project. I didn't design this condo itself, and I never planned on living here full-time, so it's not *mine*, in that sense. It's just a penthouse condo and it hasn't sold to anyone else yet so, until it does, I use it as a home base when I'm in town. If it sells, I'll use one of the others. And actually, my local real estate guy says he's got somebody sniffing around."

"So just from music, how much would you be worth?"

He frowned. "I dunno. Not that much, but not chump change."

"Must not be if five million dollars for a jet is something you can do."

He nodded. "It's an investment. I'm gonna lease the bus to another act, and when I'm not using the jet I'll charter it out and make bank on it. Might even end up with another one and run a little line out of the DFW airport."

I shook my head, laughing. "I would never have thought of you as a businessman."

He shrugged. "Well, it's a result of my upbringing. I grew up dirt poor. Dad and Grandpa didn't make shit. Grandpa did the grind for fifty years, saved enough to buy a little spread to retire on, and Dad did a little better, but he never invested, never saved, and turned out he had a gambling problem, so by the time he died he was broke as shit. Living with Crow when Dad was touring, I wasn't…poor, per se, because the club had money and so did his parents, but it wasn't mine. They just fed me, clothed me, and housed me out of the goodness of their hearts. Dad would send

I hated this line of conversation. It made me jumpy and uncomfortable and squirmy and irritable. I hated being irritable. I paced away from him, to the window overlooking downtown Dallas. Tried to figure out a way out of it without just outright shutting him down. I felt him move behind me—heard the creak of the leather couch as his weight left it. Felt the air swirling with his presence behind me. He said nothing, didn't touch me—just stood behind me. I turned. Put my back to the floor-to-ceiling window. Gazed up at him.

Myles North was the most beautiful man I'd ever seen. Six-three, lean and hard, with thick messy hair a reddish-brown mahogany. Eyes blue as the sky, blue as arctic ice, but warm and fiery and fiercely intelligent and untamed and radiating a boyish playfulness and a ravenous sexuality. Everything about Myles turned me on, but his eyes almost more than anything. Almost. I mean, his hands, his mouth, and his cock turned me on more than anything, but his eyes were right there with them, firing me up and making me horny. Although, in some ways, the horniness his eyes gave me was more…cerebral, or in my heart, than in my body. Which was weird, and scary. Like everything about him.

His body was wicked. Delicious. Hard, shredded. Jupiter was the band's personal trainer, and one of the

trucks which followed the tour around was a semi dedicated entirely to fitness equipment, a fully mobile gym,
and the guys all spent significant amounts of time working out together. Charlie and I had met them during
an off-week, or what Myles called a "de-load" week,
when they didn't lift at all. Since then, Myles had spent
at least thirty minutes working out every single day,
maintaining peak physical condition. He was a madman
on stage, wild and radiating intensity, jumping around
and running back and forth along the stage, leaping from
speaker stacks and basically going nuts for an hour or
two, which required intense amounts of energy and
fitness. That combined with his exercise routine and the
healthy diet they all maintained—again due to Jupiter's
influence—meant all of the guys were fit and strong,
but Myles was…absolutely shredded. Instagram fitness
model level shredded—not bulky, just strong, fit, and
hard, with ultralow body fat.

"What?" he said, smirking.

"Nothing." I batted my eyelashes at him. "Just,
you know…looking at the sexiest man I've ever seen."

He lifted one eyebrow. "Ever?"

"Honestly, yeah." I sidled closer to him, so only
an inch separated us. "Ever. And I've seen a lot of sexy
men."

"Just looking at me, huh?" He hooked a finger
through the belt loop of my cutoff jean shorts.

"Well, no." I felt the flutter of unease settle as I entered more familiar and comfortable territory. "Just looking, and considering…other stuff."

"Such as?"

I shrugged, demure and delicate and innocent. "Oh, just…things." I reached down and peeled my shirt up, off—no bra, the tight T-shirt lifting my breasts and letting them fall with a heavy bounce as the tight white cotton let them go.

His eyes widened, as if, despite us having sex at least once a day every day since we met, he still couldn't get over my body. Which felt…*really* good. "I'm on board so far," he muttered.

I pushed his shirt up and off, because I liked looking at his ripped chest and abs. Now for the fun part: I sank to my knees and slowly unbuttoned his fly. Lowered the zipper. His bulge sprang out against the gray cotton of his boxer-briefs. Tugged his jeans down around his ankles—he lifted a bare foot and I slipped the leg off, then the other. His underwear next, and then he was gloriously naked for me. Tanned skin stretched tight around hard muscles, broad flat chest, an eight-pack razoring down to a sharp V-cut, which framed the most gorgeous male member I've ever had the privilege of laying eyes on. Long, but god, so thick. Thick enough to make me gasp every time he slid into me. Straight as an arrow, flat up against his belly.

Well, right now, he was still only partially erect—thickening but still dangling forward and pointing at the floor. This was one of my favorite things, him floppy, just begging for me to get him hard. Didn't take much—he was staring down at me and watching me, anticipating, soaking up the sway of my boobs, and he was slowly hardening.

Not fast enough.

I slid my hands up the backs of his thighs. Cupped his buttocks, held the taut hard globes in my hands and kissed his thigh, just above his left knee. An inch higher, then across to his right thigh. Higher. Back and forth, kissing my way up one thigh and the other, alternating. To his hipbones. Licking his salty firm flesh, over his abs, under his belly button. Ran my tongue down his V-cut. He twitched, cock jerking, the tip lifting. His hands dangled at his sides, fingers curling into fists as he anticipated what I was going to do next. Like he didn't know. Silly man.

I fitted the broad round head into my mouth. Slid him in, tongue fluttering.

"Fuck, Lex," he growled. "Love your mouth, babe."

I smiled at him—with my eyes, at least, my mouth being otherwise occupied. Let him fall out. He pointed straight forward, now, half erect. I licked him from root to tip along the underside, lifting him with my tongue and then rolling my mouth over the top to plunge him deep. Away. Flopping out again. Fingernails tracing designs on his buttocks, squeezing, palming. Nuzzling his cock with my nose, my lips, my chin. Toying with him.

Now, finally, he was fully erect, eight inches of perfection nearly as thick as my wrist. I moved to take him in my mouth again, but he caught my chin with one hand. Applied gentle pressure to lift me to my feet.

"No more of that." He palmed my breast, flicking my nipple until I hissed in pleasure. "Got other plans."

I pulled away from his touch, back to the window. Unbuttoned my shorts and wiggled out of them. Naked, writhed up against him. "Oh yeah? What plans would that be, Myles?"

He reached down between my thighs. Felt me, slid a fingertip along my seam. Found my clit, already engorged and sensitive. "Well, first, I think you need to come."

I swallowed hard as he feathered just a single fingertip over me, swirling in gentle circles. "Keep that up and I will, and soon."

He brought one of my hands to the apex of my thighs. "Got a better idea. You do it while I go get a condom."

I used two fingers with gentle pressure, going slow and light as he walked away, his hard ass moving in a delicious rhythm. I bit my lip as I tried to go slow, but my need was a pulsating wildfire within me, nearing crescendo already. I fought it off, and pushed down the need to come. It was futile—I was a hair trigger under the best of circumstances. He was in front of me, swaggering toward me, huge hard cock standing up on end, swaying with each step, waggling at me as he approached, as if that magnificent organ was waving at me, beckoning me. He had a condom in his hand, a gold square packet. I waited for him to approach, till he was inches from me, our skin nearly touching.

I waited.

Drew it out.

Let him want me—let him watch me as my fingers moved in slow circles around my clit. I was buckling, my resistance crumbling under the tsunami of orgasmic pressure rolling within me. My movements deliberately slow, light soft delicate touches, I felt myself rising. Felt my core tightening. Bit my lower lip. Kept my eyes on his, reached one hand to his shoulder to brace myself as I curled forward, knees buckling, spine bowing forward as the climax began to sear and sizzle and bolt through me.

"Myles," I breathed. "I'm gonna come."

He snagged my wrist. "Not yet you're not."

I growled at him. "Don't you deny my orgasm, damn you."

He laughed. "I'm not—switch with me." He gave me the condom and when I took it, he placed one big finger where mine had been, and he was not so light, not gentle. Not so slow. He pushed me over the edge with a single swipe through my wet center, and then his finger delved into me, gathering my essence and smearing it over me, curling inside me and finding something like a switch, like a button, taking my orgasm from a flicker of a candle to the scorching blaze of the sun. I screamed, knees giving out as the orgasm wrenched through me. Condom forgotten, I knew nothing but the overwhelming nova of climax, and he held me through it, one hand cradling my ass to hold me against him, his wrist pinned between our bodies as he flicked me to ever more spastic heights of delirium, not letting me fade from the orgasm but pushing me through it to something more, something hotter, something wilder.

I came back to earth eventually, still coming, but able to comprehend my place in the universe. Knees shaking, trembling all over, I ripped the condom packet open with my teeth and rolled it onto him.

Myles grabbed my hips and spun me in a circle. Pressed up against the window, I spread my legs apart for him, braced my hands on the glass. He fit two fingers to my opening and guided himself to me. Notched his cock at my entrance. Nuzzled in. Leaned against me, just the fat broad head inside my nether lips. His mouth tickled my ear.

"Ready, Lexie?"

I shook my head. "No."

"Too bad." He slammed into me, and I screamed.

The glass was cold against my breasts and sex and cheek—I was hard up against it, breasts smashed flat, his hand around my hip, fingering my clit from the front as he slid into me from behind. Dallas was spread out beneath us, far below, and I wondered if anyone could see us—maybe in the building across the street. I liked the idea of an unknown person watching this—it made it thrilling without being an exhibitionist thing. Myles lifted up on his toes, driving into me, and I gasped at the fullness of him inside me, spreading me apart, splitting me until I ached, burned. I would never get used to his cock, how impossibly huge it was. I mean, could the man be any more of a rock star god? Messy hair, beautiful voice, skilled guitar player, and a cock like a horse. And I had every beautiful inch inside me as his hips clapped against my ass.

"Lex, baby, *now* are you ready?"

I nodded against the glass. "Yeah, Myles. Now I'm ready."

Another thing I was fucking addicted to, dammit.

The phone silenced. Rang again immediately.

I plucked his hand off my breast. "Go."

He groaned, but wrenched himself away and swaggered naked and perfect into the living room, answered the phone, standing nude in the middle of the room—I just stared at him, feeling just as fortunate and lucky and giddy to get him naked in my life. I mean, look at him. The muscles of his back rippled, his ass flexed into taut marble bubbles as he moved his weight from foot to foot, his bicep flexing as he lifted the phone to his ear. Legs like trees, a little hairy. Hair was a mess, but perfectly so.

Damn, damn, damn. The man was incredible.

And I, stupidly, impossibly, wanted him *again*. Right now. I could jump on that cock right now and come just as hard, enjoy him just as much. It was a problem, how insatiable he made me—I was already running a sex-drive of nearly nymphomaniacal levels, and Myles North put me into super-hyper-ultra turbo drive.

All I wanted to do was fuck him, again and again.

If only because as long as we were fucking, we weren't getting anywhere near discussions of my past, my issues, or putting labels on what Myles and I were or were not.

I wondered if he would ever catch on to that. I hoped not. But he wasn't dumb—far from it. I had a feeling my days of sexuality as avoidance were numbered—I'd squeeze every last bit out of the time I had left, though. And then some.

Because I was a seriously fucked-up woman. I wondered if Myles knew...and hoped like hell he didn't.

"Perfect. I'd like to leave for Alaska as soon as possible, so get whatever paperwork done that's needed, and let me know when we can take off."

"Sounds good," Murphy said.

"Same," Callahan echoed.

I ended the meeting and turned to see Lexie emerging from the bathroom, a towel around her head, another around her torso cinched under her armpits, cleaning out her ears with a Q-tip. Despite the fact that I'd had her less than an hour ago, the sight of Lexie Goode in nothing but a towel was arousing enough to make my dick twitch. And by twitch, I mean stick straight up, hard as a rock. She wasn't even naked, dammit. But the towel was tiny, a negligible rectangle of white which when cinched around her torso barely closed, the slit in front revealing taunting glimpses of her naked belly, sex, and thighs, and when she turned around, the lower curve of her buttocks as well.

Damn, damn, and double damn, the woman was a fucking siren. Five-six, maybe closer to five-seven. Curvy as *fuck*. I mean, my god, the woman had curves for days. Brick shithouse. Her tits made my eyes bug out, and the fact that she wasn't shy about them, wasn't modest pretty much at all, and didn't mind flaunting her body made it even better—you'd think with my lifelong exposure to naked boobs that

I'd have a better grasp of boob size to bra size, but I didn't. Maybe because most of the tits I saw were naked, rarely contained in bras. Growing up touring with Dad and Grandpa, I saw more than my share of flashers at concerts and festivals, chicks walking around topless backstage. Then, as I toured myself, both as an underground performer doing the grind and as a top-bill artist selling out venues worldwide, I had way more than my fair share of groupies and backstage bunnies prancing around in various stages of undress.

I digress.

Point being, I had no fucking clue what size her boobs were, other than *big*. More than a handful, for sure. Being just barely twenty-one, her tits were perky, with small, dark areolae, plump nipples which were insanely sensitive, with lots of those delicious little bumps around the nipples and areolae. They hung low, bottom-heavy, her pert little nips directly dead center. Impossibly proportioned, I would have said, considering the tuck-in of her waist and the swell of her hips. Again, being as familiar with breasts as I was, I knew they were natural—not that I cared either way.

Her hips were…how do I say it without sounding like an asshole or repeating myself? She wasn't a delicate girl, Lexie. Not overweight at all, but given the improbable size of her tits, I'll just say she was equally well proportioned below the waist. Thick thighs, no gap, bell-curve hips, plump round ass that had a hypnotic jiggle and sway to it. If she carried anything extra, it was in her hips, ass, and thighs, and she carried it like a fucking goddess.

Her hair was black as ink, buzzed short on the sides and long enough on the top that the tips brushed just past her jaw; she was super creative and daring with her hair—sometimes it was just loose and wild, other times she would style it to brush over to one side or the other, or she would slick it straight back, or braid it tight against her scalp. Never did her hair the same way two days in a row, just however it suited her fancy that day. Her eyes were the exact shade of a milk chocolate bar, and every bit as fiery and expressive as her mouth.

She tossed the Q-tips into the kitchen trash, tugged the towel off her head, and tossed it over the back of the chair. She bent over at the waist, flipping her hair upside down and scrubbing her fingers through it vigorously, then whipped upright and flipped her hair backward. I watched this with rapt attention, lower lip in my teeth, cock hardening.

She glanced at me, lifted an eyebrow. "Whatcha thinkin' about over there, Myles?"

I chuckled. "Just enjoying the view, babe."

She frowned. "I'm in a towel."

I shrugged. "You make that towel look sinful."

She indicated my hard-on. "You, um…okay?"

I nodded. "Yeah. I'm good." I ran a hand through my hair. "But I mean, if you're offering…"

She smirked. "I just got out of the shower, and just brushed my teeth."

"Kidding, Lex." I winked at her. "Mostly."

She sidled over to me. "I mean, *you* haven't showered yet, have you?"

"Nope."

"You planning on it?"

"Yup. We got errands to run today."

She made a slow show of untucking her towel and letting it fall off, but held it so it hung in front of her, blocking my view of the goods. "So *you* could get messy."

I set the iPad aside, once again feeling that ridiculous thrill of anticipation—with Lex, I never knew what she was going to do, how she would do it, where, when, or why. She was unpredictable, especially sexually. And I fucking loved it.

And no, I'm not taking back that word.

"Yeah, I could get messy."

She tossed the towel over my groin, leaving herself naked, and sat down beside me. The towel was tented comically erect over my hard-on; she lifted the towel and set it aside. Wrapped one hand around my erection and slid her touch upward. Twisted. Down. I swallowed hard, watching her small hand gliding over my cock, twisting and plunging.

She watched, too—and seemed to get nearly as much enjoyment out of watching as I did from her doing it. Okay, maybe not nearly, but the expression on her face was one of eager anticipation. "Remember the first time I did this?" she asked.

I huffed a laugh. "How could I forget?" I couldn't help but reach out to fondle one of her breasts, and my hard-on got harder. "Backstage at that festival outside Chicago, the day we met. Backstage was fuckin' semitrailers with makeshift lights and old couches."

"Charlie and Crow were, like, thirty feet away, and the whole backstage area was swarming with techies and roadies and groupies and other bands." She went slow, each stroke unhurried. "Do you have any idea how shocked I was when I got my hands on this?" She squeezed my cock as an indicator of what she meant. "I had to start out with my hands because I honestly wasn't sure I'd even be able to get my mouth around it."

"It's not *that* big," I muttered, laughing.

"Yeah-huh."

"Nuh-uh," I countered in faux-childish, combative tone.

She met my eyes. "Myles. Do you realize I can

barely get my jaw around it? To the point that it's, like, nearly comical."

"I don't find it comical at all, Lex."

"I said 'like nearly.'" She glanced down, where her fingers only just barely closed around my girth. "I have a small mouth and small hands, granted. But still."

I shook my head. "You're just trying to stroke my ego."

"No, I'm stroking your cock. Your ego doesn't need stroking. It's plenty big." When I opened my mouth to protest, she just laughed over me. "Kidding, Myles, just kidding. You're honestly one of the most down-to-earth guys I've ever met, which is weird considering you're stupid rich and world famous."

"Not stupid rich, just stupid," I joked.

She frowned at me. "You're one of the smartest men I've ever met."

"I was kidding, but thanks." I was feeling it, now. The slow burn, the aching rise. The need to move, the need for more. "The first time you did this it was dark, so I couldn't really see."

"Now you can." She went to one hand only, then, short twisting strokes around the head. "You like watching?"

"Fuck yeah, I do."

"Me too." She cupped my balls in one hand and

plunged her fist down around my base, played there a while. "You're just…you have the most perfect cock in the world, and I want to play with it literally all the time."

I laughed, but it was through my teeth, thighs bunching, because I was really feeling it now. "In case I haven't made it clear by now, please, I beg you, feel free to play with my cock as much as you want." I palmed her breasts again. "It's like how I feel about these."

"These?" She let go of me, slid astride my thighs, and cupped her tits in both hands, squeezing them around my cock. "You like this?"

I groaned, watching my cock slide through her big pale breasts. "Fuck—fuck yeah."

"Just don't come on me. I'm serious. I just got clean and don't want to have to shower again."

I flexed my hips. "I won't. I hope."

"Myles, I'm serious. Don't. I like being clean."

I laughed. "I like you messy."

"I'll let you do that another time." She released her tits, stayed sitting on my thighs as she clutched me in both hands and began pumping me in earnest now—still not fast, but steadily, slow at the top and speeding up as her fists plunged down, with that crazy-making twist of her fists at the top. "Anywhere you want."

I gazed at her. "Are you at least going to let me return the favor?"

She shook her head. "You haven't fed me yet." She turned her attention to my cock, throbbing in her fists, now, aching. My hips were helpless, thrusting with a mind of their own. "Once you're clean and we're both dressed, you're taking me to brunch. Maybe I'll let you make me come once I've eaten."

"Let me," I echoed, huffing a laugh. "If I dragged you into a restaurant bathroom and started eating you out, like you'd stop me?"

She shrugged. "I don't know. You'd have try and see."

"What if we sat in a booth and I fingered you under the table?"

She bit her lip, grinning. "That's a solid yes. Eating me out in a public, unlocked bathroom? Not an easy yes." She moved her fists faster now. "You almost there, Myles?"

I growled, hips pushing up. "Yeah...shit, yeah, nearly." I smirked at her. "Why? You in a hurry? If you're that hungry, I got something for you to eat," I said, laughing.

"Dirty boy." She bent over me, took me into her mouth—one deep plunge, another, a third, and then right as I felt the edge approaching, she backed away, licking her lips. "There. Better?"

I closed my eyes briefly—but only briefly, because watching her was one of life's great pleasures,
and one of the best parts of sex with her, physical sen-
sations aside. "You ever gonna let me finish in your
mouth, Lex?"

She shrugged, but the sudden shuttering of
her expression told me I'd hit a sore spot somehow.
"Maybe. That's not really my thing. Having your cock
in my mouth, I like. Having cum in my mouth, not
so much."

"Fair enough," I said, knowing enough of her expressions and moods by now to know to let it go.

She slowed her strokes, eyes on mine. "Really?
That's it? Fair enough?"

"If it's not your thing, it's not your thing. No big
deal for me. You do plenty of other dirty, wicked, sinful, incredible things for me."

She kept her gaze on my erection in her fists,
watching as the tip sprouted up out the top of her
hand, and then began a fast soft hand-over-hand
rhythm that made me utterly crazy, immediately
gasping and growling and hips flexing helplessly upward as the need to let go rose and rose and began to
pulse. "You really don't mind?"

I groaned. "No, Lex, I don't." I let myself go, let
myself fuck her hands. "Fuck, babe—your hands feel
like heaven."

"Thought my pussy was heaven?" she asked, voice low, husky.

"It is. Different kind of heaven." I was losing the ability to make sense as she continued the quick hand over hand. "Your mouth is heaven, pussy is heaven, hands are heaven. Tits are heaven. Just you—*you're* heaven."

She didn't answer, but I saw her absorbing that. "What about my ass?"

"That's heaven, too, but I was operating under the assumption you weren't quite ready for that yet."

"Or ever." She squeezed me. "This absolutely will not fit there, and I'm not about to try."

"My tongue will."

She hissed in surprise. "Shit, Myles. You would not. Would you?"

I couldn't answer right away, lost to the rising surge of orgasm welling up within me. "Yeah—shit yeah I would. Get you naked in the shower, get you all soapy and clean, rinse you off, and I'll do whatever the fuck you want, Lex."

"You do that, I may just reconsider my no cum in the mouth rule, just for you."

"That's...holy shit, holy shit, Lex—that's a rule? Like, always?"

"Yeah. Since...well...for a long, long time." She went faster, then, seeing me struggle to hold back.

"Never had anyone lick my asshole…always been curious what it feels like."

"Never done it to anyone," I said. "But for you? There ain't a single thing I wouldn't do to make you feel good."

She bit her lip, watching me arch up off the couch cushions, butt taut, thrusting up into her hands. "Give it to me, Myles. I wanna watch you come."

"Now, Lex. Right—oh fuck, oh fuck, right… *now.*"

I had no more words, just gone, lost in the thrall of orgasm, in the feel of her small soft hands stroking me over and over, hand over hand, and then as I began to come, she let me sag back against my belly and twisted her hands in a sinuous stroking plunging rhythm that drove me wild, made me come helplessly hard. I shouted, growled, roared, felt it surge out of me. One hand continued pumping me in hard fast strokes, and with the other she cupped my balls and massaged them, slid a finger along the underside and pressed against me and I came even harder, so hard it hurt, so hard the ache of release became a hot taut wire of fire slicing through me, making me momentarily blind and dizzy and disoriented. She didn't relent as I came, but went for more. Stroked, not faster, but slower. Drawing it out. Making me arch my spine, butt up off the bed, my entire body bent in a bow, groaning through a release so powerful I could not even believe it was real.

Finally, I sagged, the orgasm conceded defeat and faded away, letting me out of its grip.

When I returned to myself, I was gasping raggedly, and Lexie was still sitting on my thighs, a small satisfied smile on her face, watching me. "Well hi," she breathed, "you're back. I lost you there for a minute."

I had a giant pool of cum on my belly, a thick stripe up onto my chest, dripping down into my navel and connecting to my sagging cock by a string of viscous white. "Damn, girl."

She laughed. "You're welcome. Now get cleaned up and feed me."

"I need a towel or something."

She fetched a wad of paper towel from the kitchen and wiped me clean, bent to kiss my lips. "There."

I sighed, gazing at her lovely, lush, naked body. "You're amazing, you know that?"

"A handjob is all it takes to be amazing?"

"That was way more than just a handjob, Lex. It was…an *experience*."

"You could call it the Lexie Special."

"Well, then, I'll take the Lexie Special…is every day too much? I was gonna say at least twice a day, but I don't wanna be greedy."

She laughed. "I'll agree to once a day, but only one condition."

I sat up, pulling her onto my lap and wrapping my arms around her. "And what condition would that be?" I asked, pressing small quick kisses to her shoulder, over her neck, along her jawline. "Not that it matters, because I agree regardless."

"You'll agree to anything?" she breathed, tilting her head up and away to offer me her throat to kiss.

"Just about," I said, taking her offer and kissing her throat all over, inch by inch. "No pegging, no threesomes—those're my only rules."

She exhaled softly. "Myles, stop, stop."

I pulled away. "What?"

She stood up. Paced away, head down, hair falling over her face. "You're seducing me and I need food. You keep kissing me like that and I'm gonna end up riding your face, and then I'll end up riding your cock again, and I'll get messy and need another shower, and you're still sticky." She picked up both towels, which she'd discarded on the floor.

I laughed. "You say all that like it's a bad thing."

She headed for the bedroom. "We had sex last night, this morning, and I just gave you a handjob. It's time for breakfast. I need my energy so I can keep up with you."

I snickered. "So *you* can keep up with *me*? Babe,

you woke me up for sex last night. If anyone has to keep up with anyone, it's me with you."

She pivoted to stare at me. "I think it's a mutual thing. We both have out of control libidos. My point is, I'm fucking hungry."

And avoiding something, I thought, but didn't say. "You had a condition, but you never said what it was."

She shrugged again, moving into the bedroom. "Nothing. Never mind."

I followed her. She rummaged through a drawer, pawing through a loose pile of thongs and lacy underwear in every style imaginable—not one pair of plain white briefs to be seen. She snagged a purple thong and stepped into it—when she was pulling it up with a sultry wiggle of her curvy hips, I pulled her back against me. "Lex."

She writhed away. "Ew, you're getting me sticky!"

I laughed, but kept my sticky belly away from her, leaning over her shoulder with my upper torso, arms pinning hers to her sides. Kissed her neck. "Don't use the never mind cop-out with me, Lexie Goode. Say what you were gonna say."

"It was silly, Myles, I was being silly. You really want a handjob every day?"

I growled. "I want you every day. All of you. Every part of you. There is not a single moment of the day that I don't want you, however I can get you. Hands, mouth, pussy, ass, tits, I want your body." I nipped her skin over the ridge of her shoulder. "I want your mind, your soul, your heart. Your talent. Your wicked, vicious, crazy tongue." She wiggled, wanting to get away, but I didn't let her. *"You*, Lex."

She fought my hold. "Okay, I get it."

Not the reaction I was expecting. I let her go. "What's wrong? I'm confused."

She stepped away from me. "Nothing's wrong. I just don't like being held like that, so I can't get away. Please don't do it again."

I watched her closely—her body language spoke of something buried way deep, even as she made it sound like a simple preference, something she just didn't care for. I guess I'd been aware and had gotten hints of this for a while now, but this was the first time she had ever said anything. "Lex. Be real for me, yeah?"

She spun around, glaring up at me. "What, Myles? What do you want from me?"

"I'm not sure how we got here, honestly. We were talking about handjobs and now you're acting like…" I wasn't sure how she was acting, which meant I wasn't sure how to finish that statement.

She clearly didn't like whatever implication she heard in that ellipsis, however. "Like what, Myles?

How am I acting? Like I don't appreciate being restrained?"

I felt this building into a blowup, and figured I'd take the easy, if cowardly way out. "I'm sorry, Lex. I won't do that again." I knew I'd just let her avoid something much deeper, but had no clue what or how to unearth it from beneath the miles of wall and layers of defenses I'd just witnessed. "I'm gonna shower."

I went into the bathroom and took a shower, taking my time.

When I got out, Lexie was dressed in a minuscule denim skirt with an aged, frayed hem, so short and so tight the bottom curve of her ass cheeks slid out from under the hem when she moved, revealing occasional glimpses of the lacy purple of her thong. Above the skirt, a white button-down shirt was tied up underneath her breasts, all the buttons open to leave her breasts spilling out—only somewhat shielded from being completely exposed by a gauzy, lacy, sort-of-translucent but not quite opaque…camisole, I think it was called. The camisole did nothing to support or constrain, and only served to highlight the size and natural movement of her cleavage with every step.

Her hair was swept to the left, messy and artfully tangled. No makeup except a hint of shiny pale pink stuff on her lips. Oh my—and some sparkles all over her cleavage.

"Fuckin' hell, Lex."

She smiled at me brightly. "You like?"

"The skirt, the cleavage, or the titty sparkles?"

She shook her chest at me. "You noticed, huh?"

"You realize I'm going to try to lick that off, later?"

This made her frown. "I wonder if they make edible titty glitter?"

I laughed. "If they do, I volunteer to try it."

"Feed me, then we can discuss the logistics of edible titty glitter."

And it was as if nothing had happened.

But down in the pit of my stomach, something was unsettled. I'd gotten a glimpse of something dark in her evasiveness and fight picking. The girl had secrets.

I already knew about her affair with the professor, and her subsequent expulsion from the university, revocation of her scholarship, and the abortion.

Which just begged the question...what else could she be hiding?

THREE

Lexie

MYLES HAD REALLY ROLLED OUT THE RED CARPET FOR me, for this trip to Ketchikan. I'd have been fine with plain old first-class commercial from Dallas to Seattle and a pond-hopper prop plane to Ketchikan. But, no. Not Myles. He wanted to butter me up so I'd make cozy with my mom and Charlie and Cassie. It was, clearly, very important to him. He had no family, so he was going out of his way to make sure I preserved mine. I got that. But I resented the interference.

What I didn't resent was the Mercedes S-Class with a tuxedo-clad driver to take us to the airport, where we parked right on the tarmac next to a sleek, low-slung black jet—like I was a movie star or some shit. This was out of a fucking movie. No one *really* did this. Yet here I was, my chunky, calf-high combat boots clomping up the movable staircase, wind whipping my hair around and tugging at the open front of my button-down.

Up, into the interior of Myles's *private jet*, which he'd literally just purchased. For this trip. For me. An eight-million-dollar jet.

My head spun.

If it was spinning already, when my eyes adjusted to the darkened interior of the jet, it damn well popped right off my neck when I took a look around. Whereas the exterior was glossy black with tinted windows, the interior was all soft gray and muted ivory shades, with a pop of crimson in certain bits of trim. A deep leather couch ran the entire length of one side, and a row of deep leather captain's chairs, in pairs, that faced the built-in tables. The rear wall was entirely dominated by a massive flat screen TV, and I saw evidence throughout the cabin of surround sound speakers. A bar occupied the front wall near the entrance to the cockpit, and it featured bottles of top-shelf alcohol, mostly expensive scotches and whiskeys. Underneath the front of the bar was a cooler with sliding glass doors, revealing rows of beer arranged by brand—clearly preselected based on band member preferences. Behind the bar, rocks glasses for whiskey and pint glasses for beer, a select assortment of wines along with appropriate wineglasses. There were cabinets along the wall perpendicular to the bar that probably contained various snacks and other supplies.

The carpet underfoot was deep and plush, vacuumed in neat lines—I felt an urge to take off my boots and socks and dig my toes into the carpet. Each pair of chairs with their attendant table framed a window. The whole interior was elegant, yet comfortable and understated...just like Myles.

I boggled. "And I thought your tour bus was luxurious. This is insane, Myles."

He moved in beside me, whistled as he took in the interior. "Damn, no kidding." He went to the nearest chair and sat down, leaned back—the chair went all the way back, a footrest extended so the chair turned into a small cot. The table folded down and out of the way as needed. "Not quite the same as my suite on the bus, but I guess the idea is the time we save driving gets us to the next city sooner, and we just stay in a real hotel."

I plopped down on the couch and took off my boots and socks, dug my toes in, and it felt every bit as good as I'd imagined. "Worth eight million dollars?"

"For what will be my home away from home?

No stops for gas, no nosy fans peeking in the windows at stoplights? Yeah, I'd say so."

"No private suite where you can take groupies after the show." I eyed him, watching his reaction.

"I'm done with that phase of my life," he said, smiling at me. "Got other plans for after shows than random groupies with backstage passes whose names I'll never know."

I didn't touch that inference. "What do you think the guys will think?"

He mused. "Hmmm. I suppose I should probably let them know what's going on, huh?"

"I mean, you guys are a band, so I think it would be a good idea to fill them in. I'll bet money they won't complain."

He shrugged. Yanked out his phone. Brought up a FaceTime group call with the other members of his band—Jupiter, the drummer; Brand, the bassist, and Zan, the other lead guitarist.

They all picked up, and Myles kept the phone tilted down and close so all they could see was him. "What's up, guys?"

"Calling to cancel the tour?" Jupiter said, a note of laughter in his voice.

Myles snorted. "Fuck no. We have twenty-two shows lined up, each one sold out, several of those back-to-back shows in the same city. We've got three dates sold out in London, two in Dublin, two in Paris. And Mick is saying he's getting requests from venues in Rio, Johannesburg, and Sydney to see if we can add dates because they're getting so many calls asking about more tickets."

"So what's up?" Jupiter pressed. "You never call all of us at once like this, not on breaks, unless it's big news."

"It is big news." He grinned. "I leased the bus out."

They didn't pick up on the inference right away. There was a long beat of stunned silence.

"You...leased the bus?" Zan said, sounding stoned out of his mind. "So we're sharing the bus with another band?"

Myles laughed. "Lay off the pot for ten seconds, bud. No, we're not sharing."

Jupiter caught on, partway. "You got a new bus?"

"Nope."

Brand went in for the win. "No fucking way, dude. No way." He laughed. "You did fucking *not.*"

"Did what?" Zan asked. "Man, why'd you have to call right after I took a massive toke? I'm not following."

"A jet?" Jupiter offered. "You bought a jet?"

Myles stood up and touched the button to rotate the screen. "Get your first look at our new ride, gentlemen." He panned around to take in the exit, showed them the stairs, the bar, then around to the couch; he paused on me. "No, she doesn't come with the bus, so don't get any ideas."

There was a chorus of voices: "Hey, Lex."

"Hi, guys." I smirked. "I don't come with the bus, but I do come with Myles."

"We know," Jupiter drawled, his voice droll. "We've heard. *Multiple* times."

I gave a cutesy little shrug. "Oops."

Myles winked at me, and kept moving down the length of the jet with the phone, highlighting the individual charging stations complete with ports for wired internet access, the changeable LED lighting running around the ceiling and floor of the entire cabin, how the seats folded into beds, the bathroom at the back complete with a rainfall showerhead and nozzles in the wall, heated towel rack, a separate smaller room with a closable door for the toilet and its own sink and mirror. He knocked on the cockpit door, peeked his head in, and introduced the pilots—all I heard was a faint buzz of voices, one male, one female, and the tinny sound of the guys saying hello; then he was outside and down the steps, panning the camera to take in the exterior, walking around the nose—he had to shout to be heard, since the jet engines were idling, and even then they were loud.

Back inside, he settled onto the couch beside me, slung an arm over my shoulder. "So. Thoughts?"

"You know, I'm stoned out of my gourd, so I may not make sense. But. Um. We sleep on the bus? I know the chairs fold out, but I don't know if I could sleep on that, like, for the night."

Myles just laughed. "No, you won't have to. When we finish a show, we'll stay the night at a hotel. Big suites for everyone, my dudes. Then, whenever we feel like rolling our fat asses out of bed, we take a car to the airport, fly to the next city, check into a hotel. Do it all over again."

"So, no more bus, at all?" Zan was still puzzled. "Only hotels?"

"Tony and Mick are putting together our hotel itinerary for the overseas tour. The bus was paid for, including the conversions and upgrades I did, so the lease makes us money. When we're not touring, I plan on using the jet as a private charter so I'll make back money there. The expense of the hotel rooms and the cars to and from will come out of our take-home pay. Tony says we're spending a bit more this way, but with the way the tours are selling out, it's gonna be fine, and a lot easier on us travel-wise. Tony's been after us to fly for a while."

Brand—short reddish-blond hair and a thick beard, tattoos all over his hands and forearms and biceps in patchwork which didn't quite yet make a sleeve—tapped his chin, the sparrow on the back of his left hand fluttering as he dragged his fingers through his beard. "Question—this is *your* jet, or is this the band's jet?"

Myles shrugged. "I mean, it's mine. But if we're not touring and you need it, let me know. Better yet, I'll make sure the charter schedule is shared with you guys so you can schedule your use of it. Tony is setting up a separate LLC for the charter, and I'm funding and expense accounting the operating costs. You'll have to make official requests to use it so the schedule doesn't get jacked up, but the jet is yours to use as much as you want. Just, you know, there's only one jet and four of us, so we gotta just be respectful of that, you know?"

Brand nodded. "Nah, it's cool, just wondering."

"So when do we get a ride on it?" Jupiter asked.

"Well, I'm taking Lex to Alaska to see her family before we take off on the overseas leg. We got two weeks before the first date in Tokyo, so we'll fly there together for the inaugural band flight. We'll fly out of LAX and I'll get you the schedule as soon as its fixed, but I figure we'll hit up Tokyo for some fun for a few days before the show."

Zan, then. "I got a question." His eyes were closed, and I saw a tendril of smoke wafting across his square of screen. "We ain't, like, gonna end up like… like fuckin'—like Ritchie Valens and Buddy Holly, or John Denver, or Stevie Ray Vaughn? Are we? 'Cause all of them died in plane crashes."

There was a chorus of groans from everyone else. "Jesus, Zan, way to kill the celebration, dude," Brand said.

"No, we're not," Myles said. "I hired two of the best, most experienced, most overqualified pilots anywhere in the world. They're dedicated entirely to this plane and to us. They rotate shifts so neither of them is ever flying more than the regulation number of hours. They're assuring me they personally check the aircraft before every flight, and I'm paying extra to have mechanics at every stop go over it, wingtip to wingtip, nose to tail. Because, fuck that, I am not dying in a goddamn plane crash, Zan, and neither are you or any of us. But it's a good question."

Their conversation wandered after that, the way a conversation between four men who spend every waking minute together for months at a time tends to do.

Then a silence fell over the conversation.

"Man, can I just say it's fuckin' weird, not having Crow in on this?" Jupiter said. "I miss his cranky ass."

Myles's face shuttered. "I do, too. It won't be the same without him, but he's got a good thing going up in Alaska. I know he misses you guys, and if he hasn't said it, I'll say it for him—go up and visit him." He rubbed the back of his head. "Matter of fact, executive decision—from here on out, every tour leg ends in Alaska, so we spend a good week or so with Crow and Charlie. I guess the crew up there is huge, and from what Crow says, they know how to fuckin' party."

"Crew?" Zan again. "What crew?"

I laughed and said, "This is going to sound a bit crazy, but my sister Cassie is dating a guy up there who's…shit. I don't know, honestly. It's complicated, and I don't know any of them. I just know my mom is dating this guy who has triplet sons, and those triplets have cousins who own a pretty famous bar in Ketchikan, and there's eight superhot brothers who all have these superhot girlfriends and wives… it's this whole thing. There's a Facebook page about them, and one of the brothers is dating or married to Harlow Grace, and there's a pair of twins dating twins, and one of the twin couples is the music group Canary, and…" I sighed. "Cassie is all, like, *you are part of the family* now, and Charlie and my mom are saying the same thing."

"You sound annoyed," Jupiter said.

Damn his observant ass.

I shrugged. "Not annoyed, just weirded out.

Like, my mother and two of my four sisters are all ensconced in this new 'clan' whom I've never met. It's just weird and I don't know what to expect."

"A whole big family to click into," Myles said, eying me. "Sounds like a good thing from where I'm sitting."

"Canary? I love Canary," Zan piped up. "Bishop's Pawn was the shit, too. I know those guys. I played in this band in San Francisco before I joined you guys, and I played at this dive bar with Canaan and Corin. Those dudes are wicked talented."

I threw up my hands and laughed. "Everybody knows them except me! It's crazy."

Jupiter was chewing on something. "You're talking about the Badd family. Baxter Badd used to…" he trailed off. "Well, that's a different story."

Myles seized on that. "What? What aren't you saying?"

Jupiter was uncomfortable. "Years ago, before I was in the IFBB, I was just this aspiring bodybuilder. Broke as shit, is what I was. So, to make ends meet, I'd do underground fights. I was big and I grew up rough, so fistfights were daily for me, and I came across this guy who told me I could make a grand in one night whether I won or lost." He shrugged. "Turns out I was good, damn good. Won most of my fights."

Myles blinked. "Holy shit, Jupe. Why the hell is this the first I'm hearing of this?"

Jupiter shrugged again. "I'm not ashamed of it, but it's not something I advertise. For one, they're illegal as fuck. Two, I'm already kind of a scary guy, and if folks find out I used to beat the shit out of other guys for money in underground bareknuckle boxing matches they'll probably end up making assumptions. I just don't advertise it."

"Holy shit." Zan was laughing. "No wonder I'm scared of you, Jupe."

"You're scared of me because you weigh a buck-fifty soaking wet, and I could break your arm with one hand."

Zan nodded seriously. "No shit. You could. I thought Bax played football, though?"

"He did that too, but had to quit or something. I don't know the story." Jupiter paused. "I just know I demolished everybody I ever fought...except Baxter Badd. That motherfucker was faster than lightning and hit like a fuckin' freight train. He tore me a new asshole and wasn't even sweating. I fought him six rounds, but by the end of that fight I was just...a bloody wreck. Couldn't see, lip was busted, missing a tooth, and then he broke one of my ribs and that was it. Worst pain I've ever felt in my life was when he went in for a second hit on my broken rib—didn't know it was broken, either of us. Until he hit me again and I fuckin'…I went down like a sack of bricks. No chance of getting up. I'd done him pretty good, but he was the clear winner. And I'm just saying this to you guys, but he's the only person on the planet you couldn't pay me any amount of money to ever, fucking *ever* step into a ring with again."

"That bad?" Myles asked.

Jupiter's eyes were wide. "You don't fuckin' know, man. He was a one-man wrecking machine. I wouldn't want to put money on Crow in a fight between those two, is what I'm saying."

Myles whistled. "I'd back Crow against Satan himself."

"Me too," Jupiter said. "Baxter Badd is just…on a different plane of existence."

"So if you met him again…?" Myles asked.

Jupiter waved his hand. "Ah, it was a fight, a paid fight. I've got nothing but serious respect for the man. He's out of the fighting world now too, I guess. Running a gym up there, nowadays."

The cockpit opened, then, and the pilots emerged, in matching captain's uniforms. "We're ready to go, Mr. North," the male pilot said.

"All right guys, I gotta go," Myles said. A chorus of goodbyes from the band, and then Myles ended the call. He gestured to me. "Captain Alan Murphy, and Captain Rebecca Callahan, this is Lexie Goode. She'll be flying with us a lot in the future." He eyed me. "I hope."

We all politely ignored that, me especially—and I stood and shook hands with the pilots, finding myself impressed with the relative youth of the female pilot. "Pleased to meet you, Captains."

The male pilot, Captain Murphy, gave the spiel. "We're going to be taking off in a few minutes, but I'd like to thank you for the opportunity to work with you, Mr. North, and to assure you that you are in the best hands there are. We'll be touching down in Seattle for a quick refuel, and then on to Ketchikan. We should have you on the ferry to Ketchikan by... oh, eight or so this evening. We have great weather and good wind, so we should make good time. If anything comes up, which I don't anticipate, I'll pop on over the intercom. Your seats all have buckles, including the couch, so please buckle up until we're at cruising altitude. I'll let you know when it's safe to unbuckle."

The takeoff was smooth, smoother than any commercial flight I'd ever been on, and we reached cruising altitude a few minutes later. I half expected Myles to make some sort of move to "break in" the plane, but he just hunted around for the iPad which controlled the lights and TV; he turned the lights down, turned the TV on, selected a movie—a late nineties rom-com—and kicked back beside me, feet extended. I found it so easy to lean against his chest and forget where I was, or anything else.

Please don't bring up our conversation from this morning, I found myself thinking. I knew damn well he'd seen right through my clumsy avoidance, but it had been instinctual. Defenses had kicked in before I knew what I was doing, and now it was done. Not that I'd do anything different. He'd hit upon not one, not two, but three different triggers: blowjobs and swallowing, being restrained, and cuddling. And the nature of our relationship. And my insecurity with how he felt about me.

So more than three.

Fuck.

I'd ducked and dodged and picked a fight, and he'd seen through it all. But hadn't called me on it. I gave him kudos for that.

But right now he was a little distant.

Instead of trying to bend me over the couch, he was cuddling up and watching a movie—a girly movie, too, not a guns-and-tits-and-explosions dude movie. Which, honestly, I would have preferred. Rom-coms are too saccharine and too touchy-feely and too much about *love* and happily ever after—all the things I hate and despise and don't believe in.

But I couldn't bring myself to move out of his arms. It's not that it didn't feel good. It's not that I didn't feel at home, and safe and secure.

I didn't feel the things Myles had talked about.

No way.

I didn't do cuddles. I didn't do…this.

But I just couldn't move. I'd been awake last night, late. I'd passed out after we had sex, but then had woken up with Myles wrapped around me like an octopus, arms and legs coiling around every part of me, his cock nuzzled between my butt cheeks and his hand on my boob, nose against the back of my neck, hot breath on my spine. I'd been hot and uncomfortable with being held like that.

Yet then, like now, something deeper even than my deeply rooted disgust at *cuddling* had prevented me from moving away, from disentangling his hands, from throwing off his legs.

I was tired. It was all right, at best, being here on this jet, held and safe and comfortable. But just okay, though.

A bed, alone, a bottle of wine, and my vibrator. That's what I really wanted.

For real. And I meant it.

That's definitely better than being safe and secure at forty thousand feet, in the arms of a sexy, talented, wealthy, famous country music star who was absolutely gaga for me, who would do anything for me, who looked at me like I was his sun, moon, and stars, who gave me more and better orgasms than all the other men combined in my past.

Yeah.

I didn't believe it myself, but a girl can try, right?

And it was totally logical and sane to be trying to convince myself of that in the first place.

Right?

Right.

FOUR

Myles

SHE FELL ASLEEP HALFWAY THROUGH THE MOVIE. IT WAS only when she fell asleep that her tension receded at all—until then, she'd been stiff as a board, every muscle tensed, as if just relaxing on the couch with me was some awful punishment. It seemed to make her uncomfortable—as uncomfortable as when I brought up the status of our relationship. Or asked about her past. Or acted like I felt anything for her beyond sexual attraction.

Granted, my sexual attraction to her was off the damned charts. Believe me when I say I've considered every position and angle I could have her on this jet, and that I've been sitting here, while she slept, imagining them all. As if I hadn't fucked her stupid last night, and again this morning, and then less than an hour after fucking her this morning, she'd given me a handjob to end all handjobs which, until Lexie, I hadn't thought was even a thing, apart from having been a typical teenage boy. Until Lexie, the last hand-job I'd gotten was at sixteen with my first girlfriend, and that had been the first thing we'd done beyond kissing and over-the-clothes groping. Lexie made it... sensual. Erotic. Not just jerking me off, but...some-thing else. Something way, way hotter.

The Lexie Special.

I considered her statement from earlier this morning that she didn't do blowjobs. Meaning, that she didn't swallow. I mean, sure, that's her preroga-tive. Totally her choice, and no problem on my end with it. And I'm in no way slut shaming her, but it just seemed out of character. She was hypersexual. She wanted me as much as I wanted her—she insti-gated sex as much as I did if not more. She used her mouth on me, and to incredible effect. But it was always part of something else, and never to finish. I didn't know what to make of it. I wouldn't push it, because if that's a line for her, I respect that utterly. But considering how much of a sexual creature she is, it just strikes me as...odd. There has to be a story behind it.

But good luck getting that story out of her, though. I knew that all too well.

She never talked about herself. I wasn't even supposed to know about the affair and the abortion—I'd overheard the story as she delivered it as an outburst, spontaneously and angrily, to her sister Charlie. There'd been nothing else of her past related to me in the almost three months I'd known her. I'm not saying I'm gonna propose any time soon, but I've got real feelings for the girl, and fuck if I know what they are or how to deal with them, especially when she spooks if she gets so much as a whiff of anything smacking of feelings.

She had some shit buried deep. I wondered if her family even knew, because she is cagey as shit about it, whatever it is.

I mulled it over, wondering if I'd ever get anything real out of her. Was this "thing" we had doomed to be nothing but a run of mind-altering sex with a woman I was falling in love with real fucking fast? Was it fated to end before it became anything real because she was…shit, I didn't even know what? Afraid? Afraid of commitment, of me, of my fame, of feelings? Had she been hurt by a guy? That seemed likely, given her history of hookups and casual sex and dearth of information about any past boyfriends.

I think I was the closest she'd ever gotten to a regular relationship. She had lived with me for two months; those months have been telling, and I know they were wearing on her. Making her antsy. Cagey. Anxious to move on before she can't help but start having feelings for me.

Or maybe she already did have feelings but was trying to stifle them and ignore them.

Feelings. It was weird that *I* was the one angling to talk about shit, because I normally hated talking about shit. I liked to play music, perform, hang out with my band, and party. And have sex.

With Lexie.

Until I met her, my list of likes would have stopped at "and have sex."

But now, I just can't fathom wanting sex with anyone else. It wouldn't be…enough. No one could scream the way she does. No one could clench her pussy around my cock the way she does—with vise-grip power, squeezing me so hard even if I wanted to hold out, I couldn't. When she came, when she started squeezing those tight-as-fuck pussy muscles around me, I just fucking lost it. Gone.

That's just sex, that's not to mention the way she looks at me—her sense of humor, her sense of style. Her boldness, her vicious tongue. Her fierce independence. The way, every once in a while, I'd get a glimpse of something soft and sweet and tender inside her.

My thoughts were disrupted as she flipped to one side and rested against my chest, snorting delicately. She pillowed her cheek on her hands, sucked in a deep breath, and let it out with an adorable, piggish little *snurk*. She would deny snoring, but she does. I'll never tell her, though.

I had to piss like crazy, but no way I was about to dislodge her—not when she's finally snuggling.

Shit, man. Me, snuggling, and happy about it? I barely recognize myself, sometimes.

The intercom crackled as Captain Murphy came on: "We've been cleared to approach for landing, so please buckle up, Mr. North, Ms. Goode. We'll be touching down in Seattle shortly. Thanks."

"Lex," I murmured. "Gotta wake up. Landing soon."

"Mmm."

I jostled her gently. "Lexie. Babe."

"Mmm-mmm."

"Lex, we're landing soon. You have to buckle up."

She shook her head, rubbed my chest. "Sleeping. You shushy."

I laughed. "Come on, silly girl. Don't make me tickle you."

She tightened. "Don't. Tickle me and I'll punch you in the nads. I hate being tickled."

"You gotta buckle up, hon. We're landing."

She struggled to a sitting position, rubbed her eyes. Scraped her hands through her hair, messing it up and somehow making it even sexier. Stretched, arching catlike, spine bowing inward, pressing her breasts out and up. Teasing. God, the woman's tits were the most fantastic pair I'd ever seen in my life, and I absolutely never got tired of them, or used to them. Never would, either.

She caught me staring, and smirked. "You're ridiculous."

"What?"

"You literally see, touch, and taste my boobs multiple times a day, every day. Yet you're still staring at me like you're dying to get me out of my top."

"Hey, what can I say? I'm a tits man, and you have the best tits in the world."

"In the world?" she said, sounding skeptical.

"In the history of the world."

She shook her head, snorting derisively, but I caught a hint of a pleased and flattered smile as she turned away to buckle up. "You're just biased."

"I am not. I'm a boobs expert, and it is my expert opinion that your boobs are the best ever."

She rolled her eyes. "You know I'm plenty confident in my body, and that I'm not jealous. So just be real, okay? You're honestly saying, of all the women you've seen and slept with, my body is your favorite?

You're not just saying that because you're currently sleeping with me?"

I debated calling out that phrase—currently sleeping with—but didn't. "I do mean that."

"And you've mentally compared."

"Yes."

"Who else is in the running?"

"Well, everyone else is a distant second and third or whatever."

"No bullshit, no flattery."

"You really want details?"

"I really do."

"Okay, well, I played at a festival with a bunch of other up-and-coming country music stars. And one of them was this new girl named Britt Aubrey. Gorgeous girl, and super talented. She's probably second, in terms of best body and just overall most beautiful."

She blinked at me. "I know her. She's amazing, good with a guitar and a crazy powerful voice. And sexy as hell, to boot. You're saying I'm *more* beautiful—better body, face, hair, everything—than Britt Aubrey?"

"I'm saying of all the women I've known and been with, Britt Aubrey is the only one who can even try to hold a candle to you," I said as I looked out the window and saw the blue Pacific and the Seattle area below. We would be landing very soon.

She waited until we'd touched down with a squeal and bark of the tires, and then the rushing roar as we slowed to a taxiing roll. "Are you curious where you stand on my roster?"

I shot her an arrogant grin. "Since you're asking, I'm gonna guess somewhere near the top. I mean, I *am* Myles North."

"Myles North and full of yourself." She unbuckled as we taxied. "But yeah, top of the list would be understating things."

"So, answer the same question. Who's on the list?"

"Well, nobody famous for me, except you, obviously. When I was at U-Conn I went with some friends to a frat house kegger at Penn State, and banged the Penn State football team's star running back. Until you, I'd have put him as the best by far. Tall, jacked, sweet, and hung like a damn horse."

"And I can compete with tall, jacked, and hung like a horse?"

She snorted as if I'd asked a stupid question. "Yeah, Myles. Tall, shredded, and hung like…well, like an even bigger horse. He was, umm…like, a pony. You're a draft horse. In the penis department, I mean. He's got you beat in the big muscles department, but I don't typically go for the super swole guys anyway. They tend to be obsessed with muscles to an unhealthy degree, in my experience."

"I tried for years to get bigger, under Jupe's tutelage. But I'm what they call a hardgainer and eventually, after literally years of lifting wacky heavy and eating thousands and thousands of calories a day, Jupiter was like, you should just quit fighting your body and go for shredded. So that's what I did. I just can't get big, or if I did, it would have to be under the kind of insane dedication which, as a professional touring musician, I just don't have the time for."

A few minutes later I felt the jet jerk to a stop "Well, let me just say that I *really* approve." She eyed the shower, visible through the open door—a sliding pocket-door. "That looks like a fun shower."

"Maybe we can play in it, later. On the way out of Alaska."

She licked her lips, eyes going predatory and seductive. "Do we have time now?"

I laughed, because the captain came on the intercom at that moment. "Welcome to Seattle, you guys." It was Captain Callahan, this time. "We're just refueling, and will be back in the air fairly quickly. If you'd like to take a longer break and stretch your legs or get some real food, just let us know."

I glanced at her. "Up to you."

She shook her head, sighing wistfully. "Seattle is on my list of places to explore, but under the circumstances I'd rather just get to Alaska and get this over with."

She sure was eager to be done with this, which was odd, considering how close she was with her family; I got it though—she had a difficult story to relate, and wasn't looking forward to her mother's reaction, especially.

I keyed the intercom. "We'd like to just get to Ketchikan as soon as possible, thanks."

"Sure thing, boss," Captain Callahan said. "We can be airborne in about forty-five minutes."

"So…about that shower," Lexie said, after the connection to the cockpit was closed.

I laughed. "Babe, for what I have in mind for you and that shower, forty-five minutes ain't anywhere near enough."

Her gaze heated. "I like the way that sounds."

"You know what I can do in the next forty-five minutes?" I tugged her toward me, pushed her backward to lay on the couch. "Pay you back for the orgasm."

She hissed as I reached up under her skirt and yanked her thong off. "Myles, I…oh…*oh*." I opted to dive right in, tongue going straight for her clit. "I don't keep track. There's no tab or record."

"I know—*you* don't." I made her gasp, already arching—she was a hair trigger when it came to the first orgasm, and slower to come every time after, but tended to come harder with each subsequent

climax. "But I do. I'm a believer in a three-to-one ratio, so by my own personal reckoning I owe you at
least three."

"I...oooh fuck, yeah, right there, just like that."
She clutched at my hair as I found the sweet spot,
tongue circling and fingers curling inside her. "I like
this ratio."

I murmured a laugh even as I continued to lick
her closer and closer to climax. "I bet you do," I
muttered.

"We're—oh fuck, oh fuckfuckfuck—we're almost to one. Right....right...oh god, oh god, oh fuck
oh god...right *now!*" She arched up off the couch
and I followed her through it, tasting her essence
explode onto my tongue as she blossomed into a
thrashing, hip-thrusting, hair-tossing, teeth-gritted
orgasm. "Fuck, MYLES! God, what are you doing to
me oh god god oh god so fucking good oh god—"

"Making you come, that's what I'm doing."

I let her fall back, kissing her hipbone, her thigh,
across her sex, kissing all over her skin, licking and
nipping and teasing as I allowed her a few moments
to recover, and then as her breathing evened out, I
started all over again; this time I went slow, building her up gradually, licking fast and then slow, all
over and then targeted, shifting tactics every time
she started to really get into it. Then, when she was

gasping and groaning and her hips were pushing against my mouth, I went hard and fast with tongue and mouth to take her to the edge, only to back her away at the last second. Then back up, closer to the edge, and away. Edging, edging. When she was snarling at me and yanking at my hair and begging me to let her come, I finally let her topple, screaming and crying over the edge.

She clasped at my face, gasping raggedly as she twitched and thrashed through it. "I think that counts as two," she breathed. "Fuck, Myles. Where the hell did you learn to go down? Because you're *so* fucking good at it it's ridiculous."

I laughed. "Self-taught, babe."

She pulled at me, tugging me upward. "I'm serious, I think that was two at once. I'm…oh shit. I'm done. I've already come twice this morning."

"Are you complaining?"

She laughed, wiping at my mouth with her hand. "You have pussy juice on your stubble. And hell no. I've never gotten off so much as I do with you. It's a beautiful thing."

I wiped a thumb over my lips, and then popped the thumb into my mouth. "Yum. Tastes like you."

She sucked in a deep breath, held it. Shook her head as she let it out. "For real. However you learned to give cunnilingus, you learned really, really well."

I handed her the purple thong, watched as she wiggled into it. "I just pay attention."

"There had to have been someone who was instrumental in helping you learn how to pay attention and what to do."

I sighed, laughed, and looked at her. "You really want to know about weird shit, you know that?" Especially for someone reticent to share her own past. "Her name was Helen. It was when Crow was in prison and I was doing the dive bar grind on my own. I ran out of money in a little shithole town in Oklahoma and had to spend a week there till I could play another weekend of gigs so I could afford gas to keep going. There was this waitress at the bar I played at—Helen. A little older than me, I was, shit, nineteen? A kid. She was thirty-something. Single, just sort of stuck in a dead-end job in a dead-end town. Hooked on drugs, I think, but was in a sober spell when I was with her. I couldn't afford a motel and there wasn't one in town anyway, so I was staying in my van. She caught me napping there, and invited me over. I stayed the week with her, and if anyone I ever slept with really actually *taught* me anything, it was Helen. And good god, did she teach me. That was a wild-ass week, man. She worked at night, so she was a night owl like me. I'd hang at her apartment while she worked, writing music and wishing I had booze, playing, practicing. She'd come home from work and we'd just fuck like crazy till dawn. And yeah, she wasn't shy about showing me how she liked it, you know? I've always been a quick learner and there's nothing I like more than appreciation and approval, so I'd use what she showed me to get her going. I never forgot what she taught me, and I guess what she liked is pretty universal."

Lexie was still lying back on the couch, legs across mine, spread apart, skirt up around her hips. "Lucky me that she taught you so well."

"What about you?" I asked. "Anyone stand out as having taught you things?"

She sat up, then. Tugged her skirt down, stood up. "I have to pee."

And she was gone.

What a shock. I share, ask the same question in return, and get ignored. It was getting annoying, honestly.

When she came back, we were taxiing toward the runway for takeoff, so I made a visit to the bathroom to get cleaned up.

I let the question go, but filed it away as another oddity, another example of how she avoided sharing personal information at all costs.

She, for sure, had something major in her past that she never, ever talked about. It was becoming more obvious, every time she avoided an encounter, that it was something big, something buried deep. It hurt, and it irked me, because there was nothing I'd kept from her. I'd been totally open about my short-lived coke addiction, my exes and my sex numbers, and that one time I thought I had an STD. All of it was weird and embarrassing, and a bit painful, but there was nothing I wouldn't share with her, if she asked.

I wanted the same in return.

If I pressed her, though, I had a feeling I would face a major explosion, and a pissed-off Lexie Goode was something I knew I really, really didn't want to encounter. But how long could I allow her to avoid this issue, whatever it was? Was it worth it to me to press the issue? Was I willing to risk what we already had? She'd bolt, if I pushed too hard—I knew that for a fact. It was almost as if she was just waiting for me to give her an excuse to run, no matter how good the sex was.

Even I knew, deep down, that even the best sex possible between two people wasn't enough to build a relationship on if you wanted more than just sex.

And I did.

I knew I did.

It scared me stupid, but I knew I wanted more than just sex with Lexie. A *lot* more.

I just wasn't sure how to make that happen, or if it was even possible, given how cagey she was about so many things.

FIVE

Lexie

I KNEW HE WAS IRRITATED WITH ME. I CHEWED ON THAT little problem as we landed in Ketchikan and headed for the ferry—it was a dark, overcast, cool day, but it was still breathtakingly beautiful.

Too bad I was too deep in thought to really appreciate the beauty.

Myles was no dummy. He was definitely aware that I avoided certain questions. He never pushed, but I could tell it was hard for him not to.

I hoped he wouldn't push, because I couldn't guarantee our…thing—whatever it was—would survive him pushing me to talk about certain things.

The trouble was, I wanted our thing to survive. I

liked being a thing with him. I'd never been in a thing like this or for this long with anyone. I'd had sex more times with him than with any other one person. Well, except…gah, no, fuck, fuck no. Not going there. That didn't count.

And that was why I had so many topics to avoid.

We reached the other side of the channel, and Myles consulted an email on his phone. After we collected our bags, we set out on foot.

"Where are we going?" I asked.

He laughed. "To your mom's."

"You have my mom's address?"

I'd intentionally not acquired that piece of information, because I really didn't want to be here, doing this. Chicken, coward, call me what you want, but the story I had to tell my mom and Cassie was one I was not looking forward to. Primarily because I could already *feel* Mom's disappointment in me. Oh, she'd cover it with love, because that's just how Mom is. But she'd be disappointed in me. Shit, I was disappointed in myself.

"Yes, I do." He smirked at me. "I knew you'd try to be like, oh I don't have her address. So I got it from Charlie via Crow." He winked. "We're staying with your mom and her boyfriend, Luke, I think it is."

"Lucas," I corrected. "Cassie raves about him. Says me meeting Lucas is going to be the funniest thing that's ever happened."

He frowned. "Why?"

"Because I hate cutesy demeaning pet names like babe and honey and sugar and sweetheart, and he's apparently psychologically unable to not use them with women. So I'm going to want to kill him, and they're all really looking forward to what Cassie is anticipating being the Lexie explosion of the century."

"Is that why you're so tense?"

"That's part of it." I knew that came out short and snappy, but I couldn't help it.

"And what's the other part?

"You're upset with me."

"I'm not upset," he said, sighing as we crossed a sidewalk and followed his phone's GPS navigation app's directions to Mom's condo. "I'm annoyed."

"With me."

"Yeah."

"Because there's shit I just don't talk about."

"Exactly. And there's nothing I won't tell you. Haven't told you, matter of fact."

I eyed him sideways. "Bullshit. You haven't told me *everything*."

"Sure have. Everything major."

"Worst breakup."

His answer was immediate. "Never had a real relationship, so I can't say I've ever had a breakup, per se. Closest I could come would be a girl named Tiff. Backstage bunny. Had a major crush on me."

He didn't elaborate, and I waited for him to ask me the same thing, but he didn't say anything. That left me a bit off-balance, and I found myself offering the information anyway, since it was a safe topic for me. "Mine was a guy named Nick. He was a fuck-buddy, and even that's too close of a relationship to put on it. We were booty calls for each other for a long time until he came over one night and proposed."

Myles winced. "How'd you let him down?"

"At first I thought it was a joke, and started laughing. But then I realized he was serious. I may have overreacted a little. Or…a lot."

We were walking through a condo complex, and I was aware, suddenly, that Myles was acting kind of weird. Nervous, keeping his head down. He'd put on a ball cap, which he never wore; he'd put it on as we got on the ferry and pulled the brim low. Weird.

"So he just proposed—just like that?

"I sort of yelled at him for breaking the unspoken rule number one of fuck-buddies, and that's to never make it emotional."

"So you're saying you were harsh?" he asked with a grin.

I sighed. "I feel bad, now. But yeah, I was a major bitch to him about it. He looked crushed. He left, and

I sent him a text a few days later apologizing for being so mean about it, but I just wasn't looking for a relationship and he took me by surprise."

I still remembered the guilt I felt about the way I'd treated him.

"And that was it for Nick, I imagine?"

I winced again. "Weeeeeell, not quite. I got wasted a few months later and drunk texted him for a hookup." I grinned sheepishly. "He was like, I've actually got real girlfriend now so you should probably delete my number."

"Oof."

"Yeah, oof."

Myles stopped, looked up at a building in front of us and said, "Here we are." He eyed me. "You ready?"

I shook my head. "Not even close." I let out a sharp sigh. "But, we're here, so let's get this over with."

He laughed, took my hand. "Your family is going to be happy to see you. And it will be great to see Crow and Charlie. But I don't think you have to walk in and spill your guts. We are here for a week, babe."

That term of endearment was like nails on a chalkboard, and I couldn't restrain myself anymore. "I've been trying to let you do that, call me babe. But I just can't anymore." I took my bag from him, rang the buzzer for Mom's unit, identifiable by her name printed on the label. "Please, please don't call me babe. Or anything else like that. I know it's weird, but it's a thing with me. So, please don't."

He was silent a moment. "Okay," he said, looking away.

And that was it.

I eyed him. "I'm sorry, Myles. I'm just—it's a thing."

He nodded, but he wasn't looking at me. "I got it. It's a thing. No cutesy pet names. Lex or Lexie." A pause. "I guess I thought maybe that didn't apply to me, since we're…" he trailed off. "Never mind. I thought wrong. Message received."

My heart sank—I'd hurt him. Pissed him off. "Please try to understand, Myles. I care about you. It just rubs me the wrong way and I hate it. It's not you."

He nodded, and I saw right through the fake grin he put on for me—it was the stage-Myles grin, the ten-thousand-watt mega-star grin. The smile that surely had melted the panties off thousands of women, the grin that had been splashed across tabloids and *People, Time, Newsweek, Rolling Stone, GQ, Seventeen, Cosmopolitan, US Weekly*, even a two-page modeling spread in *Vanity Fair. That* grin.

The one that hid the real Myles North from the world.

"I got you, Lex. It's cool." The wink.

I hated the wink.

You know what I hate almost as much as pet names and talking about emotions? Winking. It's stupid.

He could get away with it once in a while because he was Myles Fucking North, and for sure a future Sexiest Man Alive. But I hated it.

He did it because he knew it annoyed me, because it made me roll my eyes and huff in irritation.

This time, he did it to piss me off.

"Hello, sorry, who is it?" Mom's voice, on the intercom.

"Hi, Mom, it's Lexie and Myles."

"I was indisposed when you buzzed, sorry for making you wait."

"Indisposed," I said, laughing. "Mom, it's me. You can say you were in the bathroom."

A long pause. "In the bathroom. Yeah." She buzzed the door. "Come on up, sweetheart."

"Dammit, Mom—" I started, but the intercom was already silent and the door was buzzing.

Myles laughed. "Not even Mama gets a pass on sweetheart?"

"No one gets a pass," I growled, my ire all the way up, now. "Not you, not Mom, not the pope, or the president, or God himself. No one."

"Wow. Okay."

"And don't fucking wink at me," I snarled, my voice icy and dripping poison. "It's stupid and smarmy and you just look like an idiot."

He chuckled. "Noted."

I glared at him as we hiked the steps to Mom's floor. "What's so funny?"

He shook his head. "Nothing."

I knew I was being stupid and irrational, but I was helpless to stop myself. I was about to see Mom, and I knew she knew something was up, and I'd have to tell the whole stupid story all over again and I hated myself for it, and for Charlie for pulling me into this— and for thinking any of it was in any way Charlie's fault—and at Myles for being so damned amazing even as I was being a bitch to him, because he wasn't lashing out at me, wasn't fighting, was just accepting my bitchiness without seeming fazed.

But I knew he was upset—I knew I'd hurt him, and that I had damage control to do.

If that was even possible anymore.

I had to set that conundrum aside for the moment, because I had bigger fish to fry—namely, my mother, and her moral expectations, which I have completely failed to uphold in pretty much every aspect of my life.

Mom opened her door as we approached,

bustling out in a rush; arms open wide, and all but slammed into me, wrapping me in an unrelentingly fierce hug. It was such a warm, unexpected welcome from Mom that I very nearly got misty-eyed.

"Lexie, I'm so glad you're here." Mom's voice was a low soft whisper in my ear. "I've missed you, my sweet girl."

I hugged her back, letting myself, for a moment, just be that little girl way down deep inside who just wanted her mother's love and affection. "I missed you too, Mom." I stepped back and gestured at Myles. "Mom, this is Myles North."

He leaned in and gave Mom a brief, cordial hug. "It's a pleasure to meet you, Mrs. Goode."

Mom shook his hand. "Call me Liv, please. It's a real pleasure to meet you, too." She stepped backward into the open doorway, and then spun on her heel and led the way inside.

Mom slid her palm across my cheek, up over the buzzed sides and into the messy longer top. "I like this. It suits you." The last time I'd seen Mom in person was via video chat a few months ago, before I'd cut my hair like this. Back then, it had been one length all over, down to my shoulders; a guy I'd slept with a few times had told me he liked his girls with long hair so he had something to pull on while he drilled them from behind. Those words, verbatim.

It hadn't been the idea of hair to yank on while being drilled from behind that I'd taken issue with—I quite enjoy that very much, thank you. It was the other two words: *His girls*. Ohhhh fuck no, buddy. He'd said them while in that exact position, behind me, hands in my hair; I'd kicked him off me, jumped into my clothing as fast as I could while cursing him out with every iota of indignant rage I had within me, and marched my jiggly ass straight to the nearest salon and gotten this cut. Just as a fuck you to him. I'd gone back to his dorm room, showed him my new 'do, and gave him two middle fingers. *I'm not one of your girls, you rotten, chauvinistic dickbag.* Those had been my words to him.

I shook thoughts of that unnamed dickbag out of my mind and focused on Mom. She was wearing a men's button-down, the top several buttons undone to reveal more cleavage than I think she'd ever shown in all my life, certainly. The sleeves were rolled several times and still hung past her elbows, and her knees and hints of bare thigh peeked out from the edges of the lower hem. Her hair was messy, tangled, and wild—very obviously a case of just-fucked hair. This was my *MOM*, so...yuck.

"Mom! You said you were in the bathroom!"

She smirked at me. "*I* said I was *indisposed*, *you* said I was in the bathroom."

"You were having sex?"

She shrugged, her face carefully blank. "I'm not a nun, sweetie. I spent three years alone, mourning your father, God rest him. I moved, and moved on. I have someone in my life whom I love very much and who loves me. So yes, Alexandra, I was in the middle of—well, at the end of, if you must know—making love when you rang the buzzer."

I shuddered. "Next time, I'll just stick with my assumption that you were pooping."

She made a face that was a bizarre cross between a frown, puzzlement, and an amused grin. "You'd rather think I was pooping than making love to a wonderful man?"

I rubbed my face with one hand. "Mom. I don't want to think of either one. I'm glad you're happy, I'm glad you've found someone. I truly mean that—Dad is gone, and even when he wasn't, none of us were happy, least of all you. I don't begrudge you a happy, loving relationship with a man who treats you like you deserve to be treated. I just don't want details of your sex life."

She curled her arm through mine. "Lexie, honey, I think you'll find I'm a somewhat different woman than the one you knew. Lucas has changed me, and for the better. For one thing, I'm far more open about myself, who I am, and what I want. I'm not going to hide my happiness, nor am I going to pretend I'm not a physical, affectionate woman in a relationship with a *lot* of sexual chemistry. I'm not giving you details; I'm just not hiding it. We're all of us adults now, honey."

I nodded. "Okay, who are you and what have you done with my uptight, hypermoral mother?"

She laughed. "Lucas's favorite thing to say to me is—"

"LIGHTEN UP, LIV," I heard a deep, gruff voice say.

She laughed. "That. Come on, you two. I want you to meet Lucas."

I flipped my hair out of my face. "Well, we've already had a serious come-to-Jesus talk and I'm not even inside your condo, yet. This is gonna be a fun trip."

She patted my cheek. "I hope you brought your big girl panties, Lex. Shit is about to get real."

You could have knocked me over with a feather. "Mom! LANGUAGE!"

There was a rough bark of male laughter from inside. "Don't leave 'em standing out there all damn day, babe. Bring 'em in. I been dyin' to meet this one."

"This one?" I echoed.

"Oh boy, here we go," Mom breathed. "Lex, he's set in his ways and means nothing insulting by the things he says, so please, please don't start any drama with him. Please."

"Okay, but *this one*? Like I'm—"

Inside, Mom's condo was pretty much exactly what I'd expect from her—clean, open, hyperneat, lots of elegant lines, lots of white and black with pops of color here and there. In the kitchen, standing with a hip leaned against the island counter was a grizzly bear. Or, the human version, but with massive, bulging muscles and less fur—an older, burly, tattooed, goateed version of Jupiter. Similar height—around six-six—densely packed with mammoth muscles. Close cropped salt-and-pepper hair, warm brown eyes and a mouth twisted in a wry grin.

He was shirtless, clad in nothing but a pair of cut-off khaki shorts slung low on his hips—clearly commando underneath.

I blinked at him. "You're Lucas?"

He nodded. "Sure as shit, sweetheart."

Myles and Mom spoke in synch while looking from Lucas to me and back again: "Oh shit."

"Do *not* call me sweetheart." I set my bag down and crossed to face him across the island. "Let's just get one thing straight right now, Lucas—I am not your sweetheart or your babe or your *darlin'*—" I gave the word a thick drawl. "I'm not your honey or your sugar. My name is Lex, or Lexie. That's it. Got me, Mr. Muscles?"

He blinked at me, that same wry grin on his face.

"Yeah, I got you." He eyed Mom. "Your firecracker daughter lives up to the hype, Liv."

"I did warn you, Lucas. So did Cass, and so has Charlie."

"Hey, it's an old habit and I'm an old dog. Hard to change some things."

I frowned at Mom. "You guys *warned* him about me?"

Mom shrugged. "Sure. You're...well, honey, you're sometimes somewhat...I don't want to say difficult. Just...sharp-tongued and highly opinion-ated. There's nothing wrong with being opinionated, mind you."

I was hurt. People had been *warned* about me? "Am I really that...caustic?"

Mom smiled, but it was a little sad. "I love you, and I accept you for exactly who you are, Alexandra. But yes, you can be a little caustic sometimes."

That stung.

Aaaand...cue the irrational explosion of unrea-soning anger.

"Cool." I nodded. I felt the emotion bubbling, tried to restrain it, and lost... hopelessly. "Super cool. I'm a caustic bitch whom my mom and sisters have to warn people about. Cool." I felt it pop—the cork on my anger. "Fuck you." I pointed at Mom and at Lucas in turn. "Fuck you, fuck you..." I paused on

Myles. "Fuck you, too. Not sure why, but I'll find something. So fuck you, too."

I left my purse and my duffel bag on the floor of Mom's kitchen and stomped out of the condo—shaking with anger, gut churning, hands trembling, heart cracked and mind splintering.

I heard Mom—"Let her go, Myles. It'll be a while before she cools off enough to be capable of rational conversation."

That didn't help. Mainly because it was the truth.

I shoved the door of the condo building open and walked out into a spattering of cold rain. "FUCK!" I shouted at the sky. "FUCK YOU for raining on me."

Screw it.

I walked on, heedless of the cold and wet. Not caring that it was soaking my white shirt, turning it sheer, so my lace camisole was on show—an undergarment that provided little or no concealment or support. I also had no idea where I was going. I didn't know Mom's building or unit number. Also, my phone was back there in my purse and, I'd never been to Ketchikan before.

They don't call it unreasoning rage for nothing—my reason was shot to hell.

I stomped through puddles, feeling my hair stick to my forehead, cheeks, and chin. Feeling my shirt stick to my skin. Feeling the cold and wet make my nipples stand out as hard as bullets.

Caustic?

Opinionated? Sharp-tongued?

Difficult?

A fresh burst of anger detonated inside me, and I snarled out loud. "I'm *not* fucking DIFFICULT!" I screamed at the heavy, dark gray sky and the silver screen of hazy, blowing rain. Which was not a spatter anymore, but a torrential downpour.

I felt him.

How, I couldn't say, but I felt him.

I spun on my heel, saw Myles a few yards behind me, just walking, following. Keeping his distance. Soaked and sexier than ever for it—pale, ripped blue jeans, a tight black T-shirt now pasted to his body like a second skin over his shredded torso. Battered brown leather Doc Martens. His ball cap, with some football team logo on the front, had rain dripping from the brim.

"What?" I shouted. "What the fuck do *you* want?"

We were at the condo complex community center—empty, the parking lot without a single car. He closed the distance between us, and I stopped.

"What—the—*fuck*—do you want, Myles?" I snarled. "Didn't you hear Mom? I'm too *caustic* to be around right now."

He just smiled at me, a soft, dare I say…affection-
ate smile. "I ain't afraid of you angry, Lex. Not a bit."

"Yeah? Well, you should be."

"I'm not." He sidled closer, and I felt my gut
react, felt my core react to his proximity. Damn my
body. "I have a secret weapon."

I now had to fight to keep my rage boiling so he
couldn't win. "And what's that?"

I expected him to reference his dick, but he didn't.
Instead, he closed the space between us, and his arm
shot low around my hips, the other hand buried in
my hair, yanking firmly on my scalp. There was no
escape, none. He jerked me hard up against him, and
I felt his hard-on between us, a thick ridge of taunting
temptation. Felt his heart slamming against his ribs,
belying his calm exterior. I fought him, and he let me.

"Let—*go*, fucker!"

I didn't want him to seduce me out of my anger.

He just grinned. "Say it again and mean it, and I
will."

I opened my mouth to say it again and show
him how much I meant it, but he was too quick. He
used his grip on my hair to pull me close, yanking
my face to his, mouth slamming on mouth, lips slashing across mine hot and hard and damp and insistent,
and then before I could catch my breath or capture
my thoughts, he was kissing me like the fate of the

world depended on it, and his tongue was a slithering serpent in my mouth and I tasted him along with the faint tang of my own essence on his tongue from earlier along with the mint of the gum he was chewing. I stole his gum as we kissed, broke the kiss and spat it out. I regarded him from up close, his eyes merging into a single cyclopean eye, smelled his breath and his male scent.

Kissed him. "Fuck you," I snarled into the kiss. And kissed him all the harder.

He just laughed, crouched, both hands clutching at my ass to lift me off the ground and settled me astride his lean hard hips. One arm barred under my ass, then, and the other wrapped with boa constrictor tightness around my shoulders and cupped the back of my head, crushing me back into the kiss, offering no avenue of escape. Felt us moving, his steps jarring, the ridge and bulge of his erection behind his poor overworked zipper jolting against my center.

A pause, a pivot. His hand leaving my head and reaching away—my eyes were closed and the fervor of his slashing tongue and hungry lips allowed me no thought or comprehension of anything but his kiss, which was indeed a secret weapon against which I was utterly powerless. A doorknob twisted. More steps, now echoing in an open room. Kissing, jolting steps, each one jarring my center against him so I throbbed and throbbed and pulsed with need to have nothing between us anymore, no more jeans, no more zippers. His kiss made me insane with need, took me from rage to near-climax with nothing but the intoxicating taste and power of his damned mouth on mine.

I growled, a distinctly unladylike sound, but fuck it, I'm not a *lady*. I'm all woman, and no lady. "Dammit, Myles."

Another pause, his hand momentarily relinquishing its grip on my hair as he opened another door. I wasn't even sure if he was walking backward or forward, I just felt us moving through another door, sensed darkness through my closed eyes, sensed a much smaller room, and one smelling of bleach and old mops. His foot kicked what sounded like a bucket, and then he was letting me down to the floor in a tantalizing slide of my sex against his zipper. The moment my feet hit the floor, his hands were every-where—yanking my shirt and cami down to expose my breasts with a rough bounce, and then shoving my skirt up. I heard his zipper move, and reached out for him—felt him hot and thick in my fist and the next growl I made was one of rabid need. I felt his fingers at my opening, tugging my thong aside. I stroked him, but he knocked my wrist away, grabbed me by shoulders and spun me around. I caught up against the cold metal of a door, felt it against my cheek and chest, and he was fingering me, making me move and moan as he touched me just right. I had no chance to speak, just his body behind mine and his fingers teasing my nether lips open and then he was inside me—I cried out at the sudden splitting intrusion of his hard, thick huge cock driving into me, squelching wet and fast into me.

Bare.

Wrong.

Wrong.

He couldn't be in me bare.

No, no...

But if felt so *right*, his beautiful perfect cock so big I ached to accept him, and so long he filled me and then some, and so hard and so warm I felt his veins stuttering against my tight-stretched sex. I wanted this. Wanted him bare. Wanted him to fuck me and never stop, wanted in a sudden and desperate way to feel him come, just like this, right the hell now, bare.

But panic seared through me and I reached back, grabbed at him. "No, no! Myles—"

He was already pulling out, making me ache with emptiness and starving for him. "Relax, Lex. I know." I heard a condom packet. "Think I go anywhere without a condom when I'm with you? Hell no." His hand moved against my ass, the movement of him rolling the condom on.

I ached. Throbbed. Needed.

He teased my slit with his fingers again, tugging aside my thong, locating my opening in the total darkness—there was no light but a tiny crack near the floor, little enough that I couldn't even see my hand in front of my face. Found me, and then his fat tip split me open and I surged back against him, maybe even before either of us were ready, slamming him home, deep.

His hips slapped loud against my ass cheeks. He reached around my front and cupped both tits in one hand, a rough clutch, my nipples squeezed together in his hand. He held me upright, pushed me against the door, cheek against it. His lips touched my ear as he used his other hand to find mine, guided my fingers to my clit. "Make yourself come, Lex. Now. Right the fuck now. This is gonna be fast and I need to feel you come."

I had no choice but obey, and even that was conflicted—I wanted to do exactly that, make myself come while he was inside me and coming, but being told what to do made me want to the exact opposite. Sexual need won out over psychological, though, and I pressed the tips of my three middle fingers to my clit and whipped them back and forth in a fast light touch. It was immediate—the searing heat in my core building as I worked myself into a wild frenzy within seconds.

"You want to come with me, you better come now," I said through gritted teeth.

He clutched my tits with rough affection, lips on my ear, voice a low ragged snarl. "Right now, Lex? You want me to come right now?"

I was shuddering, shaking already—his kiss and my own anger and the suddenness of this tryst had me on the edge faster than ever and I was always quick to come at least once, and there I went—my body wanted to arch forward as I cried out through a sudden and wrenching and lightning-hard orgasm. I felt myself squeeze around him, my pussy clenching so hard the muscles ached with spastic tightness around his iron-hard cock.

I was coming, and he hadn't even thrusted once.

Ohhh fuck, there he was. He pulled back and drove back in, hard—*hard*. Our bodies met with a clap of flesh, my sex wet and squelching around him. "Fuck, Lex. You better come again."

I kept going, kept touching myself, obeying him with blind instinct and need—he needed me to come as bad as I needed to come again, needed to feel myself spasm around him as he cut loose. And even now, in the throes of this, I felt a wrench in my soul, a reminder of how fucking insanely badly I wanted to feel him come bare inside me, a stupid, foolish, weak, idiotic, crazy need. My fingers flew around my clit and I felt him moving, felt his flesh sliding against my knuckles as he entered me.

Twice, then, slow but hard.

Then, as if giving up some restraint he was fighting for, he fucked me up against the door so I slammed into it—he let go of my breasts and I felt them smash flat as he filled me, driving me against the door and lifting me up onto my toes with the force of his thrust. His lips never left my ear, his huffing breath loud, and his growls louder, his chest against my back. I felt the tremors begin inside me, and now he was moving steadily, faster and faster with each stroke. Each time he filled me, I was lifted up onto my toes and slammed against the door—he was not being gentle, not at all.

It made me come so hard I saw stars flash against the inside of my closed eyelids, or maybe my eyes were open. I was screaming, loud, throat-searingly loud. Trying to meet his thrusts, but he had me pinned against the door, immobilized. He was simply *taking* me. Fucking me.

I loved it.

And I hated myself for loving the way he used me. The way he could just…seduce and screw me right out of my rage. He knew he could, and I was helpless to stop it. Because I wanted him, no matter what. Even in the fires of my blind rage, my body reacted to his—

More infuriating still, it was more than just my body reacting and I knew it, and I fucking *hated* that truth.

Hated that I knew it, that I was still trying to deny it, hated that I couldn't' deny it—hated everything about this entire situation—except how motherfucking perfect we felt together.

How perfect he could make me feel.

The only time I felt perfect, in fact, was—

I tore that thought out of my brain before it could complete itself, threw my body back against his to take his cock hard and deep, the wrenching ache of him inside me shredding and shearing away any capacity for rational thought. Even emotions faded in sun-hot glory as our bodies crashed together.

I was crying. Weeping.

Screaming.

Wordless, not even his name—too lost in a wild ecstasy to form words.

Ecstasy became something else as his grunts became desperate, as his thrusts turned frantic. I was on my toes, and he was thrusting so hard it hurt but in the most incredible possible way, and he was fucking hard and fast, and I was jostled and jounced and slammed against the door, the cold metal smooth and slick against my cheek and tits.

"Come—come," I whisper-shrieked. "Come, goddammit! I'm coming, Myles—come with me!"

He snarled, the ragged desperate snarl of rabid wolf and I felt it shock through him. My command was the trigger for his obedience: I told him to come, and he came. He lifted up on his toes, and his arms wrapped around me, clutching roughly at tits and hips, staggering backward a step so he could lift me off the floor, arching backward so I was suspended an inch off the floor, impaled on his cock as he slammed up into me, deeper and deeper, harder and harder, not trying to pull away now, just to get deeper into me—there was no deeper he could go, he was so fully buried inside me and was so huge, so long, so thick there was nowhere else to go. I screamed again as my orgasm shredded me into sobbing pieces, and then he was coming, roaring in my ear, slamming up even harder into me so my whole body bounced upward, and I felt—*felt*, even through the layer of latex separating us the force of him emptying himself into me…into the condom—

My world tilted, lights and stars flashed, my head spun, and a scene flashed through my mind, a memory of something which hadn't happened yet:

Myles, on his knees behind me; we were on a carpeted floor, and I was on my hands and knees. A mirror was in front of us, a full-length mirror. Showing all of him, upright behind me, forearms corded as he gripped my hips, clawing at my ass cheeks as he drove himself into me. I shook all over, and my mouth was wide as I screamed his name and my tits were swaying under me with the force of his crazed thrusting and his abs were so hard-tensed with exertion they may as well have been carved from marble, and his eyes were fierce on mine in the mirror—

He was bare inside me
and I was loving it
taking every slamming thrust of his naked cock into me,
   relishing the slick smooth slide of skin on skin
the heat of him and the wetness of me
our lovemaking was poetry
a symphonic crescendo of emotion mashed inextricably
   into physicality
I came and I told him to come
and he came
a hot unending wet sticky fluid perfect filling rush of HIM
his raw love pouring into me
unguarded beyond real and filling me until
I spilled over with him
love leaking out of me, hot and wet and beautiful and mine
mine because I was his

I was crying. I slammed back into myself from whatever mad wild vision *that* was, helpless against the fraught intensity of it, crying from the wrenching fury of the orgasm still shaking me in wave after wave after wave.

He set me on the floor, but didn't pull out of me.

Remained hot and huge inside me, a hard wall of man behind me.

Lips on mine. "Where'd you go, Lex?" A whisper, small and quiet and tender from him.

I shook my head, afraid to speak lest he hear the tremor in my voice. "I…"

My knees gave out, but I had nowhere to fall because he was still thick and rigid inside me, holding me up. I sagged anyway, and was glutted on him and aching with him and somehow wanting to be able to do it all over again even as I felt him subsiding.

He wrapped his arms around my middle and held me. "Where did you go, Alexandra?"

How did he know?

"I don't *know*, Myles," I hissed. "I don't know."

"I felt you…I felt something, Lex. Don't tell me I didn't, and don't tell me you didn't."

I shook my head, because I had absolutely zero words for whatever the *hell* that was. "Yeah, I just don't know what to fucking call it."

He finally slid out of me, and I clenched around emptiness—I wanted him back, wanted him inside me, wanted him where he belonged, and dammit dammit dammit I was all flipped around and upside down and inside out.

Pulled away from him, turning to put my back to the door. Knees shaking, still, legs threatening to give out entirely yet again. He hadn't even taken my thong off. I settled it back into place, righted my shirt. Shoved my skirt down. Reached blindly for him, found him—carefully pulled the condom off of him, tied it in a knot by feel.

"Myles…" I wasn't even sure what I was planning on saying. Nothing was forthcoming and I just trailed off.

I heard and felt him zip himself up. He reached past me to open the door, momentarily blinding us both with a sudden sear of golden evening sun.

Still holding the knotted condom, I stepped out of the janitorial closet and took in my surroundings with one eye closed and the other squinting—the rain had stopped while we were in there and the sun was out but was setting. The community center was a big open room, an empty information desk with a quiet telephone and a darkened computer screen along one wall, windows lining the entire front, a Ping-Pong table and a foosball table in the middle of the room, and a cluster of round games tables with four chairs each on either side.

And, at one of the tables, was a quartet of elderly women. Each one clutched a hand of cards, a pile on the table between them. Wide eyes. They were staring at us. Shocked. Horrified.

At me, a used condom dangling from my fingers,

my shirt wet and see-through, my hair a disaster, squinting at the light like a vampire.

"Shit," Myles muttered. "We had an audience, I guess."

I glanced back at the janitor's closet and saw a garbage can. Tossed the condom into it. "Sorry, didn't know anyone was in here," I said to the women, with a tight, apologetic grin, fighting back laughter at their horrified expressions.

Oh man, they must've thought Myles had been straight up murdering me.

One of the little old ladies huffed indignantly. "Well, I never!"

Another one recovered faster. "We know, Leslie." She had pale pink hair and an American flag tattoo on her wrinkled bicep. "You never." She smiled at us. "I for one say good for you. I just wish Herb had done that to me when he was alive." She huffed a laugh. "And in a janitor's closet, bless your souls. Ah, the madness of youth."

Myles took me by the hand and led me toward the doors. "Sorry for the disturbance, ladies. We'll leave you to your rummy." That ten-thousand-watt grin—he could get away with murder with that grin.

One of the ladies gasped. "It *is* you! My granddaughter is just over the moon for you, you know." She humphed. "I better keep this little tidbit to myself. I swear she thinks you're going to sweep in any minute and whisk her away into some teenaged fantasyland happily ever after. I haven't the heart to disabuse her of the fantasy."

Myles's grin faltered momentarily, and then returned brighter than ever. "Well, I don't know what I can do about that, but I can do this…" He reached into the back pocket of his jeans and pulled out a Sharpie, strode across the room and snagged one of the extra Joker cards and scrawled his autograph on it. "You got a phone?"

The old woman pulled out a cell phone that was at least ten years old, brought up the camera. Handed it to him. He circled to crouch behind the woman and snapped a selfie with her, and then another with all the women in it.

I was weirded out by the whole thing. And I suddenly realized why he'd put on the cap and had been acting so weird on the ferry and the walk to Mom's: he didn't want to be recognized.

Until now, I'd never been in public with him—only on the bus, at his condo, or going from his car to a quiet booth in the back of fancy restaurant. No one had ever bothered him like this—I'd never been faced with the reality of his fame. Not like this.

He was a different Myles. Smooth, suave, easygoing, grinning. Fake. But still him, all him, all brightness and friendly warmth. So, not fake, just a different facet I'd never seen until now. He signed one of the other women's CVS receipt, a brochure for hot air balloon rides, and a page from a day planner. More pics. Chitchat. I saw hints that he wanted to get away, but he never let on, and they seemed to have forgotten that only moments ago he'd been making me scream bloody murder in a janitor's closet. I was completely forgotten. They had his undivided attention, listening, nodding, laughing.

Finally, he eyed me. Smiled apologetically at the group of women. "Well, I should get this one into some dry clothes," he said, nodding at me. "It was nice to meet you all."

They gave a chorus of nice-to-meet-you as he ambled back to me. I heard whispers from them, along the lines of *my, isn't he handsome*, and *what a lucky girl she is*.

What a lucky girl I am.

I saw him with new eyes, then.

He wasn't just my Myles.

He was Myles North.

Rock star god. Not a rock musician, but still every inch the rock star. Famous enough to get stopped for selfies and autographs in the community center of a tiny condo complex in suburban fucking Ketchikan, Alaska.

He wasn't *my* Myles at all.

He wasn't my anything.

I let him walk me out the door, and then sped away from him. He didn't stay with me.

"Um, Lex?" His voice stopped me.

I turned. Saw him gesture in the opposite direction. "This way, ba—" he cut off, stopping himself. "It's this way."

More mixed up than ever, I ducked my head and moved past him. Made it about twenty feet before he jogged to catch up to me, stopped in front of me, and grabbed me by the shoulders. Not holding, not restraining—he'd learned that lesson, clearly.

"Wait."

I rolled a shoulder, away from his touch. "What, Myles?"

"What's the deal? Are we going to talk about what just happened?"

"Which part? My tantrum at Mom's, Lucas, and you? The fact that we just fucked—*loudly*—in public, in a closet, within earshot of four little old grandmas? Or—or maybe you want to talk about the fact that you signed autographs and took selfies with fingers that were literally *just* inside me? Or maybe you want to talk about whatever the *fuck* it was that happened in that closet...which I still have no words for, and the answer is no, *fuck* no, I do *not* want to talk about *that*, at fucking *all*." I stomped past him, aware I was basically one big walking meltdown. "I have to go apologize."

He didn't follow, and I stopped. Glanced back at him. "But you first. I'm sorry, Myles. I apologize for my outburst and my behavior. It was really wrong."

He shook his head. Seemed...either confused or disbelieving; walked over to stand in front of me. "Lex, you can't—you can't avoid everything all the time, forever."

I raked my hand through my hair. Reached up and snagged his hat, settled it on my head backward. "Sure I can. Been doing it successfully for years. Don't plan on stopping now just because it's inconvenient for you." I sounded breezy, felt anything but.

"Goddammit, Alexandra—"

I whirled on him, stabbed a finger at his nose. "Ohhh no. No no no no no. My mother is the only human being on the planet who gets to call me that, because she gave birth to me. You're not her, so you don't get to use that name, especially not in that tone."

I gave him no opportunity to respond—I bolted, stomping in my shit-kicker boots across the parking lot. I had no clue if I was going in the right direction, and honestly didn't give a shit. I was *not* having this conversation with him, not now, not ever.

I hated apologizing. Hated it.

But I knew I'd blown up on people who didn't deserve it, and I had to make it right.

Didn't mean I had to like it.

"Lex, hold up."

"No. We're fighting."

He didn't try to catch up. "Why?"

"Because you seduced me out of my tantrum, and it worked, damn you. Also, that's *my* strategy and you can't have it." I knew how childish and stupid I sounded.

He laughed. *LAUGHED*, damn him.

I let out a wordless howl of frustration and annoyance, knowing my anger and my whole entire fucked-up-ness was only going to build, and build, and build, because I was just so fucked in the head and heart about so many things, and didn't have the ovaries to woman up and face any of it.

SIX

Myles

THE POOR GIRL WAS COMING APART AT THE SEAMS. SHE HAD so much going on in her head, so many issues and she was refusing to deal with any of them. I'm not a shrink, but I can see pretty damn well that she's a mess. A beautiful disaster, but a disaster nonetheless. She needed support. She needed someone who could just…be there. Not be afraid of her titanic temper. Not take her outbursts personally. Someone who could help her find a sense of calm and control. Someone who could distract her.

I wanted to drag her stories out of her, drag the hard, painful truths of the past out of her. But I couldn't do that. I didn't dare force her to talk. Couldn't force her to trust me.

So, all I could do was try to maintain calm and reason, and do what I could.

Which included giving her space to stomp off her anger. Let her be mad at me for stealing the thunder of her tantrum and co-opting her sex-as-distraction strategy.

I followed her at a distance, making sure she didn't get lost in the condo complex, and letting myself relish the sweet view of her swinging ass in the tiny little skirt. So plump, so round, so juicy, filling out the denim until it was stretched so taut it was a wonder the seams didn't fuckin' split with each sultry step. And those thighs—damn. I loved watching them slide against each other, the jounce of the muscle, loved imagining and remembering the way they felt curled around my face as I devoured her.

How the hell I could be hornier for her now—after that epic fuck session—than I had been before, I wasn't sure. But I was.

I didn't dare let my libido take over entirely, or I'd end up doing something really idiotic, like trying to copulate with her under a damn bush or something. She just eradicated my self-control, my judgment, logic, reason, everything. Sexually, mentally, emotionally, she just…short-circuited everything I thought I knew about myself. Made me crazy. Unpredictable at best, and without any vestige of self-control at worst.

Capable of…well, dragging her into a janitor's closet in an occupied community center and fucking her until she sobbed and screamed. I think my ears were still ringing, actually.

And what the *hell* had that been, there at the end? She'd been coming, and I'd been coming—I'd felt her pussy squeeze me harder than it had ever squeezed, so hard it actually hurt. And she'd gone from screaming like a banshee to silent, in an instant—from shaking and writhing in the throes of an almighty powerful climax to stiff and tense as a board, but shivering and trembling, almost like a seizure. Clinging to me, every limb, every muscle tensed. Then, she'd begun whimpering, mumbling something I couldn't make out, too soft and under her breath. Desperation—it had been pure, unadulterated desperation I'd heard in her voice. That much I recognized. As if the orgasm she'd been feeling had gone past that, into something beyond a mere orgasm. It hadn't been me—it was nothing I'd done. I'd been in the middle of finishing my own and couldn't have consciously done anything anyway.

Was emotional fracture a thing? 'Cause that's what it had seemed like to me, like she was fighting back her emotions and feelings for me, fighting so hard, so desperately that she just fractured and split apart, the emotions she'd been denying and refusing to deal with coming up anyway, in whatever way they could make themselves known in her brain and soul and heart.

Or maybe I'm just crazy.

Maybe it was just a one-off, weird kind of climax.

We reached her mom's building, and she glanced at me for confirmation that it was the right one. I nodded, and stayed back, hands in my pockets, and then followed her inside.

Her mom was dressed, hair freshly styled, wearing dress slacks, low-heel wedge shoes, and a form-fitted pullover sweater. Looking sleek and professional. Lucas was still in his khakis, but he had his button-down back, the one Liv had been wearing, and he made the garment seem tiny and stretched to capacity. The man was a damned monster. He was sitting at the island with Liv, and they were both eating omelets and sipping coffee—two more plates sat on the other side of the island, each with a big omelet and several strips of bacon. I could smell a fresh pot of coffee.

I checked my phone, laughed. "I thought I'd entered a time warp, or something. Breakfast food and coffee at…nine at night?"

Lucas shrugged. "I like omelets. They're easy to make and fuckin' delicious. The coffee is half-caff. Liv is meeting with a client in an hour, because her client is a night owl."

Liv picked at her omelet, eying Lexie. "Calmed down, now?"

Lexie huffed, adjusted my hat on her head. "A little. Not really, but a little." She sucked in a deep breath, letting it out slowly. "I'm sorry for my behavior. I'm just…dealing with a lot right now." She looked at Lucas, hesitant, awkward. "I…especially you. I'm sorry."

Lucas left his stool and stood in front of Lex, towering over her, his brown eyes warm and friendly. "Ah, no sweat, Lexie. I don't take most shit seriously, just ask your mom. I could tell you were buggin' when you walked in. It ain't anything, all right?" He smiled down at her. "You need the words? Forgiven and forgotten. Already was before you ever came back, darl… ummm, Lex. Sorry, old habits die hard." He clapped her shoulder with a huge paw, a fatherly gesture. "Made you two some food. Sit and eat."

Lexie shifted from one foot to the other. "You made me food? After the way I spoke to you?"

I noticed Liv was fairly beaming, watching this exchange.

"Sure." Lucas rested both hands on her shoulders. "Told ya, I don't take much personal. You're hurtin', dealin' with some major fuckin' shit. Plus, with my past bein' what it is, I got no room to be touchy. I was an awful goddamn bastard for decades, an' I'm lucky to be standing here at all, luckier yet to stand here with an angel like your mother in my life. So Lex, my dear girl, I'll overlook and forgive and forget just about anything, because the shit I done that's been forgiven is way bigger and nastier than a pissy little outburst like you done."

Lexie didn't say anything about his use of "my dear girl," I think mainly because the way he said it wasn't as a pet name but as an indicator of depth of meaning. She just stood there, silent, staring. "Thank you," she whispered, and seemed to teeter forward, hesitating, and then with a weird sniff, leaned into him and hugged him. Lucas seemed stunned, just stood stone still for a split-second, and then enveloped her in his burly arms and just held her till she pushed away.

Lexie had her head ducked, and I had a feeling it was to hide emotions she couldn't quite shove down. She took one of the plates, the one whose omelet was slightly smaller, and sat on a stool on the far side of her mother, digging in. I sensed Liv had something to say, and that she'd prefer to say it in private.

"Liv, you got a balcony?"

She nodded, pointed. "Off the master. Lucas can show you."

I took a plate, accepted a mug of coffee from Lucas, and met Lexie's eyes. "I'm gonna take my food to the balcony. Yeah?"

She looked almost panicked at being left alone with her mom, eyes wide, fearful, nervous. But she nodded. "Yeah," she whispered.

Lucas went with me, taking a mug of his own, showed me the balcony; there was a cute little wrought iron bistro set, a tiny table and two tiny chairs. I sat at the table while Lucas leaned meaty forearms on the balcony railing and glanced sideways at me.

"So. Myles North."

I ate a few bites. "Lucas Badd."

He grinned. "Relax. I ain't gonna go all…what's that term Rome uses? Fanboy?"

I laughed. "That's a relief. It's tricky enough fending off a squealing sixteen-year-old girl with a celebrity crush. Ain't sure how I'd feel about trying to fend off the same from you."

He smirked. "I like outlaw country better, anyway." He paused. "Lived a good two-thirds of my life down Oklahoma way. Spent more'n a few hours polishing a barstool with my fat backside, listenin' to your pa and grandpa play."

I ate, washed it down with coffee. "You make a hell of an omelet." I finished, stood up to join him at the rail. "I came up on the scene doing mostly outlaw covers. It's honestly where I'm most comfortable as a performer, but the sound my fan base wants is just a little newer. One of these days, I'm gonna do a special album of covers of Dad's and Grandpa's music."

Lucas and I were content to sip coffee in silence for a while, and it was honestly a refreshing moment—the only other person I knew who was as comfortable in companionable silence as me was Crow. Lucas seemed to be the same way, and I appreciated it.

"How'd you calm her down?"

I laughed. "Not sure I did. I think you did more than me."

He chuckled. "She was spittin' nails when she left, came back only chewin' on 'em."

I shifted, unsure how to answer. "We…talked."

His chuckle was…entirely male. "Ah. The *talk*." Meaning, he understood exactly what I meant.

I ducked my head, grinning. "Sometimes it's the only thing that works. She's got a hell of a temper. I mean, I've known some folks with explosive tempers like she's got, but mostly it flares hot and dies quick. Lexie? Don't always die off so fast." Being around Lucas's Oklahoma drawl made the Texas in me come out strong, the twang in my voice deepening.

"How long have you two been seein' each other, if you don't mind me asking?"

I sighed. Found myself opening a little. "Honestly, I ain't even sure what to call what we are. She won't talk about what we are."

He nodded. "Well, I'm just an old reformed drunk, but I can tell you one thing—that there female has a hell of a lot of pain in her, and she's got it bottled up way deep down. Sooner or later, it's all gonna pop, my friend. You care about her, so you just make sure you're there to catch the pieces when it does."

I nodded. "Yeah. If she'll let me."

"Be there? Or catch the pieces?"

I swallowed hard. "Both, honestly."

"Just do what you can do. And sometimes, a woman'll push, hoping you're stubborn enough and strong enough to not push back, but to let her push without letting her push you off."

"You don't know Lexie. Shit, I don't think *I* really know her. I think she keeps a lot of her real self bottled up with the rest of whatever it is she's hiding in there. I ain't sayin' she's fake, but…"

"She's puttin' on a show to protect what she don't think the world can handle or accept."

"Right." I shrugged. "She don't let anyone get close. When she decides to push, she pushes fuckin' *hard*. And I mean, I ain't made of stone, you know? I care about that girl, a lot. But if she won't let me, how long'm I s'posed to keep hangin' around her gettin' pushed off?" I laughed self-consciously. "Man, five minutes around you and I'm twangin' like I'm a twelve-year-old Texas hick again."

"What, your label tell you to sound less like a good ol' boy?"

"Well, no. My best friend Crow and I own our own label—my band mates are minor shareholders, too. It was my manager, Mick. He wanted me to sound southern, but not *too* southern. And, honestly, the more time I spend away from Texas and around people who aren't from the South, the more the accent fades anyway. It doesn't ever go all the way away, but when I'm around someone like you who's got a thick accent, mine comes out."

"Crow's a good fella. I like him. Treats Charlie like a real queen."

I nodded. "Crow...is one of a kind. A truly rare human. And for as good as he treats Charlie, she brings the best out in him. Gives him some soft edges, and for as long as I've known him, he's been not much but sharp and hard through and through. Didn't even know he had a soft side, most of the time. Charlie's amazing. Be good to see her again."

"Best advice I can give you—and I know you didn't ask—is to just be there. And if she tries to push you away, don't let her. Keep on not letting her, and eventually she either will let you get close, or she'll opt herself out of your life, and either way you'll have your answer. But if you care about her like you say you do? You'll find what you need to put up with whatever she dishes out for as long as it takes, as long as you keep seein' something in her that's worth putting up with." He checked his phone, digging it out of his back pocket. "Well, Liv's gotta hit that meeting, and then we're meeting my boys and their girls for drinks. I know you and Lexie are welcome to come, if you want."

I nodded, shrugged. "I dunno. I'll have to see what Lex wants. I appreciate the invite. We wouldn't want to horn in on you and Liv having time with your family, though."

He waved a hand dismissively. "Nah, it's nothin' like that. Just an informal hangout at the Kitty. Probably will end up being more than just my slice of the clan, because this crew is thick as thieves."

"Heard there's a lot of 'em."

"Oh, man," Lucas laughed. "There's a whole damn passel of 'em. I got eight nephews and three sons, and each one has a girl, so that's twenty-two. Then there's Liv's girls, Cassie with Ink, and now Charlie with Crow, making it twenty-six. You guys is twenty-eight. Whenever the other two of her daughters end up here with men, it'll be thirty-two, just adults. Not to mention the growing pile of kids, and shit if I can keep track of *them*. I know the twins are talking about getting pregnant at the same time, and seein' as that's two sets of twins matched up, with history of twins on both sides, chances are they'll both end up with twins themselves, making four babies at the same time, and Corin and Tate already have one pair of twins." He laughed ruefully. "Man, now my head hurts."

"The twins? That's…?"

"Canaan and Corin, my nephews, are identical twins, and they're shacked up permanent-like with a pair of twins, Aerie and Tate, and that's respective— Canaan is with Aerie, and they're touring musicians under the name Canary, and Corin is with Tate, and they're here in town running the label Canary operates on, and some other shit I'm not sure about, and I know Crow is with them a lot, bein' into music himself." He laughed again. "Son, it's confusing as hell. You're just gonna have to jump in and figure it all out yourself. The web of connections and who's who and who's where and who's doing what is so all-fired complicated it's a damn sight above my pay grade."

I nodded. "Well, if I'm around to jump in, I'll probably be asking you for clarification."

"You're better off asking Liv. That woman knows every birthday, every anniversary of the couples who actually bothered to get hitched legal, she knows the whole thing. Taken on the role of matriarch like she was born to it. Some of the kids are calling her Mama Liv. And by kids, I mean the grown ones. None of the youngsters are old enough to talk yet, or not well."

He led the way back to the kitchen, where Lexie was leaning into Liv's shoulder, her mother's arms around her, and she was crying. Shoulders shaking, sniffling and snuffling, the whole works.

Liv saw us coming through and shook her head with a meaningful look, and Lucas and I pivoted in unison and went back where we'd been.

"Looks like they're makin' progress," Lucas said. "Liv's gonna be late, but her client ain't a stickler for punctuality himself."

"What does Liv do?" I asked.

"She's a real estate agent and interior designer." He flicked a hand at the town of Ketchikan at large. "Me, her, Zane, Bast, and Dru have an LLC, actually. I wouldn't quite call it flipping, because we don't do major renovations, but we take homes and condos that are outdated and just need a bit of TLC and spit-and-polish, and we update 'em, put 'em back on the market for a nice little profit. The boys and I do the work, Liv does the design, and she and Dru do the selling. Liv and Dru actually own their own agency, now."

"So that's what you do? Renovations?"

He snorted. "Hell, no. I just help out because I'm handy enough to not nail my own thumbs to the wall. Bast and Zane are the really skilled ones. Naw, me and my boy Ramsey are in business together—we're what we call adventure guides. Anything from local day-hikes to deep bush month-long hunts, backpacking trips, canoeing. If it takes you out in the woods and you need a guide who knows the area and woodcraft, we do it."

"Wow, that's pretty cool."

"Well, I grew up off-grid, some miles north'a here, and spent the first twenty years of my life living in and off of the forest. And Ram—well, all three of the boys were smokejumpers for a number of years. When they retired from that, Ram found himself happiest out in the woods, and turned it into a career."

"Maybe someday I can get you guys to show me some sights, out in the wild. I've done shows in Anchorage and Juneau, but I've never had a chance to do much exploring."

He nodded. "Sure thing, son. Say the word and I'll clear my schedule."

At that moment, Lexie wandered out, eyes red but otherwise back to normal. She smiled at Lucas. "Mom wanted me to tell you it's time to go. And to make sure Myles and I know to meet you guys at the Badd Kitty whenever we're ready."

Lucas nodded. "Sounds good. We'll see you kids later."

"Good talking to you, Lucas." I shook his hand. "And thanks."

He nodded, shook my hand back, and clapped me on the shoulder on the way past.

I waited until he was gone, and then eyed Lexie—she stood beside me at the railing.

Silent.

"So." I bumped her with my shoulder. "You and your mom talked?"

She nodded, letting out a short breath. "Yeah. I told her what happened with me and Marcus—the affair, the abortion, getting kicked out of school, losing my scholarship."

"And? How'd she take it?"

She sniffed, a sound sort of like a laugh but not quite. "I don't know why I was so scared to talk to her. She told me she was disappointed with my decision to have an affair with a married man, which I expected, and it's something I'm going to feel guilty about for probably the rest of my life. I mean, granted, there were rumors his wife was cheating on him with someone, but that's no excuse on my end. I always swore I'd never be the other woman, and I became the other woman. He resigned, you know. They moved to North Carolina. He's at Duke, now. He had tenure at Sarah Lawrence, and I cost him that." She sighed. "The abortion was harder for her. Mainly because she's angry and sad that I didn't tell her, didn't call her. She understood why I did it, but she…I dunno. It's hard for her, as a mother of five, to consider—" She couldn't finish. "I just couldn't even think of any other options. There weren't any, in my mind."

"It was your choice, Lex. Yours and yours alone."

"I know." She tried to smile at me, but didn't quite succeed—I'd never seen her this vulnerable, this quiet, this soft, this open. I felt like I was walking on eggshells, carefully considering every syllable, every movement, for fear of her shutting down again. "I appreciate you saying that, though. Mom…I think she would have convinced me to carry the…the baby…" this was in a whisper, barely audible, "to term, and adopt it out." A wretched sob. "It. Fucking *it*?"

I had no clue what to do or say. I just leaned closer so my shoulder was against hers, hip to hip, thigh to thigh. Just there. Quiet and letting her speak.

"I couldn't have." She was breathing carefully, slowly, measured. "I couldn't have done that. I know I'm, like, this emotionless ice queen, but…deep down, I'm not. Not really."

"You're not an ice queen, Lex. You just keep certain things inside."

"Certain things. Nice dodge, Myles." She sighed

bitterly. "I'm an ice-cold bitch, with an extremely limited range of expressible emotions. I'll party it up and have fun with the best of them, tell jokes and be silly, but that's about it." A glance at me. "Don't have to tell you about my emotional unavailability, do I?"

Truth? Or caution?

"No, honestly, you don't. I'm…well aware."

"I wish I knew how to be different, Myles. I really do."

"I mean, you could try? A little bit a time, you know? Like, it's baby steps to the elevator, Bob. No one expects you to turn into this emotional mush parade overnight, or at all. But just…open up a little." I nudged her temple with my forehead. "Like you are now."

"Thank you for…for recognizing it." A pause. "I'm afraid this is probably a freak one-off event, Myles. Mom can get me open, to some degree, but I'm gonna close up any second now, so you better grab your pearl while you've got the chance."

"I guess if there's any pearl I'm interested in grabbing, it'd be an explanation for what happened in that janitor closet, at the end there. Something happened with you, Lex. I know it did. I felt it."

She swallowed hard. Twined her fingers together in tight shifting knots, picked at her cuticles, making fists. "I…shit. Of course it'd be that."

"There was something, wasn't there?"

She nodded. "Yeah."

"Tell me? Please."

She rubbed her face with both hands. "It's complicated. And I don't think you're going to like hearing some of the explanation. But I gave you the opening and you took it, so I'll answer." A long pause. "I don't know how to start."

"Just the truth, whatever it is, and don't worry about how you think I'll react, or what I'll think."

"Brutal truth?"

I nodded, held her gaze. "Always, Lex. Always."

"Fine. So you've probably figured out by now that I don't ever let anyone raw dog me. That's been a rule of mine for forever. Hard and fast rule, never broken it, ever."

I frowned. "Never?"

"I still to this day have no clue how I ended up pregnant. A one in a billion chance, I guess. I've got an IUD, and I'm still well within the effectivity range, since I'm on the nonhormonal kind which last for like twelve years or something crazy. And I used a condom, and I mean literally every time." She glanced at me. "That moment you were bare inside me, that was, and this is the literal honest truth, the only time I have ever voluntarily allowed a man inside me without a condom."

"I wouldn't say you allowed it."

She tore her gaze away. "Well, it still happened. And that's the salient point, here. You were bare inside me. That's what started it." A silence. "Because I…I liked it. A lot." She was whispering. "I wanted to keep going like that. I've never, ever wanted that with anyone, ever. Not Marcus, not anyone."

"Marcus is the closest you've come to having feelings for someone, I take it?"

She nodded. "Yeah, that's true enough."

"True enough?"

"True enough for the purposes of this conversation."

"Meaning, that's a dead-end line of questioning, where I'm concerned."

She sighed, took my hat off, set it on my head, and scrubbed her hands in her hair. "I need a shower, dammit." A huff. "Fuck, fine. So, there was Jimmy Nawrocki. I had a major crush on him, my sophomore year at U-Conn. Huge crush. Mainly sexual infatuation, and that only got worse when we…well, we spent a week in a hotel together between semesters."

I laughed. "A whole week? Damn."

She smirked. "It was a good week."

"I'll bet."

"What's your record?"

"Record for what?"

She bumped me with her hip. "Longest sex marathon. Not a single session, but most number of back-to-back sessions with the same person without leaving."

I hummed. "Without leaving? That's tricky. I'd say Helen, because basically we hooked up every moment we were together, stopping only to eat, sleep, and go to the bathroom, and that was a week. But she had to go to work, so that eliminates her based on your criteria." I shrugged. "Probably it'd be Britt. She performed before me, I went immediately after her, and we hung out, partied, and had fun with other acts most of the night. Ended up at her hotel, and stayed up for…god, nearly three days I guess, essentially just having sex or waiting for me to get hard again. Passed out for twelve hours, woke up, got room service, did another almost three days straight, drinking and fucking. It only ended because we both had gigs."

"So, I've got you beat on total time, but you've got me beat on longest amount of time without sleeping between." She laughed. "'All right, we'll call it a draw.'" She said this in a bad English accent.

I smirked at her. "You quoting Monty Python at me now?"

"Nick, that friend with benefits I told you about. That was his favorite movie. We watched it at least once every time we hooked up. I can quote the whole thing."

"So."

She snapped her fingers. "Didn't work? Damn."

"Not gonna distract me that easily."

She sidled closer; turned to face me at an angle, pressing her breasts against me. "How about this?"

"Why don't you have sex without a condom, Lex?"

She frowned, but didn't pull away. "Obvious reasons—infections and pregnancy."

"And?"

A shrug. "It's too…personal. Too intimate."

I nodded. "I get that." Slid my arm around her waist. "How's this tie into what happened in the closet?"

She bit her lower lip, heaving a deep breath—and what that did to her cleavage did threaten to distract me. "You were bare, and it felt good. Too good."

"And?"

Another sigh. Damnable swelling cleavage stole my gaze from the deep lush brown of her eyes. "And then, when you were coming, I had this…I don't know. Vision, maybe. It felt like a memory, but it wasn't real, it obviously hasn't happened, but it felt like it. I don't know. It was fucking weird, is what it was."

"What did you see?"

"Us," she whispered.

"Us, how?"

"On the floor of what I assume was a bedroom. There was a carpet and a full-length mirror. I was on my hands and knees, and you were taking me from behind. We were so beautiful together, Myles. So perfect." Her eyes closed, her voice took on a dreamy quality, as she related what was still obviously a very powerful memory. "I felt you inside me. You were bare. I could feel *all* of you. Every inch. Every vein. I could feel your balls tapping against me as you slid in, so fucking deep. It was…glorious. Better than anything. What made it so goddamned powerful was… was the sense of…of belonging. To you. You inside me, bare like that." Her voice shook, broke, steadied. "Then, as you came, in real life, like, in that actual moment, I felt you come in the—the dream, memory, whatever. I felt it, the flood of you. Being filled by you. And it was just…it was too fucking much. It was so beautiful and so right it fucking hurt."

"Jesus, Lex." I had a raging hard-on and a welter of confused emotions.

She looked at me, tears in my eyes. "Myles, I—"

The fear in her eyes, the wariness…told me everything I needed to know.

"Don't worry, I won't ask you to make that a reality." I sounded cold and I knew it.

She closed her eyes, relieved or hurt, I wasn't sure if was one or the other or both. "Myles, that's—"

"You wanted it, it felt beautiful and right, but you're not about to let it happen. That's what made it so hard for you, right?" I felt cracks seam the tender inner sanctum of my heart. "Because letting that happen would be letting me in."

She straightened, and I saw the moment the clamshell snapped closed. "Yep. You guessed it." She pushed away from the railing. Turned and went inside. "I'm going to take a shower and change clothes. Mom wants us to meet her and Lucas at some place called Badd Kitty." And with that, she walked away.

I watched her go.

I'd already had sex with her twice today, and got a handjob to boot. She'd come…god, six times? More, maybe. I wasn't sure.

So maybe that was why I didn't invite myself into her shower. That had to be it. A mere surplus of sex. Maybe there was such a thing as too much of a good thing.

I didn't believe myself for a second. Desire wasn't the issue, for me. Nor was biology—I was rarin' to go right this minute.

Taking a shower was her running away. If she let me into that shower with her, she'd run the risk of giving in to what her body and heart wanted but her mind was too terrified to allow. So, she ran.

From me, from us. From herself.

And I let her.

SEVEN

Lexie

I DIDN'T HAVE THE COURAGE TO INVITE HIM INTO THE SHOWER with me. I wanted to. No matter how frequently I had that man inside me, I always wanted more. I'd always had an out of control libido, an insane capacity and need for sex. Just physiologically, where most women seemed to run out of energy, get sore, need a break, or just plain get tapped out of libidinous drive, I don't. I just don't. Myles North is pure jet fuel dumped on my sex drive. What was already a wild inferno, he turned into an uncontrollable supernova. It honestly scared me.

And then there was the emotional aspect of it all. I wanted…a whole bunch of things I couldn't even begin to quantify or name.

I wanted to be held; I wanted to feel safe—like I had on the plane ride here. Like I had every night since meeting Myles.

I wanted to feel him raw and bare inside me, feel him lose control, feel him desperate and wild and all fucking mine, in my arms, above me, behind me, beneath me, all around me, everywhere in me and through me. I wanted to—

Fuck.

I wanted to love him.

To be loved by him.

Standing in the shower, coming to that realization, I fucking lost it.

I fell to the floor of the shower and sobbed. Again. For the second time today.

Because I just could not figure out how to let him in. I could not tell him how I felt. Admitting to myself how I felt about Myles was terrifying enough, but there was no possible way I could tell him. Telling him I was falling in love with him meant I would have to reveal more secrets.

And lordy, I had some doozies.

Secrets which not even Mom, Charlie, Cassie, Torie, or Poppy knew about. Secrets no one knew except me and the person involved.

Secrets that I did not even dare to think about.

Eventually, the water started to lose its heat and

I forced myself to my feet, finished my shower, then turned off the water and stepped out, toweled off.

I borrowed Mom's hairdryer and did my hair in a tight topknot, minimal makeup, and dressed in a pair of saffron yellow peasant slacks—tight at the waist and ankles, low-rise, and voluminous and blousy and flowing around my legs. Above, I wore a bright leafy green piece of thin linen which tied up around my neck and around my back, and was entirely open down between my breasts to where it was knotted over my diaphragm. I put some nude-colored nipple pasties on, just so I didn't start a riot with Mom's new "family," along with some strategically applied double-sided boob tape to make sure the girls didn't totally escape the negligible constraints of the top.

Leather sandals completed the outfit, and I was ready to go.

When I emerged from the bathroom, which was en suite to the bedroom Myles and I would be sharing, he was in the process of removing his damp jeans, shirtless, barefoot, messy hair. Fucking glorious. My heart started palpitating immediately upon seeing his broad back and taut, muscular ass and powerful thighs—he was facing away from me, kicking the jeans off and swearing under his breath as the damp denim stuck to him. God, he was beautiful with his collage of tattoos, his wild damp hair, skin golden.

When he was finally free of the wet jeans, he kicked them across the room with a shout of triumph, and snagged a clean pair. He shrugged into a tight white T-shirt, and threaded a faded, worn, tanned leather belt with a big platinum Texas-shaped buckle into his jeans. He snagged a clean ball cap from his duffel—this one white and orange with the Longhorns logo, then sat on the bed, tugged his socks on, and his trusty boots—in all the time I'd known him, I'd only ever seen him wear two different pairs of boots: one a pair of floppy-sided, square-toed, scuffed and stained tan leather cowboy boots, and the other a pair of Doc Martens, brown and shiny, often polished, but scratched and well-worn. Despite his wealth, he was a man of simple tastes, and was dedicated to comfortable, familiar clothing.

Dressed, he stood up, settled a deep sigh, and just stood there a moment, not realizing I was behind him. I stepped carefully closer, and I noted the moment he realized my presence—his shoulders straightened, his head lifted. I pressed up against him from behind, slid my hands up his belly over his shirt. "You look every inch the country star, Mr. North."

He chuckled. "I was going for average Joe."

"You couldn't pass for an average Joe if you tried, Myles. You just exude star power. It's just in your DNA."

He twisted his head, sniffed at me, inhaling deeply. "God, Lex, you smell so fuckin' good."

I leaned closer, so his nose slid along my throat. "Lavender and vanilla perfume."

He inhaled deeply, and my skin pebbled. "Been driving me crazy, tryin' to figure out what the scent was." He inhaled again. "Fuckin' love the way you smell, Lex."

I shivered. "I'll wear this scent more often, if you love it that much."

He growled. "Best be careful, wearin' it around me. Makes me fuckin' horny as hell."

"Myles, seriously, what *doesn't* make you horny?"

He nipped my throat. "About you? Not much."

I shivered again, laughing as his hot breath and sharp teeth moved down my throat to the hollow where my throat met my breastbone. "Stop, Myles, or we won't make the get-together."

"Well damn, what a shame that would be."

I felt my hand lift, slide along his cheek, tracing his rough three-day stubble. "We have to go, Myles. Mom really wants me to meet them all."

He sighed in resignation, kissed my shoulder. Straightened. "Fine, fine. I'll be good." Another unexpected nip to the side of my neck. "For now."

"You be good now and *I'll* be good later."

"Sexy Lexie, you're *always* good."

Two words, one a compliment that I valued under most circumstances and the other simply my name—together, said as a nickname, were like being doused with cold water. Worse, like having acid thrown on me. I writhed away, shuddering convulsively, nearly gagging; instant panic attack.

"Do not ever—*fucking EVER* call me...*that*... again." I whirled, and I knew he saw the deadly serious venom in my eyes, in every line of my expression. "*Never*. Do you understand me?"

He blinked, eyes wide, hands up in surrender. "Jesus fuck, Lex, yeah, I got it. I apologize. I didn't know."

I swallowed hard. Turned away to blink the hot salty mist away. "Thank you," I whispered. "I can't explain, I just..."

He was behind me, hands gingerly resting on my shoulders. "It's okay, Lex. You've got triggers. It's okay. We'll uncover 'em as we go along and I'll learn them. Breathe, okay? It's all right, Lex."

I shook my head. "You had no way of knowing. Just please don't say that again."

"I won't."

I tried to steady my breathing. Waited for the questions with shoulders hunched as if waiting for a blow. They never came. I turned and stared up at him. My eyes were still damp. "You're not going to ask?"

He shook his head. "I know better."

"Dammit, Myles, that's not fair."

He pulled me close, wrapped me up in a hug. A warm, enveloping, platonic, safe embrace. Just held me. "I'll wait, Lex. I know you got shit you can't talk about, won't talk about. I ain't blind. It's deep, and it's big, and it's painful, and I doubt you've ever talked about it. I ain't gonna ask, now or ever. I want to know—I *need* to know. But you gotta decide if you trust me, if I'm somebody you want deep enough in your life to give me your secrets. Only you can decide that. I ain't pushin', Lex. Not gonna. Just so we're clear, I am asking you to try to trust me. To give it to me. Talk to me. But this, right here, right now, it's the only time I'm gonna say it. It's up to you, Lex, and I'm strong enough and patient enough to wait for you to figure it out on your own time."

I let him hold me and didn't try to respond. I had nothing to respond with. Eventually, the panic attack lessened, faded away, and left me. When I could, I pushed away from him. Drew a deep breath, and let it out slowly. I stared up at him and tried to find something to say. "Myles, I…"

He touched my lips. "Don't have to say anything, Lex. Just wanted you to know where I'm at." He took my hand, twined his fingers with mine, and smiled at me. "Ready?"

I sighed again—I didn't deserve him, the way he treated me. But I was going to take it, because it felt too good to deny myself. "Yeah, let's go."

———◆———

Badd Kitty turned out to be Badd Kitty Saloon—a supermasculine place, but in an inviting, appealing way. Faded, reclaimed wood for the floorboards and walls, weathered, aged, rusted, reclaimed bits of tin, copper, and steel for trim and odds and ends, a long polished bar running the entire length of the interior on one side, real double-hinged batwing doors in front of the bathrooms and kitchen; forties and fifties pinup posters on the walls, along with movie posters from spaghetti westerns, Charles Bronson movies, and old black-and-white horrors like *Psycho*, *Nosferatu*, and *Creature from the Black Lagoon*. Other decorations included an entire antique motorcycle on one section of wall, a pair of Old West pearl-handled revolvers and a gun belt, and an assorted collection of antique tools and weaponry. There were lots of two-tops and four-tops in the middle with plenty of space between the tables and a space for people to dance and mill around. Booths lined the wall opposite the bar.

Interestingly, there were only two TVs in the

whole place, placed on either end of the bar, and neither was tuned to Sports Center, but instead both were playing what looked like *The Good, the Bad, and the Ugly*, with the volume up enough that if you were sitting near the TV, you could actually hear it. There was music playing everywhere else, an old Elvis Costello tune I recognized but couldn't have named.

The bar was busy, but I soon realized that it was only immediate Badd and Goode family members and attached significant others and kids in attendance; there was actually a sign on a stand as you entered which stated the bar was closed for a private event.

And good golly Miss Molly, what a crew it was. Every male I saw was more mouthwateringly hot than the last—I'm not ashamed to say that if the entire collection of men in this room were to do a nude or mostly nude calendar, I'd be the first to buy one and hang it in my bathroom for the purposes of visual stimulation while twiddling my bean. Because *damn*, the men were hot. The sheer volume of muscle and testosterone and insanely perfect male sexiness was so overwhelming I had to fan myself, and restrain myself from running into the bathroom and doing something inappropriate with myself—or better yet, with Myles. I mean, the testosterone and sexiness levels were off the charts.

And then there were the women.

I have a healthy self-esteem, okay? Facts are facts, and I'm hot. I know what I look like and I'm not intimidated being in a room with other beautiful women.

But...the women milling around in the Badd Kitty Saloon? Each of them was incredible.

Faces so beautiful they could start not just fights but whole wars.

Bodies that made mine seem downright frumpy.

Perfect hair in shades ranging from blond to brown to red to black like my own.

Mesmerizing eyes.

Brilliant smiles.

Geez, what a group.

Myles and I were standing in the entrance, taking it all in, and I glanced up at Myles. "Wow."

He snorted in disbelief. "No kidding. Wow. I mean, where do I look first? The men make me feel like a ninety-pound wuss, and the women make me feel funny in the pants region."

"Right? I mean, god. Check out the monster dude behind the bar talking to Mom. He makes even Jupiter look small and puny."

"Must be Baxter, the one Jupe was telling us about."

I couldn't take my eyes off him. He was the

physical embodiment of a comic book superhero. "He's scary as fuck." I eyed the crowd again. "I won't be mad if you feel a little overcome by lust at some of these women, I gotta say."

He shook his head. "Check out the strawberry blonde with the ice cream-colored skin and the freckles, over there with the blond Adonis."

I followed his gaze, and was dumbstruck with marvel. "Dude."

"Right?"

"I think I have boob envy."

He guffawed. "You got no reason to envy *any-one*, Lex. But yeah, she's fuckin' *stacked*."

"Is that how you'd describe me? Stacked?"

He smirked at me. "Jealous?"

"Nah." I shrugged. "Just curious."

"She's not just stacked, she's *fuckin'* stacked. It's a level up." He eyed me, his gaze raking over my rather prominently displayed tatas. "You, Alexandra Goode, are not just fuckin' stacked…" he trailed off. "I'm trying to think of what would be one step up from that."

"Well, I'm not sure I know how men rank their categories of boob size, so I can't help you there."

"Myles! Lex!" A female voice from across the bar. "Get in here and meet everyone!"

I turned my gaze to see Mom standing on the

rung of a bar stool, hand on Lucas's shoulder for balance, waving at us over the heads of the crowd. I waved back, took Myles's hand, and we wove our way through the gathering of sexy men, gorgeous women, and more than a couple of toddlers hanging on to adult legs. Despite being a bar and everyone except Mom and Lucas being young and beautiful, it was a surprisingly familial, comfortable atmosphere. Not a party, just...a family get-together.

Myles glanced at me as we approached Mom and Lucas. "Pretty chill, actually. I was expecting either a lame reunion atmosphere, or some kind of crazy party. This is cool. Just family and friends chilling. Like a backyard barbecue, but in a bar."

"So...not the time to do Jaeger shots and dance topless on the bar, then," I joked.

"Uh, probably not. That's later."

A tall guy with long hair in a low ponytail overheard me, and grinned. "I mean, if you wait till later, Liv and Lucas take the youngsters to one of the houses and put on kiddie movies, and things in here get a little crazy. So if Jaeger shots and dancing topless on the bar is your thing, nobody here is gonna get pissy about it."

Lexie laughed. "Good to know. I was joking, though." She shrugged. "Mostly. I *have* been known to flash while drunk, but I don't think I'll let myself go that far at a family get-together." She stuck out her hand. "I'm Lexie Goode."

"Lucian Badd." He gestured to the woman beside him—about my height, dark skin and dreadlocked hair making her mixed race all the more beautiful for it. "This is Joss Mackenzie."

Lucian and Joss both turned to Myles, and he shook both of their hands. "Hey guys, nice to meet you. I'm Myles."

"Yeah, I know," Joss said, laughing. "I think by now everyone in the bar knows Myles North is in the house."

"So what am I, then? Chopped liver?" A woman's voice, a familiar voice.

One I'd heard in half a dozen of my favorite movies. I turned, and there, live and in the flesh, was Harlow Grace. Oscar and Emmy winner, A-list star, and one of my heroes, because she isn't afraid to speak her mind. She's classy, elegant, outspoken, opinionated and unapologetic. She has the kind of star power that allows her to choose her roles, and she's played the gamut, from ditzy bombshell arm candy villain-bait to hard-charging journalist, and everything in between. She's never done a nude scene, has publicly stated that she will not, and it's written into her contract, yet she still manages to be sexy, a Hollywood sex symbol. She's released sexy, provocative photos, professionally done, on her website, for free, and even a nearly nude full page spread in *Maxim,* and a *Sports Illustrated* swimsuit edition feature. She is not afraid of her body and not afraid to show it, but it's on her terms. And that's what I find heroic, especially in today's society.

I squealed, and gripped Myles by the arm. "It's Harlow!"

He eyed me with amusement. "Did you act like that before you met me the first time?"

I laughed, poked his ribs. "Ohmygod, I was *so* much worse. I admire Harlow as an actress and role model—but I had a huge, major crush on you."

"You did?"

I frowned. "Um, duh?" I stared at him. "Do you think I jump into bed with just any celebrity I happen to meet backstage? I met Harry Styles backstage once and he invited me to hang out with them after, but I was already going to a party with some friends so I didn't because they were my ride, and it was *Harry Styles*, whom I admit I also had a little bit of a thing for, even if I'm not a huge fan of his music."

Harlow was watching this with amusement. "Once upon a time, I'd have taken that opportunity with Harry, had it been offered to me. He's cute!" She grinned at Myles. "And you're Myles North. Holy shit. I'm a huge fan."

I blinked. "Wait. Do celebrities get celebrity crushes?"

A tall, lean, clean-cut guy with tattoos on his forearms and heavy-rimmed glasses stood next to Harlow. "I think for a celebrity, it would simply be considered a normal crush." He paused. "But then, a celebrity is a celebrity, regardless of who they are, objectively speaking, so from that perspective, yes." He glanced at Harlow. "What is your opinion, Low?"

"Hmm. Interesting question. I mean, yeah, I'd still consider it a celebrity crush. I suppose I am technically a celebrity, but so is Tom Hardy, right? I've never met him, and he's super famous, and I think he's mega hot. So it would be a celebrity crush." She grinned at me. "So I guess that makes the answer yes, celebrities get celebrity crushes."

The brother with the glasses seemed puzzled. "You find Tom Hardy attractive? Who is Tom Hardy?"

She patted his shoulder. "An actor. A very talented, very good-looking actor."

"And you have a crush on him?"

She sighed, looked at him with love. "A celebrity crush is different than having a normal crush on an average person, love. It just means you really admire and are attracted to them, as a star. Being famous, it's assumed it's unlikely if not impossible that the crush would ever be anything but an idle fantasy. So it's not a real crush like you're thinking."

He was still frowning. "But you're a star. You could meet him at a press junket, or on the red carpet, and become his girlfriend with ease. You are famous yourself and thus have access a not-famous person would never have. So it is not an impossibility for your celebrity crush on this Tom Hardy individual to become a reality."

She leaned into his side and pressed her lips to his ear. Whispered something that mollified him—and more, judging by the way he shifted awkwardly.

He was odd, and serious, and earnest, but clearly totally in love with Harlow, and she with him.

I extended my hand. "You must Xavier Badd."

He was puzzled. "We have not met. How do you know my name?"

I gestured at Harlow. "It's a well-known fact that Harlow is engaged to Xavier Badd, a robotics genius, Silicon Valley start-up darling, and inventor of fascinating devices which I've always wanted, but have never been able to afford."

Harlow laughed, nuzzled him. "What she means is, you're becoming famous yourself, baby."

"Famous because of my connection to you is not famous for me," he said. "But I suppose that is a natural risk of being romantically entangled with a woman of your elevated social status."

I laughed. "You're funny."

He didn't laugh with me. "I was not joking."

"I…um. Oh."

He blinked, frowned. "I am not comfortable in such large gatherings, so my social capacity is somewhat hampered. My apologies." He turned to Harlow. "Please excuse me, my love. I need some space."

She just nodded, kissed him with quick familiarity. "Go up to the break room and tinker. I know you brought a gadget with you."

He nodded. "I have my briefcase. I'll just catch my bearings and return when I'm able."

I watched this exchange with curiosity. When Xavier had vanished into the crowd and up a flight of steps, Harlow smiled at us. "He's on the autism spectrum. It makes big parties like this hard for him." She smiled proudly. "He's done a lot of research into ASD, and we have a charity foundation which we do a lot of work for, funding research and promoting awareness. He does a lot of speaking engagements on the subject in schools near where we live down in LA."

"So is that why he talks like…"

"Like an eighty-year-old Ivy League professor, stuck in the body of a superhot twenty-three-year-old? Yeah. If you were to ask him something he knows a lot about—which is just about everything—you'd hear him go into real lecture mode. He's literally one of the smartest people on the planet." She gestured after him. "When I say go tinker, he's going to pull some gizmo out of his briefcase that a billion-dollar robotics lab couldn't conceive of in a hundred years, which he invented for fun while doing, like, quantum physics or something."

I felt a little dizzy. "Wow. So robotics genius isn't just an online magazine tagline."

"Oh no," Harlow said. "It doesn't even begin to scratch the surface of the genius of that man. He can quote all of *The Iliad* and *The Odyssey*...in the original Greek. He can quote Marcus Aurelius...in Latin. His most recent language project is teaching himself both Old and Middle English, at the same time. It's a side hobby for him, learning obscure or dead languages. He says after he's literarily fluent in Old and Middle English he's going to teach himself Sanskrit because he heard it's challenging."

I laughed. "How do you keep up with him?" I asked.

Harlow just cackled. "Intellectually? You don't. You just try to not get carried away in the flash flood of his intellect. It makes daily conversation interesting, that's for sure."

I saw a quartet of dazzling beauties behind Myles: a pair of male twins and a pair of female twins, one with a toddler on her hip; the men were, like all the Badd men I'd seen so far, tall, lean, and muscular and devastatingly handsome; the women, again, were in a class all their own in terms of sophistication and beauty. The women made me feel frumpy and slutty, and the men made me feel weak in the knees and guiltily turned on.

The circle Myles and I were part of—Lucian, Joss, and Harlow—expanded to include the twins. The men: same height and build as Lucian and Xavier, both had the grizzly bear-brown hair as the rest of the family. Both sported tattoos and piercings, wore ripped jeans and Sharpie-decorated Chuck Taylors and concert T-shirts.

The women were a combination of Blake Lively and Marilyn Monroe, slender and elegant and sophisticated. Both were dressed like they could have stepped out of a *Vanity Fair* fashion ad—sleek and daring and revealing without being overtly sexual, highlighting their bodies without displaying.

Harlow saw me eying the female twins. "Don't worry, I feel the same way around them."

I blinked at her. "Sorry, what?"

She indicated the two blond women. "Them. They're so freaking perfect they make you feel…tawdry. Right?"

I boggled. "But you're…"

She arched an eyebrow. "An absolutely ordinary

woman with self-esteem issues, especially as regards to the width of my hips." She smoothed her hands over her hips, which were almost as generous as mine, and then gestured at the twins, whose hips were quite a bit more slender. "They don't mean to be perfect, they just can't help it."

I laughed and realized one of the twins was staring at me.

I waved. "Hi?"

"Lexie?" the female twin with her hair up guessed. "He's Myles North, which based on what Charlie has told me, makes you Lexie."

I tried a tentative smile. "Um. Yeah. My infamy precedes me, I guess."

The male twin with the undercut, the father of the toddler, nodded seriously. "Oh yeah, for sure. She was all like, god, that sister of mine. What a bitch. You're gonna hate her. Please punch her for me."

The other twin elbowed him. "What my idiot twin, who thinks he's funny, is trying to say, is that Charlie has told us very good things about you."

I frowned. "She has?"

The longhaired one nodded. "She has. How cool you are, how much we're all going to love you."

"That you're bringing one of our music idols with you," the other said.

Myles snorted. "I'm ain't worthy of being

anyone's idol, guys." He shook their hands, one and then the other. "I'm Myles."

"No shit you're Myles," the jokester twin said. "I ate too much cheese yesterday so I'm majorly consti-pated, otherwise I'd be shitting myself, meeting you."

"Two things, Cor—one, fuckin' gross, dude. Nobody needs to know you're constipated. Two, quit fanboying the man. Get—it—together." This from the other twin, the last three words emphasized with a light but loud backhand-forehand-backhand slap.

"Slap me again, bitch, and I'll hogtie you and force-feed you Lena's pureed peas."

"You said a bad word, Daddy," I heard a tiny voice say from around my knees—a little boy of four or so, with his dad's brown hair and his mom's eyes. "You gotta give me a dollar."

Corin glanced down, ruffled the boy's head. "Hey, kiddo. Didn't know you were standing there, bud." He frowned. "How do you know I said a bad word?"

"Because whenever you get mad about stuff you say *sonofabitch* real loud and Mommy gets mad at you and you gotta give me a dollar."

Corin restrained a smile. "You're right, that is a bad word. But if I owe you a buck for saying it, you owe me a buck back because you said it too." He shrugged. "So I'd say we're even."

The little boy shook his head firmly. "Nuh-uh. I only said it to say you said it. I didn't really say it."

Canaan smirked. "He's got you there, bro."

"No!" Corin said. "It still counts. Saying it is saying it, regardless of your intention."

And then the twins were arguing about swearing, until the boy tugged on Corin's pant leg. "Daddy? Daddy!"

Corin broke away from his argument with his brother and glanced down. "Yeah, bud?"

"I gotta poop."

Corin laughed. "Well? Go! You know where it is."

"But it's a big one, and I gotta go now."

Corin's eyes widened, and he scooped his son up and whisked him off horizontally, making airplane noises while the boy laughed hysterically, interspersed with sing-song chants of "poop poop poopy poop."

I watched the proceedings with amusement and said to Myles, "I wasn't sure what I was expecting to find at this family party, but not this."

Myles waved at the reduced circle around us. "Nice to meet you guys. Canaan, I think, right? Maybe we can get together for a jam session before I skip town."

The remaining twin nodded. "Yeah, I'm Canaan. And a jam session sounds like an awesome idea." He hesitated. "Did you bring Betty-Lou with you?"

Myles shook his head. "Nah, I keep her in a tem-perature- and humidity-controlled storage case. I have a new guitar I'm dying to break in."

Canaan's eyes widened. "You have it with you?" he breathed, his voice awed and reverential.

Myles frowned. "You know about the guitar?"

"I was with Crow when he finished it. I know literally nothing about it because that man is the most tight-lipped human being I've ever met in my fucking life, but I know musical instruments and I know that was one hell of a special piece, and I've been dying to hear what it sounds like." Canaan shook his head. "It was a masterpiece, and I mean that. Like getting a Stradivarius, but directly from the maker himself."

Myles didn't answer right away. "Yeah, that's a fair comparison. River Dog was a true master artisan."

"Wait, River Dog was a person? I thought the name was just, like, some sort of cool reference to a myth or some shit."

Myles laughed. "Yeah, Crow's not real forth-coming with information, is he? River Dog is Crow's grandfather, deceased now, God rest him. That gui-tar was the last thing River Dog ever made, and he died before he could actually finish it. He taught Crow everything he knew, but when he died Crow sort of…turtled a bit, I guess, refused to touch it. Until he moved here." He scanned the bar. "Where is the sonofabitch, anyway?" Myles then glanced around his knees. "Shoot, anymore kids around for me to owe a dollar to?"

Canaan laughed, shaking his head. "Nah, Lucas, the one who had to poop, is with Corin, Liam is over there being fed cheese sticks by Eva, Harlow has Lena, and that's all my kids. Brock and Claire have Nina with them over by the stage, Mara's two boys are playing the Switch with Eva and Bax's son over there in the back booth, and Dru and Bast's daughter is... actually it looks like she's trying to braid Ink's beard. And that's the lot, I think."

Myles frowned. "That is a lot of kids."

Canaan laughed again. "We're a lot of people and we all really like having sex, I guess."

Myles cackled. "Okay, well I'm gonna try to watch my language regardless. Good to meet you. I'll meet up with you about the jam session." He tugged my hand. "Come on, let's go say hi to your mom and sisters. And where the...heck...is Crow?"

Ink, a six-foot-seven giant covered head to toe with tattoos, currently having his beard clumsily braided by a little girl heard the question and gestured. "Kitchen. Him and Claire are fixin' up some snacks."

Cassie was sitting beside Ink and she leaned over and showed the girl how to merge the braids. "You're gonna be a braiding expert soon, Delia."

"I always want to braid Daddy's hair, but it's too short. And Mommy says I'm too rough to braid hers, but she still lets me. Uncle Ink's beard is the funnest to braid. It's soft and scratchy at the same time, and sticks together. Mommy's hair is all slippery and hard to braid."

Seeing Cassie, tough and hard-nosed and independent and as fiery as me, being all sweet and Auntie-like to this little girl was weird. Cassie saw me, kissed the little girl on the head and helped tie a rubber band around the very tip of Ink's braided beard, and then hopped down from the stool and rushed over to hug me. "Lexie! God, it's so good to see you."

I hadn't seen her for a while but the first thing I noticed was that she was…different. All my life she'd been all muscle and bone and athletic, toned female physique. Now she was…softer. I wanted to say bigger, but that would sound judgmental. And softer wasn't right either. Stronger. Not as hyper-lean and shredded as she'd always been. More muscular, and so yes, physically larger. But because of it, her diminutive size was offset by muscularity and just…feminine softness.

"You look so good, Cass!" I said.

She smiled, pushing back from the hug but not letting go. "You think so? I'm heavier than I've ever been in my life, but…I feel *good*, Lex. I'm teaching fitness and dance classes now, you know."

"Mom told me in her latest epic novel of an email," I said, looking my sister over. "Honestly, in my personal opinion, you look *way* healthier and more feminine now. Not that you were masculine before, but…whatever you're doing suits you."

She snorted. "What I'm doing is eating actual food and living an actual life. I lift weights and dance and teach, and I go for runs with the other girls sometimes, but I'm not obsessed with my weight anymore. I realized I had been. My whole life, I had to stay under a certain number or I'd lose my spot in the troupe." She looks around at the room. "I'm so, *so* much happier."

I grinned at her. "I think it's the happiness as much as anything. You're like, glowing." I frowned. "It's not a pregnancy glow, is it?"

Cassie's eyes widened and she jokingly made the sign of the cross. "Heaven forbid. No. I'm not anywhere near ready to be a mom yet."

"Well now you did it," Ink rumbled. "Now we're gonna get you pregnant."

"And there goes sex for you, big guy," she teased.

"What's sex?" the little girl piped up. "Mommy says I'm too young to know."

"Crap," Cassie breathed. "I, um…"

"Your mom is right, little one," Ink answered. "Auntie Cass should watch what she says around little ears."

"Mommy says I have the biggest ears in the world," the girl said. "But I checked and they're not big at all. So I don't know what that means."

"It means you hear things you shouldn't," Cass said. "And then repeat them and ask questions adults have trouble answering."

"Auntie Cass, huh?" I mused.

Cassie laughed. "If you're part of the clan, you're an aunt or uncle to the little ones. You don't have a choice. You're inducted, and thus expected to spoil, corrupt, and snuggle all the various children."

I looked around—it seemed very few of the children were with their parents, and seemed to think nothing of climbing up the leg of the nearest adult, regardless of who it was, and that adult would pick the child up without missing a beat and incorporate him or her into the conversation. It was odd, supremely, to see these men with the tiny children, the ones like the triplets and Bax especially, who resembled WWE stars in terms of raw athletic bulk, with the gorgeous, alpha-male sex factor of the kind of men who played superheroes on the big screen. None of them were dads yet, I didn't think, but they were clearly each growing comfortable with kids, since I saw one of the huge triplets tossing up and catching a little black girl with tight ringlets and bright eyes and a squealing laugh.

I watched. "Who's that?" I asked.

"The big blond guy with the wanna-be Duck Commander beard? Or the little girl he's tossing in the air?"

"Uhh, both?"

"The blond with the beard is Ram, Lucas's son."

I racked my brain for what Mom had shared in her emails. "Uhh, Ramsey is the outdoors one, right? Him and Lucas own a hiking guide company."

Cassie grinned. "Correct! We all call him Ram, though, not Ramsey. And the little girl is Nina, Brock and Claire's daughter." She pointed at the adults in question: a tall man built somewhere between the monster physique of Bax and the lean whipcord of the twins, with his brown hair swept back and to the side, clean shaven, and so devastatingly handsome he would put every GQ model ever photographed to shame; the woman was tiny, barely over five feet, with blond hair cut straight across at her chin.

I was trying to figure out how to politely ask the obvious question, but Cass answered it for me.

"Claire can't have kids—not sure why. They adopted Nina a year, year and a half ago. Took them, like, over a year to get through the adoption process, I guess."

We watched Ram throw the little girl ever higher, much to her delight. Cassie turned back to me. Then eyed Myles. "My sister clearly has no manners or she'd have already introduced us. But, I mean, you're you and so obviously I know who you are, but still."

Myles held out his hand. "Myles."

"Cassie. The other bitchy sister."

I cackled. "The *only* bitchy sister. *I'm* a perfect angel."

She flipped me off, and then went way too serious way too fast. "Mom gave me the Spark Notes version of what happened, but said I should talk to you myself."

I huffed. "The Spark Notes version is I had an affair with a married professor, got caught by his wife, who was the dean's daughter, got kicked out, lost my scholarship, and had an abortion." I turned to see several faces regarding me with interest, and realized I'd said all that rather...loudly. "Well...shit. Now everyone knows."

The tiny blonde came over. "I got knocked up at nineteen, had a miscarriage and had to have a D-and-C afterwards. The D-and-C resulted in what's called Asherman's syndrome, meaning I'm infertile and will never have a biological baby of my own." She watched Ram still playing with Nina. "We adopted her seventeen months ago and I've never been happier."

I blinked. "Wow. Um...wow."

A tall woman with auburn hair that was closer to red than brown was next to her. "I was stood up at the altar and ended up here in Ketchikan by mistake, met my husband Bast, fell in love, and never went back."

A woman with long thick black hair in a complicated braid entered the circle. "I'm from an obscenely wealthy upper crust East Coast family whom I've disowned and will never see again, because I love Baxter—who was an underground prize fighter when I met him, and I've actually been to one of his fights, before he quit doing it. Got all bloody, too."

"Zane knocked me up the same week we met, which was a week of epic fucking, I must say, and I'm still not sure if I know what I'm doing most days because I never thought I'd be able to fall in love, much less be a mother and a wife." This from a tall curvy blonde whose tits and ass were nearly as bangin' as mine and the tall strawberry blonde's—who was also now joining the circle.

Said strawberry blonde leaned against the other blonde—this was getting confusing—who'd just shared her story. "I was a dedicated hookup artist with a cold dead heart, a wandering vagina, and zero future. Then I met a man named Ramsey, messed around with him a few times, and it turns out the dick was so good I couldn't walk away, so I stayed with his dick…and the rest of him."

I snorted, because that sounded like something I'd say.

Next was Aerie, the other blond twin, with Tate beside her once again. "We hooked up with the twins sort of out of curiosity regarding what it would be like with them. Tate got pregnant, and our mom disowned us, loudly and publicly, in Badd's Bar and Grill. We gave up modeling careers to be here with them."

"Actually, I think we disowned her just as much," Tate said.

Joss chimed in, next. "I'm an orphan. I was homeless for a very long time. Almost got raped. And I was a virgin when I met Lucian."

Harlow, appearing from somewhere. "I never told Xavier who I was when we met. He didn't know, and I liked it. I liked feeling like a normal girl. So I never told him, even though I knew he was different and that whatever we were doing wasn't going to be just random sex, because it was clear he was a virgin. I kept my fame a secret from him until things blew up, and it's only because he has such a kind and forgiving and understanding heart that we're together. After that deception, he had every right to forget me, but he didn't, and here I am."

A short, curvy girl, who looked like she was related to the giant Ink—jet-black hair and skin color and facial structure that made her Native American—held up her hand. "I was a secret tattoo artist, because my mom refused to allow me to do anything except go to college and get a real degree and a real job, so I could be the first and only one in the whole family to do so, even though I didn't want to. I did go to college, and I did get a degree, and I did get real job at a law firm, but I hated it and it wasn't until I met Remington that I found the courage to do what I was truly passionate about."

Another blonde—this one not quite blond and not quite brunette. Tall with a damned near perfect body. "I lived a life of being the good girl, doing the right thing for the right reasons all the time. I couldn't stand Roman the first time I met him...or the second, or the third. Or...quite a long time after that. Couldn't stand him, and at some point would have said I hated him...but was absolutely bonkers for him at the same time. As Izzy would have said, I wanted the dick in the worst way."

"Kitty!" the statuesque, potty-mouthed strawberry blonde said. "I'm shocked at you."

Kitty just laughed. "The rest of you are rubbing off on me."

I looked around. Looks like all the women had told me their stories, or the Spark Notes version anyway.

Cassie nudged me. "I got in a car wreck which

ended my professional dance career *and* my relationship with my fiancé, who turned out to be gay. Moved here with Mom like a dog with its tail between its legs, and Ink saved me from walking straight into the Passage because I was anger-walking."

"My fiancé cheated on me with my overweight middle-aged boss. I quit, moved, and then went on a cross-country road trip with my sister, and did the craziest thing I've ever done—fell in love with a badass biker and moved here with him." She smiled over her shoulder at Crow, who was standing behind her with a giant glass bowl of guacamole in his hands.

Mom walked through the circle to me and placed her hands on my shoulders. "My husband of twenty-five years died, and I moved here for a change of scenery and pace, to start over. I met a strange, gruff, rough, enormous, foul-mouthed, beautiful disaster of a man named Lucas, and we did things my daughters would probably not appreciate hearing about, which made me realize how unhappy I'd been in my marriage before Darren died. I had to accept that, digest it, and then figure out how to fall in love all over again, as a middle-aged woman, well past her prime, with five grown daughters."

"Ain't shit about you being past your prime, woman," Lucas growled.

Mom sighed, smiled. "Thank you, Lucas." She

stayed focused on me. "The point of all this, my dear love, is that there is no story about yourself you could tell which we all here would not understand, sympathize with, and do everything in our power to help you through. You are among *family*, Alexandra."

My throat was hot and tight. I didn't know *any* of these women except Mom and my sisters, and the only men I knew were Myles and Crow.

So...

Family?

My family was scattered across the country—or had been until recently; now Mom, Cassie, and Charlie were here in Alaska, Torie was still in Connecticut wasting her life away with a bong and a waitress's apron, and Poppy was in New York dodging the reality of having to either woman up and chase her real dream, or give up on it. And me? I was...I had no fucking clue what I was. Or where I belonged. Or what I wanted to do.

Or who I wanted to do it with.

Should I move to Alaska with Mom, Cassie, and Charlie? Live with my mother again? Live with one of my older sisters and their serious boyfriends? But do fucking what?

I looked around—the entire clan's eyes were on me, every single one. And there was...love in those eyes. Acceptance. They didn't fucking know me, so how could they love me? How could they accept me? They didn't know me. They all—Mom, Charlie, and Cassie included—thought they knew my worst, deepest, darkest, most painful secret...the affair and abortion.

If only it was that simple.

If only it was as simple as not having a career plan or goals. Well...it was not like I had career plans beyond college; the plan was always get the degree and figure "then what" when then became now. I always assumed if I put off the notion of a career long enough, something would just...happen. I'd end up doing something.

But now even that had been taken away.

I was adrift.

I was at a loss.

I had nothing. A storage locker full of...shit. Clothing, mostly. A shitty fourth-hand futon, a thrift store coffee table, a mattress and bed frame, some books, some posters, some knickknacks from my childhood, a few photos of family, some notebooks full of old poetry and song lyrics. Some cassettes and CDs with self-recorded attempts at being a singer-songwriter.

That's it—the sum total of me, if you count my possessions as me. If you count my personality and my achievements as me, I'm even less. I'm a partially educated twenty-one-year-old woman with no real world skills or work experience, no degree, not even an interesting romantic history to point to—just a collection of dirty stories from sleeping with any half-decent looking dude who caught my momentary fancy.

"You all think you know me. Like it's so easy to just...*know* someone. Like, I told you a few stories about my shitty, fucked-up life and because you're all *so* amazing, you can all just *accept* me and fucking *love* me." I glared icy daggers at Myles as I said that. "You don't fucking know me. None of you fucking *know* me."

"Lex, honey—"

I whirled and stormed away. "That includes *you*, Mom."

I walked out into the gloomy leaden sky, into the drip-drip-drip of a solid drizzle. Running away from everyone who thought they knew me, who thought they cared about me. Running away to...

What? Who? Where?

Nothing, no one, nowhere.

EIGHT

Myles

WE ALL WATCHED HER GO, AND SILENCE EXPANDED throughout the bar in the wake of her departure, the only sound the faint croon of an old Tony Bennett tune.

"*That* is one fucked-up female," one of the Badd men said.

Whack! The sound of a hand smacking a chest. "Baxter! Be compassionate."

"I am compassionately saying she's got some serious damage she ain't dealt with. Fuckin' all of us know from painful personal experience that when you don't deal with your shit, your shit has a way of hunting you down and fucking you up until you quit runnin' and face it." He looked at me, incredulous. "Dude—the fuck are you still standing here for? Go, motherfucker!"

I went—at a run. She wasn't hard to find, as she hadn't gone far. Just across the street to the end of a dock where a mind-bogglingly huge mega yacht, an ocean-going, full staff and crew kind of yacht, was docked. Lexie was sitting at the very end of the pier, her feet kicking into space, her shoes beside her.

She didn't turn around. "I am *not* discussing any of what just happened, Myles, so if that's why you're here, you can just fuck right off."

I plopped down beside her, moving her shoes to the other side. Propped my hands behind me, and watched a cruise ship that was anchored offshore, all lit up. I didn't say a thing.

She finally eyed me, not turning her head. "What? What do you want, Myles?"

"What do I want?" I laughed. "A lot of things. Gotta be more specific."

A bitter, angry sigh. "With *me*, Myles. Here, now, in this moment—what the fuck do you want? Why are you sitting here, not talking?"

I shrugged. "Just keeping you company."

"What if I don't fucking *want* company?"

I looked at her. "Then you say to me, 'Myles, you sexy, understanding hunk of a man, I really just need some time alone. Could you please give me a little bit of time and space? I'll come find you when I'm ready.'"

She lifted her chin. I saw her wheels turning. Deciding. Did she really want to be alone? Or did she just not want to be questioned?

I held her gaze. "Have I, at any point, demanded answers or stories or explanations from you?"

"Myles—"

"*Have* I, Alexandra?"

"You don't get to—"

My temper flared. "The fuck I don't! I think at this point I absolutely have earned the right to use your full name, Alexandra Rochelle Goode. Answer the goddamn question—have I *ever* demanded *anything* from you?"

"No," she whispered.

"And I'm not doing that now."

"But you're—"

"Sitting next to an upset woman who I care about a lot."

"Dammit, Myles."

"No, not dammit Myles. I give a shit about you, Lex. Bare minimum, you gotta let me have that without fuckin' fighting me on it. I give a shit about you—how you feel, what you want. You know who else gives a shit about the person that is Alexandra

Goode?" I gestured angrily back at the bar across the street. "Every fucking body else back there. Most especially your mom, Cassie, Charlie, and Crow. So all I'm sayin' here is, you're not fuckin' *alone* in dealin' with whatever hell it is you're holding on to."

"I'm not—"

"I got a motherfucker of a bullshit sniffer, Lex, so don't give me that. Yes, you fuckin' are. I'm calling you on it. It's as plain as the nipples on your tits that you're harboring some seriously fucked damage inside you."

She sniffed a laugh. "As plain as the nipples on my tits, huh? Isn't the phrase supposed to be as plain as the nose on your face?"

I laughed. "Sure. But noses are boring, and while you've got a cute one, as far as body parts go, I much prefer your boobs. So I went with that."

"Ah. Fair enough." She nodded. "Anyway. You were saying?"

"I said it. It's as obvious as whatever you want to say is real fuckin' obvious that you're holding on to some deep, dark, fucked-up, painful shit. I see it. I know it. I don't know what it is, and I'm damn certain nobody else does. That's fine. It's your life, your history, and your choice to share or not. But know this, Lex, and hear me real goddamn clear: I will wait. I will continue to care about you. I will continue to not let you push me away. I will continue to let you deflect the hard conversations into sex and humor. I'll let shit stand, for now. I'll wait." I fixed her eyes with mine. "But I can't do it forever. Eventually I'm gonna need either truth and reciprocation, or to be cut loose. I ain't sayin' now. I ain't giving you an ultimatum. I never will. But it's inevitable. Same for your mom, your sisters, and anyone else in your life. Hard truth is, Lex, folks can only be kept at arm's length for so long, and then they quit tryin' to get any closer."

She swallowed hard. "Fuck." She blinked, her eyes wet. "So what are you saying, Myles?"

I shrugged. "I'm saying what I said. No deeper meaning, nothing left unsaid. I care about you. Could I have feelings that go deeper than just caring about you? Sure, I *could*. Maybe I already do. I don't know. What that means for you is up to you. I will not ask about *anything*, Lex. You've made it crystal fuckin' clear you will *not* discuss your past beyond safe surface shit. Okay. Your choice. The wrong one, if you were askin' me, which I realize you're not. But still, your choice. Do I want more with you? Somethin' deeper? Yeah, I do. But I'm gonna take what I can get with you, and if that's nothin' but the best sex of my life, so be it. I'll take it and I'll fuckin'…I'll treasure it. But just know that I'm offering more. It's not unconditional, though. I do have a condition for offering you all of me—and that's all of you in return." I stood. Gazed down at her. "I'll leave you to your thinkin' and stewin', now. I'm going back to the bar and I'm gonna hang with the crew, drink some whiskey, have some laughs, play with some kids, get to know Cassie and your Mom. As far as I'm concerned, this conversation is over. I'm not opening it again. I'm not gonna say or do shit to push or ask or plead or pull. I've said my piece, made myself pretty damn clear. Ball's in your court. I will accept without question whatever you choose, Alexandra. But that's a double-edged sword. This is me chasing you, this is me pursuing you. You try to play hard to get from here, you won't find me chasin' you." I drilled my gaze into hers. "I fuckin' *care*, Lex. I *want* to know, I *want* to be there. I want more than just sex. But like I said, I'll take what you're offering until it runs out and I'll milk it for all it's worth."

I walked away without a backward glance. "Your move, Lex."

———◆———

"Where's Lex?" Cassie asked when I reentered the bar.

I gestured. "Out on the dock. I think she needs to…shit, I don't know."

Cassie stared at the door as if she could see Lexie.

"She's kept us all at a certain distance for...years. I never really realized how distant until now."

Charlie was standing behind Cassie's chair. "She hides it with her sarcasm and being funny and super, like, bold, but I think deep down she's..."

"Insecure," Liv said. "And I just wish I knew why."

Charlie sighed. "She told me she had a dream of moving to Nashville and becoming a singer-songwriter."

Liv blinked. "She did?"

Charlie frowned. "You didn't know? How do you not know that about your own daughter? I mean, Mom, I'm not trying to, like, think I know anything about being a mother, but that seems like something you would know."

She shook her head. "No, and I feel horrible for not knowing that about her." The pain on her face was agonizing to see. "You say she *had* a dream. But she doesn't anymore?"

Charlie shook her head. "No. She told me one time when she was like seventeen and close to graduating that Dad came into her room while she was practicing her music, and told her that she needed to face reality that she just wasn't talented enough to make it as professional musician, and that she needed to find a more practicable and realistic goal for her future."

Liv blinked, and a tear trickled down her cheek. "No. No, no way. He didn't."

Charlie shrugged. "That's what she said."

"Oh, Darren." Liv wiped at her cheek. "How could he crush her dream like that?"

Cassie laughed bitterly. "He never believed I would make it as a professional dancer. He paid for the lessons, went to the recitals, but he never really believed in me. He never told me I wouldn't make it like he did Lex, but I knew that he didn't really think I could do it. He was always like, sort of just waiting for me to fail, to come to my senses. I knew it. I also knew that dance was the only thing that made sense to me. It just...defined who I was. I've learned to define myself other ways now, but then, it was all I had, so I believed in myself despite Dad not believing in me." She smiled at Liv. "And you were there for me, so that made a huge difference."

Liv shook her head. "I was there for you. But clearly not for Lex. Darren just...how could he crush the dreams of his child like that? How *could* he?"

Cassie shook her head. "I don't know, Mom. Like, what's weird is, I loved him. He loved us and I assumed that my whole life. I didn't feel, like, UNLOVED, by him. But it just felt...shaky. I don't know how to put it—I think I'm still working through it."

"Dad was an asshole, that's what it is," Charlie

said in an uncharacteristic outburst of anger. "He tapped out. Gave up. Stopped trying. With you, with all of us. Why, I can't even begin to understand. But it's an undeniable truth. And I'm getting the impression that of all of us, Lexie suffered from that the worst."

"He was musically talented," Liv said, musing half to herself. "Once upon a time, at least."

Cassie stared. "He was? How? I never saw him with an instrument, never heard him sing a note unless it was in the car or the shower, and he wasn't bad, but I wouldn't have called his singing voice exceptional."

Liv sighed. "He played the guitar, acoustic and electric. He was in a band. A pretty good one, too. Back when he was in high school. He actually took a gap year to try and make the band work—of course, back then nobody called it a gap year, we just called it not going to college. His dad gave him a year to make a go of being in a band instead of going to college. He was lead guitar and did backup vocals, and he was… really, really good. He could play almost anything— The Allman brothers, ZZ Top, Black Sabbath, even a decent cover of some Jimi Hendrix songs. The band did well, for a while. Started gaining notoriety in the local scene where we grew up in Connecticut, started booking gigs on the coast and even a few in New York. But they never quite got the break. They got close, got heard by some producers a few times, but never got the contract offer. And then the year came and went, and his dad forced his hand. Choose—pursue the band, but if you do, I won't pay for college when you realize your band isn't going anywhere and you don't have a future."

Charlie winced. "Ouch."

"And let me guess," Cassie said. "He chose college?"

Liv nodded. "Gave up music, went to college, got a job, made that his career, and that was it. I don't think he ever looked back." She was staring up, to the left—remembering. "He never talked about music. He enjoyed listening to it, but after he quit the band, he never even thought about it again, as far as I know. Not with me anyway."

I rubbed the back of my neck. "I know this is your personal family business, but from an outsider's perspective, it seems to me like he never really did get over it. Just shoved the dead dream down into the back of his head. For you, Cassie, your dream was dance, and when his own dream didn't pan out he was skeptical anyone else's could. Your dream being different from his meant it didn't hurt him as much. For Lex, having a dream that had been *his* dream? It must have cut. He was jealous. Sorry to seem like I'm shittin' on his memory, but…he cut Lexie to the bone when he said what he did—and I got no reason to think she was lyin' or makin' that up. I don't think she recovered from it. And for the record, Alexandra is goddamn *talented*. I've only managed to tease a few little snippets out of her, and even that little bit blew me away. Just her and her little ukulele in the back of my bus—she was hesitant and quiet, but she…" I growled a sigh. "She's got real talent. I'm sayin' this as a professional, not as someone who has feelings for her."

"And you think her dad killing her dream is what has her so upset?" Liv asked me. Her eyes were sharp.

I knew I owed her the truth. "I think that's part of it, but not all."

Liv tilted her head to one side. "What else would there be?"

"I honestly don't know. She won't talk about it." I shrugged. "Not to me, not about the past, but I know there's something. You don't walk around with the kind of anger she's got without somethin' big lurking way down deep."

Liv's sigh, then, was pained. "And I have no idea what it could be—which means I missed something *huge*. Something beyond the fact that she had a dream and the talent to pursue it, and her father crushed it because of his own insecurities."

"I wish I could offer more insight, but she keeps me at bay as much as she does everyone. And I confess I don't know what to do."

"I've seen her with you," Charlie said. "She's different with you. She's let you in farther than anyone, including us. So, speaking for my family, I think, I would just say…please don't give up on her. I think if anyone has a chance of getting her to open up and find some kind of healing from whatever it is that hurt her, it's you."

I felt my heart flip. Felt a heavy burden on my shoulders. "I'm tryin'. This is all new territory for me, and hell if I know what I'm doing. But I care about her and I'll keep holdin' the line with her until she won't let me no more."

———————◆———————

It was something like two in the morning. I was buzzed, but only pleasantly so. I hadn't seen Lex since earlier on the pier. The party had picked up as the evening went on—by some kind of unspoken agreement, the men all spent the early part of get-together doing the bulk of the kid-wrangling while the women congregated and drank and talked and laughed; the men still had fun, but it was obvious they were holding back. And then, when the kids became cranky and difficult, the women took over. And then, eventually, those with little ones all carted the kids across the street to the yacht—which belonged to Harlow and Xavier, it turned out—and it was just the men in the bar. And that's when shit got a little nuts.

The casual sipping of beers became glasses of whiskey, and the oldies and classic rock became hip-hop and modern heavy rock, and the whiskey on ice became shots, which became passing bottles around. And eventually the party moved up, onto the roof, which had been turned into a whole other hangout area with a separate bar and a small stage area and lots of couches with lots of corners, interspersed with those tall outdoor heaters for warmth.

I found the guys all to be the epitome of cool, but no two were the same. Bast was gruff but easy-going, Bax was loud and vulgar and hilarious, Rome was a lot like Bax, Brock was chill and prone to deeper conversation, Lucian rarely spoke at all but when he did everyone shut up and listened, Remington was sort of in between Bax and Bast— able to cut loose and be goofy and loud but not quite as dedicated to being the center of attention; Xavier spoke for no more than five minutes but was insanely cool nonetheless, and Ramsey was distant and aloof but he loosened up as the night wore on and the booze flowed. Ink was fascinating and intim-idating, and of course, Crow was Crow, and by god it was great to be with him again. I really missed him and now that he was up here in Alaska with Charlie I wanted to find a way to get up here more often.

Canaan and Corin were absent for a bit of the night, and when they came back it was with armloads of instruments. Several guitars, a wooden box of some kind, a mandolin, and a didgeridoo. Canaan handed me a guitar, Crow another, and Corin sat down on the box. At first Crow and I just stared at the guitars in our hands.

"Um." Crow eyed Canaan. "I make 'em, I don't play 'em."

"Bullshit!" Canaan sing-songed. "I know you play. Heard you play when you were finishing that guitar you made for Myles."

Crow shifted, still wasn't buying it. "I didn't make it, just finished it. And that was just fuckin' around, not really playing."

Sitting beside him, I sighed. "Crow, you ain't still stuck on that bullshit, are you?" I gestured around. "This ain't a stage, brother. This is a bunch of guys, and zero pressure. No one's askin' you to record or perform. Just...jam, man."

Canaan, to his credit, sensed the breadth and depth of the unspoken but clearly ongoing debate between Crow and me. Just waited.

Crow stared at me. Then the guitar. Slowly, he relaxed, and settled the guitar on his thigh. "You ain't gettin' me on stage, motherfucker, so don't try."

I felt as giddy as a little kid—I'd been trying for years to get Crow to do more than just write music on his own. He rarely even let me see him play when it was just the two of us—he'd record the music on his iPhone in the middle of the night, alone, and I'd show it to Zan, and we'd arrange it and put my lyrics over it, and that was how the songs got written. So, this promised to be fuckin' amazing.

Crow slid his hand up and down the neck of the guitar, making the strings *zzzzhhhh* musically, finding the balance, the weight, the feel. His right hand rested flat on the strings, and then he plucked a few strings, no pick, finger style, open chord. Then he tried a few transitions, a few slow chords, learning the guitar's sound and personality. It was a beautiful piece, a sexy blond Taylor custom with a rich honey sound.

He glanced at me. "What are we playin'?"

The twins were watching me, waiting, and I guess because I was the famous musician, I was lead. Even though Canary was a hell of a well-known act. Whatever. It was just a jam session.

"How about..." I let my own fingers start plucking a tune, which turned into the percussive low notes of a Johnny Cash song—"Get Rhythm."

It was a fun, rollicking tune, and Corin quickly found the beat on his box drum—hell if I knew the name of it—and then Corin had a mandolin in his hands and he was picking a quick circle around the melody, weaving harmony above and below me, and then Crow was playing, effortlessly mirroring and matching me. I knew the song cold, ever since my days as a cover artist.

Johnny Cash turned into a Bruce Springsteen song, and after I'd started it, Crow surprised me by taking over the lead and I let him, amazed at his facility and skill. I knew he was good, but...he was *good*.

Canaan was a wizard—he also had brought a banjo as well, and seemed equally as talented with the banjo as he was with the guitar and the mandolin.

How long we'd been playing, I wasn't sure. I just knew the hours flew by, and I felt more at ease than I had in years, even with my band.

Then I felt her.

I twisted in my seat on the couch and saw Lex, standing in the doorway of the stairs to the roof, her ukulele case in hand, and a look of raw, ragged longing in her eyes. She wanted to play.

I grinned at her and waved her over. "Come on, Lex!"

We weren't playing a song at the moment, just sort of noodling, each one of us playing whatever we felt in the moment and making it work. At some point, most of the women had joined us as well—all except Mara and Dru. Aerie had a ukulele as well, and had been sitting and listening. And now, seeing Lex, she brightened. "Come on, Lex! I'm too chicken to join in on my own."

Lex hopped onto the couch and sat between Aerie and me. "Oh you are not chicken. You're Canary, and you've got a fucking Grammy."

She pointed at Canaan. "*We're* Canary, and *we* have *three* fucking Grammys, but Cane is the real talent. I just plink my little uke and sing a few little songs. This much talent in one place? It's intimidating."

"You know I don't like it when you're overly modest, babe," Canaan said. "And we're just jamming. Nothing to be intimidated by."

Aerie pointed at me and then Crow. "The boys I'm used to. Myles North is like, almost as famous as Harlow, and Crow is an entity unto himself with that guitar."

Tate, who had her cello out and was rosining her bow, grinned. "Shut up and play, Aerie. This is a once-in-a-lifetime jam session."

Aerie glanced at Lex. "Well? You in?"

Lex eyed me. "I don't know."

"She's in," I said. "She just needs to hear something she knows."

Lex frowned. "You're speaking for me, now?"

I grinned, and let the melody playing become "I Need You" by Tim McGraw, a song I knew she knew and loved, having heard her hum it in the shower more than a few times.

"No," I answered. "I just know you."

The others picked it up immediately, Corin with the beat, Crow with the lead, me flowing around him and Canaan with the banjo making it sound kinda bluegrass. Aerie started in on the lower range of her ukulele, and Tate plucked her strings with her fingers to mimic a bass note. Which left Lex.

And the vocals.

After a moment of watching and listening, Lex closed her eyes. She sighed, a low, tight sound, not quite relief, but something more painful, fraught. As if she was giving in to something forbidden. And joined in, hesitantly at first.

We were all bound in this moment—all of us. They'd all heard the conversation we'd had about Lex and her dad, so we all knew what a big deal this was for her. She'd clearly never stopped playing, because after her initial hesitation, her fingers began to *fly*. Virtuosic, fluid, finding the melody for herself and putting her spin on it, soaring above in high range in counterpoint to Aerie's lower thread.

I knew the song. Knew the words. Mind like mine, mind for music, the lyrics are just there, and that's a song I'd heard a thousand times, a song I'd sung a million times myself—always solo, just me singing Tim's part and always half wishing in the back of my mind and at the very bottom of my heart for someone to sing the harmony, to sing Faith's part with me.

This was that moment.

Her voice found mine, wrapped around it. She had a surprisingly soft, quiet, smooth voice, contrasting with her loud, bold personality. She sang with her eyes closed, leaned over her ukulele and played her part without thinking, sang with depth and passion.

She wasn't just singing, she was performing.

She just didn't know it.

The professional in me was watching her carefully, and I knew she was not just talented. She was a once-in-a-generation talent. Raw vocal power that didn't need to be loud to be perfect. Each note was effortlessly flawless. Not sure this makes any sense, but her voice was just liquid. Sweet as honey and strong as whiskey, yet it moved and breathed.

Her face, already beautiful, *shone* when she sang. Radiated pure joy as she performed with me. Her fingers flew, and the song neared its end.

Her eyes opened and met mine.

I knew the song we'd do next, and I knew it'd surprise her. I also knew she knew it—I'd heard it on her earbuds as we traveled, a song she tended to listen to regularly.

"Just Give Me A Reason" by Pink and Nate Ruess.

I plucked out the melody, and I saw her recognize it.

"Damn you," she whispered.

"Never said I'd play fair, darlin'," I said, grinning with an ease I didn't feel.

This moment, playing with her, it was heavy. Beautiful, deeply meaningful...but fuckin' heavy.

She sang, and no one else played. Just my guitar, her voice. Stripped down to the barest bones. Lexie fell into the music, dove in and swam deep. The soft quiet voice she'd used for the Tim and Faith song was replaced by a low, powerful one, not quite a belting voice but close. Strong, impassioned.

When it was my turn, I made sure my voice stayed in the backing harmony, letting her be the focus. She didn't play either, just held the uke with her hand on the strings, palms flat on neck and bridge, head ducked, curled over herself and rocking as she found the power in her voice to let loose, to belt the lyrics as they were meant to be sung, with passion that could almost produce tears. When she got to the chorus and sang about being not broken just bent, I heard her shake, almost crack, and keep going.

Stronger for the breaking.

When the song ended, there was total silence.

"Fuck me," I heard Bax breathe, awed.

Canaan nodded. "Music's next great duet has been born, and we watched it happen."

Lexie seemed to come awake; shaking off the stupor being in the zone like that can put you into. "What? What do you mean?"

Aerie leaned close to Lexie, wrapped a slender arm around Lexie's shoulders. "You don't realize, do you?"

"Realize…what?"

Aerie kissed Lex on the cheek. "That you just found your purpose in life."

"My…purpose?"

I held her gaze. "How do you feel right now, Lex? Honest. No filter, no bullshit. Right now. How are you feeling? What are your emotions?"

She swallowed hard. "My hands are shaking. My whole body is shaking, like an adrenaline rush times a thousand. I…my *soul* is shaking. I feel…" She closed her eyes and then opened them and stared up at the endless wash of Alaskan summer stars. "I feel like I'm more alive than I've ever been. Like I'm finally awake."

"You understand what that is, right?" I didn't wait for her to answer. "It's your soul finding its home."

She shook her head—disbelief, not disagreement. "It was a couple songs. No big deal."

Corin, who had a more caustic sense of humor than his twin, just snorted. "Bzzzzt!" he buzzed. "Wrong answer, try again—big deal. Way big deal. Biggest deal ever. It wasn't just a couple songs, it was you finding the real *you* that you been hiding from your whole fuckin' life."

Lex scoffed. "You're on drugs."

"The video evidence, if you please, Señora Claire." Corin gestured with a dramatic roll of his hand at Claire, who'd been recording it.

Claire stepped forward and squatted near Lex, cueing up the video and handing it to Lex. Who watched the entire three song video silently, eyes wide.

"I…" She seemed to have to gasp for breath. "I sound…like *that*?" Her eyes went to mine, still disbelieving. "That's me?"

I nodded. "That's you, Lex. The real you, *all* you."

Liv had been hanging on the outside of the circle, watching and listening. She now came through, parting the sea of Badd and Goode with her slender form. She was crying, tears sliding down. Aerie saw her coming and moved aside to make room for Liv, who sat down and wrapping Lexie up in a Mama Bear hug.

"Your father was wrong, Alexandra," Liv whispered. "He was so, so wrong."

Lex pulled away, glanced at Charlie. "You told her?"

"Of course, silly," Charlie answered. "Did you think I wouldn't? Was I not supposed to? Would you have?"

"It hurt so bad, Mom," Lex whispered, choking back a sob. "I thought I knew pain, but when Dad told me I was never going to be good enough to be a professional musician, I...I think part of me died. Because at that point in my life, my music was all I was living for, all I *had* to live for."

Liv reared back as if slapped. "All you had to live for? What do you mean?"

Lex shook her head. "No, no. Nope. Not going there."

"Lex."

She shot to her feet. "No. Not another word. Not talking about that. Not with you, not now, not with anyone, not fucking ever. Yeah, I'm a fucked-up mess. Yeah, there's a reason. Dad breaking my spirit and crushing my purpose in life is a big, huge, massive part of it. Yeah, there's more. No, I'm not going to talk about it, so fucking forget it." She grabbed her ukulele case—hard-sided, black, and hand-painted all over with pastel daises and roses and pieces of lyrics—latched her ukulele in it, and moved for the exit. "I appreciate what you're all trying to do, I appreciate your...your support. But this was a mistake."

"You can run, but you can't hide!" Corin called out. "The Badd Clan has officially adopted you, Alexandra Rochelle Goode! You'll be back, and we'll all be here for you when you do."

"I appreciate the sentiment, sweetheart," Tate said, rubbing his shoulder, "But I'm not sure that was the best way to express it, in that moment."

"Sure it was. We're like an infectious disease. Once we're in you, you can't ever get us out." He pointed at each person in turn, everyone who wasn't Badd by blood. "You all showed up and fell in love, not just with one of us, but with all of us." He pointed at the stairwell, down which Lex had vanished. "I can tell when someone's gotten bit by the Badd bug, and she has. She just has to run away from it for a while. Sometimes it just takes a minute to really feel it."

"An infectious disease, Corin, really?" Canaan whacked him on the back of the head. "I'm not a fucking disease, you idiot. You are, maybe."

"We're identical twins, you moron. Whatever I am, you are."

I glanced at Claire. "Can you send me that video?"

She nodded. Then her eyes widened. "Does that mean I get your personal phone number?"

I laughed. "Yeah. And you can even use it to message me."

"I'm getting Myles North's phone number," she said, doing a silly little dance.

Harlow faked a pout. "God, what*ever*. The second another famous person comes along, I'm no longer special. I get it."

Claire shoved Harlow. "You're old news now, bitch. I've been in the bathroom with you, helping you pee because you were drunk off your ass on tequila. You are officially no longer a celebrity, but a sister. Sorry."

Harlow hugged her, laughing. "It's fine, I'd rather be a sister anyway."

Claire faked gagging, pushing Harlow away, who clung like a leech, laughing. "Too sweet, too sweet! Keep hugging me and I'm gonna barf." She pretended to shudder as Harlow let go. "I'm allergic to sentimentality."

Claire handed me her phone, and I put my name and phone number in it, and then she sent me a message; I saved her contact info and she immediately sent over the video. I had an idea brewing, but I knew I'd need a bit more footage for it to work. The trick would be to get Lexie to play and sing again, and to let me record her, and then put her out into the universe.

But first things first…I had to find her. Again.

NINE

Lexie

MYLES, AND EVERYONE ELSE, SEEMED TO REALIZE I'D been pushed to the max, and backed off the personal shit.

The rest of the week was just plain fun—the most fun I'd had in years, if I'm honest. Every day the Badds shut down one of their bars and had everyone over. They had several bars, it turned out—the original, Badd's Bar and Grille; a second location co-owned by Bast and the triplets, Badd Kitty Saloon, where we'd met the first night Myles and I arrived; Badd Night, a third location owned by Bast, the triplets, and Zane, and was more of a live music venue than a mere bar. The newest location, and the first outside Ketchikan, was The Badd News Bar in Anchorage, which the triplets, Bast, Zane, and the two sets of twins all co-owned, run more as a franchise with Badd management oversight.

Every night that week was different, because not everyone showed up at the same time every night. It all depended on kids and work schedules and other obligations, but everyone showed up at some point, and every night, after the kids were in bed, the musical people ended up sitting together and jamming. And honestly, I fought it at first. I tried just sitting and listening and pretending my fingers didn't want to play, that my voice didn't want to lift. But it was a futile fight. After the first night, I knew I was hooked. I knew Corin was right, knew Myles was right.

I'd played and written songs consistently since Dad's disastrous talk with me, but it was like a dirty secret. Something I hid from everyone, my roommate included. If I could have hidden it from myself, I would have. Because I had believed Dad. I'd believed him. He'd told me I sucked, that I should give up, and I'd believed him.

I'd given up.

But music wouldn't give me up. During college I'd be lying awake half the night, restless, irritated, exhausted. And eventually I'd roll out of bed, grab my ukulele, and find somewhere to be alone. The communal bathroom was usually the best place—I'd sit on a toilet and play, sing, and hate myself for it. I'd sing my songs, sing the songs I was listening to on the radio and couldn't get out of my head. Sing the songs I loved, my old favorites, the classics. I learned new ones. It was a habit, like a secret drug habit. One I couldn't quit, no matter how hard I tried. I'd go two days, three, but I'd always end up with my ukulele in the dorm bathroom or under a tree outside, singing and playing, and hoping no one was listening.

And then…Myles happened.

Back on the bus, during his tour when we'd first met, he'd bribed me to play for him. He'd told me he'd give me an entire night as my own personal sex slave if I played one of my own songs for him. I hadn't been able to resist that offer, so I played him a song I'd written a few months before, as a way of expressing some feelings for a guy I'd been struggling with. I'd been quiet, timid, nervous, and he'd listened, and told me I was talented and that he wanted to play with me sometime. I'd told him he could play with me anytime, and that, of course, had led to a really long, fun night. I'd given the man a hell of a tongue workout, that's for sure. I must've had at least a dozen orgasms that night, hadn't let him get even one until I'd been ready to pass out, and then I'd finally let him plow me as hard as he wanted. I think he'd probably thought I'd want something more creative, more acrobatic, or something most men would find degrading or emasculating. But really, at the end of the day, I'm a simple girl. I just want to come as hard as I can, as many times as I can, for as long as I can, until my body stops letting me come. And good goddamn, but Myles North could make me come like no other man ever has, and I took full advantage of that.

That had been the start.

Playing for Myles.

Then we'd sing along to songs together, sharing an earbud.

He'd play a song and I'd sing along. I'd let myself play my ukulele now and then, in front of him.

But that was it. Nothing major.

Then I'd heard them jamming. Heard his distinctive guitar style, his unmistakable voice. I heard other voices, other instruments. And I'd been pulled physically, bodily pulled, as if by a rope around my waist. Up, to the roof. Ukulele in hand. I'd *had* to play. *Had* to sing. It had been impossible to resist the need. Like an addict being offered a free hit of the purest grade substance.

While I'd played, I had been *alive*.

And it was terrifying.

Because now I was truly addicted.

To the rush, the aliveness, the attention. I needed

more. Like any drug, the more I used, the more I needed. And every night that week, I got hit after hit. Sitting in the circle surrounded by Crow and Myles and Tate and Aerie and Canaan and Corin, playing every song we knew and jamming improv jazz style when we ran out of songs we knew. Singing, and having people watch and listen and *validate* me. Pay attention to my singing and playing as if I was *good*. Like I had something of value to add. Being appreciated for my talent.

Being appreciated for *me*.

Not for my body or, for my sexual prowess.

Which was, honestly, the only thing I ever let anyone see, aside from my bold as brass balls, take-no-shit attitude.

Which was a front.

Fake.

I'd been faking for years, and you'd think it'd just be real by now, but I wasn't.

I mean, it was me, it was the only me that existed anymore. But deep down, there was another Lexie. And music was bringing her to life.

Playing for people—being *seen*, being *heard*—was breathing life into her.

And that, more than anything, was what terrified me, was what kept me awake into the smallest hours of the morning, no matter how late I went to bed.

Myles was true to his word: he never made any-thing deep or personal. Never asked me to talk about myself or my past, even when we were alone and naked together and nooking in the afterglow. He would just hold me and let me pretend we weren't snuggling, and that I didn't love snuggling in his arms more than just about anything in the world, including the sex itself, which was in turn better than sex had any right to be.

See, my pretenses were vital to my worldview:

I had no heart;

I didn't know how to love or have feelings;

All I knew was sex;

I had no talents beyond sex;

Sex defined me as a person and as a woman, and I was okay with that;

I didn't want, have, or need a purpose in life;

My secrets would stay secret forever, because I could not and would not ever trust anyone enough to reveal them.

But Myles was eroding my belief in my pretenses.

Chipping away at my ability to hold on to them.

Good thing I'm the stubbornest woman alive. He could chip away forever, but he'd get tired of it eventually. He'd said so himself. I just had to outlast him and eventually he'd give up.

And that was what I wanted.

I dared not admit to myself that *that* was yet another pretense, because that one was rooted way down deep, way under the rest, hidden under the others.

That week was, honestly, one of the best of my life. Myles and I had very little time alone, what with Mom and Lucas being up at the crack of dawn every day, and being hauled all over Ketchikan for day trips with Mom, and hiking with Lucas, and impromptu recording sessions for Myles and Crow at the twins' record label/studio, where Myles and Crow put down acoustic stripped-down recordings of their favorite songs as well as a few Myles North originals, including a handful of songs Myles and Crow had written on the spot. A surprise release, Myles was calling it, but it wasn't a Myles North album, it was a one-off: Myles & Crow Unplugged.

Damned Myles and damned Crow—they sweet-talked, bribed, threatened, and coerced me into playing on two songs with my ukulele and sing harmony.

And damn, damn, and double damn if the songs on which I appeared didn't sound…fucking amazing.

Despite me, my insecurities shouted.

Because of me, my newly reborn dreams whispered.

I was both dreading and anticipating the resumption of Myles's tour. It was going to be a whirlwind, and I'd get to see places I probably never would have otherwise. It'd be just me and him again, mostly. Close quarters, lots of alone time. But that also meant more time for Myles to sink his hooks into me. More emotional attachments for me to pretend I wasn't forming.

I was in denial, and I knew it.

I had shit to face, and I knew it.

But I had every intention of avoiding as much as I could for as long as I could. Because deep down, despite the bluster and bravado of my personality, I'm a coward. Afraid of being hurt even worse. Of being rejected. Of being used. Of being betrayed. Of putting my heart in someone's grip and being crushed.

Of baring my secrets, because to put them out there would make them real all over again and I'd spent years forming a nice hard calcareous exoskeleton of emotionless armor to keep the dark agony contained. To bring them up and out, to really deal with them meant breaking open that shell, and once the shell was compromised, my tender, sensitive insides would bared to the vagaries of what life had taught me was a cruel, wicked world.

And if the world was cruel and wicked, it seemed like a good strategy was to be cruel and wicked in the name of self-preservation.

Myles disagreed, clearly, because he kept teasing little nuggets of sweetness and tenderness out of me, damn the conniving asshole.

Like when we spent an afternoon with Zane and Mara—Zane was a former Navy SEAL, and exuded calm, deadly confidence underneath a hard-ass veneer, a demeanor that his wife seemed to have made it her mission to soften. Mara was every bit as tough and capable as Zane, and I discovered she was a former combat medic, which made sense. That afternoon, Myles and Zane decided to head off to the docks to do some shore fishing, leaving me with Mara...and their two kids, one of whom was a little baby girl.

And I, being a twenty-one-year-old single girl prone to sexual misadventure and hard partying, with little to no exposure to young children, had absolutely no clue what to do when Mara plopped the little girl into my lap.

"Here," Mara said. "Play with her. My boys are way too quiet, which means they're doing something apocalyptically destructive."

I gaped, mouth flapping. "Wait, I—I don't know the first thing about babies!"

Mara laughed. "Don't drop her, and don't let her

swallow anything. Let her sit on your lap and be slob-
bery. It's not as hard as you think."

And then she was gone, and a few minutes later I
heard her bellowing angrily—apparently her assumption had been correct. And there I was with a baby.
How old, I couldn't have said. Old enough to sit up on
her own but not walk, old enough to eat mushy food
but still need formula. Old enough to gum and slobber and slurp all over my fingers and my necklace and
my shirt. She was cute, but…what did I do with her?

"Um." I held her on my lap, hands around her
waist, making sure she didn't topple over suddenly.
"Hi."

"Ba. Ba-ba-ba." She whacked me on the cheek,
laughing.

"It's not nice to hit, you know."

"Dad-da-da."

"I don't know where your dad is. I don't even
know for sure *who* your dad is, because I'm relatively
certain you're not Zane and Mara's."

"Mama."

"Mama is upstairs dealing with those two boys,
who seem to each have the destructive capacity of a
category four hurricane."

"Ma, ma, ma, ma." She grabbed my necklace, a
choker with a dangly chain and clover pendant, and
stuck in her mouth.

"I don't think you should chew on that, kiddo." I looked around for something to give her to play with, and spotted a giant plastic key ring with giant plastic keys in bright primary colors. "Here, chew on this, Gummy the Slobber Queen."

She took it, stared at it intently as if deciding what to do with it. And then promptly began assaulting me with it, cackling hysterically.

"Why you little bitch! Wait—I can't call a baby a bitch, can I? Not nice, Lexie. Be nice to the baby. If your first word is bitch, I'm going to be in trouble."

Whack! Whack! The keys smacked me on the nose, shoulder, and eyebrow, each whack accompanied with baby laughter.

Which only grew more hysterical when I pretended to take the keys and then give them back, with a peek-a-boo type rhythm and boo to it. "Give me that! Here you go. No, no, no, give me that!"

And then she scored a direct hit to my eyeball, and that game was over, much to Mara's amusement—she'd been watching for who knew how long.

"Tate has been trying to stop Lena from hitting for weeks, but it's her favorite game," Mara said.

"So she isn't yours. I wasn't sure."

"No, she's Tate and Corin's youngest. Tate and Aerie are helping the boys finish mastering the album you guys recorded, so I'm hanging out with Lena."

"And what did your boys get into?"

"Marco and Isaac are the most conniving, destructive, hyperactive human beings I've ever known," she sighed, and I could tell she meant that with every ounce of love she possessed. "They got into my makeup, found my MAC lipstick, and drew penises all over my vanity mirror. And on each other. And my marble countertop. And my antique claw-foot soaking tub which Zane just installed six months ago."

I put my hand over my mouth. "You're kidding."

"I wish I was. They claim a kid at school taught them how to draw dicks, and now they draw dicks on everything. Like, I think they think they've invented penis-based humor."

"Their names are Marco and Isaac?"

She nodded. "Marco is the oldest, and he's named after Zane's best friend, who died in combat. Isaac is the younger one, and he's named after a friend of mine who died when I was a teenager."

"So Zane really was a Navy SEAL? Like he did secret combat shit?"

She laughed. "Yeah. He's worked really hard to leave that part of himself in the past, these last few years. Having Marco and Isaac has helped him relax and soften a bit, but...yeah." She sighed. "He still wakes up with bad dreams sometimes. Usually about the day Marco was killed."

I shuddered. "I cannot even imagine."

"Be glad you can't," she murmured.

"You too, huh?"

She shrugged. "I saw my share of gnarly shit, but my job was to fix people. His…not so much." She smiled at me, because while we'd been talking Lena had gotten drowsy and had fallen asleep, her head pillowed on my arm. Even asleep, she was slobbering on me. But god, she was cute as hell. "She likes you."

I laughed. "She fell asleep on me. Not sure that counts as liking me."

"You don't know babies. Lena hates sleeping. She'll fight falling asleep tooth and claw. So her falling asleep on you is actually a pretty clear sign she feels good with you."

I felt uncomfortable with that. "Well, that's makes one of us comfortable with me," I said.

But the joke fell flat. Mara just gazed steadily at me. "I'm not that much older than you, so don't take this the wrong way, but…you remind me a lot of myself before Zane."

I sighed. "Is that right?"

"Closed off, scared shitless of my own emotions. Die-hard hookup artist, zero plans to let anyone in."

I wanted to retort, but couldn't think of anything that didn't sound petulant and defensive. "And then you fell in love with Zane and now you're a brand-new

woman?" Well, shit. So much for not sounding petulant or defensive.

She laughed, though, not insulted at all. "Yeah,
in some ways. Mainly because I found something I
wanted and I was willing to let go of whatever was
standing in the way."

"Zane's tender yet manly love?"

She snorted. "Hell no! Regular access to the best
dick I've ever gotten!" She laughed. "And no, that's
not entirely a joke. I stayed for the sex, and the falling in love was just a terrifying and life-changing side
effect."

I laughed. "Terrifying and life-changing side effect. Sounds about right."

"I fought it hard, Lexie. Hard as I possibly could,
as long as I could."

"But eventually the love was just too strong to
resist?"

She snorted again. "Wrong again. He knocked
me up, and that just...broke my resistance to him."
She narrowed her eyes at me. "Real life isn't a
Hallmark movie. It's messy. Hard. You're faced with
scary choices. Mine was to have the baby alone, or to
risk being with a man I barely knew, who scared me
shitless. Not having the baby wasn't a choice for me.
Nor for him."

I blinked, swallowed. "So it worked out for you."

Mara nodded. "Yeah, it did. But it was a hell of a risk. I put my heart on the line, all the way. My whole life. Moved here, to be with a man I'd known a few months at most. Got absorbed into his family, which as an only child of an absent father and a mother I basically walked away from when I joined the Army, was a lot to deal with."

"And has it been worth it? Worth the risk?"

Her answer was immediate and definitive. "Absolutely."

Something to think about, at least.

The last day in Ketchikan I was alone with Mom, Cassie, and Charlie for most of the day—on Myles's insistence; he got Ram, Lucas, Brock, Ink, and Zane to take him into the deep brush for some boy time in the woods with things that went boom. Most of the day was easygoing—spent getting mani-pedis, lunch, browsing the touristy shops, and light chitchat. It was later in the day, back at Mom's condo with big glasses of wine, that the conversation took an expected turn.

"So, Lex." Mom was sitting on her white leather love seat, knees curled under her thighs.

I sighed, took a fortifying sip. "Here we go," I muttered. "So, Mom."

"You and Myles are leaving tomorrow?"

I nodded. "He has a show in Tokyo next week. Not sure which day, but being the first show of this leg of the tour, the band needs a few days to practice."

"And you're going with them?"

I nodded. "Yeah. I'm actually pretty excited about it. I'll get to see places all around the world. I think it will be fun."

Mom seemed to be carefully considering her words. "But you and Myles aren't…" She hesitated. "A thing."

I paused for a moment and looked at her directly. "I mean, sort of. I don't know what we are—there are no labels for it."

"You lived with him in Dallas for two months, after several weeks on the road with him. You brought him here, to meet us. And now you're going on a world tour with him."

I shifted uncomfortably. "Yeah. So?"

"That's a *thing*, sweetheart."

"I know it's a thing. It's just it's kinda new and I'm not sure what the next weeks will bring."

"Seems like you really care about him, and it's totally obvious he cares about you."

I took another long sip of wine. "What's your point, Mom?"

Charlie held me with a level gaze. "Her point is either shit or get off the pot."

"Screw you, Charlie. Just because it was easy for you doesn't mean it is for me."

"It wasn't easy, Lex, it still isn't. Worth it, but not easy. I'm not saying any relationship is easy, I'm saying you're playing a game and it's not fair to him or to yourself."

I eyed Cassie. "And what's your take on it all?"

She shrugged. "Myles is great. He likes you. Give him half a chance and I'd say he'll fall in love with you faster than you can blink. And damn, but you could do a hell of a lot worse than Myles North, and not just because he's rich and famous. He's just a good, solid person. But none of us know what's behind your real, deep down hang-ups, and what it's doing to you. You've alluded to things in your past, but none of us know a damn thing them and, honestly, that makes us feel shitty—I know it does Mom—but we can't make you talk about something you're not ready to talk about. So you're just sort of stuck, because you'll never get anywhere in life or relationships until you woman up and deal with your shit."

"I agree with what Charlie has just said, and I can only add that we are all here for you, no matter what, but must we curse, girls?" Mom said.

"Yes, Mom, we must," I snapped.

She flinched. "No need to snap at me, Lexie, I'm not the bad guy."

I sighed. "I'm sorry, Mom. It's just that from the moment I got here; everyone was all up in my business. Literally, everyone, and that's a *lot* of people to have up in my personal shit, none of whom I know from Adam. Then Mara wants to give me advice, and now this…intervention. I don't want to talk about my drama, I'm not *going* to talk about my drama, and I would appreciate it if I could just be left alone to deal with it my own way."

"The problem, Alexandra," Mom said, her voice gentle but direct, "is that you're *not* dealing with it."

"Is that so terrible?" I asked.

"You have many, many people who care about you, who have wisdom to offer from life experiences which either mirror, or are very similar to yours, people who could help you. But you won't let us. None of us. Not even me, your own mother. Is it so terrible? No. But when you push hard enough for long enough, eventually those who love you have no choice but to just leave you to your own devices." She set her wine aside. "There's just one problem with that, Alexandra. Myles will eventually give up—push him away long enough, and he'll walk away. The Badds, the men and women of this clan, they'll let you stay aloof and won't push or chase. It's not their way. They offer everything they have and everything they are, take it as is or leave it, but if you say no thanks, they'll let that be the answer, out of respect." She leaned toward me. "I'm your mother. I *cannot* and *will not* let you push me away. I will not let you walk away from me. If you want me to give you space to figure things out, I'll do that. If you want to just handle things on your own, I can do that too—it's painfully difficult to watch your child hurt and struggle and not be able to help, but I'll respect your wishes. What I won't do is just leave you alone. I'll be here, waiting, when you need me. As long as it takes. No matter what it means. I'm still your mommy, even when you're an adult, Lex. So push all you want, but you won't ever get me to just *leave you alone.*"

I swallowed hard. "I know, Mom. But some things I can't just…dump on your lap, like here, fix it Mommy."

"Yes, darling, you can."

"You can't fix this," I whispered.

"Perhaps not fix, perhaps not erase. But help. Support. Advise. Barring anything else, I can just commiserate and love you through it."

"And you know what else?" This was Charlie. "I think I know Myles enough to know that what Mom said goes for him, too. He's all in for you. You just have to jump out of your little tower of isolation and solitude and safety and trust him to catch you."

"I can't," I whispered, my voice rough and ragged. "I don't know how."

"It's simple," Cassie said. "You just jump. There may not be a happy landing, or there may be the best landing ever. You have no way of knowing what's at the bottom, and that's the scariest thing in the world. But when your walls are crumbling and life is flooding up all around you and you've got nowhere else to go, you're left with no choice. Jump, or drown." Her eyes were bright and direct, with characteristic Cassie frankness. "You're drowning, Lex. Time to jump."

This intervention was getting way too close and I was beginning to panic. "You don't know what you're talking about," I hissed, and shot to my feet, leaving my wine, my mother and sisters, and all but ran out of the room.

Outside. Into the cool of a Ketchikan summer night—a sliver of moon and a silver wash of stars above. I just walked and walked, who knew where. I walked for a long time, miles probably, got lost, turning this way and that, until I knew I was hopelessly lost, but too upset to care.

Finally, I stopped walking and took stock of my surroundings. Nothing. Darkness. No streetlights, stoplights, nothing. I could see a mountain or tall hill on one side, and water in the distance on the other. Close by were buildings disguised as low dark bulks.

I could see cracked streets, a chain link fence and deserted parking lots.

And, suddenly, I was scared.

Especially when I heard footsteps in the distance, approaching rapidly. At a quick jog. I tried to hide in the shadows, but as the runner approached and became a huge, hulking form, he saw me and angled toward me.

"Lex?" A low rough growl.

"Y-yeah?"

The figure was wearing a sleeveless hoodie, shorts, and running shoes. Massive shoulders. Improbably tall. He tossed back his hood. "It's Bast."

I sighed in relief. "I kinda got turned around."

He looked around and barked a low laugh. "I'd say. You turned yourself around into the ass end of nowhere."

"How do I get back?"

He pulled wireless earbuds off his ears, turned them off, tucked them in a pocket, and headed back the way he'd come. Gestured for me to follow him. "This way."

"You can just give me directions—I don't want to interrupt your run."

"Nah. Ketchikan is pretty safe, but no point taking chances."

"Bast, for real. I can take care of myself."

His only response was a bearlike growl, which seemed to indicate that the conversation was over. And, looking around, I decided having a big male escort wasn't such a bad thing. We walked in silence for a long time. And eventually, I huffed.

"So? Where's your advice?"

He chuckled. "We got some nosy folks in the crew, don't we? Can't leave well enough alone when they see somethin' that needs fixin'. They mean well, but it can be overwhelming sometimes."

"No kidding."

"Ain't my style. You talk, I'll listen. You ask me my opinion, I'll give it. But I'd just as soon walk in silence if you're into that."

"I'm good with silence."

"All right then."

And he was as good as his word—nothing but our footsteps in the darkness as he led us unerringly back to the bar; I knew Mom's condo was not from here. There was the loud buzz of a seaplane coming in, lights blazing, approaching low and quick, nose up. A few dozen feet above the water the engine cut out, and I watched it float in silently, the floats skimming the water and sending white spray to either side. Then it was sluicing easily across the surface, making for a specific dock, slowing seemingly as if by magic, and then turning to slow and stop right up next to the dock.

"Damn," I said. "In the dark, no power, perfect landing. I don't know shit about flying, but I know that was impressive."

Bast chuckled. "That's Brock. Used to be a stunt pilot. He was flying before he could drive. A no-power night landing is child's play for him. He can knock the cap off a beer bottle with a wingtip. Seen him do it."

"So Zane is a former Navy SEAL and badass combat guy. Brock is a stunt pilot. Bax, from what I hear, used to be an underground bareknuckle brawler, former professional football player, and is now an internationally renowned personal trainer. Canaan and Corin are successful musicians. Lucian owns some business from what I understand…"

"And dabbles in black-and-white close-up photography." He snapped his fingers. "There's a word for it. Macro? Macrophotography?"

"Hell if I know." I laughed. "Xavier is a genius robotics inventor." I eyed him. "What about you? What impossibly cool thing do you do?"

"Me?" He shrugged, laughing good-naturedly. "I'm just a bartender."

"I find that hard to believe."

He shook his head. "For real. I manage the bars. More paperwork and less pulling beers these days what with four locations but, at the end of the day, I'm just a bartender." He eyed me. "Don't forget Rem, Ram, and

Rome. Smokejumpers—ultra elite wildfire fighters—
they parachute out of a perfectly good airplane *into* a
wildfire too hot and too remote for the *other* elite wildfire fighters. Rome helps me run the bars, Remington
is a tattoo artist, and Ramsey is a deep brush, big game
hunting guru."

The guys were trooping down the dock, laughing,
hanging on to each other and throwing elbows—they
were too loud, like some of them had had too much
to drink. Brock had flown and was hanging back at the
plane, tying up, and Lucas, huge and broad, was walking straight and staying quiet, watchful; I knew from
Mom's emails that he was a former alcoholic, and had
taken it upon himself to be a watchful, sober presence
for the others as much as he could. Playing catch-up
for years of neglect was how Mom said he'd phrased it.

Which left Zane, Ink, Ram, and Myles, four of
them sauntering together down the dock, howling
with laughter at something—knowing men, I guessed
I was probably better off not knowing.

Bast glanced at me, at the guys, and then lifted his
chin at me. "You good?"

"Yeah, thanks. Sorry to have ruined your run."

"Nah, I was just stretching my legs, gettin' some
fresh air." He smirked at me. "Next time you take a
pissed-off walk, just stay next to the water. That way,
you can just walk back the way you came."

"I will. See you later." I hesitated. "Hey, Bast?"

He paused, turned back. "Yo."

"Thanks. For the silence, I mean. You don't know how much I appreciate it."

"Sure thing, Lex." He waved, and headed off into the darkness.

I waited for Myles and the guys to reach the end of the dock.

Myles saw me, grinned. "Lexie! Lexie, baby. There you are." He swayed a little. "Waiting for me, were you?"

I laughed. "Yeah, Myles. Just standing here in the dark, waiting for you to come back."

He latched onto Ram's shoulder for balance. "I think you're being sarcasmic." He blinked. "Sarcasmic? Is that right?" A laugh. "Shit, I'm lit."

I moved to his side, leaned up against him. "Yeah, you are."

He stared down at me, deep brown eyes dizzy but intent. "You mad?"

That stung a little, that Myles's first thought upon seeing me was to ask if I was upset about something. Wanting to alleviate his worries, I lifted up and kissed his cheek. "Mad? Hell, no. I'm glad you had a good time."

He sighed. "I don't get like this often. Party a lot after shows, but I stay cool." He belched loudly. "'Scuse me. But I felt like with these guys? With *these* guys? I could maybe be a little less cool. It's hard bein' cool all the time."

Zane laughed. "You are far from cool, my dude. I'm onto your little secret. You're just a big dork." He cackled. "But that's okay. Your secret is safe with me." Zane sounded like he was a little less lit, but then he missed a step, standing still, and I realized he just sounded like it.

"I'm not a dork," Myles protested. "But people got this—this idea that a rock star oughta be cool. Like, *cool*. So I'm cool, for the fans. But you guys are *real*. And the real me isn't cool. I'm just, just like…this guy, you know?" He swayed way back, and I caught him. "Whoa. Gettin' the spins."

"Getting the spins?" Ink rumbled. "You had the spins half a fifth ago, little man."

Myles glared way, way up at Ink. "Who are you calling little, you damn tree?"

Ink rumbled a deep laugh. "You're funny."

Ramsey let out a fart. "Everybody's little compared to you." He seemed to see me for the first time. "Oh, hey."

I laughed. "Hi, Ramsey. That was disgusting, by the way."

"You heard that, huh?"

I laughed. "Heard it? I think they *felt* it in San Francisco."

Ink chortled. "You oughta hear mine. You'll really feel those."

"No, thank you." I patted Myles. "I'm heading back, all right?"

"I'll come with you," he said.

"No need. I know the way from here, and it's not even that late."

He leaned on me. "But babe, babe. Sorry, Lex, I mean. Sorry. Um. I've been drinkin' since ten this morning. About ready to pass the fuck out. And plus, I ain't sure I can walk in a straight line."

"I'm not sure you can walk at all."

Lucas rested a big hand on Myles's shoulder. "I'm heading that way, too. So if you need help, I'm here."

Myles looked up at Lucas. "You got it, dude." He laughed, eying us expectantly. *Full House*. No? Nobody? I used to love that show. Crow's mom would let us watch TV and drink sodas, and we'd always watch that, and…what was the other one? *Step by Step*. Ahh, the nineties, man." He waved at Ramsey and Ink, as if they were far away. "Bye, guys. You're the coolest. Thanks for making me feel welcome, and not famous."

He saw Brock, then, ambling up to the group. "That was a hell of a flight, man. I want you to know I appreciate you staying sober and flying us."

Brock laughed. "Ah shit, he's going maudlin." He

glanced at me. "Quick, Lexie, get him out of here before he starts crying on our shoulders."

"I'll do something on your shoulder," Myles said, and cackled.

"Gross, dude," Brock said, laughing. "Not on my shoulder, you're not." He grinned, gesturing at me. "On hers, maybe."

I flipped him off. "Don't you volunteer me for that, motherfucker!" I laughed, though, making a joke of it.

Myles wobbled, eyes on me. "No, I thought about that, but she's too classy for that. Wouldn't want to." He smirked at me, winking. "I got other plans, anyway."

"Yeah, passing out and hoping you don't piss the bed," Brock laughed. "And good luck with that, man. You are *lit*."

"I never piss the bed. Well, not since I was super little. I did get so drunk this one time that I shit myself, though. But I was like, a kid, and Crow and I had gotten hold of a bottle of Everclear. That was a bad time."

"Well, you better not shit on me while I'm in the bed with you," I said. "You shit on me, I'll never have sex with you again."

Myles held his hand up to his heart. "I solemnly swear I will not poop the bed."

I laughed, and angled him away, toward where Mom's condo was. "Come on, rock star. Let's go."

"Not a rock star," he mumbled. "I'm a *country* star. 'S different." A muzzy laugh. "Rock stars are sissies. They think they can hang, but they can't. Bring a rock star to a country show, and he'll wimp out. We know how to fuckin' *party*."

I eyed Lucas. "You want to take his other side? I think this fella's reached his limit."

Lucas moved around to prop Myles up on his other side, and Myles grinned at each of us. "It's a sandwich. Except the meat is on the outside, and the white bread in the middle." He grinned at Lucas and then at me. "Big meat. Sexy meat." He poked his belly. "No meat. Just a skinny kid from the ass end of Texas."

Lucas laughed. "One foot in front of the other, Myles."

And, step by step, we got him back to Mom's. Up the stairs, into the condo, where Mom, Cassie, and Charlie were watching a movie—they paused it as we entered and regarded Myles with amusement.

"Wow, someone had a good time," Mom said.

Myles wobbled his head, now finding it hard to hold it up. "Too good. This is tradition, though. Last night of freedom before going back out on the road, I get bomb-faced. Because on the tour, I gotta be the *man*. The honcho. The boss. Gotta wear the belt and twang but not too much, and sign for fans, and be *on*. And I love it. I do." He blinked at Mom. "I do. I love it. But it's hard, sometimes. So I go a little cuckoo, the night before I go on the road." His eyes go serious. "I don't do this much." He looked at Lucas, and Mom. "Don't want you to think littler…lesser…not as good of me. I stay cool. Just not tonight."

Lucas clapped him on the back. "If you can keep it under control the rest of the time, I got no issues, son. You're entitled to cut loose now and then."

Myles nodded. "Gotta cut my bladder loose, is what. Back teeth are floatin'."

I helped him, with some effort, into the en suite bathroom, where he pissed for approximately twenty minutes, braced with two hands on the wall behind the toilet. He shuffled, only partially dressed, to the bed. And flopped in.

I helped him undress, brought his feet up and onto the bed. Tucked him in. "Sleep good, rock star."

He seemed oddly lucid, his eyes on mine. "Thank you for taking care of me."

"You're awful polite when you're hammered, you know that?"

He rested a hand over his eyes, and flopped one foot on the floor—to keep the world from tilting too much. "Ready for Tokyo, Lexie?"

I sat on the edge of the bed, toyed with his hair. "No, not really."

He was silent a while. "You're really not pissed that I went off and got hammered?"

"I'm not your wife, for one. And for two, even if I was, I wouldn't begrudge you a night out with the guys, cutting loose and doing irresponsible guy stuff. I'm not jealous. I'm not controlling. I'm glad you had fun with them. They're good people."

"The best."

"Why didn't Crow go with you?" I wondered.

A sigh. "He said he was doing something important. Wouldn't say what, but that I had to know it was important if he was missing a tour send-off bender." He hummed. "Wonder what he was doing? I miss his ass. He been my best friend and my brother since I was just a little redneck."

"You've never been a redneck a day in your life, Myles."

He chortled. "You didn't know me back then. I had a mullet. For real. A rattail. Thought it was the coolest thing in the world."

"You did not," I cackled.

"Did too. Long one. Ask Crow, sometime." He was silent a long time, near to snoring. "Lex?"

I was about to grab water and Tylenol for him, but turned back. "Yeah?"

He slid his forearm off his eyes, peered one-eyed at me. "Glad we came."

I wasn't sure I agreed, but I didn't disagree. "Yeah."

"I see why your mom and sisters ain't leavin', now that they're here."

"Me, too."

"If I wasn't touring, I'd be here." He paused, long and slow. "'Specially if you were here."

I really had nothing to say to that—thankfully, I didn't need to. He passed out, then, and I heard him start snoring. I grabbed the water, the pills, and slid into the bed beside him. I was a long time falling asleep, thinking about everything everyone had told me this past week, and wondering what the hell to do about any of it.

TEN

Myles

I WOKE UP GROGGY. DIZZY. THIRSTY. I CRACKED AN EYE open and saw water and pills on the bedside table. Thank god. I took the pills, and guzzled water until my mouth felt less like a desert. That done, I stumbled into the bathroom, and took a long, long piss. I made my way back to the bed.

And there she was.

Lexie.

Sleeping.

Facing away, the sheet lining her curves. God, she was gorgeous.

I was way too hungover to get an erection but yet, as I slid into bed and curled up behind her, I felt myself responding. It was…a unique sensation. Being in bed, and so utterly happy to simply be in bed, getting to go back to sleep, getting to feel Lexie's lush, plump backside squishing against me, her skin soft as silk and smelling like vanilla and lavender. I was majorly hungover, and I was dizzy, and had an achy head and gut, but I was so happy to be here with her.

I slid back under the veil of sleep, my hand on her belly, just under her breasts.

I woke up later, who knew when, feeling less hungover.

Naked.

Hard as a rock, my cock nestled neatly between Lexie's ass cheeks. My hand on her tit, the lush big handful overflowing my palm, her nipple perky against my thumb. Her breathing was such that I knew she was awake.

"Mmm," she hummed, sleepily.

I couldn't stop my hips from moving. "Mmm," I hummed back.

She sighed, and slid her backside against me. She was naked too, all bare skin and plush curves. "You're alive," she murmured.

"Barely."

"You were pretty blasted."

"Yeah."

"You were cute." She wiggled back against me. "How you feel now?"

"More alive. Less blasted." I thumbed her nipple. Flexed against her. "Lucky to wake up to this."

She turned her head to the side, a small smile on her face. "Oh. And what do you plan to do with this?"

I didn't think. Just acted out of need, out of instinct. Slid my hand to her hip, to her thigh. To her knee. Lifted her leg aside. Felt her opening nestling hot and slick against me. "This." And slid into her.

Bare. She was wet and tight and softer than anything, and so perfect. She moaned as I moved inside her, as I slid deep, felt her wrap hot around me and clamp. There was no way to hold back—just me and her, this moment, our perfect union, bodies joined and matched and moving together like puzzle pieces fitting into place.

I moved, filling her, feeling her spasm around me. Felt her fingers find her center, helping herself along as I slid sinuously in and out. Her breasts provided the perfect handhold, and I kneaded them, one and the other and both, thumbing her sensitive nipples.

It wasn't slow, or long. I was there faster than I thought possible, and wanted nothing more than to topple over the edge as I felt her squeeze and throb and clamp. She bit her lip as she restrained a scream, writhing against me, clenching around me, and that was my undoing. I pushed into her, hips slamming against the juicy bounce of ass.

Gritted my teeth and groaned. "Lex," I breathed, "Oh god...Lex."

I was there, seconds from the edge.

She gasped, breathed a curse, and suddenly I ached, throbbed against nothing. She'd rolled away, snatched herself away from me. I didn't have time to react, to even understand what had happened, and then she was resting her cheek on my belly and I was in her mouth and she was stroking me with one hand and cupping my balls with the other doing something to them that had me aching harder than I'd imagined possible.

Her mouth was tight and wet and insistent, and took so much of me, and her fist slid fast and soft around me and I was groaning, aching, throbbing.

"Lex..." it was all I could manage. I had to warn her. "I...fuck. I can't hold it."

She hummed, backed away and sucked a deep breath. Whispered against my throbbing erection. "Let me have it, Myles."

And then I was in her mouth again and I had no chance, none. It was too good. Not as good as if I'd gotten to give her this where I wanted to be, buried deep inside her with her mouth on mine and her orgasm in synch with my own.

Close, but not as good as that would be.

"Coming," I grunted. "Lex, I'm—oh fuck!"

Both hands stroking and pumping me, and her mouth was sliding around my head and she was sucking and her tongue was wild and slithering and circling, and I was aching to explode. I couldn't. I knew she didn't do this.

"You don't want it, Lex," I growled, holding back with every ounce of control I possessed, holding back until it hurt.

She pulled back, drawing her mouth off of my cock with a loud *pop*. Licked the tip. "Yes, Myles. I do."

"What?"

"You arguing?"

I pulsed, fighting the need to come. Hips pushed up, helplessly thrusting into her hands. Balls felt like they were boiling over, aching with pent-up heat. "No, but you don't do this. You don't have to."

"Don't have to," she murmured, smiling up at me. "Maybe I want to." She licked me from root to tip, turned her head sideways and ran her teeth and tongue and lips along the side of my cock. "Maybe I changed my mind about what I want to do to you. To do *with* you."

"Fuck, fuck, fuck." Everything hurt, ached, throbbed, pulsed. I'd long since gone past what I'd thought was my capacity to hold back. "Lex, I swear. Just…do what you did last time. Let it go on me. I don't need this."

"But you want it." She pressed her lips to the tip, kissing it sensuously.

I closed my eyes, because if I had to watch her lovingly kiss my cock, I'd lose the battle. "Yes, Lexie. I do want it. But what I really want is to come inside you, bare."

"That's the one thing you can't have," she whispered. "I'm giving you this instead. Because I want to. Stop fighting it."

And then she took me deep, lifting up and pulling me away from my body and swallowing around me. She was squeezing me with her fists, hard, preventing me from coming even if I'd wanted to let go. Around my shaft, another hand around my balls, pinching off my ability to come. Her mouth went wild on me, then, bobbing fast, tongue slurping, taking me deep so I heard her swallow around me and gasp for air, and I had to watch.

"Fuck it," I snarled. "Fine. But I'm gonna make you come with me."

I reached forward and snagged her hips, lifted her up and settled her ass on my chest. She shifted so she was sitting on her shins, and lifted her ass into the air, presenting her sex to me—and I gratefully, willingly, eagerly pressed my mouth to her and tasted her. Slid my fingers inside her slit, found her magic spot and massaged it while I devoured her, hard and fast, bringing her to the edge more swiftly than she'd ever gotten there.

"Oh fuck, Myles—Jesus, what are you doing to me?" she gasped, pushing back against my mouth. "Fuck, I'm gonna come already!"

It was mere seconds—her hair trigger pulled so fast she didn't even know she was coming until she was already there. She screamed, writhing against me, hands squeezing hard around me so hard I grunted in surprise, her mouth paused above my cock. She came, and came, screaming, whimpering, thrashing against me...and then plunged me into her mouth and let go of her grip on me, used both hands around me, sliding and pumping as fast as she could, and my orgasm was ripped from me. I growled through gritted teeth, and then as I felt the cum rise and the heat blast through me and the pressure release, I had no words but her name, chanted as she took me and took me, took all I had and then some.

I came, and it was an explosive eruption so potent I thought it was going to paralyze me, my back arching, cock pounding with the volcanic heat of climax. I filled her mouth with my cum and she swallowed, but not fast enough, and I came again and it spilled out past her lips and trickled down my shaft and she gasped and swallowed around me and I pulsed again, hard, and again, and again, and each time she gulped around me and more thick milky cum trickled past her lips and down my shaft. Each pulse shredded through me with wrenching power, until I couldn't even whisper her name, couldn't thrust, couldn't do anything but let her hands do the work of pumping hard and fast around me, and then she slowed, and her palm cradled my balls and she pressed fingers to the sensitive sliver of skin just behind my sac and massaged as she used her hand to twist and slide around my shaft and her mouth suckled around the head, and I wasn't sure if I was coming again or coming still, but it was another wild hot crushing pulse of body-wrenching climax, and I didn't think I had anything left inside me to come, but somehow I did and she took that too, letting it spill out.

Finally, after an eternity of climax, she let me go and I collapsed back onto the bed. Lexie rolled off me and pivoted, bringing her head to my chest. She smiled up at me.

"That was…a *lot* of cum," she murmured, laughing. "Like, whoa."

I was limp, floppy. "Uh, huh."

She palmed my jaw and brought my face to hers, kissing me on the cheek. "You dead?"

I nodded sloppily. "Uh-huh."

She lifted my now-inert cock, let it flop back to my body in the mess. "Looks like you need a shower."

I shook my head. "Can't walk. Legs are jelly."

She laughed. "It was really that good?"

I nodded. "Uh-huh. That good."

"Better than the handjob I gave you back in Dallas?"

"Yeah."

She traced her fingertip through the sticky mess pooling on my skin. "You mad I didn't swallow it all?"

I laughed. "No, Lex, I'm not."

"Just glad I didn't leave you hanging?" I heard the edge of defensiveness.

I cupped her cheek. "It was perfect, Lex. Everything we do together is amazing and more than I could ever have thought possible."

"Even if I'll never let you raw dog me?"

I frowned. "Not usually one to argue with vulgarity, but that makes it sound like it's something… dirty, and not in a sexy way."

She sighed. "You know what I mean."

"I know you're trying to put distance between you and me and the emotions of being totally bare with each other, Lex. And I'm not going to push it." I held her face, thumb grazing her cheekbone. "Yes, I want that. Desperately. You say it'll never happen, and if that's the case, I can accept that. I know you're dealing with a lot, Lex, and I'm not going to put anything more on you."

I slid out of bed, bringing her with me, stood up and carried her into the bathroom. Set her on the marble bench in the shower, turned on the water. Let it run hot. Adjusted it to a tolerable temperature and tugged her by the hand to stand her up. Kissed her neck. Her jaw. Her breastbone. She was holding her breath, resting her hands on my shoulders.

"My turn," I said.

"Your turn?" Lexie breathed. "For what?"

"To make you come so hard you see stars."

"You already did."

"Not good enough." I reached out and snagged the bar of soap. Lathered it up and began running it over her skin, starting at her shoulders. "Not to equalize what you just did to me. I feel like I owe you at least three more orgasms for that."

"I told you, I'm not keeping track."

"And I told you I do." I ran the bar of soap all over her, lathering her breasts, her diaphragm, down her belly.

I ran the soap over her hips, all over her thighs from back to front, avoiding her ass and core—saving them for last. Letting the water run over her, sluicing onto her head and neck and shoulders, letting her stand in the stream and luxuriate in being washed. Taking my time, scrubbing and massaging all at once. Brought the lather up to her sex and went to my knees. Pivoted her so she could brace against the wall, because I planned on making sure she'd need to brace herself. I took my time washing her core, nudging her thighs aside and using the gentlest touch I could. Kneeling behind her, my arms around her hips, the soap running over her slit, my other hand working in the lather and letting the rivulets of water rinse it all away. Then I brought the soap around to her backside, massaged the globes and scrubbed them, working my way inward. I leaned forward to kiss her back, her hips, tasting the clean water on her skin. I ran the soap and my other hand in slow slides inward, parting her ass cheeks. Over the tender knot. Just a pass of my hand, at first. The soap. Again. She gasped as I lathered the inner curve of each cheek and the parted seam between, and massaged the tiny virgin knot of muscle.

"Ohhhh fuck, Myles. You're doing *that*?" she gasped. "Now?"

"Uh-huh," I murmured.

"Ohhh fuck."

"Better hold on to the wall, babe."

She clapped her hands against the marble wall, leaning forward and arching her back inward to press her ass outward. Eager. I set the soap aside and gathered water as it ran over her shoulders and spine and hip, splashed it over her ass, rinsing her clean. And then set about kissing: spine, hipbones; ass cheek, upper swell of her thigh. Working my kisses inward. She was moaning as my lips and tongue dared and delved closer and closer, moaning from anticipation. I hesitated, and then took my first taste of her. She gasped, a sharp shrill whimper, and one hand left the shower wall, reached back to scrabble at my head, and I took that as encouragement. I slid my fingers between her thighs, up, found her clit and circled it hard and fast as I used my tongue against her ass to make her writhe. She lifted up on her toes, away from me even as she pressed her ass back against me, and I devoured her harder, faster, more vigorously than ever, head whipping from side to side and my fingers circling in a blur—she screamed, bit down on it, and her voice cracked, broke, and she dissolved into weak-kneed dipping, shaking, whimpering breathlessly, coming hard. I pushed her through it and to another, sliding my fingers inside her, delving in and smearing her with her own essence, returning to her clit until she broke apart again.

And that was when she lost the battle.

Her knees gave out, and she slid down to the floor of the shower. Trembling. Shaking all over, gasping for breath.

She lifted up to watch me splash water on my face, and rub my mouth clean.

"Holy shit," she breathed.

Watching her lose control had been almost as arousing as anything she could do to me, and I was achingly hard for her again.

She saw this. Moved on all fours across the shower floor, toward me. I clambered to my feet and she followed me. Stood in front of me, breasts brushing my chest. Her breathing came in ragged pants, her chest lifting with each one. She was wild, aroused beyond all control. Her hands shot out, clawed, and hooked into my pecs, shoved me up against the wall. Fingers trailed down my cheeks, clutched my jaw. Eyes on mine, hers alight with aroused ferocity. Panting. Holding still, in the way a lioness freezes before she pounces.

And then she lunged at me. Lifted up, hooked one knee around my hip, heel on my opposite thigh, and sank down onto me. I growled wordlessly, feeling myself slide into deep wet soft perfection, felt her clamp around me, clenching spasmodically as she shook from the aftershocks of two potent back-to-back orgasms and quaking her way to a third as I drove up into her. I was beyond all control. All thought. I was alive with need, not for climax now, not for release, but for *her*. For intimacy.

For this.

She lifted up on her toes and I cupped her ass and lifted, and we set her down together, onto me. Lifted in synch. She slammed her mouth onto mine and stole my tongue, sucked it into her mouth, and drove her hips against mine. I gasped, feeling her slick wet heaven sliding around me, squeezing me, and I knew nothing but Lexie, but this, but us.

Pushing, thrusting.

Needing more.

I palmed her ass in my hands and lifted her all the way off the floor, stepped forward to press her back to the opposite wall, and she clung to my neck and writhed on me and her heels scrabbled desperately at my ass and she was a wild thing, a feral cat, all claws and teeth, nipping my neck and earlobes and shoulder, clawing at my back.

"Myles," she breathed, those two syllables a broken, ragged plea.

I was so close. Drowning in her.

I had one brain cell operating enough to know what she meant with that single desperate plea of my name.

I set her down and wrenched control over myself—found it from somewhere within. Slid out of her. Stepped away. Shaking.

She whimpered, this time from loss, from confusion, from I wasn't sure what.

I was shaking all over, every muscle tensed hard. I turned away from her. Head ducked, fists clenched hard.

Felt her behind me, palms sliding over my belly. "Myles, let me—"

I gripped her wrists in both hands. Shook my head. "No."

She leaned against me, breasts squishing flat against my back. "I'll suck you off again."

I didn't let go. "No. Not this time."

"Why?"

"Because I…" I ached, hurt, physically as well as emotionally. "I want something you can't give, Lex. It's not about the act. It's about what it means. I'm not going to take it. It's not going to happen on accident, in the heat of the moment." I twisted, keeping a grip on both of her wrists. "You're either going to want what I want, or you're not. We can do plenty of other things, Lex. Just not that."

"You're not being fair," she whispered, and I heard the hurt and confusion and anger. "You don't know, you don't understand."

"I know that." I let go of her hands, cupped her face in both hands as the water ran cool. "And I'm still not asking. But I have to hold some part of myself in reserve, Lex, or I won't survive this. I'm offering you everything I am without reserve. If you take that offer, you get all of me. If you can't and won't, then I have to keep something back."

"It's one thing, Myles. That one act of you coming inside me without a condom—I just…I can't do that."

"I know. And, like I said, it's not about the act, Lex. It's really not. You make me feel *so* fucking good, every time we're together, no matter what we do. It's not about coming inside you bare. I don't want that to, like, mark you or some macho possessive shit, or because I'm obsessed with how it feels."

"Then what is it about, Myles? Because I don't fucking understand."

"It's about you holding something back. It's about you not being willing to tell me *why not*. There's nothing I won't and haven't told you. Nothing I won't do for you, nothing I won't give you if you ask for it. You're not with me for my fame or my money, and I'm well aware of that. But if you asked me for fucking anything, I'd do it. Want a house? I'll buy you a mansion in fuckin' Monaco, or a penthouse in Paris. Say the word. Want a Ferrari? I'll go pay cash for one right this fuckin' second. You don't want any of that shit, and I know it. That's almost more frustrating, because there's not a goddamn thing I can do, not a goddamn thing I can give you to earn the trust I want from you. Because the raw truth of it is, it's not about me. I wish it was, because then I could fuckin' *do* something. If I was an asshole and my behavior was shitty, I could fix that. If I was this or that or whatever, I could fix it. I could be better. Do better. Be a more generous lover. Buy you presents. Take you on vacations. I don't fuckin' know. But it's not—fucking—about—*me.*" I swallowed hard, eyes burning. "And that sucks. Because it means I'm out of options. All I can do is take what you're willing to give, because I'm a fucking addict for you now, Alexandra. I'm hooked on you, and there ain't another drug in this world that'll be the fix I need to live. It's you, darlin'. You or nothin' at all."

I backed away, then. Turned away. Shut off the shower. Snagged a towel from the rack and used it to gently, lovingly pat and dry every inch of her perfect skin. Her hair was still wet, and I hadn't really gotten clean, just rinsed off. I tossed the towel onto her head, and she laughed, muffled, and then went quiet as I used exquisite care to towel her hair. I pulled the towel off of her face, smiling as her hair went *poof*, into a frizz explosion in a thousand directions of straight up. I wrapped the towel around her torso, tucked it in around her chest. Wrapped her in my arms. Pulled her close. Kissed her, slowly, gently, putting everything I hadn't had the words to say into the kiss. It was a delicate burn of a kiss, all heat and no fire, sweet as honey.

I pulled away, leaving her breathless, and just smiled down at her.

I turned, and walked away.

"Damn you to hell for that, Myles North," I heard her whisper to herself, and I could tell she was shaky, almost tearful.

ELEVEN

Lexie

THAT MORNING WE WERE BUSY PACKING UP AND SAYING a few dozen goodbyes; that, at least, was a saving grace. It was absolute hell not dwelling on what had occurred only minutes before.

Mom and my sisters and Crow were the last group we said goodbye to, and then we all piled into a giant black Suburban borrowed from…someone in the clan. Lucas drove us to the ferry with our single bag each, and Mom tried in vain to pretend she wasn't about to get all emotional that I was leaving again so soon.

Because we were flying private, we didn't have to go through security or parking, which Lucas thought was just the greatest thing ever. We parked right on the tarmac near the idling jet, and Myles invited everyone aboard for a quick peek.

"Dude, Lex, I am so fucking jealous," Cassie said, sprawling out on the couch. "*This* is how you do international travel. For real."

I just grinned. "It is pretty pimp."

"The pimpest." She held out her fist to Myles, and they tapped knuckles; then, Cassie's eyes went serious, fiery. "Take care of my sister, Myles North."

He nodded. "I absolutely will."

"Don't give up on her," she said.

"Cassandra, goddammit, not now," I snarled. "Seriously? Can no one give it a rest for one day?"

"Alexandra, goddammit, yes, right now," she shot back. "I'm just saying my truth because who knows when or if I'll ever see him again, so this is my chance. I like him for you, Lexie. And just for the record, if you don't take the chance while you've got it, you're a moron." She stood up, wrapped me up in a tight, fierce embrace. "I mean that with all the love I have for you." She held me at arm's length, her eyes damp. "And that, just so we're clear, is a fucking lot."

Mom sighed. "You don't need to swear to make your point, girls."

"Yes, we do," Cassie and I said in unison.

I shoved Cassie away, but it was playful and loving and only partially serious. "Shut up, dork."

She just shook her head and let Charlie take her place at my side.

She just hugged me tight. "I love you, Lex."

I waited, but nothing else was forthcoming. "That's it?"

She laughed. "Yeah, that's it. Everything's been said several times in several ways, so there's no point me piling on. I love you, I support you, I'm here for you. That's it."

I sniffled. "Thanks, Char-Char. You're the best."

Cassie scoffed incredulously. "Oh, *she's* the best? Is it because she dropped her entire life to come do an epic road trip with you? Because I could have done that."

"But ya didn't," I sang.

"Whatever," Cassie said, but I knew she was teasing.

Out of the corner of my eye, I saw Crow and Myles standing close together, foreheads bumping, murmuring in low tones. Crow grabbed Myles by the back of the neck, shook him. Shoved him away in a rough gesture of masculine affection. Stopped near me. His dark eyes burned into mine. He closed me up in a hug.

Whispered, his voice rough and raspy. "Don't fuck with his heart, Lex."

I swallowed hard. "Doing my best, Crow."

"Sometimes our best ain't enough, darlin'. Sometimes, you gotta go past just doin' your best." He tapped me on the nose, just to annoy me. "You'll be alright."

And then it was just me and Mom—the girls and Crow had trooped off to check out the plane and Myles had followed them.

She hugged me, too. Hard. Tight. Mama-bear fierce. "I love you with all my heart, Alexandra Rochelle. Don't you forget that."

"I *know*, Mom." I swallowed hard. Then I said the words that did not at *all* fucking come easily or naturally: "I love you, too."

She pulled away, and lost the fight against tears. "I'm sorry I failed you, Lex. I hope someday you can tell me."

Fuck, fuck. NO.

"Mom...shit." I closed my eyes. Felt them burn, hot and salty. "Don't. Please don't."

"Can't help it, baby girl. I'm your mama. I worry for you."

"I'll be okay. I'll figure it out."

"It's just..." She rested her cheek against mine. "You don't get all that many chances at true happiness in this life, Lex. I'm on my second, and I know I won't get another. I'm taking it and I'm running with it, and I am *not* letting go, not for a damn thing. No matter what. Because, Lexie, honey, Lucas *loves* me. Being loved like that? There's nothing like it. And it's worth *everything*."

Swallowing was hard, breathing was hard. Being me was hard, in that moment. I clung to her. "I hear you. But it may not be possible for me. And I can't really explain why. Not yet."

"I'm your mother, Lex. Why not?"

I shook my head. "I can't."

She sighed and let me go. "Okay. Someday?"

I shrugged, blinked hard. "Maybe. We'll see."

She walked me to the stairs and we hugged again. Charlie, Cassie, Crow, and Lucas went down the stairs and reached the tarmac. They all piled into the Suburban and headed for the ferry, and then it was just me and Myles at the bottom of the steps, waving goodbye to everyone. He grabbed my hand and we ran up the steps, pausing at the top to look back. Seeing my damp eyes he said, "Okay, Lexie?"

I shrugged. Nodded. Shook my head. "I don't know."

He chuckled, kissed me on the temple. "Fair enough." He cast one last glance at Ketchikan, visible in the far distance, across the Passage. "Well? Ready for this?"

"Not even a little."

"Too bad. Tokyo, here we come."

We touched down in LA, and were joined by band members Brand, Zan, Jupiter, and their manager Mick. Mick had been planning on getting his own ride to Tokyo, but decided to check out the new ride, and so I met Mick—who looked to be in his late fifties with salt-and-pepper hair in a ponytail which was doing a poor job of hiding male pattern baldness. He had a brilliant white smile and an easygoing manner, and I was sure he had lots of stories to tell about his career in talent management.

It was a long, boring flight; the guys turned on a shoot-em-up movie with lots of boobs and explosions. They didn't drink all that much, and Myles not at all—I think he was still feeling it from his bender the night before. I sat with Myles, half watched the movie, and read a book. It was…well, homey. Except for the occasional blip of turbulence, it was remarkably like being in a fancy condo with some guy friends.

The problem with boredom is that it left me way too much time trying not to think about this morning.

Him, bare inside me. How perfect it had felt.

How badly I'd wanted him like that, how badly I wanted him like that all the time.

I tried to not think about how he'd tasted. There'd just been too much to swallow, and it had almost been hotter for that.

He probably didn't realize the panic attack I'd had the entire time I had him in my mouth—how I'd fought it, hard. I'd fought to keep breathing, to ward off the terrible, dark, evil memory. I'd kept my eyes on him, reminding myself this was Myles. No one else—just Myles. Sweet, sexy, amazing Myles.

Myles who had looked at me, during and afterward, as if I'd given him a gift he could never repay.

He had no idea how hard that had been for me.

I'd wanted to stop and just cry, not because of him or anything he'd done, and not because I hadn't enjoyed how he tasted, how he felt, how he'd reacted—because I had enjoyed that. But because I'd been fighting a battle he knew nothing about and I wanted more than anything in life to be able to tell him.

But I couldn't.

It was ingrained, imprinted. Seared into me—never tell.

No one. Ever.

He'd know.

Logic told me otherwise, but logic was utterly helpless in the face of some things.

Myles nudged me. "Hey."

I jerked, pulled out of my reverie, and shut the book. "What? Hey."

"You were somewhere around Mars, it looked like."

"Just…thinking."

He'd been on his iPad with a Bluetooth keyboard attached, clicking and clacking, answering emails, plugging back into work mode. He eyed me. Glanced past me, at Mick, who was sprawled out in a chair, staring out the window at the clouds. "Mick."

Mick glanced up, nodded at Myles's gesture to join us. Mick crossed the isle and sat down opposite Myles. "What's up?"

Myles opened a window on his iPad—a YouTube window. The title of the video was "Myles North with Crow and Lexie Goode" and it was an original song we'd done for the acoustic album.

"Mick, I want you to check out this video we made up in Alaska. Give you a little taste of what's coming for the band."

"Oh shit. Really?" I watched the video along with Myles and Mick. "You made a video?"

"When Corin realized several people had been recording our jam sessions, he got them to send in all the footage, then stitched it together into video, and tracked the song over it. Fuckin' genius."

"It's…live? Like, it's out there?" I felt faint.

He pointed at the screen. "Went live on YouTube this morning, and it's got six million hits already."

"Fuck." I sat back, rubbing my face. "Six million?" I couldn't quite believe it.

Myles laughed. "It'll have a hundred million by tonight, guaranteed. Especially once I post it on my socials. It hasn't even hit any of the big sites, yet. Once it does, watch out. My fans have been after me for years to get Crow on something. I'm always talking about how talented he is, but the reclusive fucker has been impossible about it until now. He'd never go on stage with me, but this is a good compromise." He grinned at me. "The thing that really makes this video, though, is you, Lex. Straight fuckin' fire."

I shook my head. "I wasn't ready for that."

He chuckled. "You never are. You helped make the album, you knew I was publishing it."

"Yeah, but that was just my name and voice as a session player. Not my face."

He held my hand. "Believe me, you're ready. This is just the beginning for you."

"Myles, until this week I've never played in front of anyone, ever."

"I know this week was a bit of a trial by fire. Now you just jump in and trust me."

"Jump in?"

"And trust me."

I swallowed. "Myles, I don't know."

"Lexie, I do." He squeezed my hand. "The future is now, and you're it."

"That is crazy."

"Not really." He laughed. "Just trust me in this. I won't let you down."

"I'll try." I knew he had plans, and if I knew what they were, I'd be shared shitless. So I didn't ask, but I had to admit I was just a little bit excited.

Tokyo was nuts. Busy, crowded, loud and super fun, and the people were so polite. We spent two days just seeing the sights—usually through the tinted windows of a limo; being whisked from place to place, always entering through the back entrance. Seemed like a lot drama to me, but Myles took it seriously. We ate in fancy restaurants and simple little holes-in-the-wall, went to shows, nightclubs, and one night Myles even got me drunk enough on sake to do karaoke, which he then recorded and put up on his socials. Suddenly I had my own following and hashtag, and he showed me thousands of comments of people wanting to know who I was, and if I was going to be on the tour. Thousands of comments—I could barely get my mind around it.

He scrolled through them, and had to scroll for what seemed like forever, just so I could see how many there were.

It didn't seem real.

I didn't really believe it.

And then Canaan and Corin sent over another video, edited from more of the same footage, and this one was just Myles and me in a duet, with footage of us together. A lot of the footage was from when we did the duets at Badd Kitty. The video racked up hundreds of views within seconds of going live, millions within hours, and then it got picked up and spread around. The number of people who had seen it was higher than I could fathom.

The count was more than most of Myles's band videos, including the ones he had Grammys for.

This was crazy…and exciting all at the same time.

But I couldn't believe this was because of me—it didn't seem real. Or right. I was no one. I'd done nothing. Sang a few songs into a mic, in a little studio in Alaska.

And now?

#Lexie&Myles was trending on Twitter.

Then, our two days of playtime in Tokyo was over. We showed up at the venue—the Tokyo Dome, a place with fifty thousand seats. Empty, for now.

The stage was still being set up—lights, sound, effects—it was a whirlwind of activity. Once the sound was up, Myles and the guys settled into a sound check, found their marks on the stage, and then went through their set list.

The setup and rehearsals took a few days, but it was becoming a familiar routine for me—I'd sit side-stage, a bottle of water near me, watching the techs bustle and the guys play, stopping as they missed a note or messed up a chord or forgot a lyric. The day before the show, they went through the entire set from start to finish in a full dress rehearsal, necessary after more than two months off, to make sure the show went off without a hitch.

The last night, before the big show the next day, after their rehearsal, Myles sat down with me at the side of the stage.

He was sweaty from jumping around the stage, shirtless, a towel around his neck, chugging a bottle of water. "Hey, you."

"Hey yourself," I said. "You guys look and sound great."

"We're all right," he said. "A little rusty. We'll do a quick run-through tomorrow, and we'll have it down by then." He winked at me. "You know who looks great? You."

I snorted. "Quit winking. It's smarmy and

stupid." He was quiet, and I knew he had something to say. I poked his ribs. "Well? Out with it."

"I want you to do something for me."

"No promises. But what?"

"Practice some songs. Your own. Your favorites. The ones that really show the world who you are. Your best songs."

"My songs, like my own personal ones?"

He nodded. "Yeah."

"Why?"

He just stared. "You know."

"I'm not going on stage with you."

He chugged more water. "You are."

"I can't play in front of fifty thousand people, Myles."

"You can."

"I'll suck."

"You won't," he said with utter confidence. Not a shred of doubt in him.

"I'll mess up."

"They won't know."

"I'll embarrass you."

"Never."

"Myles, I can't."

"Lexie, you can." He crumpled the plastic bottle, twisted the top back on to suction it closed, and tossed it into a nearby trashcan. He turned to face me, and took my hands. "Listen to me, Alexandra."

"The full name, is it?" I went for breezy, came off snarky.

"Eyes."

I begrudgingly met his gaze. "What, Myles?"

"I believe in you."

I swallowed hard. "Okay."

"Hear me. Don't look away. Don't give me fuckin' attitude." He was serious, harsh. "I—believe—in you."

I blinked, my eyes were wet with tears. "Please stop."

"You need to hear it. Know it. I believe in you." He gestured—Jupiter, Brand, and Zan were standing, watching, listening. "They believe in you."

"Sure as fuck," Jupiter said. "You're the real deal, Lex."

"We're with you all the way," Zan said.

Brand: "Word."

I shook my head. "Thanks, guys, but..."

"But nothing. Has anyone ever said that to you? Anyone ever make you believe it?" He held up his phone. "Believe the millions of views your two videos have gotten in under a week. Nobody even really knows who you are, yet. Those numbers are organic. They are all yours. My reach, sure, but it's *you*. They want *you*."

I shook my head. "I can't, Myles, I'm too scared."

"You can." He touched my chin, so I had to look at him. "I'll be right there with you, every single moment. Promise, my heart to yours."

"Why are you forcing this?" I asked, my voice raspy.

"Because you'll never jump if I don't push you. The only way you'll ever fly is if I push you out of the nest, because I know you can fly." He cupped my jaw, his smile so tender it cut like a razor to my heart. "Because I believe in you."

"Dammit," I whispered. I shot to my feet and did what I always did—I ran.

He let me go. I only went as far as the limo, because I'd learned my lesson about running off in strange places—no Bast to rescue me here. I sat in the limo and let myself cry for a few minutes. I'd been keeping it pent up for too long, and it had to come out.

He believed in me? How could he? Why? I didn't deserve this.

All those silly dreams as a girl, sitting in my room with my guitar or ukulele, playing my silly little songs about teenage crushes and heartbreak and loneliness and being misunderstood by the big, bad world.

Those silly little dreams, the ones where I'd sing into my mirror, recording myself on Dad's old boom box, and later on my computer, pretending I was singing for thousands of people, to a sold-out stadium. There'd be flashing lights and people screaming my name.

I'd just wanted to be *seen*, back then.

I didn't know what fame was back then. Now, having been around Myles, I had a much clearer idea about what it meant for him, but shit, I had no idea what it meant for me. I'm about to find out, I think. I can feel that, and it's terrifying.

God, there are so many things to be scared of, and they're all piling up and coming to a head.

All those silly little dreams, crushed in a moment by a father's careless words: *"You're just not talented enough, Lexie."*

All those silly little dreams.

And here was Myles North, superstar, top of any list of sexiest men alive, top of any list of most talented performers. Award winner. Showstopper. Globetrotting multi-millionaire.

A man who kept his *four* Grammys in a box in a storage unit, because he cared more about playing music than he did anything else.

Except for me.

He believed in me.

I couldn't ignore that.

But I wasn't sure I could be what he wanted me to be.

He wanted to love me.

He wanted me to love him.

There would be a moment, soon, when I'd have to make a choice—believe his words, or Dad's.

You're just not talented enough, Lexie.

or

I believe in you.

All those silly little dreams…

About to come true.

If I could find the courage.

TWELVE

Myles

S HOWTIME.

I was keyed up as fuck—feeling higher and wilder than if I'd bumped a couple lines. I hadn't—I was stone sober.

The dome was packed to capacity. House lights were low, house speakers playing modern country. The jabber of tens of thousands of voices overlapped in a million ways, and I knew from experience I wouldn't have been able to make out a single voice or conversation even if they had been speaking English.

I was jumping up and down, shaking my hands. My T-shirt was already damp and sticking to me, and I'd taken my hat off and put it on backward and forward a dozen times. Hands shaking. Knees shaking. Gut churning. Head spinning. Lyrics ran through my head, and I sang them as they occurred to me. Went through scales, up and down, tongue twisters.

Then the music cut out. The stadium lights dimmed.

Darkness covered everything. I heard Jupiter move, saw his broad outline swagger to his set, straddle the stool. Twirl his sticks.

"Ready boys?" he called.

Brand and Zan were there, plugging in. "Ready," they both called.

"Myles?"

I let out a breath. Glanced at Lexie, standing next to me. "Kiss me for luck."

She clutched me by the shirt, yanked me to her, and kissed the jitters right out of me. "Kill 'em."

And shoved me toward the stage.

God, she looked hot. Booty shorts—cut-off denim, white fringes, ripped back pockets, just barely cupping the lower edge of her perfect ass. Knee-high cowboy boots, red leather, glittery, pointy toed. White button-down tied under her boobs, cinched tight to keep them in, mostly unbuttoned. Hair swept to one side, minimal makeup.

Fucking perfect.

She had her guitar and ukulele, and I'd heard her in the hotel room, all night and all day, going over songs. In the bathroom, alone. Refusing to let me be with her as she played.

"Myles?" Jupiter again, voice pitched low. "They're going nuts, bud."

I leaned over and kissed her once more. Grinned at her, and then snatched the cordless mic from the stagehand, the guitar from the new tech...whose name eluded me in the adrenaline of the moment. Good kid, though. Swung it by its strap around my shoulder, headstock pointing down and jogged out on stage.

"Hit it, Jupe."

As practiced: a full half a dozen beats, BOOM—BOOM—BOOM—BOOM—BOOM—BOOM...

And then the lights kicked on, brilliant and blinding, and Zan and Brand hit the huge opening lick of "Hookups and Hangovers" and the crowd, already howling and clapping and whistling, erupted to a deafening roar. I stood at the very front and center of the stage, arms raised overhead, a huge grin on my face—the one I thought of as my show-biz grin, million watts, the one that had landed me on magazine covers and lured probably way too many women into my bed. Brand and Zan twisted out the opening—Zan's six string electric howling as he trotted his fingers through a complicated ham-mer-on series of notes, Brand with his huge bass thumping and growling. And then they silenced their strings and Jupiter kicked out the beat, a steady pound on his bass drum and a quick clacking tapping interlaced rhythm of his sticks on the snares and snare rim. I stomped my foot on the stage in front of the mic, hands clapping over my head, and within a beat the crowd was stomping and clapping with me.

Stood up close to the tilted-down mic, swung my guitar around and led us back into the melody as I sang and the crowd sang with me, and we went through it all again because they like short verses and catchy choruses they can sing along to.

And then it was muscle memory and autopi-lot, feeling alive as you only can on stage in front of tens of thousands of people, fingers stinging from the strings and sweat pouring down, ears ringing, my whole body shaking with the adrenaline rush of performance.

Song after song, all the hits, the crowd singing along in a strange mixture of English and Japanese. Having performed here a few times already, I knew a few phrases in Japanese, learned after laborious rep-etition, and I sprinkled them throughout the perfor-mance—*"thank you, Tokyo!"* and *"are you having a great time?"*, and things like that. I wasn't one for talking to the crowd all that much, especially now that Crow had retired as my tech. I missed that fucker.

All of a sudden it was the end of the set, an hour and a half gone in the blink of an eye. I was saying goodbye and thank you in English and Japanese, trotting off stage with my guitar in hand, the guys joining me just off-stage. We were all sweating like pigs, but as we hit the wings we all crashed together in a sweaty group man hug of laughter and back slapping. The lights were still down, the sound system silent, and the crowd was more deafening than ever, demanding an encore.

Best fucking feeling in the world, that—crushing a set and being begged for more.

We let 'em howl for a few minutes, and then we four butted our heads together, arms around shoulders.

"Three-song encore, boys," I said. "'Heaven Is You', 'Claim to Fame', and 'This Ain't a Breakup'." I grinned at them each in turn. "And then I drag Lexie on stage."

"Hell fuckin' yeah," Jupiter said. "Just you two?"

"Yes sir," I said. "You guys okay with that?"

Brand and Zan were enthusiastically all right with sharing the encore with Lexie.

We jogged on stage in the darkness, finding our marks via the glow-in-the-dark taped X on the floor.

"Heaven Is You" started with a bold, thunderous bass solo from Brand, and then we all kicked in at once as the lights came on and deafening applause became ear-piercing cheers of approval at our choice of encore opener. All too soon we'd shredded through our three songs, and the lights stayed on as the boys trooped off stage, Jupe throwing spare drumsticks out into the crowd, some close and some as far back as he could fling them, Brand and Zan tossing picks to the front rows. I stayed on stage and handed my Fender to Alyn—the new tech whose name I was still learning—and accepted, not Betty-Lou, this time, but the guitar I'd named Na'ura, after Crow's Mom.

The crowd, sensing something different than my usual show ending, settled and sat, silent.

I gestured at the cameraman, and he scuttled closer. "Get a good shot of my new guitar," I said into the mic; I glanced up at the side-screens to make sure he was getting a good close look at it. "Ain't she a beaut? She's named Na'ura. All of you remember my guitar tech and best friend, Crow?"

The crowd's affirmation was loud and enthusiastic.

"Well, he's retired as my tech and taken on a new adventure." I lifted the guitar. "Making these. Now this one here is a special piece—not only is it the first guitar he made, it was the last one ever made by his grandfather, River Dog who, if you know anything about custom acoustic guitars, was the maker of some of the hardest to get and sought after customs in the world. And this is the grand prize. He died before he could finish it, and Crow, my brother in every way except blood relation, finished it and gave it to me. You guys here in beautiful Tokyo, Japan are the first audience in the whole wide world to hear me play it."

Alyn brought me a stool and a sound tech brought out a second mic for the guitar—it was a classical acoustic, no amplification. I settled on the stool, snugged Na'ura on my knee, and finger-picked a melody that the crowd soon recognized as the opening to "Sing You Home," the first slow ballad I put out, and the only one to really ever make any waves, chart wise.

"Ya'll know this one," I said. "Sing along."

I moved through the song, eyes closed, playing from the soul.

Let the last note quaver through the dome, and the kind of silence after a song like that is the perfect kind of silence.

"Got another special treat for you," I said, after a moment. "So just...hang on for me for a quick second."

I held the guitar by the neck and strode off stage. Lex was there, clutching her ukulele for dear life, shaking. I stand in front of her. "Ready?"

She shook her head slowly. "No."

I wrapped my arm around her waist and pulled her toward the stage. "I got you, Lex. You can do this."

She stumbled, resisting, and then as we hit the stage beyond the curtains, she found her feet and I heard her breath catch. "Holy shit," she murmured, her eyes wide. "That's a lot of people."

The sound tech rushed out two more mics, setting them up for her vocals and uke, and Alyn brought her a stool, and she was there at the mic, on stage. I turned sideways to face her and the crowd.

"This is Lexie," I said. "A very special woman in my life, and one of the most talented humans I've ever known. She's a little nervous, since this is her first time on stage, so can you guys give her a big ol' Tokyo welcome?"

She stumbled backward a step at the sudden assault of noise from the crowd that washed over us in waves the moment I said her name, and the cheering became a chant—*Leeex-EEE Leeex-EEE Leex-EEE*!

"They know your name, darlin'," I said, sure to get the words picked up by my mic. "Say hello."

She sucked in a breath, exhaled too loudly and too directly into the mic, and she reared back at the white noise it produced. Frowned. Tried again. "Hey, everyone." Deafening applause. "Myles, uh...he said you may not mind if we play a song or two together."

The crowd became louder, wilder.

"Sounds like a yes to me," I said. "So. You pick the song, and I'll play along. Whaddya got, Lexie?"

She swallowed hard. Stared down at her ukulele. Breathed in and out slowly for a few beats. "Um." Another beat. "I wrote this one back in college. Most of my songs are kinda sad, so, you know, sorry if it's a downer. This is, um, this is called 'What You Don't See.'"

She started a gentle, slow melody, and I waited till I'd gotten the gist of its movement and then set a line lower on the register of my guitar, slow and sad and moving around her part.

She smiled at me, acknowledging what I was doing. Then faced the mic, closed her eyes, and I watched sadness slide over her features as she started to sing:

"Dance for you
Move for you
Shake my hips and purse my lips
Fake a smile and all the while
I've got a secret
Not a dirty one,
Nothing you can see
Won't notice it if I let you strip me down
Won't know about it when the lights come on
You wouldn't like it if I told you what it was

I've got a secret and I plan to keep it
Hide it behind the club lights
As I dance for you, move for you,
Shake my hips and purse my lips
Fake a smile and flash my style
Let you see the skin and the curves
So you won't see what's underneath
I could bare it all for you
And you still wouldn't see a thing
Except the naked me
You won't even know what you're missing
Won't ever care about what you don't see
The thing you miss
What you overlook
Under the lips you kiss and the clothes you rip
Under the lace and the latex
Past the silk and after the sex
What you don't
What you can't
What you'll never see
Is the real me."

Her voice was low, rough, pained. She wasn't just singing this song; she's baring herself through it. Lost in it. Just as hurt singing it as she was when she wrote it. Hers was not technically perfect voice, but it was a powerful one, mesmerizing for its quiet mystique.

She wasn't loud, in this song. The crowd was utterly silent, on the edge of their seats trying to hear.

The song ended, the notes faded into ether, and she went quiet, opened her eyes. Another stunned moment, and then the crowd was wild, emitting a wall of sound that went on and on.

I grinned at her. "I think they like you, Lexie."

She smiled shyly. "Thanks, everyone."

"How about another one?" I said.

She sighed. Hesitated. Held my gaze, as if debating something internally. "I, uh, I do have something. It's recent, and, um, actually it's about you."

"Me?" I said, grinning. "Why Lex, I'm flattered."

She laughed. "Don't be too flattered until you hear it."

I faked a shiver. "Uh-oh. Should I be scared? Is it a takedown piece?"

She shook her head, laughing at me. "Nah, nothing like that." She wiggled on her seat, adjusted her tuning. "It's called 'The Ugliest Me'."

The melody to this one was faster, higher, brighter, and showed off her finger work skills, and I stayed quiet, letting her show off. Which, honestly, she wasn't trying to do, she was just playing the song. I kept my palm over the strings and watched her, let her have the spotlight, the moment, all to herself.

"I'm a faker, boy

A baker of lies
A maker of secrets
Master of disguise
I'm a mason, boy,
Builder of walls
Stacker of bricks
Thicker than skin
And harder than steel
Miles high and fathoms deep
Hiding what's real
And all while you sleep
Restless and listless
Tired and wired
I lay in the bed beside you
And build all over again
The walls you got past a few minutes ago
You know my weakness
If only you knew how often I'm sleepless
Putting back up what you took down
Hardening everything you softened
Burying what you dug up
Because I'm a faker, boy
A baker of lies
A maker of secrets
Master of disguise
I'm a mason, boy,
Builder of walls

Stacker of bricks
Thicker than skin
And harder than steel
Miles high and fathoms deep
Hiding what's real
And all while you sleep
I want to let you in
Wish you could see
Wish I could say
Wish I could show you
More than just the pretty me
Wish I had the courage to be
Wish I was bold enough to be
The ugliest me
To tear down the walls and the secrecy
It's not that I don't trust you
It's not that I don't want what you're offering
It's just that I'm afraid to show you
Afraid to reveal
Afraid you won't like
Afraid you won't love
The ugliest me."

Silence.

Never in my life has a silence been so penetrating.

"Wow." I felt myself choking. "First time in my life I've ever been speechless."

Sneaky thing, that move. Blindsiding me with emotions like that, on stage, when I can't answer the way I'd like.

No applause. They were too moved, too stunned.

And then it hit all at once.

The standing ovation.

Not just a trickle-down, a few here and there—all at once, everyone, in unison got to their feet.

What a way to end the first show.

I stood up, took her hand, and walked her to the front of the stage. Stepped back and left her there. Let her soak up the fact that all this was for *her*.

It went on for what felt like minutes, and then I led her toward the curtains, pausing at the mic. "Thank you, love you guys, goodnight."

She stumbled as I led her off-stage, and I had a feeling she was shell-shocked. Got her off-stage and away from the lights and the bustle, to a quiet sliver of darkness between two semi-trailers for our set and sound equipment. She slumped backward against the trailer wall and buried her face in her hands, and began shaking.

I wasn't sure at first if she was crying or laughing, but it soon became clear she was definitely *not* laughing. Sobbing.

"Lex?"

She shook her head.

I crouched in front of her. "Lex. Why are you crying? That was fuckin' amazing. They *loved* you."

"I wasn't...ready," she said, hiccupping. "I fucked up like six times. Skipped an entire verse of the first song."

"Not even I could tell," I said. "They fuckin' *loved* you out there, Lex. That was a show-stealer."

Her head went up, eyes fierce. "I didn't *want* to steal the show from you, Myles! I wasn't *ready*!"

"You're never ready!" I shot back. "You would never have been ready. You think I was ready? I went from dive bars to stadiums in record time. I had no idea what I was doing, but I knew it was what I was meant to be doing."

"That's you," she snapped. "Not me."

"It *is* you," I said. "That's what you're meant to do, Lex." I cupped her face. "You can't tell me that didn't feel amazing while you were out there."

"It felt like I was about to barf and piss myself at the same time. You did the grind, Myles. Day after day, week after week, year after year, playing, learning how to perform, being in front of people, doing what you love to do, what you chose to do. You were an overnight success that took—what?—a fucking decade of slogging along in dive bars to achieve?" She tapped her chest. "I didn't have that. You think you went from dive bars to stadiums in record time? I went from not ever having played on a stage before, with no one even knowing I'm a musician—" she gestured at the Tokyo Dome, "to *that*. Never playing for anyone, never being recorded, nothing. Playing alone in a bathroom because I can't help but need to play and sing…alone in a bathroom because…because I fucking *suck*, Myles. I'm nothing. No one." She was sobbing, words scraping out past harsh breath and ragged sobs. "My dad said it, and he was right. I'm no good. They didn't love me—they loved *you*. If they liked anything about me, it's just because of *this*—" and she cupped and shook her tits, "and this," and slapped her bare thigh near her hip, "and *this*," and she tugged on her hair.

That made me angry.

"You really believe that?"

"Of course I do, Myles," she said, far too calmly. "It's the truth."

"You think fifty thousand people, seeing you from stadium seats, at least half if not more of them straight females, were cheering the way they were because of what you *look* like?"

"Giant screens, remember?"

I hunted for words. "Lex, that's…" I turned away, at a loss. "I have never seen anyone play the way you do, sing the way you do. You're *made* for this, honey." I spun back, grabbing her shoulders. "Lex, listen to me. You are *talented*. Beyond talented. You're a natural. Sure, you were nervous. You think I'm not? You think you're *ever*, no matter how many times you do it, *ever* totally ready to go out and perform in front of fifty thousand people? Pro tip, darlin', you're not. I get nervous every single night. I get the jitters. The butterflies. The shakes. I get off stage and I'm shaking, every single night, because it's scary as hell and it's a fuckin' *rush*." I stared her down. "Yeah, so you messed up. I fucked up at the Grammys, Lex. The *Grammys*. I was so fuckin' nervous I forgot the words to a verse and improvised an entire solo, and it was awful. The guys had no idea what I was doing, and neither did I. Everyone knew I'd fucked up. I got torn apart for a shitty performance—the same night we won four fuckin' Grammy's. I fuck up all the time. Forget words. Mess up a solo. I tripped on a cord once, and nearly took a header off the stage—Brand somehow kept playing with one hand and yanked me back on stage with the other."

She shook her head. "Not the same."

"No, maybe not. Point is, we all get nervous and we all fuck up." I let her go. "Lex, you have to learn how to believe in yourself."

She laughed bitterly. "Yeah, okay. Let me just put that on my little ol' to-do list—" her voice went sarcastic and she mimed writing something on an

invisible notebook. "Note to self—be less of a co-
lossal fuckup. Also, *believe* in yourself. All you need
is faith, trust, and a little pixie dust." She glared at
me. "You got pixie dust, Myles? Because I don't."
She slapped my chest with both hands. "This isn't *A
Star Is Born*, Myles. You're not going to shove me on
stage and make a star out of me. Not everything has
a happy fucking ending."

"It can, though," I said, stung by her words. "If
you let it."

She turned away, shaking her head.

"Lex—"

She turned back to me, suddenly sultry. "You
want a happy ending, Myles?" She pressed herself up
against me, eyes burning with sexual promise, leaning forward to give me a glimpse of the tits she was
pushing against me. "I'll give you a happy ending,
and you don't even need a massage first."

"Lex."

She cupped my crotch over my zipper—despite
my mixed emotions, my body responded. "Yeah,
that's what I thought. You want to have a happy ending?" She ripped open my zipper. Reached in and
hauled me out, fisting my cock. "This is the happy
ending you want."

"No, it's not." I growled. "Quit."

She bit her lip, her smirk a succubus smile. "Ah,

wait, I know." She dropped to her knees. Brought me to her mouth, spoke in a whisper, her lips sliding against me. *"This* is what you want."

I grabbed her wrists, pulled away, and lifted her to her feet. "No," I snarled. "That ain't what I fuckin' want, Lex."

She wiggled against my hold. "Let go, Myles."

I let her go, but zipped myself up—with intense difficulty and very real pain as I fought to bend my hard cock into my jeans. I faced her. Seething. Angry. Confused. "You can't distract me with sex this time, Lex. I ain't askin' about secrets, I'm just askin' for you to fuckin' be *real* with me. You *loved* being on stage. You know it, and I know it. I know what that looks like, and I saw it out there in you. I saw a woman with massive fuckin' talent doing the thing she was fuckin' born to do, and doing it like she'd been doin' it her whole life. I saw fifty thousand motherfucking people watch you sing your heart out and fuckin' slay them all dead with how incredible you sounded. I saw that, Lex, and nothin' you say can make it less true."

"If that's what you think you saw, then you're blind."

"No, I'm seeing more clearly than ever." I gave her the full force of everything I was feeling. "The ugliest you, Lex? It's this, right here. You not believing in your own worth and refusing to hear otherwise." I was quiet, calm, but I knew my words cut like a knife. "I see it, Lex. I *see* you."

"You don't. You can't."

"I do, and I can." I cradled her face, brushed tears away with my thumbs. "I see the ugliest you, and I still care." I swallowed hard. Said it. "Still fuckin' love you, Lex."

A ragged, raw, agonized sob tore out of her. "You *can't!*" she screamed. "You don't know!"

"What?" I shouted back. "What don't I know?"

"Everything," she choked out. "Fucking *everything.*"

And then she fled, turning a corner and vanishing into the crowd of techs and stagehands and the whole small army of people it takes to put on a show of this scale. I wove and pushed my way through the crowd, a few steps behind her. And then, in a moment straight out of Hollywood, a taxi appeared from nowhere, stopped, she got in, and was gone in a moment.

Without her purse.

Without her phone.

Without money, cards, or ID…

With no clue which hotel we were staying in.

In a city she'd never been to, in a country whose language she spoke not a single word.

Whatever demon was she was fighting, the thing had her on her heels.

I managed to get a taxi not long after, but by then she was long gone and I had no idea where or how to go about finding her.

THIRTEEN

Lexie

THIS WAS STUPID…IT WAS BEYOND STUPID.

Maybe one of the most stupid things I'd ever done in my life.

Coming to Tokyo, sure; getting on that stage, absolutely. Not to mention calling Charlie to rescue me in the first place, and ending up at that festival, in the back of a semi-trailer with my biggest celebrity crush, doing wildly inappropriate things with a total stranger. That was definitely a dumb move, not to mention falling hard and fast for my celebrity crush.

And then, running away like this?

Fucking idiotic.

My entire life was a mistake.

I was a mistake.

Here I was, alone, in the middle of Tokyo without a single thing—no purse, no phone, no money, not even the name of the hotel we'd been staying at.

I was fighting a panic attack.

And losing…big time.

After managing to get out of the taxi without paying, I ended up just walking aimlessly, looking in store windows, stopping here and there to rest my feet, sitting on a bench watching the rush of humanity that filled the streets even at this late hour.

Wishing Myles was here to save me, and simultaneously dreading seeing him again. Having to face down another epic blowup.

He'd seen right through the fake.

He'd said the L word.

Fuck.

I got choked up and angry and panicked all over again just thinking about it.

I couldn't even read the street signs or the names of businesses. Couldn't understand anything anyone was saying.

How would I find him?

How would he find me?

I could strip naked and stop traffic, get myself arrested and hope they could somehow get him to come bail me out. It was a tempting thought.

All you're good for, that evil little voice inside said.

I hated that voice.

I had been so *alive* on that stage. He'd pinpointed it with scary accuracy. It was as if I'd finally taken my first full breath after a lifetime of never truly opening my lungs all the way. As if I'd been asleep my whole life, and performing had finally woke me up. The greatest rush, the greatest high.

I felt it all in spite of the fear and the nerves.

God, standing at the front of that stage, watching fifty thousand people scream...for *me*. My name. For my music. My voice. Me.

It had been, legitimately, the greatest moment of my life.

And that evil little voice of doubt had stolen that fragment of joy.

From me. And from Myles.

And he'd *still* found the wherewithal to give me the raw, courageous truth of his feelings for me—knowing exactly how I'd react.

That cut me to the bone.

Yet I couldn't penetrate my own emotional walls. I couldn't fathom giving him that emotion back.

I couldn't tell him my secret.

It was too painful. Too dark. Too horrifying.

I was sitting on a bench and massaging my

blistered feet, not paying much attention to the people walking past.

"Lexie?" a small female voice asked in a thick accent. "You singer?"

I looked over, and a teenage girl was standing off to one side, phone in her hand, and a hopeful, joyful expression on her face. I had no clue how to react. I managed a small smile and said "Um. Yeah—yes, I'm Lexie."

"Selfie?" She held up her phone. "Please? You take selfie?"

God, it was embarrassing—she knew more of my language than I did hers. I knew "Domo arigato, Mr. Roboto" and that was about it, and only a vague idea that *domo arigato* might mean thank you. Possibly.

She could communicate with me.

I smiled. "Um. Sure?"

She squealed, waved at a group of girls standing nearby, giggling and taking photos. They all hustled to stand near me and the girl snapped about fifty photos in several bursts. "Thank you!" she said, facing me and giving me a short bow.

"You're...you're welcome." Baffled at the interaction, I almost missed the opportunity. "Wait!"

The girl, now in the ring of her friends, turned around. "Hai?"

"Um." I had no idea how much English she'd

understand, but I knew this was my only chance. "Can you tag Myles?"

"Tag?" She held up the phone. "Twitter?"

I nodded. "Tag Myles North."

She lit up. "Okay!"

I pointed at the nearby intersection. "And a photo of the street signs?"

She was baffled, but agreeable "Okay?" it sounded like *ohh-KEHH*. She took a photo of the intersection. "Tag?"

I nodded again. "Thank you."

She was thinking. "You lose place?"

I nodded. "Yeah, I'm lost."

She spoke in rapid-fire Japanese, took me by the arm and hauled me to a nearby cafe filled with people. She was taking a video and jabbering rapidly, showing the cafe, the windows, the intersection, me, her friends, and then suddenly I had a pink drink in my hand and I was sitting with the group of Japanese teenagers who were all staring at me like I was *someone*, chattering to each other and giggling behind their hands, whispering. The girl who'd approached me sat beside me, showed me her phone.

Her social media stream was on the screen, and she tapped her latest posts—the photo of us, the street sign, and then her video—the likes, shares, and the retweet numbers were shockingly high considering how recently she'd posted it. I was impressed. And that was when I saw what she was pointing to: a comment under the video. A tiny thumbnail pic of Myles from one of his album covers, with his name and blue checkmark. *"Thank you! And tell her to stay put!"* This was in English on a feed dominated by her native Japanese characters.

I felt an absurd burst of relief, so powerful that I compulsively hugged the girl. "Thank you! Oh god, thank you so much!"

She was surprised by my hug, uncomfortable. Stiff, awkward. She shifted away from me, smiling and laughing, but obviously deeply uncomfortable. "Ohh...okay!"

I moved away. "Sorry." I grinned sheepishly. "What's your name?"

She nodded, looking anywhere but at me. "Okay, okay." She finally met my eyes, my gaffe forgiven. "Emiko."

"I just...thank you, Emiko. Thank you."

She laughed. "Hai, hai."

There was a commotion, then—people in the cafe responding to something going on outside—a crowd gathering. I tried to see, but the crush and rush was too thick—so I moved to the window.

Myles.

Stepping out of a blacked-out SUV, still in his

jeans, boots, sweat-stained white T-shirt, and backward Dallas Cowboys hat, the outfit he'd worn on stage. He was ringed by people thrusting dozens of receipts and hats and photographs and scraps of paper at him, coming from all directions—there were four security guards around him, but they could barely keep the gathering chaos at bay.

Myles was absolutely at ease. Smiling, shaking hands, posing. Signing with a big black Sharpie. Never hurrying. I saw him glance over the heads of the crowd, lifting up on his toes—his eyes met mine, and I saw longing in them, relief.

Another slip of paper was waving in his face and he turned to give that person his attention—and for that moment, as he bent to listen, smiling, turning to pose for a selfie, that person had his entire attention. A genuine smile—not the megawatt magazine grin, but the real Myles smile.

I expected him to sign a few autographs, pose for a few selfies, and then escape.

But he didn't.

The crowd grew, and the security guards did their best to keep him from being crushed, but he didn't turn anyone away, even when the crowd continued to grow.

How long?

Half an hour? A full hour?

I wasn't sure.

Seeing him in front of a sold-out crowd was one thing.

This was another.

And the way he handled it hit me hard, for some reason.

He *cared*.

He made eye contact with each person. Didn't shy away from being clung to for a photo, and that photo becoming two or three, or more. He signed everything handed to him. Smiled for each person, wrote their name on the autograph. Not just a scribble of his initials.

Finally the crowd began to thin and his security was able to gradually move him away from the SUV and toward the door of the cafe where I was. I moved to the door, and a hulking American security guard in a black suit and mirrored Oakleys hooked his arm around my shoulders and hustled me into a walk. "This way, Miss Goode."

"Uh, okay." I halted. "Wait!" I went back in and grabbed Emiko by the hand and brought her to Myles. "Emiko, this is Myles; Myles, this is Emiko, the girl who helped you find me."

He seemed to know hugging strangers was a cultural no-no, because he didn't try, as I had. "Thank you so much, Emiko. I was worried sick."

Emiko was over the moon, chattering in Japanese and jumping up and down. Finally, she settled enough to take several selfies and a short video with Myles, and got him to sign a scrap of paper.

And then she was waving at us with a huge grin, and we were finally alone.

"That's us," Myles said, gesturing at the SUV.

The bodyguard guided me to it, shielding me from the press of people with his own body. opened the door just wide enough to admit me, then closed the door and leaned over to whisper to Myles, who nodded and signed another hat, took another selfie.

Myles did all this despite the exhaustion I saw in his eyes, and in the lines of his body. He had just performed at a huge show, using all the energy that entailed, and then I put him through the stress of running away in a foreign city. I felt worse than I ever had in my life, but the worst of it was that I couldn't control myself.

On top of that, I realized just how careful he had to be about going out in public. He rarely went out in public, knowing he would be inundated by the kind of thing I had just witnessed.

Knowing someone is famous is one thing.

Seeing the effect of it is another.

I had a lot to think about as I sat in the back of the SUV with Myles, alone with my thoughts.

Finally, after what had to have been an hour, he waved goodbye and slipped into the car.

I buckled up and silence descended on the hushed interior of the luxury SUV. The security guards were split between the front seat of this SUV and an identical one behind us.

He wasn't looking at me.

I didn't know what to say.

"Smart thinking, getting that girl to post that video." He finally looked at me, and I could tell he was hurt, angry, and at a loss for words.

"She saw me sitting on a bench and wanted a selfie with me." I laughed. "I was about to say how weird and awkward it was, but then I just watched you do it for an hour straight."

He gave a sort of half laugh. "First taste of fame, huh? Get used to it. Before long, you'll be doing that," he said, gesturing behind us.

I didn't want to argue, so I said nothing in response to that. "Thank you for coming to get me. I'm so sorry to have put you through that."

"Yeah."

Silence.

Finally, after forty-five minutes through brutal traffic, we arrived at the hotel.

That had been the worst, most uncomfortable silence of my life.

The silence continued as we took a private elevator up to the suite .

We arrived directly into a massive penthouse with a multi-million-dollar view of Tokyo spread out below. Ultramodern, all stark lines and contrasting black and white and chrome with pops of color and muted shades of gray.

There was food waiting—a huge spread of food. Seeing it made me realize how hungry I was.

Myles made up plates for us and we ate…in silence.

I had no clue what to say, or how to break the silence without bringing up questions and creating more arguments. Myles didn't deserve that. So I kept silent and Myles seemed content to let it be, as well.

For the first time since I met him, we went to bed without sex.

Awkward, tense. The knowledge of so much unspoken between us.

So much he wanted that I had no clue how to give.

So much he deserved to know that I couldn't tell him.

So, he went to bed, and I sat in the bed beside him, exhausted and utterly unable to sleep.

I heard him snoring, and hated myself for everything.

FOURTEEN

Myles

I WOKE SOMEWHERE NEAR DAWN, FOR REASONS UNKNOWN. I didn't have to pee, I wasn't thirsty, wasn't hungover. Just…awake.

At 5:01 a.m. local time.

Jet lag, maybe, but I was used to that, and I could generally fall asleep whenever I needed to. And god knew after the show, the hours of hunting Tokyo for Lexie, and then signing autographs and posing, the awkward silent drive, the tense silence in the penthouse here—I should have been dead beat. But I was wide awake.

And that's when I heard it.

Lexie—singing, playing a guitar.

I saw her, on the balcony off the master suite. Sitting in a chair, leaning back on two legs with the chair back resting against the corner and her feet on the railing. Guitar across her thigh. City light bathed her in a dozen shades of glowing shadow. She was nude, under the guitar, from my angle, I could see the swell of her breast pressed against the guitar, the curve of her thigh as it rounded under on the chair. Her eyes were closed, her head tipped back, and she was singing the saddest song I'd ever heard.

There were no words, just a haunting aria of loneliness and brokenness, laced through with a low delicate melody on the smaller, higher strings—no fancy chords or finger work, just a slow melody that carved a hole in your heart and left the bitter taste of sadness its place.

I grabbed my phone, brought up the external camera, no flash, and hit record. I could just make out her outline; see that she was naked without seeing anything except her and the guitar.

I recorded until she stopped, hands squealing on the strings, and I heard her sniffle. She was playing my first guitar, an old Yamaha I'd gotten thirdhand; I could tell by the sound of it. It was old and battered and hard to keep in tune, but I'd written some of my best songs on it, and still liked to play it when I was feeling melancholy. Interesting that she'd chosen it—Betty-Lou was with me, unlocked at the moment, as I'd spent a few minutes playing before I went to bed; Na'ura was here in the hotel, too, also unlocked as I hadn't gotten a more protective case for her yet.

She opened her eyes, perhaps alerted by that sixth sense that told her she was being observed—looked over and saw me sitting up on the bed.

"Hi."

"Hey." I wasn't sure if I should tell her I'd recorded her and decided against it. I would figure out what to do with it later.

For now, I couldn't take any more awkwardness. I left the bed and went out onto the balcony—it hot and humid outside. I was naked, like her; we were both habitual nude sleepers, and had established that early on.

She watched me, holding the guitar in place across her torso. "You heard?"

I nodded. "It was beautiful. Haunting."

She shrugged. "I wrote it when I had some things to express, but no words for what I wanted to say."

"Well, you said it loud and clear." I hesitated. "And I guess I just…I'm sorry for whatever happened to cause you to feel that way."

She shrugged. "Thanks, but it's just life, I guess."

I was leaning against the railing, facing her. "Couldn't sleep?"

Shook her head. "Not a wink."

"Lex, I…"

She carefully set the guitar aside. Set the chair down on all fours. Sat up, hands on her thighs, naked, gazing up at me. "Myles, can you just, please, for right now, just don't—"

I knelt and tipped the chair back up on the hind legs and balanced it as she'd been; she squealed in surprise, and then found her balance. I slid my fingers around one dangling ankle, lifted her foot, and draped it on my thigh. Then the other. Held her eyes. She understood what I was offering: distraction. Another avoidance of the topic. I ached to know the source of her pain, but I knew she had to offer the story on her own terms.

When—or *IF*—she would ever be ready.

Until then, I could offer her nothing but myself. My patience. My understanding.

And this.

A distraction.

An escape, if only for a moment, from everything.

I was going to give it to her on *my* terms, though.

I didn't plunge right in and devour her. I took my time—kissed her calf, her knee. Lifted her leg and licked the tender underside of her knee. The inside of her thigh. So close that my nose nuzzled her soft warm seam, and then I kissed over it. I kissed my way down her other thigh, and now she was breathing slow and deep, watching me.

"Myles..."

"Lex?"

"I..."

I knew it was going to excuses and prevarication, so I slid my tongue up her slit. She was distracted, as I knew she would be. She gasped, and I teased her clit with the tip of my tongue, and then went back to kissing the insides of her upper thighs as I dragged a fingertip up her seam and down, up and down, teasing in, and in, and deeper, until I was sliding through her wetness and she was hiking her hips up in a silent request for more. I flicked her with my tongue, and then delved my finger deep, and she cried out. She was usually quick to come the first time, and I was determined to draw her out, this time. Once, but so hard she wouldn't know what hit her.

So I drew her out. Teased and tickled, licked and kissed, never settling into a rhythm, fingers sliding in, curling, withdrawing—but *slowly*. When I gave her my tongue, it was as slowly as I could move it; fat flat licks to her slit, upward and inward, ending at her clit. She gripped my hair and groaned, held my head between her thighs and thrust hard against my face, legs splayed apart with her heels locked together around the back of my neck.

"Myles, god Myles, I need to come."

I kissed her clit, a soft wet suckling of my lips. Backed away to grin at her, three fingers penetrating her in a slow arrhythmic squelching slide. "Nope."

She growled, pushing her pussy against my hand, needing what I refused to give her. "Please."

Slower, then, fingers moving in and out millimeters at a time. I flicked her clit with my tongue and she flinched, hips flexing helplessly. "God, oh god Myles—please, I'm so close. I need it so bad."

"Mmm-mmm. Not yet."

I continued to tease her until her hips were flexing wildly and she was gasping and growling like a trapped wildcat, trying desperately to grind hard enough against my evasive tongue to take the orgasm I wouldn't give her.

"You want me to beg? Is that it?" she snarled. "Fine, I'll beg. Please, Myles—*please!*"

I kissed her clit again, made out with her pussy until she was on the verge. "Nope, not really turned on by begging."

She mewled in frustration as I left my mouth inches from her and went back to teasing her with my fingers sliding in and out in no set rhythm. "Then *what,* Myles? What do you want? You want me to suck your cock and swallow all your cum? Is that it?" She tried to reach for me, but I wouldn't let her move, held her in place and dove in, twirling my tongue around her clit until she cried out raggedly, sobbing. "Oh god oh god oh god, Myles, *please*—what? What the *fuck* do you want? Do you want me to let you fuck me bare? What? Tell me what you want!"

What I wanted was her to make love to me.

I wanted her to take me inside her, and cling to me, come around me, and whisper my name as we came together, bare or not. I wanted to hear her come apart and tell me she wanted me and needed and loved me. I wanted her arms around me, her legs scissoring around my hips, and her breath in my ear.

I wanted what she could not and would not give me, and she was so hung up on the no condom thing that she was missing the truth of what I really wanted: *her,* the real true raw bare vulnerable Lexie Goode, given willingly and openly.

So, instead of getting something that she wasn't ready or able to give, I drove her to the edge of madness and held her there. Licked and fingered her to the cusp of climax and kept her there, begging and pleading and crazed, thrusting and thrashing, crying and sobbing, tipped precariously backward in the chair and unable to totally give in.

When it was obvious she couldn't take any more, I picked her up out of the chair and carried her in my arms into the bedroom and set her gently on the bed.

"Myles?" she panted. Eyes wet, breasts heaving. "Please?"

I knelt at her feet. I gazed at her, and let her see the love in my eyes, let her see what I felt, what I'd told her I felt.

I cupped her ass to lift her higher. "Now, Lexie."

And then I devoured her hard and fast and wild, and she screamed louder than she'd ever screamed, spine arching off the bed, bridged upward with her feet digging into the mattress, pussy grinding helplessly against my mouth, wetness bursting on my tongue as she exploded. Her teeth clenched down hard on her scream and it became a ragged whining growl as she came and came, sobbing through it.

When it finally released her from its tidal sway, Lexie collapsed to the bed, panting. I slid up her body and lay beside her, brought the covers up around us and cradled her in my arms, pillowing her head on my chest.

"Sleep now," I whispered.

She couldn't even murmur in response.

I fell asleep holding her, feeling her twitch as she fell into slumber.

I woke to sunlight streaming hot and yellow on my closed eyelids and the sounds of the city blowing in through the open door to the balcony.

And something hot and wet and soft moving on my cock.

I moaned, fluttered my eyes open. "Mmm?"

I looked down, and saw Lexie outlined under the sheet that was draped over my waist. Felt her hands cradling my balls and cupping my shaft as she went down on me, slow and deep.

"Lex..."

She hummed a negative. Batted the sheet away. Reached up and found my hand, placed it on her head. Pushed down on my hand. Encouraging me to guide her to what I wanted, how I wanted this.

Sleepy, disoriented, already rising to the verge of orgasm, I was helpless to stop, to resist wanting this. Her mouth felt so good and I'd gone to sleep with a painful erection that hadn't ever entirely faded.

I gave in, and tangled my fingers in her hair, guiding her to slow down, to go shallower, and then deeper. She swallowed around me, gagged a little, and I held still and brought her shallower yet, not wanting or liking the gagging sounds. She stroked me, cradled and massaged me, and I lost myself in her soft wet mouth, gasping and panting as she took me to the edge.

"Lex, I'm gonna come," I breathed. "Right now, fuck, right *now*—fuck!"

I tried to pull her away, but she went deeper, and I felt her mouth around my base and her throat around the head and I couldn't stop myself from coming, from letting loose and I felt her swallow, gulp, her hands both wrapped around my cock as she backed away and pumped me wild and fast and I came again, and she swallowed and her tongue swirled and I felt like I was being ripped apart in the best possible way.

I felt dizzy and faint, light-headed as the orgasm blasted through me.

She didn't stop there.

Kept her mouth on me, held me in her hands and licked and kissed as I seeped and faded, aching, blissful and spent.

Finally she crawled up my body and rested her cheek on my chest, not saying a word.

And neither did I.

I was conflicted.

That had been one of the best—in fact, *the best* blowjob I'd ever gotten, including the first one from her that was the only other one even close in comparison. It had alleviated the boiling ache in my balls. It had felt *good*.

But it wasn't what I wanted.

I wanted *her*.

I wanted *us*.

I'd take blowjobs any day and every day, and thank her with as many orgasms as she could handle. But that was meant to be her way of thanking me for last night, or this morning, or whatever it was. It was meant to stand in for the intimacy she was too afraid to give me.

We couldn't even have sex without some excuse behind it, because the kind of sex I wanted with her meant more than fucking, more than hooking up. So much more. And she wouldn't dare let that happen.

So she skirted the issue with oral play that in no way satisfied me, or her. I knew that, but I wasn't sure she was allowing herself to recognize it.

I wanted to be stronger—to have the courage and fortitude to deny her the oral distractions.

To force the issue.

But I wasn't that strong.

So I said nothing. Just held her. Let the mountain of unspoken *everything* and *more* pile higher between us.

"Myles, I…"

I touched her lips. "Shush, Lex."

"But—"

"Are you ready to talk?" A thick, telling silence. "Thought so. So just…let it be, for now. Okay?"

"This isn't how I want things to be, Myles."

"Me either. I said my piece. Rest is up to you."

"I don't want to lose you."

"I went after you, yeah?" I touched her cheek, rolled to an elbow and gazed down at her. "I found you. Brought you here. Gave you space. Didn't push nothin'. I'm *here* Lex. I ain't goin' nowhere."

"But if I can't eventually give you what you want, you will."

I shook my head. "It ain't about condom or no condom, babe. That's the least important thing on the planet to me. It's about what it represents. It's about vulnerability." I held her gaze. Let her see as deep into my heart and soul as she dared look. "It's about there being an *us*."

She had nothing to say to that, and that told me everything.

———⋅✦⋅———

Moscow.

No matter how I tried, I couldn't get Lexie on-stage—she flat out refused, and became angrier than she'd ever been when I tried to force it. So I let it go.

Moscow was followed by three dates in Germany, and more refusals to perform. I would hear her playing my guitar or her ukulele, knew she was writing new songs, testing out melodies and snatches of chorus, tweaking. I knew music was coming back to her and that she wanted it.

Paris, Barcelona, Lisbon. Some of the most beautiful cities in the world, and I made sure she saw them. We took time away from everything, just me and her in a blacked-out SUV, seeing the sights and hitting little cafes, sipping wine. The shows were all sold out and every single one was a huge success. We were making big bank on this tour and Mick was thrilled.

We haven't had sex in over a week. I refused to let her blow me instead of being intimate, and she refused to let me go down on her unless she could do the same to me.

It was all falling apart.

She refused to perform.

Hid in the bathroom or sat on the balcony playing my guitar and ignoring me.

Ignoring calls from her mom and sisters.

She was coming apart.

We were coming apart.

It was all disintegrating. Dissolving. Breaking at the seams, crumbling at the cracks.

Prague. Four a.m. local time.

She was asleep. Well, passed out—that's the other thing: she's started drinking herself to sleep and I hated it.

But I couldn't just...leave her here, obviously. Couldn't and wouldn't stick her on a plane ride home. On a certain level, this whole thing was nuts. Why was I putting myself through this? Why was I continuing to accept her endless parade of bullshit? Especially now, as she increasingly fell apart.

Because at night, as she fell asleep, she'd cling to me. Clutch me close and tight and hard, and nuzzle against me as if I were the only thing holding her in place, keeping her together. She'd wake up and sigh, and wriggle against me, fall back asleep, and in those moments of tenderness and sweetness, I knew why I was doing all this. And sometimes, there'd be hints of sweetness from her. She went off exploring on her own, and brought back souvenirs for the guys and me, and another time went out while we were rehearsing and doing sound check and came back with a bottle of local whiskey and junk food. Little things, but gestures like that meant something, coming from Lexie.

I didn't know what else I could do. And then I had an idea. It would mean breaking things wide open. It was risky. It constituted an invasion of her privacy. She'd be angry with me—beyond angry. She may never talk to me again, if I did this. Yet, I felt I had to take that chance—that if I didn't bring things to a head, we'd never have a future together.

I unplugged my phone, grabbed the bottle of whiskey she'd gotten me, cracked the top and took a slug. I was still wide awake after our concert tonight, so I took the bottle and my phone out on the balcony and closed the door behind me. Sitting on a chair, I got comfortable and brought up the video of Lexie I took a couple weeks ago in Tokyo.

I watched it...again. For the tenth or twentieth time.

God*damn,* she's good. I knew beyond a shadow of a doubt that if I posted this to my socials, it would go viral. Millions of views in a matter of hours. She's *gorgeous.* Her voice is haunting. It's a hypnotic, mesmerizing video.

Pure talent. Pure unadulterated star power, raw and unpolished.

I uploaded it to my socials. I hesitated.

I could lose her over this.

But I was losing her anyway.

She deserved her time in the sun—and the world deserved her music.

She was too afraid of...of fucking *everything* to put herself out there.

This video—more than her appearance on the Myles & Crow album, more than the other videos, even more than her encore with me in Tokyo—would put her on the map.

I turned to look at her. Sleeping in my bed. Our bed. A hotel bed. Arm across her face, an empty wine bottle on the bedside table.

I had to shake her out of this.

This was the only way I knew.

I hit the publish button.

In a matter of minutes, she's on my socials, pinned to the top of my website. It's out there.

No going back now.

FIFTEEN

Lexie

WE WERE ON THE PLANE FROM PRAGUE TO OSLO and I finally, begrudgingly, went through the eight billion notifications on my phone. Calls from Mom, Charlie, and Cassie. Emails from Torie which I flagged and set aside for later because Torie was a mess I didn't have the energy to deal with right now. A voicemail from Poppy:

"Hey Lex. Just, you know, checking in. Miss you, girl. I'm, um, thinking pretty seriously about finally dropping out and moving to Alaska to focus on art full-time. Mom says Eva du Maurier lives there, and she's one of my art idols, so maybe I could get some pointers or something." A pause. "I saw your video. And, damn Lex, that was some ballsy shit. How you have the courage to put something like that out there, I'll never know. But for real, I had no clue you're so damn talented. I remember hearing you sing in your room a lot, but that video...damn. It's on a whole other level. Anyway, I miss you; hope to talk to you soon. Bye."

Video?

What video?

Then I checked the text messages from Mom and the girls in Ketchikan.

Mom: *Why didn't you tell me about the video? You're amazing, Lex. A little risque, perhaps, but amazing. It has so many views already!*

Charlie: *OMFG!!! LEX! The video. Call me!*

Cassie: *Holy motherfucking shit, Alexandra. You have the biggest ovaries ever, girl. I can NOT believe you let Myles take and post that. Everyone is talking about it—everyone. You're blowing up, Lex. Big time.*

I opened Twitter. My account suddenly had a blue check, my follower count was in the millions, and I had more comments and retweets and tags and shares than I'd ever seen.

And there, at the top, was the video in question. I played it, and I dropped the phone on the table in front of me, hand over my mouth, heart stopped.

It was me.

On the balcony in Tokyo. Naked, wearing not a

stitch except the guitar. You couldn't see much, given that it was dark and the only light on me is ambient city glow and my bits were covered by the guitar. But it was obvious I'm naked in the video, and it was provocative, sexy. My leg was propped up on the rail, and I was leaning back in the chair, head tipped back, eyes closed. Plucking that lullaby I wrote for myself. Singing the wordless song.

It was the most haunting thing I'd ever heard, and it was hard to believe it was *me*.

I checked it on YouTube: less than twenty-four hours and it had over seventy million views.

My head spun.

It was posted under Myles North, the official, verified artist account. Yesterday…or this morning, early.

I looked up, and Myles was watching me. Zan, Brand, and Jupiter were huddled together on the couch, watching something on Jupiter's iPad, laughing as if it's inappropriate. Not the video, then. And studiously acting like they have no idea what's going on over here.

"How—fucking—*dare* you," I hissed. "You had no right to record that, and even less right to fucking *post* it for the world!"

He looked…sad. He knew this was coming. He knew exactly what he was doing.

"Why?" I snarled. "Tell me that. Why? The truth."

"Because you won't. You won't play. You won't try. You're too scared. And you're too fucking talented to keep your music hidden from the world. The world deserves your talent, but you're too fucking scared to put yourself out there."

"That's my choice, not yours!"

"I disagree. You know that people love you. You've seen it." He stabbed the screen of my phone angrily. "Look at the fucking comments, Alexandra. Fucking read them!"

Omg so talented!

She's beautiful AND talented? Can I plz be her?

That voice tho! She's incredible!

Can we get a version of this in full light? Without the guitar? Damn.

I've never heard anything like this in my life. More!

I don't know who this chick is, but she's got the most amazing voice I've ever heard. When does her album come out?

I saw a video of her performing with Myles in Tokyo, and OMG! She's my new favorite artist. Where can I buy her music?

And on, and on. Hundreds and thousands of comments. Some basic likes, some gushing comments. Some telling me to put on clothes for my next video. There was even a comment from a well-known Nashville producer: "*Have your people call my people, we'll get you signed.*"

My eyes stung. "Great, they like me. You still had no right."

He nodded. "I know."

"And you don't care?"

"I'm sorry, Lex. I know it was an invasion of your privacy. But your talent *belongs* to the world. Not hidden in a fucking bathroom. I'm not going to let you squander the talent you've been given. I'm not going to let you hide in the goddamn bathroom just because you're scared. You can hate me if you want. Never talk to me again. I knew the risks when I put it up. I accept them. Because you *want* this. I know you do. You just don't think you deserve it. But you do."

"Fuck you, Myles."

He blinked hard. "I'm sorry, Lex."

My phone rang and I answered without thinking. "Hey, is this Lexie Goode?"

I fought back sobs. "Uh, yeah. Who's this and how did you get this number?"

"This is Benny Frey, and I represent RCA records in Nashville. I got your number from Mick, Myles's manager. I'd like to speak with you in person to discuss some opportunities we have for you."

"I…"

"I'd also like to congratulate you."

"For…what?"

"Seventy-six million views in twenty-four hours. It's a new world record."

"It is?"

"You didn't know?"

"I didn't know…" I laughed bitterly. "Yeah, you could say I didn't know."

"You're probably fielding a lot of calls right now, so I'll let you go. But I'm going to text you my info and you get hold of me when you're ready to talk. I know you'll be getting other offers—talent like yours only comes along once in a really, really rare while, but I know I speak for all of us at RCA when I say we'd like the opportunity to match any offer you may receive."

"Thanks?"

A laugh. "Call me, whenever, wherever. Or just look me up in Nashville."

"Yeah, I…I'll…I have to process things. But thanks for your call, Benny."

I set my phone down, shaking. "What the hell was that?"

Myles laughed. "That was a top RCA exec hunting you down, hoping to be the first to snag you." My phone rang again; I went to answer it, but Myles's hand clapped over it, stopping me. "Advice? Don't answer. Let them leave voicemails. I'd put it on mute, if not turn it off. It's going to be ringing off the hook for days."

I choked. "I don't know what to do, Myles. Why did you do this to me?"

"You don't have to do anything. You wait till the major players have their offers in. Mick is getting you an agent—not mine, someone else. So you're on your own, not tied to me. Your agent fields the offers, brings you the best ones, and you accept or reject."

It was hard to breathe. "You're not making an offer? You and Crow have a label."

He shrugged. "It's just organized enough to let me put out Myles North records. I'm not set up to take on outside acts. And I guess I assumed you wouldn't want my help."

"But I…I don't know who to trust. What's a good offer? What should I be wary of?"

"Why ask me? You don't trust me any more than you do anyone else." He sounded so…bitter.

"That's not fucking fair, goddammit," I snapped. "I do trust you. I mean, you did this without my permission and I'm absolutely furious with you. But I also recognize you didn't do it out of, like, nefarious motives."

"Of course not. The exact opposite."

"I just…" I felt my eyes mist over, panic bubbling up. "I don't know how to navigate this."

"You take your time. You don't commit to anyone or anything."

I snorted bitterly. "Yeah, well, that's easy."

He seemed to physically bite down on a response, the gist of which I could guess. His phone
rang. "Mick, what's up?" He listened, gave verbal af-
firmatives, and hung up. Back to me. "Mick has his
top four picks for agents for you. All women, best in
the field. He's emailing me the info and I'll share it
with you. You pick from there, sign a contract, and let
your new agent deal with everything. She'll call the
labels and tell them she's your agent and to bring her
any offers. You ignore all other calls except those from
your family."

"Do I have to sign with an agent?"

He shrugged. "It makes life easier, if nothing
else. It's a complicated world out there, in the music industry. She'll be your guide through the murky,
shark-infested waters."

"I mean…what I…what if I don't want to—to do
this?"

He ground his teeth. "Don't bullshit me, Lex.
You're scared, angry with me, and overwhelmed. I get
it. But don't act like you don't want this." He leaned
across the table and took my hands. "Lex, think back
to the times you've performed. Remember how you
felt."

I closed my eyes, and I was on that stage again
in Tokyo, fifty thousand people *accepting* me, loving

my music. Alive. Nothing else had mattered, in that moment.

"I remember," I whispered.

"Deal with *this*," he wiggled my phone, "and you get *that*. It's why I put up with signing autographs and taking a thousand pictures with strangers, because *they're* the reason I get to do this. I deal with press and media and attention and endorsements and money and managers and agents because it lets me be on stage doing the thing I love more than anything else in the fucking world—which is performing. It's what I was born to do. I'll die on stage when I'm a hundred years old, because it's who I fucking *am*." He poked my chest. "And it's who *you* are, if you can summon the fucking courage to let yourself have it—the courage to believe in yourself and your abilities."

"I don't know if I have that courage."

"Look deeper, Lex." His voice was low and rough. "You *do*."

"My own father didn't believe in me."

"And he was a damned fool. He was *wrong*." He squeezed my hands so hard it hurt. "I fucking believe in you more than I've ever believed in anyone or anything, Lex."

"I don't deserve that."

"Not for you to decide. I decide that."

"You decide what I deserve?"

He laughed. "No—I decide what I feel for you, and how *you* feel about how *I* feel is irrelevant." He sucked in a slow deep breath, let it out. "I accepted the end of us—the end of whatever us there could have been—when I put that video out there. I did it for you, because I believe in you and because I love you."

I rocked backward. "I...I can't. I can't handle this."

I shot out of the booth and bolted for the suite in the back. Shut and locked the door, and sobbed—out of sheer, overwhelmed confusion, if nothing else.

———⊰❖⊱———

The plane landed, and I didn't leave the cabin. Couldn't.

Hours passed and what did I do in those hours?

Cry? Rage? Sleep?

No, I drank.

I escaped the only way I knew.

One bottle of wine.

Two.

I lost track after that.

The room spun around me, and I fell off the bed at some point. Hated myself for being this weak.

But it was too much.

I loved him.

He loved me.

But he didn't know my secret.

And now—now the whole world wanted me.

Wanted my music.

Almost a hundred million people had watched me in my most vulnerable, intimate state, singing a lullaby I'd written for myself, to help me deal with unimaginable pain. That pain was on display, raw and real.

For the whole world to see.

I wanted to sing.

I wanted to let Myles love me.

I just didn't know how.

And no matter how much wine I drank, I couldn't drown that out.

Waking up was a slow, painful process. My tongue was a wooden stick glued to the roof of my mouth, which was filled with sand that was on fire. Someone had put my skull in a vise, poured molten lava into my brain cavity, and was using my temple as an anvil. My stomach felt like a vat of boiling acid.

I hurt.

I also stank—I could smell my own body odor,

a rank jumble of smells emanating from my mouth, armpits, and vag.

I heard seagulls, and that was wrong somehow, but the lava-drum that was my brain was far from operational, and I couldn't figure out why I was hearing seagulls in the distance.

I also heard waves crashing, and tried to put two and two together. We must be in Oslo or somewhere near the water.

The world was swaying. Back, forth…back, forth. Lulling. Soothing.

And nauseating.

Suddenly my stomach was heaving and I was gonna hork.

I grunted, trying to at least roll over instead of vomiting on myself. I managed to flop sideways, and the swaying worsened, as if I was on a boat.

"Oops, don't fall out." A voice. Male. Deep. Familiar. A voice that somehow meant hugs and kisses and snuggles and comfort. "Here, I got you."

"Puke." It was all I could manage, and my voice sounded like a raven with a sore throat.

I heard movement, felt a hand at the back of my neck, holding my hair aside. Something touched my forehead, the rim of a bucket or something…just in time. Out came the hot filthy acidic flood, my stomach twisting itself inside out. Grit, bile, liquid guilt and shame.

"There you go. Get it all out."

I thought I was done and tried to breathe. Got a breath, and then my stomach churned, twisted, and it started all over again in a gushing bitter stink.

After a few moments without any more vomiting, I heard a bottle cap twist and felt something pressed to my lips.

"Here. Water. Sip it, rinse and spit." I knew him. Brain wouldn't offer up a name, not even my own, but I *knew* him. Trusted him.

I tried to obey, but swishing was beyond my abilities, and it spurted out of my mouth. I heard a male chuckle. "Babe, you are still *so* fucked up." A towel touched my mouth, chin, throat. "There. Now try again."

I did, and managed to rinse my mouth and spit it out. I took a sip, and then more, and then more. Then the bottle of water was pulled away. "Best take it slow until you see how it sits."

"Uuuurrrgggghh, god, I feel awful."

"Yeah, I bet you do, but you'll be all right. I'm here."

Somehow, hearing that soothed me. If he was here, I'd be all right. I wanted to cry, from everything, but I couldn't. Staying awake impossible.

I woke again, and felt a little better, I felt less tired and my stomach was more settled.

"Gonna puke again?" I heard him say.

I shook my head. "Don't...don't think so."

"Hey, you can actually talk. We're gettin' somewhere."

"What happened? How much did I drink? Jesus."

"I found two empty wine bottles, and my bottle of Johnnie Blue was significantly less full. So, a fuckin' lot."

"Shit. I don't even remember the whiskey."

I felt his hand on my head, affectionate, checking my temperature. "I was worried you were gonna have to see a doctor. You had alcohol poisoning, for sure. Thank god it wasn't lethal, but it definitely did a number on you. You've been in and out of consciousness for days."

"Oh my god. I can't believe it. Where are we?"

"Don't worry about that. When you can function normally, we can talk. I'm gonna give you some Tylenol and you're gonna sleep again."

I took two pills with more water, but this time the water had a flavor to it. "What was that?" I tried to open my eyes—the brilliant sunlight hurt like hell, so I closed them again.

"Water with electrolytes. I'm trying to rehydrate you."

"Didn't taste like Gatorade."

"Fuck that. That shit's sugar water. This is some shit Jupiter uses, no sugar, no junk, just straight electrolytes and natural flavoring."

"Oh."

Except for the sound of seagulls and crashing waves, silence enveloped me, and I was drifting off to sleep.

"Myles?"

His hand on my cheek. "Yeah, darlin'?"

"I'm sorry. I'm so sorry."

"For what?"

"This?" My attempt at a rueful laugh ended in a pained moan. "For me. For everything I've put you through."

"You're not getting rid of me that easily."

That made my eyes burn. "I don't wanna be rid of you, either."

"Coulda fooled me," he said, and then sighed. "Quit worryin' about it, Lex. Just rest. We've got all the time in the world."

That wasn't right either, but my faculties were still offline and I couldn't figure out why.

I fell back asleep.

The next time I woke up, I was me again, but with a terrible headache and a cotton mouth and an oily, acidic stomach. I even opened my eyes.

Overhead were…leaves? The ceiling of the room was like straw, thick and woven together, coming to a point. Beams of hand-hewn tree branches supported the roof, and the walls were somehow different. Mostly I could see open space through which was impossibly blue water that went on forever. I realized I was in a hammock, which explained the swaying.

There wasn't much in the room. A bed, a small three-drawer bureau. Bedside table. A partially ajar door leading to a bathroom. The room was open concept—bedroom, sitting room, and kitchen all in one. It was simple and rustic, in a tropical way.

There were sunglasses—my own—on the bedside table. A note: *Put these on.* And a smiley face. An arrow pointing toward the bureau. *Look in there. Wear what you find.*—M

The letter of his initial was done with a swooping series of loops and flourishes.

I put the sunglasses on, because even in here, it was bright. I realized I was naked, which could be explained by me having barfed on myself at some point, but also it was Myles and he liked me naked, and knew I slept better nude.

I made it to my feet and found myself surprisingly

steady. The bureau contained four bikinis in various colors and styles, all in my size; none of them actually mine, all with tags. A gauzy floral cover-up dress, what appeared to be a sarong of some sort, and...that was it. Four bathing suits, two cover-ups. Oh, and a pair of flip-flops on the floor by the bureau.

I saw no bags, neither mine nor his.

Nor did I see him.

I chose a bathing suit—royal blue and *very* small. Basically just a sliver of fabric just wide enough to cover my nipples and not much else, with ties that went around my neck and back. The bottom was a triangle that *mostly* covered my vagina, but if I wiggled wrong, my hoo-ha would swallow the fabric. I mean, damn. He was not sending any subtle messages with this, was he?

I could rock it, though. And look killer doing it—there was a full-length mirror, and despite gross, oily, tangled hair and smeared makeup and an overall haggard appearance, my body looked pretty damn fine.

Sunglasses, bikini, flip-flops...a fresh bottle of water from the fridge. Which, I noticed, contained whole, healthy, natural foods and no booze. Probably for the best.

I stepped outside onto the porch of the hut, which, I discovered, ran around the entire perimeter of the hut. I mean...where the hell was I? This was a tropical paradise for sure. Fiji? Bali? Somewhere like that. If the door facing the ocean was the front of the hut, an island was behind it, low and hilly and jungle covered. No walkway, no pier, no connection to the mainland. Just this one hut, on stilts, on the water.

And nothing else.

The seagulls were calling, and the ocean surf crashed against the island shore in the distance. There was a constant, gentle, warm breeze. The sun was hot and bright and invigorating.

I saw a ripple in the distance—I watched, and after a few minutes, I knew it was Myles, breast-stroking through the water straight toward me. There was a ladder descending into the water, and he swam to it and climbed up.

Naked as a jaybird.

"You were swimming out there, alone, naked, in broad daylight?" I asked.

He grinned, shook his head to fling the water off, wiped his face. "Yep." He gestured around. "A producer friend of mine is friends with some billionaire tech dude. He owns this." He gestured at the hut. "Meaning, the island as well. It's one of the most solitary, remote places on earth. There's a diesel generator on the island, which we can crank up if we need electricity, but we won't. Plumbing is covered. Propane stove. Plenty of food and water."

"And this is…where?"

He shrugged. "I don't know exactly. We're on an island in Indonesia. That's all I can tell you. I asked my friend if we could crash here, and his friend gave our pilots the coordinates."

"When did we get here?"

He chuckled. "Yesterday morning."

"*How* did we get here?"

"Plane from…wherever the fuck we were in Europe, can't remember right now—to an airport a few hours from here, and then we rented a seaplane and Callahan flew us here."

"And we're here…why?"

He shrugged. "To take the bull by the horns."

I felt my heart skip. "What's that mean?"

He was utterly serious, eyes burning and intense. "It means I postponed all my shows for the rest of the tour. Refunds to all who ask, vouchers for upgraded seats to everyone who kept theirs. It means there's no way off this island for two weeks. No boat, no plane. No phone service, no internet. Just you and me, and our issues, and all the time in the world."

"Myles…"

"You damn near drank yourself to death, Lex, and that's no joke. I had a doctor check you out before we left Europe. He wanted to admit you, intubate you, and IV you, but said as long as I watched you carefully and made sure you were hydrated when you recovered, you'd be okay." He was frowning, hard. "I ain't no stranger to partyin' harder than I should. I've woken up with hangovers from hell. Done shit I shouldn't. But this? This was different."

I rested my forearms on the railing, watched the sun glinting off the waves. "Yeah, it was. I've gotten crazy wasted before, but I've never been passed out for *days*."

"Well, to be fair, I don't think you'd been sleeping much before that."

I shook my head. "No, not for more than a few hours a night." I hesitated, swallowed. "Too...too much of everything to be able to sleep."

"I needed a time-out. You needed a time-out. I can make up the shows. I can afford to refund the tickets." He gestured. "So, here we are. Hell of a place for a time-out, huh?"

I sighed. Tried a smile, and failed. "Yeah, I guess. It's beautiful, all right. Peaceful." I turned, rested a hip against the rail, and faced him. "So. Where do we start?"

He eyed me, his expression neutral. "Well?" He knelt, slid my flip-flops off my feet, stood and plucked my sunglasses off my face, setting both aside. I got excited, despite still feeling like shit, because things had been off between us lately and I hated it. And this felt like him making the move on me I so desperately wanted.

His hands clutched my waist.

His lips touched mine. Soft, quick. Not a kiss, just a touch.

"First thing is...this." And he tossed me off the side of the balcony into the water. I hit with a splash, sprawling into warm ocean brine, gentle waves rolling over me. I heard a splash nearby, and surfaced to see Myles beside me, hair in his eyes and a grin on his face.

"I'm way too hungover to swim, Myles."

He laughed. "Nah, best thing for you." He wrinkled his nose. "Plus, you stink."

I laughed, then sniffed my pit, and reared back, gagging. "Yikes. I may need more than a dunk in the ocean."

"Yeah, like soap and a toothbrush. And shampoo." He kicked to get closer to me, wrapped an arm around me and twisted to his back, taking me onto his front as he floated, kicking away with me on his chest. "But for right now? Just chill. You got nowhere to be, no one to answer to, no one to perform for."

"Except you."

He shook his head. "You don't owe me shit, Lex. We ain't here for me to force a story out of you. I was worried about you, so I took you away from everything." He spat water out of his mouth, one hand on my ass, the other pulling at the water, his legs kicking steadily. "You wanna fuck, we'll fuck. You wanna talk, we'll talk. You wanna dig out your secrets and let me help you carry them, I'll listen and I'll cry for whatever pain has you so fucked up, and I'll hold you and help you figure out the way forward. You don't want to do any of that? We won't."

"What if I just want to go home?"

His eyes pierced mine. "And where would home be for you, Lex?"

I clung to his shoulders and swallowed hard. "I...I don't know."

"You can leave anytime you want, but the only place to go aside from the hut is the island, and there ain't much there but the generator hut and other mechanical shit, a little caretaker's hut, a storeroom for backup supplies, and a storm shelter. Other than that, it's just a little rock in the middle of fuckin' nowhere, with perfect weather and a little hut to sleep in."

"We're really stranded here for two weeks?"

"Yep."

"What if there's a hurricane?"

"Well, it ain't typhoon season, I'm told, and if there was, we'd ride it out in the shelter. It's stocked with rations to keep four people alive for a week."

"Oh."

"Any other questions?"

"Why are you naked?"

He grinned. "Well, I only been skinny-dipping once before, and it was at night in a lake and I was a kid. There ain't nobody for a couple hundred miles, and I figured hell, why not? It's fun. Freeing."

"So why am I wearing a bikini?"

He shrugged. "Wanted to provide you with some options."

He glanced over his shoulder. "Here we are."

"Where?" All I could see was a patch of ocean just like the rest of it. The island in the distance, the hut a little closer, and not a thing else anywhere.

He quit swimming and somehow was resting on…a sandbank, shallow enough that we could sit on it and be up to our waist in water. "Came out here earlier, just to hang out while you were sleepin'. Peaceful out here."

I slid off him and sat in the water. Stared around me at the utterly serene setting. "Thank you," I said.

"For what?"

"Taking care of me. Bringing me here." I swallowed hard, choking up. "For…for being you."

He brushed at my cheek. "I won't say it, because I don't want to freak you out. But…I care about you."

That didn't help my mixed-up emotional state; made it way worse—because I had only one possible response. "I…it's selfish. But…I wouldn't mind if you…if you told me how you feel."

"Why's it selfish?"

I stared out at the water rather than at him. "Because I…I can't give you that back. I just don't know how, Myles. I want to. I swear to god, I do. But I don't know fucking *how*."

He nodded. "Well. You don't have to know how. We can figure that out. That's why we're here, Lex, to figure things out." He pivoted, brought me so I was sitting between his knees. "I love you, Alexandra."

Tears. A lot of them. "I hate crying. I never cry."

"Why?"

"Because it…it doesn't do anything. Makes things worse."

"There's a reason."

I nodded. "It's…tied up with everything else."

He was quiet a long, long time. He reached out, slowly untied the neck of my suit top. "Doing this so you can feel true freedom, not as a sexual advance. Just so you know." The back of it. The sides of the suit bottoms. Plucked both pieces off me and let them float away. "Tide'll bring 'em to the shore, and we'll get 'em later."

It was freeing. Exhilarating.

I couldn't help but grin. "I'll be right back."

I kicked off the sandbank and swam around. It

was the best feeling in the world—like nothing else. I'd been skinny-dipping—in lakes, private pools, hotel pools; my personality was all about being a daredevil, an exhibitionist. But this was different. No one to impress or be caught by, just me and Myles and the seagulls. The seagulls didn't care, and Myles was in love with me.

I swam back to him. Let my legs dangle in the deeper water with my upper torso on the sandbank. "Is there a difference between loving me and being in love?"

He tilted his head; let his eyes rake over my body. Nodded after a minute. "Being in love can be temporary. I can say I was in love with Britt Aubrey. We both knew that was nothing but a fling, but there were feelings. I coulda seen myself with her. But it was physical. She was gorgeous and we were both young people with the world at our feet and careers to conquer. It was a rush, wild and fun. But not much more. It'd have faded. Excitement over her body would have eventually gone away, lust for her with it. When that's gone, what's left?"

I hated the sound of that. "So what's that mean for me? You're gonna get bored of me?"

He shook his head slowly. "No, Lex. Yes, your body is far and away better than hers. But even you will age. Someday you'll be past your prime and

getting old. So will I. And what's left then is what matters." He splashed water idly. "I know *you*, Lex. Your
soul. Your mind. More than just your body, more
than just your humor or your flirty nature or your
incessant need for sex. I know that you're afraid. That
you're hurt. I know that under the bold girl with the
big brass balls is someone sweet and kind and tender
and even shy. I know you love performing more than
anything, but you don't think you can have it, that
you're good enough, that you deserve the attention.
I know you have things you're literally *dying* to not
be secret anymore. But you're too afraid to trust me.
Because you've been hurt, bad. Somebody fucked you
up, Lex. I see it. I don't need the story to know that.
I know you need me to prove to you again and again
that I'm here, and that I ain't goin' fuckin' nowhere.
No matter what."

"You didn't answer the question." I kicked gently,
floating. "If attraction fades, if physical desire fades,
what's left?"

"That's the difference between loving you and
being in love. We ain't had sex in, what, two weeks?
For folks like us who have hyperactive sex drives,
that's a *long* fuckin' time. And it's taught me a hell of
a lot about how I feel about you. Because what's left,
in terms of my feelings for you, without sex, is raw
emotion. And the drive to *do* and to *be* that's more

than feelings. Because even feelings ain't enough. To hear my dad tell it, he loved my mom somethin' fierce. And she him. But she had demons, I guess, and couldn't and wouldn't wrestle 'em, or let Dad help her. Don't know what it was, because Dad would only talk about Ma when he was lit, and he wasn't often alone with me when he was like that. They loved each other, is my point. But it wasn't enough. She ran off on us because she couldn't handle it. Him, me, us, life, I don't fuckin' know. I just know pure emotional love wasn't enough."

"Did you know her?"

He shrugged. "A little. I got a memory of her. Tall, beautiful. I get my hair color from her. She was quiet, but intense, I think. I remember bein' in a little farmhouse in East Texas, Ma fixing a sandwich for me, singin' some old song. That's about it. She left when I was real young." He paused. "You know, I won't say I ever treated women like shit, like possessions or meat or just a place to put my dick, but Dad and Grandpa were both single. Mom left, Grandma died before I was born, and Dad and Grandpa were just single touring musicians. So their relationships, such as they were, weren't much but physical, with whoever was available to them. Then I spent time at the compound with Crow's folks and family, and most of them had pretty fast and loose notions of relationships. That's all I've known, and it's how I lived. Love was for books. Movies. Hallmark and Hollywood. But then I met you, and I realized real fast it was…it was somethin' different. I saw how Charlie 'n Crow figured their shit out and that told me a lot."

"You're saying a lot, but—"

"What's left when the physical is gone?" he interrupted. "What really matters? The fact that I'm here, an' I'll always be here. That I won't go fuckin' nowhere, no matter what. I *choose* you, Lex. For me, for my life. Whatever that looks like. I don't need shit back from you. It's me giving what I got to give, and you can take or leave it, but I ain't takin' it back. And I ain't goin' nowhere."

I laughed. "You've never sounded so Texan in all the time I've known you."

"Strong emotions do that."

I twisted onto my back and let myself sink under the water, rolled forward and kicked away; knifing through the gentle swells, I held my breath and swam, hard, until my lungs burned. I surfaced, spluttering—I'd swum quite a ways, and Myles was just lounging on the sandbank, watching me. I treaded water for a moment, and then flopped to my back and backstroked back to Myles.

"Feeling better, huh?" he called.

"Not sure if it's the sun or the water or the swimming or the combination of everything, but yeah, I am." I kicked myself up onto the sandbank and sat beside Myles. "I need to eat something, I think. And I need time to process what you're telling me."

He nodded. "Sounds good. Let's head back." He scooted across the sand to the deeper waters. "This happens on your time, Lex. Your time, your way. I'm playing this your way, all right?"

I laughed. "No, you're not. You're forcing my hand." I followed him, swimming beside him.

"Well, yeah, to an extent, because you won't tackle your shit. I want more from you and for you, and you can't do that until you take your demons on."

"You don't know what you're talking about," I said, turning and spitting out salt water.

"Yeah, I fuckin' do." He paused, and we swam in silence until he reached the hut and climbed up.

I spied my discarded bikini floating underneath the hut, snagged it, tossed it up on the porch, and climbed up. Myles was inside, still naked, dripping, pulling food items out of the fridge.

"Wait," I said, leaning against the railing in the sun. "I thought the electricity was on a generator that's not running."

He pointed at the roof. "Solar panels on the roof work the fridge, and the lights if we need 'em. The generator is if we need electricity for longer than the solar can provide. If we don't use the lights or plug anything in, the fridge can run on solar indefinitely."

"Are you going to just be naked the entire time we're here?" I asked.

He shrugged, nodded. "Why not?"

I bit my lip, watching his taut ass and rippling back muscles shift as he fixed us a plate of cold cuts, cheese, and fruit, along with two bottles of water. Desire for him ripped through me, and I restrained it with effort. "Yeah, why not…"

He laughed. "If you're having trouble with me being naked, I can put on some trunks."

"Trouble? It's no trouble."

He glanced at me, noting the way my eyes followed his junk. "Lex."

I jerked my eyes up to his. "Yeah?"

"This is all about you. Whatever you want, whatever you need. The only thing we're not going to do is keep avoiding issues and using sex to do so."

"Well take away all my strategies, why don't you," I grumbled.

He sat on a chair, handed me one of the sweating bottles of chilled water. "You're brave and bold and strong in just about every aspect of your life, Lex. I won't accept weakness and cowardice from you in this, where it really counts the most."

"You won't accept it, huh?" I knew I sounded petulant and angry. "Why's it up to you?"

He sighed. "Don't be combative, Lex. Please?"

"It's the only way I know."

"Maybe it's time to start learning new strategies, then." He smiled. "You can practice on me."

"Why?"

He rolled prosciutto up with a slice of cheese. "Because you're better than that. You're worth more than that."

"Says you."

"Yeah, says me." He handed me the rolled-up cheese and meat. "Would you agree I know you as well as if not better than anyone else?"

I ate it, not looking at him. I nodded, eyes downcast. "Yeah, at least as well as anyone else I know. Weird, considering how brief a time I've known you."

"But we've spent every single moment of that time together, waking and sleeping."

"You say you know what you're talking about when you tell me I have to face my demons."

"Because I do." He paired cheese with a strawberry. "I've got my own demons, and I've had to face them so I can be a whole person."

"Like?"

He sighed. "This is what you call being open and vulnerable, so pay attention." A pause to chew and to think. "My mother abandoned me. Gave me mommy issues. Trust with women issues. Why do you think I've never had a real relationship? I don't trust women to care, to stay, to be trustworthy, because the one who should have, didn't. I already told you the closest I ever got to a real relationship with a girl was Britt Aubrey, and I know she wanted it to be something. She said as much. It freaked me out. I ran so fast I left tire tracks. It just scared me. She wanted more. She wanted it to be something besides a hookup at a festival. I was honest and said I didn't think I was ready for that, and it wouldn't be fair of me to pretend I was, because I didn't want to hurt her. But the reality—the truth was, I was too chicken back then to face—that I *did* want more with her, but I didn't trust her. Didn't trust her motives. Didn't trust that if I put my heart into something with her, that she wouldn't crush it when she got sick of me, like my mom did."

I wasn't sure what to say to that, so I said nothing, just listened.

Also, why did my heart feel weird at the knowledge that he'd been in love with Britt Aubrey? Why did that make my stomach flip? Why did I not like the idea of him wanting something with someone else that he claimed to want with me?

"I loved my dad and my grandpa, but I didn't exactly have a normal or stable childhood. I'm more at home in a dive bar than I am a house. I've never had a home. Dad rented an apartment month to month when he wasn't touring, and when he went on tour, he let the apartment go and we lived in his van. And then I lived with Crow, but that wasn't really my home. And even then there was a lot of moving around. I've always just been a vagabond, you know? So that's issue number two—I got no clue what a home is." He let a silence breathe between us. "I don't trust women, I don't understand love and don't know what it's supposed to look like, and I ain't ever had a real home. Grew up wandering and ain't ever stopped, and I ain't sure I know how. Those are my demons." He fed me a blueberry. "I'm choosing to trust you, which, I gotta be honest, you're not makin' easy. I'm choosing to believe that loving you will be worth it, that I can figure *how* to love you, and what that looks like. An' if you and me can figure this thing out and our future takes us to a point where we're ready to decide on a home, I'll figure that out too. It's all scary as hell, Lex—but to me, you're worth the risk."

"What if I'm not?" I whispered.

"My decision, and I think you are." He held my

gaze. "Make no mistake—you have the power to totally crush my heart, Lexie. But I'll take that risk."

I blinked hard. "Don't put that on me."

A laugh. "Too late, sweetheart. It already is."

I shot to my feet and stalked away, around to the backside of the hut, facing the island. I breathed hard. His heart…was in my hands. He couldn't have been any more open or direct about that.

If I didn't have the courage to deal with my shit, to become the woman he needed and wanted me to be so I could love him…I'd crush his heart.

Fucking enormous burden. Thanks, Myles.

I heard and felt him behind me. He didn't say anything, just stood and waited.

"This is a fucking lot for day one, Myles."

He sighed. "Yeah, you're right. Let's just take today and shelve the whole conversation."

"And do what?" I asked.

"I can think of a few things," he said, smirking.

My instinct was to reach for him, but I didn't. I couldn't even smile. "Normally I'd be all over that. But…you're right. We have to—*I* have to tackle the shit I've been avoiding for years. And I can't do that if I'm letting you distract me with sex."

He chuckled. "If *you* let *me* distract you with sex?"

I gestured at him. "You, all naked and sexy

and tempting and coming at me with innuendos." I sighed, rubbing my face with both hands. "Just don't even know where to start."

"Today, you relax. Swim. Read a book—there's a shelf of paperbacks in there, and I brought my e-reader which has all sorts of stuff downloaded on it. There's a basket of assorted magazines in the bathroom, too." He gestured at the island. "We can swim over there and explore the island. Or you can just sit and do not a damn thing at all. Sun yourself. Get a tan. Sleep."

I nodded. Hesitated. "I...I think if I'm going to have a chance at sorting through all this in my own head, I'm just going to need some time and some space." I eyed him. "I'm normally a really social person, and I'm not normally a 'give me space' kind of person. The opposite, usually, but—"

He slid up behind me, wrapped his arms around me; and even though I could feel his manhood against my buttocks, and his hands were clasped just under my breasts, it was a nonsexual thing, an embrace. Comforting and nothing else.

"You don't have to explain, Lex. You can tell me you need space to think. It ain't gonna upset me or offend me or make me think you need to be away from *me*. I get it. I really do. I'll be around, but you take the time you need."

"Why are you so understanding?"

He laughed, kissed the side of my neck. "Because I *want* you to do what you need to figure this out, Lex. Also, I think being understanding is a pretty big part of showing someone you love them. I ain't an expert by any means, but it makes sense to me."

I leaned back into him, soaking up the comfort of his embrace, and the feeling of knowing he had no expectations. "What would you say if I told you I wanted us to not have any sexual contact for right now?"

"I'd say we'll both need to wear bathing suits, because you bein' naked all the time is gonna make that real fuckin' hard for me."

I wiggled my ass against his limp sex. "Doesn't feel all that hard to me right now."

He growled. "You just said no sex, woman. Don't set me up for failure."

I sighed. "Sorry. Habit. Plus, I'm having similar trouble with you being naked. Believe it or not, I'm attracted to you, and seeing you naked is not doing anything helpful for keeping my hands to myself."

"Joking aside, I'm with you on making sure what happens between us is focused on the mental and emotional stuff, rather than the physical."

"We've got the physical down, I think," I said.

"Yeah," I agreed, laughing. "I'd say we do."

He let me go. "You still hungry?"

I shook my head. "Want to wait and see how that sits first. I still feel queasy and a bit hungover."

He held my arms, kissed my cheek. "There's no right or wrong way through this, Lex, except not dealing with it at all."

"Which is what I've been doing for years."

"And now it's caught up to you."

"I won't drink like that again," I said. "I promise."

"Don't promise me, promise yourself."

"I want you to know. I realize how scary that must have been for you."

"It…wasn't awesome."

I twisted, and it was very difficult indeed to not fall into the easiest thing—his lips, his skin, his muscle and hands, his cock and his heat.

I managed it, though. Barely. It took all I had, but I managed to pull away, to not touch him, and face the water, letting my thoughts finally—after years of suppression and avoidance and blocking it out—return to the darkness inside me, to the old terrible memories, the deep wounds.

I dredged it all up, bit by bit. Sat in the old agony, and let it flow over me.

Knowing I was safe.

Knowing I was loved.

SIXTEEN

Myles

THIS TIME, SHE WASN'T AVOIDING ME. SHE WAS LOST, though. In thought, in herself, in memory. I saw her crying and sat near her in case she needed comfort. She held my hand but said nothing and so I let her have the silence of my presence.

At one point, late in the evening of the first day, she dove off the porch and swam away, and I watched her breaststroke to the sandbar and sit there well past dark, sitting, thinking.

I was wearing my swim trunks as part of our agreement to wear clothes for the next while, and she'd put on bikini bottoms but no top, which didn't help my sexual urges, much. I held out though—didn't touch myself, or her. It was going to be worth the wait.

She returned to the hut when stars were bright and the moon was brighter, and sat outside for a while. Eventually she came inside and slid into bed behind me, wrapping an arm around my middle and pressing her breasts against my back. I immediately got a monster hard-on that I struggled to ignore. Her hand clung to my belly, low, and I fought the need to feel her hand clasp around me.

With effort, I ignored it all and fell asleep.

Day two was more of the same—she spent a while reading a paperback, but I saw her turn the pages only fitfully, her eyes staring off into nothing for long periods of time. I made her an omelet on the propane stove, and she accepted it with a smile, but said nothing.

Sometime past noon, she swam off again, and I let her go. Her mood was dark, and tense. No longer tearful, she seemed angry, now. When she came back hours later, her eyes were reddened, tear tracks staining her cheeks.

She sat beside me on the bed, where I was lazing, dozing. "Can we go explore the island? I need to do something besides sit and think."

"Sure," I said. "There's a little rowboat tied to the back of the hut. Why don't we put on some clothes and row over?"

It was hotter on the island, away from the constant cooling breeze we had being right on the water. There was a trail leading inland, and we followed it uphill, winding toward the peak. We finally reached the top, sweating bullets and panting like mad. The view was spectacular, and we could see the little hut down below. We headed back down and found the generator, storeroom, and storm shelter. We checked them out, and by the time we'd seen just about everything there was to see, it was getting late in the day.

"Ready to go back?" I asked.

She nodded. "Yeah. I need a shower and something to eat."

So, we rowed back and I fixed us food while she showered; she emerged with her hair wet and dripping, naked, eyes red again.

"Couldn't see the point in getting a towel wet," she murmured. "I can just lay out there and air dry."

I wanted to ask if she was okay, but it seemed like a dumb question. "You want to eat out there? Or…?"

She shook her head; seemed to hold her breath, considering her words. "I wouldn't mind if you sat with me."

So we ate out there, sitting side by side on easy chairs, watching the stars come out and the moon slide up overhead, larger than any moon I'd ever seen, full and round and brilliant silver. After a while, the only light on us the stars and moon, I heard her suck in a deep breath.

"No interrupting, okay? No questions. No comments. Don't be sympathetic. Just listen, okay? I've never spoken of this and it's going to take all the courage I have to talk about it now. So just…just let me get it all out."

"Okay."

She reached out a hand—I extended mine and tangled my fingers with hers.

A long silence ensued and I waited through it.

"When I was eleven, I decided I wanted to be a musician," she said. "I asked Mom and Dad for music lessons. They gave me an old acoustic guitar of Dad's, a library book on guitar for beginners, and told me to try on my own. So I did. I taught myself some basic chords, learned how to play kid stuff like 'Three Blind Mice' and 'Mary Had A Little Lamb' and whatever. When I could play six basic songs all the way through without messing up, I gave Mom and Dad a recital. I had it all planned out. I'd even made little recital programs on Dad's computer. My sisters were all there, and it was a big deal for me. I played my songs without messing up, and when it was over they all clapped and cheered. I felt amazing. I begged my parents for music lessons, and they found me a private music teacher, Mrs. Pruitt. She was about a thousand years old and had hair that was so white it was almost blue, and she could play the most amazing classical pieces on the piano. I didn't want to play the piano—I wanted to play the guitar. Taylor Swift was just popping up on the scene, getting noticed and stuff, and I wanted to be like her."

A long silence.

"Mom and Dad made me take piano for a year and a half, until I finally went apeshit on them, pitched a tantrum about how I hated piano and that I wanted guitar lessons and singing lessons so I could be like Taylor. I got so mad, you don't even know. I got grounded for, like, weeks. But when the grounding was finally over they found me another music teacher. Before I started the lessons they sat me down and told me that I had better be one hundred percent serious and committed, because this teacher was one of the most expensive and sought-after private music teachers on the East Coast. John David Henley."

"Heard of him," I muttered.

"Anyone in the music business has. He's given vocal lessons to some of the most famous musicians in the world. Very prestigious. And he happened to be only an hour away. I was ecstatic."

"They figured music was just a phase, huh?"

She shrugged. "Probably. We were pretty well off, so they could afford it, but still, it was superexpensive.

I remember hearing them argue about it, one night. My dad was like, I could buy a Corvette for what I'm paying that guy, but Mom reminded him that I was so happy, that I'd been serious about this for two years, blah, blah, blah. So, I was thirteen—the same age as Taylor when she got discovered, and I figured I had it made. If she could do it, I could do it, too." A pause. "The first lesson was amazing. He had me sing a bunch of songs and play the guitar for him, and was like, oh yes, you have a natural gift. I can work with you and help you. If he didn't think you had the talent, he'd tell your parents it wasn't worth his time or their money. Lessons with him were ultraexclusive. So, because I had the talent, the lessons began. I had a second lesson, then a third, and soon a month had gone by. Mom would drive me down to New York for my lesson each week and after that first month I really felt I was learning a lot. I practiced all the time at home, and I just loved it."

I said nothing as she paused again. Summoning her courage.

"Shit, this is hard." She propped her foot on the chair and picked old flaking toenail polish off her toes. "He gave lessons out of his house, a walk-up brownstone. He had a formal waiting room right off the front door; you know how those old brownstones were built—sitting room on one side and dining room on the other, kitchen behind, and bedrooms upstairs. Well, the sitting room was his waiting room. It had dark brown floors polished so you could see your reflection in them. Busts of famous composers sat on the mantel of the fireplace. There was a giant cage with a blue-and-gold macaw in it—Bob Dylan was its name. Antique furniture, the kind that's impossible to sit on. Across the hall from the front door was the music room—what in most houses of the type was the dining room. He had a full grand piano in there, several guitars, a harpsichord, and an accordion. He could play like ten instruments, and taught them all. A rare musical genius, I guess. There were window seats in the sitting room and music room, with gauzy white lace curtains. The place seemed like it hadn't changed in a hundred years, or more. Even the electrical outlets were old. So, I'd sit in the waiting room and wait for my lesson as the previous student finished. Sometimes, there wouldn't be anyone there, and I'd start right away, other times I'd have to wait twenty minutes or more for my lesson. I had to be on time, but the lessons always started when he felt like it. If a student needed extra drills on something, he'd drill them until they got it right, and everyone else's lesson would be thrown off schedule. It used to drive my mom crazy."

Lexie was silent for a few minutes and I knew she was working up to the real story.

"I didn't notice this until much, much later, but within a month or so of beginning lessons with him, he never scheduled anyone right before or after me. I'd walk in and he'd be ready for our lesson. Our time would be over, and Mom might be running late, and we'd play a song together or just talk. He was easy to talk to, Mr. Henley." I heard her swallow. "Six months went by. I was getting really, really good. I could play some pretty advanced classical pieces on the guitar, and some modern stuff. My voice was getting stronger, and my technique and breathing and all that, my throat voice instead of my head voice. And...and one day, I had to pee during our lesson. That was a big no-no. Students weren't allowed any distractions. I held it as long as I could, but I had to go. So he let me—and the only bathrooms were upstairs. He told me the best bathroom to use was in his bedroom. I just had to pee, so I didn't think about it. When I came out, he was in the bedroom and the door was closed."

My heart clenched. "Fuck."

Her voice was tiny and soft—like the girl she'd been. "I wasn't sure what was going on or what he was doing. But he was there, and in front of the door, and said maybe the lesson could wait. He had something else he wanted to show me. He said—he said I was a special student, and...and there were things we could do that would help him teach me even better.

I was wearing a little skirt, knee-length, denim. A T-shirt. Nothing special, nothing revealing. I'd never even held a boy's hand. He…he put his hand under my skirt and touched me over my underwear. I didn't know what to do. I was too scared and confused to speak, and he was so close all I could smell was his cologne and his wool sweater. He touched me, and I said nothing, did nothing. And…and then he put his finger inside me. And I could feel something happening to him. To his pants. Didn't know what it meant. I just knew he was touching me and it felt wrong, but I just…I had no voice. No words." I dared not even breathe. "He told me I was his favorite student. And that we had a special relationship. Special to us. Only for us. No one needed to know, not even my parents."

A long, long silence. A sniffle.

"Mom picked me up, and I pretended I was fine. I didn't know how to tell her. And he'd told me not to. He'd told me before that he could make me famous, and he could make me like Taylor. He knew people. He said to just do what he told me and he could help me. And I just…I wanted to be a famous musician. So I didn't tell Mom, and certainly not Dad or my sisters. Plus, I had promised them that having music lessons was not just a phase, that I was serious, and I knew Dad especially would be mad.

"Charlie was busy being the golden oldest child

getting straight A's in everything, and Cassie studied dance at this prestigious dance academy which was the same day and time as my music lesson in New York. So when I got in the car, Cassie was there too, and talking a mile a minute about plie this and arabesque that and she was going to be lead next year and she had a solo and blah blah blah. How could I tell Mom what had happened? I couldn't. And my younger sisters were just little kids, and if Mom wasn't driving us to lessons she was taking them to soccer or book club or Poppy's art tutor. She was always busy. I wanted to tell her. I was scared and it had felt wrong and it made me feel gross, but there was just never a moment to be alone with her.

"And then it was the next lesson. He acted like nothing had happened. And then we began our work for the day, but Mom was late. She was usually late picking me up because Cassie's teachers were sticklers for students leaving on time, so Mom always picked her up first and I was always waiting."

I desperately wanted to comfort her—she sounded so sad and so broken.

She just squeezed my hand as hard as she could, as if to reassure herself that I was here, beside her, and that she was here with me.

"So, after a few minutes he asked me if I'd told anyone about our special *lesson*. I just shook my head, and he was like, good, because if anyone found out it would be very bad, and mostly for me. And he wanted to make me a famous musician, but if I told anyone, he wouldn't be able to do that. And then he touched me again." She faltered. "Then he said it would be better to have our special lesson upstairs. I knew he was going to do something I wouldn't like, but I—I went along anyway. I don't know why. I was so scared—I hadn't told Mom what had happened last week and now it was happening again. Mom would never believe me now. Why didn't I say something, right? I know it doesn't make any sense explaining it now, but back then, it felt like I had no choice. He made me take off my skirt. And my underwear. And he touched me again."

Another heavy silence.

A sniffle.

"My shirt. Everything. He locked the bedroom door. I remember my heart was pounding so hard it hurt, and my throat was…just closed. Hot, tight. I couldn't have made a sound if I had tried. I was naked, and no one had seen me naked since I was a little girl, and that was my parents. I was shy, back then and I didn't like even changing for gym class, and now there I was, naked in front of this grown man who had touched my privates. He…said we were going to have another special lesson, and I had to stay very quiet and do exactly what he told me. He made me lie down on his bed, and…pose for him. He took pictures with a—one of those cameras that print the picture…what are they called?"

"Polaroids."

"Yeah, a Polaroid. He showed it to me, and said I was so beautiful." Her voice was…wet, and thick. Hesitant. "He stood next to the bed and took off all his clothes. I'd never even seen Dad all the way naked, so that in itself was a shock, but then he grabbed my hand and put it on his dick. It was already hard, but when he made me touch it, it got even harder. So big, so…ugh. Horrible. Thick, hairy. Wrinkly. He wasn't young. But clearly still…vigorous." A shudder, a gagging sound. "So, uh. Yeah. He climbed up on the bed, and knelt over top of me, said this was going to hurt a little, and then he put it in me. I could tell even then he was trying to be gentle but he was too excited. Gentle didn't last long." A broken whisper now. "It hurt. So much. And then he started…the only way to put it is he fucked me. I couldn't make a sound—I didn't know what was happening and it hurt and I was terrified and it was just…so fucking *wrong*. But I couldn't stop him. Couldn't even speak. I never said no. I let it happen. That's how I felt, then, and for years later. Deep down, I still believe I *let it happen*. I should have said something or done something. If I'd said no, please stop, please don't…would he have… would he have not raped me? I didn't say anything, but that's what it was…rape."

A long, dark, ugly, vicious silence.

"I wish that was the whole story. Touched a couple times, fucked once, and then I got the courage to stop it." A bitter, hateful laugh. "Nope. Not by a long shot. He…it took him a long time. He was breathing heavily and…and I realize now that he could get it up but had trouble keeping it up. So he…he stopped. Knelt over me. Made me—" She broke for a moment, unable to continue. "He forced my jaw open with his fingers and put it in my mouth. Came in my mouth. I remember that moment more clearly and vividly than any other—that first time. It tasted sour and so bitter. There was so much I couldn't swallow it all, and I couldn't breathe. And he wouldn't stop. He just kept whispering, *yeah baby, you like that don't you. Take it, baby. Take it all, sweetheart.*" A pause. "Thus my aversion to pet names, baby and sweetheart specifically. Those were his words for me. From then on, I was never Lexie to him, I was sweetheart. And when he was fucking me, it was baby."

She was curled up on the chair in a tiny ball; she'd yanked her hand away and had her arms wrapped around her shins, rocking. Whispering. I had to strain to hear.

"The abuse didn't stop. And I couldn't tell. He told me if I told anyone, I would get arrested and go to jail. I wasn't sure I believed him, but it was scary enough of an idea that it worked. He told me it was our secret and if I told anyone, our special relationship would be over and he couldn't help me be famous anymore, and no one would believe me anyway. All true, I now realize. Just the truth, only twisted so it seemed like a threat." A ragged whimper of a sob. "Every week. For years.

"I withdrew, socially and emotionally. I was already shy, and that only made that worse. I never left my room. I stayed in my room every moment I could, playing, practicing. I was so good, back then. I really was. He was an amazing teacher, truly. He could get the best out of you, he could make you play and sing with a passion you didn't even know you had. I think I thought if I was good enough, I'd get discovered somehow and whisked away, and the abuse would stop, and I'd never see him again. But it never did. He'd fuck me, until he was ready to finish and then he'd come in my mouth. Thus my aversion to that. But he never used a condom. Never. Probably part of why he did things that way. Obviously, knocking up his teenage student would put a damper on things, so he was very, very careful. He never even got close to coming inside me."

Pause. A choked sound.

"Except once. The last time. I was seventeen. I was getting too old for him, I now realize. His sweet spot was thirteen to sixteen. Most of his female students were in that range, and I always wondered how many he did this to." A breath, a sob. "So, I was seventeen, musically talented. I was applying to colleges, but figuring I'd leave for Nashville the day I graduated.

"Anyway, he'd been sick the week before, so we'd skipped the lesson. For four years it was the only reprieve I'd had except holidays. When I arrived, he didn't even pretend we would have an actual music lesson. He locked the front door, pushed me into the sitting room, and just...went after me. Pushed me over the couch, yanked off my underwear, ripped them, and hurt me in the process. And just..." a ragged, horrible sound. "Just *railed* me. Bare. As always. Right there in the sitting room, those lacy curtains barely obscuring anything. He was just...an animal. And this time, he didn't stop. He came inside me, and it was the worst thing I've ever felt in my life. He was...he was on top of me, and he said...I remember the smell of his breath and the way his voice sounded when he said *'yeah, baby, you've always been my favorite, Sexy Lexie,'* and that was when he came, calling me Sexy Lexie. Somehow, it was worse than all the other times combined. Why, I don't know. I think maybe because I knew by then how pregnancy worked, and that I'd probably get pregnant. Being seventeen, Mom had had the talk with us girls, and boy was it detailed. We talked about our cycles, and if we were going to have sex it should be protected, but that we should also understand our fertility cycles. Typical Mom overachieving situation. But thanks to that, I knew I was at my peak fertility. And he'd come inside me. Without a condom. And that I was going to get pregnant."

She sobbed, and I reached out, wanting to comfort her, but she waved me away.

"Just listen. I'm…I'm okay. It's just a terrible memory. Just listen." So I sat on the floor next to her, dying to comfort her, touch her, hold her, be angry for her. "He finished and told me to go to the bathroom and clean up. I did, and when I came back, he had a Plan B pill. I realized then he'd been planning this, and he was ready. He told me to take it. Watched me take it. And that was when I just…lost it. I slapped him. Hard. I was shaking so bad, I could barely function, and it was a rage unlike anything I'd ever felt, before or since. Just…*hate*. I hit him and hit him, and he tried to stop me but I was just…insane. And that was when he hit me back. Just full on punched me across the jaw. Knocked me clean out. When I woke up, he wasn't anywhere to be found, and my jaw hurt so bad, and, I still…I still had his cum leaking out of me. So I went home—I was driving myself by then. I made up some excuse about a fight at school or something— not sure Mom believed me, but she didn't push it."

She reached out, took my hand, squeezed.

"I never went back. I stayed at school and lied about going. My parents had been mailing him the payment for years, and I guess he kept cashing them even though I wasn't going. He wasn't about to raise any flags, obviously. I was about to graduate and I'd been making plans—I'd been accepted to a bunch of colleges and universities, but my plan was to move to Nashville and work and get a job as a honky-tonk gig player and write songs and all that. I'd been talking about it nonstop, because I was just so excited to get *away*. I figured once I could get *away* I could start over. Be someone else. Be a Lexie that hadn't been raped every week for four years, and never told a soul. I could become someone else, somewhere else. And that was when Dad came up to my room while I was playing and told me I'd never make it, that I just wasn't good enough." Quick, sharp pause. "If he hadn't died, I don't think I'd ever have forgiven him for that. I still haven't, really, but his dying changed things."

"God*damn*," I breathed.

"Yeah." She huffed, a laugh that was sad and angry and bitter. "Raped by my music teacher, and my own dad killed my dream. That day, then and there, I gave up on music. Went to U-Conn. Gradually, I started reinventing myself. I was painfully shy, modest, introverted, hated myself and didn't trust anyone. Halfway through freshman year, I just…I was sick of being that Lexie The Victim. I said fuck this, and decided to be the exact opposite. Threw away all my clothes, and went to thrift stores and bought all new clothes—short skirts, revealing tops, see-through stuff, booty shorts. Cut off old jeans and khakis, I stopped wearing a bra. Started just saying whatever went through my head. Started just being a bitch to people I didn't like, or to anyone who pissed me off. It felt *good*. Like I was reclaiming myself. I was no longer a victim. I did what I wanted. Started drinking. Going to parties. It was at a party that I had voluntary sex for the first time. In a bathroom of a frat house, super drunk. But it was good. It felt good to do that voluntarily. I did it again at the next party. Then sober, and that was even better. Because every time I had sex, I was trying consciously to erase the memory of John David Henley. I couldn't drink him away; I found that out real fast. But sex? Sex did the trick. The more I hooked up, the more I could replace memories of Henley with other guys. Guys I'd *chosen* to fuck." She sighed slow, deep. "It became the new me. Bold, aggressive. Exhibitionist. I'd dance on tables, flash the whole party. The wild college girl stereotype. I'd do keg stands in miniskirts with no underwear on. I had no standards—as long as I was remotely physically attracted to the dude, I'd fuck him. My only rules were condom, every time, and I'd never blow a guy to completion. I gave plenty of BJs, but I'd never let them finish in my mouth…for obvious reasons. It became sort of my calling card, I think. I had a reputation, and guys knew things about me. I was the crazy slut who'd fuck anyone and give amazing BJs, but you couldn't come in her mouth."

That made me feel…uncomfortable. I'd always prided myself on not being jealous or possessive. But somehow, this was different. I said nothing, however.

"I chilled out a bit at Sarah Lawrence. I realized I didn't like the slut label, and started campaigning against slut-shaming, women's rights, equality, all that, as well as being a little less overall slutty. But only a little. I believed in all that women's lib stuff, still do, but…I don't know…it was misplaced passion. I'd created this whole persona, this Lexie who was one big spiky armored shell. All slutty and a show-off and a flasher and a skinny-dipper in public pools in broad daylight, someone who could outdrink football players, and all that. It was a persona, my armor against the world. And then, at some point, it just stopped being a persona and was just *me*. Because I'd forgotten how to be the other me, the quiet shy little victim girl who let her music teacher sexually abuse her for four years." She laughed. "I don't even think that Lexie exists anymore. Henley fucked it out of me."

She turned on the chair and faced me. "So. There's the story, the secret I could never tell. You are the only person, aside from Henley and me, who knows about it."

I looked at her, love and compassion in my eyes, fighting for the right words. "Lex, I…I don't know. I want to hunt down and kill that fucker, slowly. I want to get Crow to come with me, because that guy can be colder than fuckin' ice. I want to hurt that motherfucker, and make the hurt *last*."

"That won't fix me," she said.

"I know." I sighed, rubbing my face. "It's just how I feel at this moment. I want to kill that guy. I hate that that happened to you."

"Not as much as I do."

"Obviously." I reached out, and she let me take her hand. "I know there's nothing I can do to change that, or to *fix* you. I think…I think you should see a therapist. And I'm not joking. I have had therapy in the past and I know it can help."

She reared back. "You have?"

I nodded. "Yep. In Dallas, between tours. My partying on tour was becoming a problem, and my lifestyle of taking advantage of groupies was, too. I don't mean take advantage in a nefarious way, they were always throwing themselves at me, and I only hooked up with the ones who threw themselves at me. I just mean the opportunity was there and I took advantage of what was offered."

She squeezed my hand. "I know, Myles. You don't have to explain that."

"After what you just told me, I feel like I probably should be more honest about that part of my past."

"I can smell a predator a mile away. But you're a *good* man, Myles." She smiled at me. "A really good man. The best. And a sexual predator is the last thing you are."

"I want to be able to help you, Lexie. I want there to be something I can *do* to make it better."

She slid off her chair and onto mine, and curled up on my lap, her head on my chest. Snuggled close. "You can do this. Just hold me."

"This I can do."

"It means more than you understand, Myles." A soft breath of relief. A sniffle. Tears in her voice. "I can't believe I told you."

"I'm glad you did. Thank you for telling me."

"Was I at fault? For not saying something right away?"

I knew I couldn't give her the knee jerk pacifying answer. "Honestly, no. You were thirteen. He was in a position of power. He had your dream in his hands. He was the authority, and you were a child. A girl. Someone who didn't know any better, who was put in a horrible, impossible position. I mean, obviously, for your own sake, I wish you had been able to tell someone, but I know from having heard similar stories that telling may not have made it any better or even ended things. Having met your mom, though, I'd like to believe she would have believed you."

"I can't tell her, Myles."

I pulled back. "What? Why do you say that? I think you should. She needs to know."

"It'll crush her. She'll take it as her own failure." A sniffle, a sob. "I was good at hiding it. She couldn't have known, but I do admit she knows there is something I'm hiding."

"There's a part of me, possibly a cruel part, that wants to say she should've just *known*, and that maybe she is a little culpable. That she should have been paying closer attention to you. That your mood changes, your withdrawal, were signs that something was wrong."

She shook her head. "I don't know."

"That's a different conversation."

"Yeah, it is." A sigh. "I'm tired, now."

I lifted her, stood up with her, and carried her into the bedroom. I lay on the bed with her and cradled her from behind, holding her tight.

I drifted, and thought she was long since asleep.

"Myles?"

"Yeah, Lex."

"Now that you know, you have to promise me a few things."

"Okay?"

"You won't tell anyone else. It has to be on my terms, and my time."

"Of course, Lex. It's your story to tell, not mine."

"Thank you."

"And the other promises?"

"Just one."

"Yeah?"

She hesitated. "You can't feel sorry for me. You can't tiptoe around me, or try to baby my feelings." She twisted. "You can't be afraid to touch me. To have sex with me. You can't hold back from being aggressive like you are, like I like so much. I like that. It doesn't re-victimize me, I don't have flashbacks." A pause. "Well, the first time I swallowed for you, there was some of that. But it's better now. And I think the more I do things he used to do, the more I'll put him in the past."

"Lex, you mean—"

She rolled to face me and touched my lips. "I *chose* to blow you, and to let you come in my mouth. I knew what I was doing, and I did it for both of us. For you, because I was being skittish and weird about other sexual stuff, and I wanted to give you something you'd like to make up for it, and for me so I could get rid of the stigma of that act. I even thought that maybe you'd stop trying to find out what had happened, stop trying to make me...do this. Which I realize now was what I needed to do more than anything. So the point is, Myles, when you came in my mouth, yes, I was fighting fucking awful flashbacks the entire time. But it was *you*, and I knew it. The next time, it was just you and me, and I enjoyed doing that to you and seeing your reactions. How much you liked it. And I'll do it again because I like making you feel good, I like watching you go crazy."

"Jesus, Lex. Now I feel bad."

"Please, please don't. The worst thing you could do is feel bad. About anything we've done together, or for me."

I sighed. "Yeah, I get that."

"What I choose to do, I do because I want to." She rested her hands on my chest, and I tightened my hold on her. "I will have sex with you bare, Myles. I will. To erase the last of what happened."

"Not just for me, though."

She sighed. "Yes, for you. But for me, too. It will be…" She blinked, swallowed hard. "Because when we do that, it'll be making love. Something I'd thought was impossible for me."

I smiled at her. "I like the way that sounds."

"Me too." She let out a breath, soft and contented. "Do one thing for me, tonight, please?"

"Anything."

"Just hold me, like this, all night."

"Easy."

"And maybe…" she hesitated, swallowing hard. "And maybe, at some point, you could tell me you love me. I like how that feels." She snuggled closer, tucking her head under my chin. "Not now. Not when I expect it. But when I don't."

I laughed. "Funny girl." I kissed the top of her head. "There's nothing I'd like more, Alexandra."

"Call me baby."

"Right now?"

"Yeah."

I touched her chin, kissed her lips. "Lex, baby. You are so strong. So brave. And I'm proud of and amazed at the woman you are, for all you've come through."

She blinked. "Dammit, you weren't supposed to make me cry again. I've cried more today than in my whole life."

"It's okay to cry, sweetheart. It doesn't make you weak."

"Sweetheart, too." She sighed, and it was a relieved, almost happy sound. "From you, it's okay. I don't hear him."

"We'll erase him from you, bit by bit, together. As long as it takes, whatever it takes."

"Promise?"

"I swear on Betty-Lou, my most prized possession."

She took that seriously, as weird as it was—she knew what that guitar meant to me. "What did I do to deserve a man like you in my life, Myles?"

I laughed. "I wonder that about you, Lex." I ran my thumb over her lips, wanting to kiss her, but knowing she just needed to be held. "I think we're made for each other. We just...deserve each other."

"I can't say I'm suddenly *okay*, but...I feel closer to okay than I have since I was thirteen."

"I'm so happy for you, Lex. You deserve that."

She slipped her arms up and around my neck, toying with the back of my head. "Sleepy time now."

"Okay."

And so we slept.

SEVENTEEN

Lexie

IT WAS LATE MORNING WHEN I WOKE UP. I WAS RESTED and contented—I remembered the night before with crystal clarity and knew with utter certainty that telling Myles had been the first and biggest step to healing. I knew also that the road to true healing would be long, and yes, I'd have to see a therapist to really root out all the shit I'd buried so deep and for so long. I knew I had to tell Mom, and that it would crush her maybe worse than Dad's death had, that she'd interpret it as the worst failure of her life. And I wouldn't be able to deny it completely; the truth was I did blame her a bit for somehow not *knowing*, and protecting me.

One thing I did know for sure was that Myles loved me—truly loved me. He, more than anyone, had seen me at my worst and still loved me. That thought brought tears to my eyes. Without him I wouldn't be where I was today…confident about the future.

And I knew that I loved him. With all my heart. I loved him.

I let all this roll around in my head as I woke up. Myles was outside and I could hear him splashing around. I got up and looked out and saw him swimming up to the hut, saw his hands, and forearms, and then his whole beautiful body, naked, with the water sluicing off him, over his abs and down his sharp V-cut. My tongue stuck to the roof of my mouth, and my thighs involuntarily clenched together as heated need pulsed through me.

It still didn't seem possible, or even right, that he was mine. That in a second he would enter this hut and I would get to do whatever my imagination allowed.

I couldn't believe that I could be his.

That I *wanted* to be his. It wasn't about possession, I now realized—it was about *belonging*. And what a difference. Subtle, but powerful.

He shook off, brushed the water from his skin and ran his fingers through his hair. Stood with his face to the morning sun, smiling—happy to just be alive, I think.

Then his eyes opened, and he turned and looked at me—still covered with the blanket.

He smiled at me—bright, happy, loving. "Hey, beautiful. Sleep good?"

"Amazing." I couldn't help but smile back.

He didn't quite frown, but his brow tightened. "How are you feeling?"

I smiled to soothe the worry. "I'm great, actually. I feel like a huge burden has been lifted off me. I know it's not all suddenly, like, all better. Or fixed. It's going to take time. I'll have regressions, and flashbacks, and the memories are still *there*, but…it's not a secret anymore. Now you know, and you accept me anyway."

"Accept you, and love you more than ever."

I melted a little bit. Felt warm. Tossed off the blanket. Felt the warm rushing buzz of satisfaction as his eyes narrowed with desire and his chest lifted, and his cock immediately twitched, and began hardening.

"More than ever?" I whispered.

He nodded, jaw clenching as his eyes raked over my nude body. "Yeah. Way more."

I blinked at him, lazily sultry, smiling. "Come here and show me."

He prowled toward me, cock swaying and growing with each step. Muscles shifting under his skin. Eyes devouring me. He was a vision of male beauty, dominant alpha sexual aggression that

combined perfectly with sweetness and understanding. I wanted him more than ever—wanted to kiss
every inch of him and hold him and be held, wanted
to ride him and be under him. Wanted to feel him inside me and hear him whisper three words…

And whisper them back.

We crawled onto the bed and he paused at my
thighs.

I reached for him, bringing him up to me. "No,
not that, not now." I cupped the back of his head
and pulled at him—he knew what I wanted, what I
needed, and he kissed me.

Kiss isn't the word.

His mouth sang against mine, a song without
sound, a melody of lips and tongues and teeth, and
the chorus was his soul matching mine. I let myself
want nothing but to kiss him. To feel just this—love
through lips. He knew it, and didn't push us past it.
Just kissed me, and kissed me. I scoured his hard
shoulders and broad back with my hands, dug my
fingers into his hair and ran my nails down his spine.
He braced over me with one hand and held my face
with the other, a gesture of such sweet possessive
intimacy that it stole my breath—I didn't need to
breathe, because he was the oxygen in my lungs. I
clutched at the hard taut bubble of his buttocks and
spent a few moments there, just enjoying the feel of

it in my hands, cupping and squeezing, digging my nails in and just petting it for the beautiful thing it was. He just kissed me. As if we'd never kissed, as if everything that had happened between us had been a dream, a rehearsal, and this, finally, was the real thing.

Each moment the kiss went deeper, and the deeper we went the more my heart opened. Blossomed. Brightened, as if the sun was finally rising—no, that's not right. The sun has always been shining, I'd just had the shutters and blinds closed all this while. He kissed me, and put all his soul and all his heart and all his love into the kiss, and the shutters and blinds of my heart opened. Burned away, so the sun could finally shine in and brighten the corners and chase away the shadows.

His love was the sun.

I let my eyes burn with it, with a molten swell of emotions that was beyond happiness, beyond joy.

He finally came up for breath and saw the tears on my cheeks. Wiped them away with his thumb. "What's this?"

"Good," I breathed, stopping him from wiping them away. "It's good."

That was all I had words for.

The rest had to be shown.

I knew what I wanted, and I knew exactly how

I wanted it. I pushed gently at his shoulder, and he rolled to his back. He knew where I was going with it—his hands gripped my waist and as I rolled he lifted, and then settled me on his belly. He stared up at me.

"This okay?" I whispered.

He ran his hands up my thighs, over my waist, up my sides—cupped my breasts. "More than okay."

I held his eyes, hoped he saw in them the fullness of what I felt shining out. I leaned forward, braced my palm on his chest. Lifted my hips. Bit my lip, eager for this and a little nervous as well. I reached between my thighs and found him, thick and hard and ready; took a moment to appreciate the feel of him in my hand, plunging my fist down around him, thumb and forefinger leading the way to his root. He let out a gruff moan.

"Love the way you touch me, Lex."

I just stroked him. "Like this?"

"God, yeah."

His hands roamed over my shoulders, down my back. Curled over to cradle my ass. "You are so fuckin' beautiful, Lex. You take my breath away."

I laughed, taking my time touching him, enjoying the feel of him; drawing out the moment I would take him naked inside me, nothing between us. "I take your breath away, do I?"

"Yeah."

"Then let me give it back." I sealed my mouth to his, bent over him with my breasts pressed against his chest.

He growled, and I moaned, because one of his hands had left my ass and was sneaking its way to my sex, finding my clit and circling gently.

God, I did *not* need the head start this time.

I couldn't wait anymore. Didn't want to. The fear of being with him bare was gone. Residual nerves, sure. But I knew he loved me, and this time I was choosing this.

I guided him to my slit, snugged him inside me, just barely within me.

"Hold on, wait," he murmured.

I waited.

"I love you, Alexandra."

Already choked up and fraught with a thousand wild and intense emotions, hearing that, right then, at the moment I needed to hear it most, broke me. But in a good way. I started laughing and crying at the same time, blinking through the tears and laughing. "How do you always know what I need to hear?"

He lifted up, kissed me. "Because I *see* you, Lex. I'm yours and you're mine."

"Belonging," I whispered. "Not possession."

"Exactly."

I was still laughing and crying in some strange

mixture of emotional overload, and he was almost but not quite inside me, splitting open my nether lips with a teasing intrusion, a seductive promise of what I wanted, what I needed more than anything...

This.

I sank down on him, and he speared deep, his hardness sliding into my softness, and I cried out with a wild unbelieving groan of homecoming bliss, and my tears and laughter became a wild whimper of everything. I clung to his neck and rested my forehead on his and was too overcome by sensation, and fullness, and him, and us to even be able to kiss him. I sat on his hips with my shins beside his thighs, my breasts draped on his chest, clutching at his face with my hands and breathing him—just *feeling* him.

He was still and quiet, his breathing deep and even. His hands rested with loving and affectionate possession on my ass.

I rolled my hips, a slow shallow movement. Testing. And oh *fuck* it was so much, with Myles, like *this*. With his love for me making this a new and beautiful thing, erasing the old and the painful and replacing it with the glory of *us*. Stilled again, I clung to his neck and breathed his scent and his breath and his heat, and writhed just a little, getting him deeper. Until he was as fully within me as he could physically be, and he was bare inside me, and so thick and so huge and so hard that I could feel all of him, every throbbing inch.

He growled, hips moving, and I knew it had been a long time and I suspected he hadn't even helped himself out in that time, so I knew he was close already and needing me to move. I just…couldn't. I needed to luxuriate in this moment.

I tugged on his lower lip with my teeth and kissed his chin and clung to him and whispered—"I'm sorry, Myles. I know you need to move. I just…I need…I need this. I need to just feel you—feel *us*."

His hands slid soothing lines and circles up my spine to curl over my shoulders and then down my back with lightly scratching nails, returning to my bottom, which he squeezed and caressed and petted. "Take what you need, Lex. All the time you need. I'll wait forever. I can't promise I can hold out for long, but I'll do my best."

I moaned as I lifted up, letting him slip out of me most of the way, held him there, and then sat down slowly to take him in me again. "I don't care about orgasms right now, Myles," I breathed. "For the first time in my life, sex isn't about getting the O… it's about just…*us*. Feeling us together. Come when you need to come. I don't care if I do or not—I know you'll take care of me. I just need to…to live in this moment as long as I can."

"Yeah, love. That's all that matters. You and me and this moment."

But I couldn't just sit on him either. I had to feel *more*. I rolled my hips and felt him slide through me. In, and out, slow, gentle, unhurried. All of him beautifully bare inside me, and then the aching space of emptiness as I drew away, and then glutting on him as I took him into me again. My face near his, his breath on my lips.

And now I had to kiss him.

I tasted his tongue and the salt water on his lips and I took his breath for my own and let my hips define their own rhythm upon him—slowly rolling him inside me and rushing through then pulling away so I could take him in again, and each time he filled me I cried out with renewed ecstasy. He was moaning, a soft almost boyish sound of pleasure, the moan fading as I drew away and becoming louder as I plunged down on him. The moans became a whisper of my name, and then a chant, almost sang in a rough voice—*"Lex...Lex...Lexie, oh god Lex, yes my love..."*

"Call me baby, call me love, call me sweetheart, call me darling," I murmured to him, moving with slow consistent rhythm. "Tell me how much you love me. Tell me how good I feel."

He let himself move now, too, his hands on my hips, gripping roughly and helping me to slam down, encouraging me to move faster, harder, even as I resisted so I could make this last forever. "I love you so fuckin' much, Lex, baby—you feel so incredible like this. I love watchin' you ride me, darlin', love to see you feeling good on top of me. I wanna watch you come, baby—come for me, Lex. Touch your pussy, make yourself come so I can hear you scream. Come for me, Lex, right the fuck now, baby. Come for me and scream my name and tell me you love me while you're coming on top of me."

"Oh fuck—*Myles*," I gasped, bent forward to crush my upper body onto his, forehead on his chest as I rolled my hips in a faster rhythm and slid my hand between our bodies to obey him—because his order was exactly what I wanted, what I needed.

I touched myself and felt lightning gather low in my belly, building to quaking thunderheads. He moved, gave me the speed and friction and rhythm and fullness I craved, and my circling fingers gave me the clitoral stimulation to fling myself to the edge, closer to the wild hot screaming threshold of orgasm, and my thighs shook and my belly tightened and my breasts heaved and trembled as I gasped helplessly, my ass slapping down on his thighs to meet his roughening, desperate thrusts.

"Myles," I whispered, my voice too ragged and lost in emotion to speak properly. "Don't stop, baby, please don't stop, I'm so fucking close."

My fingers flew wildly, and his thrusts were hard and fast and shook my whole body with vigorous force, and I loved each one, loved each naked thrust of his cock into my aching clenching sex.

"Come for me, Lex. Please, I need to feel you come."

I was crying again and didn't care, now, because it was all too much. I was there. "Ohhh god, oh love, oh god Myles—*now, now, now!*" My voice broke as I came, and sobs racked me as white-hot lightning seared and crackled and shot through me, centered in my core and making my whole body seize, thrashing, and then a scream was wrenched out of me as I found my voice.

I heard him roar, but the rushing in my ears of my hammering pulse was so loud even his roar was drowned out, and I was blinded by lights flashing behind my tightly squeezed eyes, and I couldn't move, was paralyzed by the ripping intensity of my climax—

And I felt him loose his own orgasm. Felt his cock throb, swelling thicker inside me, felt him push up so his spine was arched off the bed and his heels were scrabbling at the mattress and lifting me up higher even as I collapsed on him and clung desperately to him and shook all over and felt my pussy squeezing and I bore down, squeezing harder and his cry went ragged.

I felt him come.

"Oh fuck, yes, Myles, I fucking love you Myles, I love you, oh god I love you," I said, my voice ragged and broken and wet with tears and shaking with awe. "More, Myles—give me more, give me more."

He sank down to the mattress, and I pulled away, up—his hands clawed into my ass, clutching with mad bruising strength, and he jerked me down, hard, thrusting into me, pouring his cum into me in a hot flood of thick spurts, growling and gasping with each one, and I felt them, accepted his orgasm into me and squeezed around him and rode him frantically as my own orgasm continued, expanded, broke open into another, a harder one. I sat up, then, balanced on him and leaned backward, head tilted up, breasts thrust to the ceiling, and his hands covered them and squeezed them and then he pinioned my hips and helped me roll and ride and lift up and slam down. He was still throbbing inside me, still pouring rush after rush of seed into me and I was screaming and he was groaning—

And then his eyes flicked open at the same moment as mine did, our gazes locking as our mutual orgasm finally released us, and we stilled. I sat on him, squeezed around him and felt his cum seep out of me around his pulsating, subsiding erection.

"I love you, Myles," I whispered, no longer saying it from the wild insanity of climax, but in the tender glow connecting my soul to his. "I love you."

"I love you more, my sweet, darlin' Lex." His voice was soft and rough and low and awed and thick with his emotional Texan twang.

I laughed, and fell forward, wrapped my arms around his neck and he clung to me, hands on the back of my head and neck, clutching at my ass. "Hold me. Don't let go, not ever."

"I won't, I can't."

We gloried in the afterglow. How long? I couldn't have told you. Yes, it was messy, but I didn't care.

And then at some point, after a timeless beautiful eternity of dozing in his arms, I felt him thicken and swell against me, not quite inside me anymore. And I writhed against him until he was ready for me and we lay on our sides and I accepted him into me and we moved like that, face to face, my thigh over top of his, slow and tender the whole while, gasping together in almost-kisses. We came together without a word, and he overfilled me yet again and I loved it all the more.

He told me he loved me as he fetched a towel and cleaned me as well as he could. Then he carried me to the bathroom and we showered together and it was just a shower, but an intimate one, washing each other and sharing the stream of lukewarm water.

When we were clean, we dove naked into the warm ocean and swam together.

We made love on the sandbar in the sun with the water lapping around us—sitting up on our knees, him behind me, his hands clutching at my breasts, as he pushed into me, and I had to reach awkwardly behind my head to clutch at him, or behind my back to find his flexing ass and pull him against me, and then as he began to reach his climax I fell forward into the water on my hands and knees, the water lapping around my thighs and low-swaying breasts and he grabbed my ass and began to just fuck me with abandon, and I screamed as loud as I could to encourage it, feeling him slam into me and shake me all over with the power of his thrusts, and he came like that, taking his orgasm without pause or thought of me, exactly what I wanted: to feel him lose control and give me all of his wild alpha dominance. And then it was my turn. We swam back, and I lay on the porch of the hut in the golden hour evening glow and he knelt between my thighs and gave me orgasm after orgasm, until I lost count and he claimed his jaw had gone numb.

And that was just the beginning.

The seaplane came after a week of nonstop love-making, and dropped off supplies, and I told Captain Callahan to come back in another two weeks because I wasn't even close to being done with Myles.

We made love everywhere there was—in the shower, on the porch, in the water, at the peak of the island's summit, in bed, in the hammock; and in every position we could think of and a few I think we made up.

If anything could heal me and erase the specter of John David Henley, it was that month in paradise with Myles North.

The only shadow on our time there was the knowledge that this perfect idyll would end and I would have to have a very hard conversation with my mother in the near future.

EIGHTEEN

Myles

I'D HAD TO RESCHEDULE FOUR SHOWS: DUBLIN, Glasgow, and back-to-back shows at Wembley in London.

Cost me a shitload of money and some pissed-off sponsors and venues, but my only concern, outside Lex, was the fans. I'd put up a video I'd taken on my phone explaining that I a sudden and unavoidable personal emergency, and that I would honor all tickets and offer full refunds to anyone who wanted them. Almost no one asked for refunds, and in the end the venues accepted my rescheduled dates at the beginning of the fall. I still wasn't sure if the Myles North band was starting another domestic tour then

or not, or if we were going to take time out to record another album, or take time off.

It didn't matter. I'd figure it out later.

For now, I had all that mattered: Lexie, her head
on my lap as she snored her way across the Pacific. The
most incredible, memorable, unforgettable month of
my life behind us, and a beautiful future ahead of us.

I knew she was still scared to talk to her mom, and
I'd offered to fly my personal therapist up to Ketchikan
to facilitate the conversation, but she'd declined, saying
she needed to do it herself.

So, we were en route back to Ketchikan—unan-
nounced. No one knew where we'd gone. The public
only knew I'd canceled four sold-out shows at the end
of my most successful tour to date, and that Lexie had
vanished with me, and I'd gone totally radio silent for
a month—highly unusual for someone as active on
social media as I was.

I'd had offers before, of course, from some of the
most highly sought-after publicists and social media
gurus to manage my accounts for me, promising in-
creased viewership and revenue, but I'd always declined.
I wanted my socials to remain authentically and or-
ganically mine, run by me personally. So, when I fell
off the face of the earth to sort out the love of my life
and the future of our relationship, it meant my socials
were silent as well.

I didn't care.

I'd post an update when I was ready, and my fans would be there, hungry to know what I'd been up to, and I figured I'd probably release some surprise new music or something.

It was a long, long flight from the South Pacific to Alaska; we stopped to refuel in Hawaii, and spent a day there shopping, as incognito as we could be.

Finally, after almost two days of travel, we were on the ferry from the Ketchikan airport. I was wearing my ball cap pulled low and mirrored aviators despite the overcast day, and Lexie was, well, just Lexie. Ultra mini denim skirt with scarlet fishnet stockings and knee-high black leather shitkicker boots, a loose, flowy silk blouse with no sleeves and a wildly plunging neckline showing the entire inner swell of her cleavage, bold smoky eye makeup, and her hair done in stiff spikes every which way, the tips temporarily dyed bright pink.

She was feeling herself, she claimed. Whatever that meant, I wasn't sure, but I did know that she seemed looser, more relaxed, and more comfortable with herself. I also knew she looked hot as fuck, and despite having spent the whole past month screwing until our privates ached, I still wanted to bend her over the railing and fuck her through the fishnets, under which I knew for a fact she wasn't wearing anything. Probably to tempt me to do exactly what I was considering.

"Down boy," Lexie murmured.

I chuckled. "How'd you know what I was thinking?" She glanced pointedly downward, and I realized I'd sprung a half-stiffie, tenting the front of my jeans. "Oh. Well, shit, woman, you can't blame me, when you're wearin' that."

"Excuse me?" A little girl's voice. I turned my body away and glanced down at the owner of the voice—a little girl of eight or so, with an eager but shy smile, and a CD copy of my very first album. "Are you Myles and Lexie?"

I grinned, and knelt to be level with her. "Sure are, darlin'."

Lexie knelt with me, keeping her knees pressed tight together and balancing precariously on her heeled boots. "Hi, sweetheart. Are you a fan of Myles?"

She held up the album. "Uh-huh. Big time. And you, too." She pointed back at her mom and dad and brother, watching from a distance, smiling. "We're on vacation, and this was in my backpack by accident, and then I saw you guys and I was hoping you could both sign it for me."

I pulled the fat black Sharpie I always carried in my back pocket, handed it to Lexie. "You first, babe."

Lexie signed carefully, hesitantly, as if she wasn't quite sure she was supposed to be signing an autograph. "Here." She pulled it back. "Wait, what's your name?"

The girl's grin was ecstatic. "Alexandra."

Lexie laughed, a bright happy sound. "No way! Mine too!"

"Really? I thought your name was just Lexie."

"Nope, Lexie is short for Alexandra." Lex added the girl's name, and an inscription: *From one Alexandra to another. Follow your dreams!*

"Can I tell everyone to call me Lexie, too?"

Lex laughed. "You sure can. I mean, I think it's a pretty cool name."

Alexandra turned to me, her eyes big. "I've listened to this CD so many times it has scratches on it and my mom says she's sick of it which she didn't think was possible because it's so good."

"You know, I think I have something very, very special I'd like to give you." I grabbed my duffel bag and dug inside, found what I was looking for and showed it to her. "This is something no one on the whole planet has ever seen or heard, because this CD is one of only three ever printed. It's all the songs Lexie and I have ever sung together, all in one place." I opened it, wrote her name on the inside of the liner, and then signed it. Closed it, gave it to her. "That, my dear, is going to be worth a *lot* of money someday, be-cause we're not making it publicly available, like ever."

Alexandra's eyes were wider than ever. "Really?"

I showed her the other two copies. "These three are it. I'm keeping one, Lexie's keeping the other, and you have that one. That's it. Forever and ever."

She frowned. "You're not making a CD together?"

"Oh, we will, and someday soon, I hope," I said. "But that's not a real CD, it's just recordings of the different times we've performed together. It's kind of like if you recorded yourself singing your favor-ite song on your mom and dad's computer, and then made a CD out of it. And that's why it's so special."

She couldn't believe it. She didn't seem to know whether to want to jump up and down out of sheer excitement, or to be overwhelmed. So she settled for clutching it to her chest. "Oh, thank you, thank you, thank you!" She looked at Lexie and then me. "Are you guys in love?"

Lexie was the first to answer. "We sure are."

"Are you gonna get married?"

I met Lexie's eyes. "Yeah, I do believe we will."

Lexie's turn to go wide-eyed. "We will?"

I reached into my duffel bag again, pulled out something I'd bought while we'd been on tour. I turned to Alexandra and showed it to her without let-ting Lexie see. "Wanna help me?"

Her eyes were so wide I thought they'd pop out. "Uh-huh."

"When I get to one knee, you show it to her. Okay?"

"Okay."

"Ready?"

"Ready."

"One…two…three." I turned to face Lexie, fell one to knee, and Alexandra held up the opened ring box. "Marry me, Lex."

Lexie shook her head, hands on her mouth. I heard awwws and sighs from the rest of the ferry, and knew this was being recorded and photographed. She nodded, eyes wet. "Yes, Myles. Yes. Of course, yes."

"I know it's soon and it's crazy, but I love you and I know this is what I want for my life. You, always and only you, every day for the rest of my life. We can be engaged as long as you want. Just marry me."

She laughed. "I already said yes, Myles."

I took the ring and slid it on Lexie's finger. Turned to wink at little Alexandra, eyes wide and starry with romance. "Thanks for helping me propose, Alexandra. It was perfect."

"Did you know?" she asked Lexie.

I laughed and said, "*I* didn't even know until this moment."

Alexandra tried to give Lexie the ring box, but

Lexie shook her head and pressed it into Alexandra's hands. "Keep it. And when you get older and some-one breaks your heart, look at this box and remember that true love is real. Okay?"

We stood up, and Alexandra held the ring box and the CD in shaky hands. She smiled at us. "Thank you *so* much."

"Of course, honey," Lexie said. "And thank *you*. You helped make this the best day of my life."

The girl ran back to her family, chattering a mile a minute in a high-pitched squeal of disbelieving excitement.

Lexie turned to me, turning her hand this way and that to look at the sparkle on the diamond. "Holy shit, Myles. This thing is *huge*."

I admired the ring on her hand; it had been breathtaking in the store but was even more so on her hand. "Four carat central diamond, with another carat and a half of stones around the setting."

She gasped. "Dear lord, Myles. It must have cost a fortune."

I just shrugged. "Don't you know, babe? I'm flush. Besides...I'd go broke giving you everything you want and deserve."

She leaned against me. "I can't believe you just proposed spur of the moment, on a ferry, with a fan."

I laughed. "Me either. But that thing was burning a hole in my bag, and it just seemed…right."

"It was perfect." She held up her hand again. "Wow. Just…wow." She turned in my arms to gaze up at me. "When did you know you'd propose?"

"The moment I heard you say the words 'I love you,'" I said. "It was just a matter of when, at that point."

She was quiet a while. "I'm one of those odd girls who didn't spend her whole life dreaming of a wedding. I suppose you can imagine why."

"We have all the time in the world for you start dreaming, Lex."

She shook her head. "That's just the thing. I don't need all the time in the world. I don't want a big production with, like, swans and a castle reception and all that shit." She gazed up at me. "I can tell you what I what want right now."

"Okay. I'm listening."

"Get the guys here—in Ketchikan, as soon as possible. I'll get Torie and Poppy here, and we'll have it on the roof of Badd Kitty. I just want to say I do and become Lexie North as soon as possible. We just had our honeymoon, so we're just doing it backward, right?"

"You want to take my name." I said it as a statement but meant it as a question.

She laughed. "Surprising to me, too. I wrote a paper for a women's studies class at Sarah Lawrence about how women taking men's names is an archaic and outmoded tradition that should be ended." She sighed. "And here I am, madly in love with you, and I can't wait to take your name so the world knows I'm your wife." She cackled. "Wife. My god. A word I never, *ever* thought would apply to me."

"That's really how you want to be married? As soon as possible, here in Ketchikan? Just family and friends and a little ceremony on the roof?"

She leaned against my chest, watching the waves clap against the bow of the ferry as we came around to dock. "Yeah. And then we can go on tour together."

"The guys have been talking about how cool it would be to redo some of our songs as a male-female duet. Write new ones as a five-piece, you on guitar and uke, us singing together. Some with me on lead vocals, some with you on lead vocals."

"I never wanted to insert myself into your career, Myles."

I laughed. "Did you not hear what I said?" I touched her chin. "The *guys* suggested it—not me. They *want* to expand. They want to update our sound. They want *you*."

"You're telling the whole real truth? I can't

believe they want me in the band, especially after all the drama I put you guys through on tour."

I sighed. Tugged out my phone and brought up a four-way FaceTime. The boat docked and we disembarked as the lines rang and the guys popped on one by one. I moved us to the side of the pier. "Hey, fellas."

A chorus of hellos.

"Once again, you're calling all four of us at once. Means you've got something to announce," Jupiter said.

I pulled the phone back to bring Lexie into the picture, and she held up her left hand.

"Surprise!" she said, grinning ear to ear.

"No fuckin' way!" Brand said. "That's wicked cool, guys. Congrats."

Lexie took the phone from me. "That's not the real reason we're calling, though. And by the way, you're the first to know. It literally just happened minutes ago."

"So what's the real reason?" Zan asked.

"Myles was just telling me you guys want *me* to officially join the band. And I need to hear it from you, because I don't quite believe him."

"Better believe it," Jupiter said. "We've been talking about it ever since the UK shows were canceled. As a band, we've sort of gotten stagnant with our sound, and it's time to change it up anyway. I'm bored as fuck of hearing Myles sing all the damn time. Plus, having a pretty lady on tour would be nice, and goddamn but you're easy on the eyes, you know? Plus, you're talented as hell. So yes, Lexie, we as a band have collectively decided we want you to join."

"We've even decided on a name," Brand said. "The North Band."

Lexie, newly in tune with her emotions, got all misty. "I don't know what to say."

"You say yes, that's what," Zan said. "Duh."

She nodded, giddy, grinning ear to ear. "Yes! We're The North Band."

They all howled and cheered, and even I felt a little choked up. "You guys are the best, you know it?" I said, taking the phone back. "All right, we gotta go. We've got to family to see and lots of news to share."

"Wait!" Lexie snatched my phone from me. "You guys have to get the next flight you can up to Ketchikan. We're having a small informal wedding as soon as possible."

"Holy shit," Jupiter said. "All right. We're all in LA at the moment, so we'll catch a flight up."

I took my phone back. "Cancel that—I'll call Callahan and Murphy and reroute them to LAX. They'll pick you up."

"Sweet. The private jet. I love that thing," Brand sighed.

"All right, see you guys soon." I waved, there were goodbyes, and the call ended. I smirked at Lexie. "There. See?"

She palmed my cheek. "You've changed my life in every possible way, you know that?"

"No more than you have mine." I glanced up and saw a huge pickup truck with knobby off-road tires, a lift kit, and a thick black bull bar slide into a parking lot nearby. "There's our ride—time to go."

She was suddenly nervous as she realized it was Lucas and her mom.

I squeezed her hand. "Lex, relax. The conversation will happen when *you're* ready. And I promise you, it will be okay."

She nodded. "I'm just scared to tell her."

"You felt better after telling me, right?"

"Yeah, but that was different. She's going to take it personally, and I...shit, I can't think about it right now or I'll fall apart. Let's just focus on the good news—we're engaged and I'm in the band."

I hugged her one-armed as I guided us over to Lucas's truck. "It's good news all around, babe."

Lucas and Liv met us on the sidewalk, and I tossed Lexie's and my bags into the truck bed, shaking Lucas's hand while Lexie hugged her mom, and then we traded.

Lexie was keeping her left hand down, hiding it.

Liv didn't want to let go of Lexie. "I'm so glad to see you," she said. "I didn't think we'd see you again for a long time. And then the tour got canceled and no one knew what was going on, and I was so worried."

Lexie brushed her mom's cheeks. "We just needed time away from everything to work things out. I had some things to deal with so we could figure out our relationship."

Liv searched her daughter's face, eyes sharp, insightful. "So, you're…you're okay? You guys figured it out?"

Lexie let a grin break over her face as she held up her hand to show her mother. "I'd say so, yes."

Liv gasped, hand over her mouth. "No!" She took Lexie's hand and examined the diamond, eyes wide. "Really?"

"Just happened on the ferry here, actually," Lexie said. "It was so sweet. I'll tell you all about it later."

Liv hugged Lexie again, crying. "I'm so happy for you. You don't know how happy. I wanted this for you so bad."

"We're getting married while we're here," Lexie said. "Like, in the next few days. Just a little family thing."

"Ya'll ain't messin' around, are you?" Lucas rumbled. "Congrats, you two. Happy for ya."

Liv's eyes were searching Lexie. "There's something else, isn't there?"

Lexie shielded her emotions—I watched her do it. "There are two things. One I can say now, the other is for later. Myles and his band have officially invited me to join them, so now we're The North Band."

Liv looked even more thrilled. "Oh my god, that's amazing!" She looked at me. "Thank you, Myles. More than I can say, thank you."

I shook my head. "That part was the guys. I wanted Lex to have her own thing, but the guys overruled me. They want her with us. And honestly, it's the most logical evolution of our band and our sound. She's joined us on tour, we've sampled our sound a few times, and this is the right thing. It's gonna be amazing. And it's all her. I just helped her see that it was what she needed to do."

"What's the other thing?" Liv asked.

Lexie shook her head. "That's a conversation for another time. Soon, but in private."

Liv looked worried. "I don't like the sound of that."

Lexie shrugged, holding back nerves and tears. "Later, Mom, okay? Please?"

Liv nodded. "Okay, whatever you want."

The next day we spent the time making the rounds with the ring and the news of the band, meeting up with everyone. Liv had a client to meet with early and Lucas had a local hike he was guiding, so we slept in and had a leisurely breakfast.

Lexie was quiet as we ate.

"What's on your mind? I asked.

"A lot." She shrugged. "Talking to mom when she gets back."

"What else? I can see you're chewing on somethin'."

She nodded. "I was thinking. I know you've got the buildings you own in Dallas, but..." She sighed, tried again. "It's hard for me to do this—to ask you for something."

"Anything. You know that."

"I know, but I've never asked anyone for anything in my life. So this is just...hard." She swirled coffee in her mug. "Can we, or I, or something...get a little apartment here in Ketchikan? Just so I can visit my family?"

I took her hand. "I've already been texting with Zane and Dru. And in fact, your mom's client this morning is actually me. All those emails I was working on, on the way here? It was with your mom, Zane, and Dru, looking for a place for us up here."

She blinked. "Wait. Really?" A frown. "Mom and Dru as realtors, but why Zane?"

"Because him and Rome have a side hustle as builders and renovators, with Lucas helping out as needed. Your mom and Dru found a place, but it's gonna need some TLC, and so she and Zane and Rome are checking it out today, going over plans. They're coming here afterwards and they're gonna show us their ideas." I grinned. "It was gonna be another surprise, but this works, too."

"I know you love Texas, Myles. I don't want to keep you away, I just…"

I snorted. "I grew up there, sure, and it'll always have a special place in my heart because of that, but there's really no one there for me anymore. It was just my home base out of convenience, because it was what I knew. Here? Your family is here. Crow is here." I held both of her hands. "Of *course* this is where I'd want us to make our…" I held my breath. "Our home."

She swallowed, tearing up. "Damn you, Myles North, you're making me so fucking emotional all the time. Thank you."

"You really think I'd settle for a shitty little apartment? Hell no. We're doing this right. This is your home, my home—*our* home. So it's gonna be fuckin' pimp. And you're gonna make it ours. Okay?"

A few hours later, Zane, Rome, and Dru left Liv's condo with sketches and plans in hand, our new home taking shape—a warehouse conversion like Zane and Mara had. Just…on steroids.

And then it was just Liv, Lexie, and me.

And we all knew what was next. Liv sensed there was something, but she didn't know what.

Liv eyed Lex, sighing. "So. Is this a good time for the other thing you had to tell me?"

Lex swallowed hard. "Yeah, I…I guess. It's not… it's not an easy thing I'm going to tell you, Mom."

I prepared to stand up. "I think you guys need privacy for this."

Lexie snatched my wrist and gripped me so tightly my bones ground together. "No, I…I don't think I can do this without you, Myles."

I sat down. "Okay. Whatever you need."

Slowly, then, haltingly, Lexie told Liv her story, almost verbatim as she'd told it to me, clutching my hand in a death grip. Sparing no details. She cried through much of the telling, but remained strong. Liv seemed unable to process what she was being told. When Lexie was finally finished Liv sat, stunned, tears streaming freely down her face.

"Can…Can I have a moment?" she whispered.

She didn't wait for an answer—shot to her feet and beelined for the bathroom. She was in there several minutes, and emerged with a box of Kleenex and red eyes, no more composed than when she'd gone in. "Lexie, I...I don't even know what to say. I had no idea."

"I know you didn't, Mom. I hid it from you, from everyone."

Liv cracked, sobbed. "I should have known. I should have *known*. Oh god, oh god, Lexie." She peered at her daughter through a screen of tears. "I'm sorry, Alexandra. I'm so, so sorry."

Lexie left my side and sat on the love seat by her mother. "It's not your fault, Mom."

"Yes, it is. I should have known."

Lexie sighed. "You know, there is a part of me that wants to blame it on you. But I can't. I hid it from you, and I'm a damn good liar. You couldn't have known."

Liv shook her head. "It's not okay. I'm not okay with this."

"Neither am I, Mom," Lexie said. "But I have to learn to be. Getting it out is a big step. It's not a secret anymore—and I've been keeping that a secret since I was thirteen. I'm free of it, now. Myles is to thank for that, honestly." She smiled at me. "It's going to take time to heal, for me, and for you, and for us."

"It explains why sometimes you were so sharp with me, almost angry," Liv said. "I could never understand, and now I do." She sighed, long and deep and painful. "I am so, so sorry I didn't protect you from that, Lexie. I should have. I feel like if I'd been paying closer attention, less busy with my career, with your sisters, with my marriage I'd have seen something…"

"There's no point playing what-if, Mom," Lexie said. "You think I haven't spent the last eight years playing what-if? What if I hadn't insisted on music lessons? What if I hadn't said this or done that? What if something I did or said made him think I wanted it? What if I'd said no? What if… what if I hadn't been too confused and scared to say no? What if I'd told you? What if I'd let you see how badly I was hurting? There's a million, billion what-ifs in a situation like this, Mom, and not a single one of them will change what happened. We just have to move forward."

"I don't know that I'll ever forgive myself," Liv whispered. "Four years. Every week for *four fucking years*." She hissed the last part, her use of a curse word a testament to the depth of her pain and guilt. "I'm so fucking sorry, Alexandra."

Lexie wrapped her mother in a hug, and they stayed like that for a long time. Eventually, both of them sniffling and teary-eyed and clutching Kleenex, Lexie held her mother's eyes. "I'm going to be okay, Mom. I survived it, I'm past it. I have Myles. I have you, and Charlie, and Cassie, and this whole crazy clan of people up here. I'm in a band! A world-touring, hugely popular, Grammy-winning band. I'm going to have a home, here, near you guys. It's going to be okay, Mom. It will."

Liv nodded. "You've had all these years to deal with this, Lex. I'm just now finding out. It's going to take me time to work through it." She took a deep breath; held it, let it out slowly. "Thank you for telling me."

Lexie rubbed her face. "You and Myles are the only ones who know. And I'd like to keep it that way, for now. I don't think the other girls need to know. Not yet, anyway. And now that Myles and I are getting married soon, I want this whole time to be happy. But I knew—I just knew you needed to know." She held Liv's arms. "And...I don't blame you, okay? I don't hold anyone responsible but him. He was a predator, and I was his prey. It happened. It's over. We move forward. We see therapists. And we just live and be happy, okay? Don't blame yourself, Mom. Please."

Liv nodded again, trying to regain her composure, and mostly succeeding. "I'll try. And yes, we'll be seeing a therapist, because you don't heal from something like this just by talking about it a few times. And god knows my mom guilt is going to keep me awake at night until I'm able to deal with it."

"Don't let it, Mom. Promise me."

Liv shook her head. "I can't do that, my love. I'm your mother. My sole purpose in life was to raise you and keep you safe, and I failed—I failed *huge*, in the worst way I could have. It's a burden I'm going to have to carry, knowing I failed you that way. I hear what you're saying, and I appreciate, but you can't shield me from the guilt I'm going to feel. That I *should* feel." She sniffed. "We'd just better not tell Lucas or Crow. Because if either of those two ever found out..."

"If any of the men in this family found out," Lexie said, "it would be ugly. And for as much as I've daydreamed about the horrible ways I'd like that man to suffer for what he did to me, I won't allow it. I won't dwell on it. It won't fix me. It won't heal me, it won't take away the pain I felt, and still feel."

"You know how hard it is for me to not hunt him down?" I said, my first words in a long time. "I want to peel his fuckin' skin off. But I know Lex is right." I sighed. "I probably should let you know, though, Lex—I had a PI find him. He's been in jail for the last four years, and will spend the rest of his life in jail. Someone spoke up, finally, and decades of abuse came to light. He's gone."

Lex nodded. "I got a letter from a lawyer when it all started coming out. But I couldn't face any of it. I was too scared and embarrassed and ashamed and... shit, a lot of things—to be able to be part of that trial. It would be everyone finding out, and no one knew, and I just wanted it to stay that way. I never did let myself find out what eventually happened to him after the trial—I couldn't face the prospect of him not being convicted." She shook herself, tendered me a small smile. "So, thank you. I feel like the door to everything is closed."

"I hope you know I would have contracted a hit on him, if he wasn't in jail," I said.

Lexie frowned. "Myles."

I shrugged. "Not sure that's much of an exaggeration. I still know people in the AzTex." I let out a breath. "But I've been assured that child molesters and rapists…well, let's just say they don't fare well in prison. So he'll get his due…for a long time."

Lexie shook her head. "Myles, thank you for wanting to avenge me, but I just want to forget it all. I don't want revenge. I just want to live my life and be happy." She reached out, and I moved to perch on the edge of the love seat. "Just love me, Myles. That'll more than make up for it."

I smiled. "That's easy, babe."

Liv eyed Lexie. "He called you babe."

Lexie grinned, laughed. "Yeah, I'm over that. As long as it's not some smarmy old dude talking down to me, Myles using words to show me how much he loves me is something I'm more than okay with."

Liv clapped her hands. "So. Happy things. Can

I please, *please* be allowed to go a little crazy on this wedding?"

Lexie pretended to be annoyed. "No frilly shit, Mom. No swans, and none of that something old, something new, something blue stuff. You know me. Have fun, but...no frilly bullshit."

Liv laughed. "Yes, yes. But you have to let me go a little crazy. You're my first daughter to get married. Cassie and Ink and Charlie and Crow all say they're waiting awhile and see no need for the ceremony." She rolled her eyes to show what she thought about that. "So now I get to plan a wedding, and I'm excited."

"Ohh boy," Lex laughed. "Here we go."

I poked her. "Have fun with it, babe. I'll give you my Amex Black card, and you can go fuckin' nuts." I leveled a look at Liv. "I mean that. Whatever you can convince her to go for, do it."

"A what card?" Lexie said.

Liv's eyes were wide. "ultraexclusive, truly unlimited credit. Like, buy literally anything."

I dug said card out of my wallet and handed it over. "See how much damage you can do, ladies." I kissed Lex. "I wanna go jam with Crow. Okay?"

She nodded. "I'm gonna stay and talk to Mom. See how much of your money I can spend."

I touched her lips. "Ours, baby. Remember that."

She kissed me back, and I had to pull away before I got carried away. When I left, Lex and Liv had their heads together, and I had a feeling the idea of a small family wedding this week was a goner. But I didn't care. As long as that woman was my wife at the end of it, it would be worth the wait and the cost. I'd sell off a condo building or two, if I had to, but I doubted they could do *that* much damage.

My wife.

Lexie Goode, my wild goddess, was going to be my wife.

Suddenly, my life had gotten even better.

EPILOGUE

Torie

MY PHONE RANG IN THE MIDDLE OF MY SHIFT, AND MY boss heard it before I could silence it.

"No cell phones on floor," he growled at me in his thick Albanian accent. "You know this."

"Sorry, Mr. Sokoli. I was running late this morning and forgot it was in my pocket."

He knew I was one of his best waitresses, so he just grumbled in Albanian and waved me off. "Table eight wants more coffee."

I hustled with the coffeepot, making sure to at least silence the phone. I felt it vibrate with a voicemail, but I got double-sat again because the girl in the back section was new and couldn't handle more than three tables at a time, so I was busy running my two tables at once in her section, plus the six tables in progress in my own. By the time we closed and I got through all my side-work, it was after eleven at night and I hadn't even had time for dinner, so my stomach was growling. I counted out my tips, tipped out the bus boy, pocketed the rest, and headed for my bike.

By which I mean bicycle. The old Camry of Mom's I'd been driving since I was sixteen—handed down from Mom to Charlie, to Cassie, to Lexie, and then to me, had over a hundred and fifty thousand miles on it—and it had finally died. Dead, done, buh-bye. It needed a new transmission, which Mr. Sokoli, who knew a bit about cars, told me would cost more to fix than the thing was worth. So I was stuck using a twenty-year-old ten-speed I'd gotten for ten bucks at the Salvation Army.

Two roommates had moved out with boyfriends, which left Jillie, Leighton, and me paying extra rent, and things had been dead lately, and…well, the truth is, I was just broke. I had two hundred and nineteen dollars in my bank account, another hundred and five in my pocket, and rent was due tomorrow and it was three hundred. That would leave me with…shit, math is hard…twenty-four dollars to my name. For food, for everything I would need until my next shift, and I was scheduled to be off for two days. I'd have to pick up some shifts. Whenever I could, I worked doubles and extra shifts and even picked up some shifts at the cafe where Leighton worked, washing dishes for cash. But I was always a day late and a dollar short.

I'd gotten partial scholarships to local colleges, and Mom had made an open-ended offer to pay for community college if I wanted, and I'd tried that for a semester, but I just...I had no clue what I would study, so why waste the time and money? I was turning twenty in a week and had no education beyond high school. No talents, like Cassie with dance or Charlie with being, like a super genius with five degrees or whatever, and now Lexie was this world superstar musician all of a sudden, and even Poppy was like the most talented artist I'd ever seen—she took photographs and painted over them, used magazine cutouts and feathers and just about anything that inspired her, and she would embellish the photograph until it was this whole new thing.

All my sisters had talents and skills and careers and futures.

And then there was me. Torie. The middle child. You'd think Lexie would be the middle, since she had Charlie and Cass above her and Poppy and me below, but somehow I was the middle girl. The quiet one. The one who never went out for the school play, never did volleyball or soccer or music lessons, or dance. I didn't paint or sing, I didn't excel at academics. I had nothing. I just…was.

I waited tables and smoked pot with Leighton and Jillie. I didn't even have a boyfriend. I'd never had a boyfriend. Max didn't count—we fooled around when we were stoned, but it was just fooling around, and I'd told him I wasn't going to sleep with him. I wasn't wasting *that* on a stoner loser like Max. I say that with affection, because I'm a stoner loser too, and he's been my best friend since third grade. But I don't love him and so we just fool around.

The bike ride home was long and cold because it was late and I'd forgotten my hoodie this morning, and then it started drizzling and by the time I got home I was soaked and freezing my tits off. Leighton and Jillie were watching *The Last Unicorn* for the billionth time, so I jumped in the shower to warm up.

And by the time I got out, I was dead tired and went straight to bed.

I forgot about listening to the voicemail from earlier in the day, or even looking to see who'd called. My phone never even made it to the charger.

So when I woke up the battery on my phone was dead. I juiced it up enough to turn it on and saw the call had been from Lexie. The voicemail was like, four minutes long, and that just sounded super boring, so I just called Lexie back.

"Torie!" Bright, chipper, happy. "Did you get my voicemail?

I sighed. "Why are you so loud?"

She laughed. "Are you stoned already?"

"No, I wish. I just woke up. I saw your voicemail, but it was like an hour long so I figured I'd just call you. What's up?"

"You really should've listened to it," she said, "because now I have to say it all over again. But it's better to say it directly to you than on a voicemail anyway, so…the story, Torie, is I'm getting married."

I blanked out. "Uh. To who?"

"Myles North."

"The country dude you were on stage with?"

"Yeah, him."

"Dude, he's hot."

"I know!"

"You're marrying him?"

She laughed. "Yeah, I know, it's a little sudden but it's, like, the most amazing thing ever."

"How long have you known him?"

"Like, four months."

"Lex, that's crazy."

She laughed again. "I know. But I'm stupid in love with the man, and we're going on tour as The North Band this fall, and I'm doing it as Mrs. Myles North, thank you very much."

"I'm happy for you."

She snickered. "You super sound it, Tor."

"I am!" I tried to sound chipper, but I'm just a mellow person, and I just woke up and I'm *not* a morning person. "I'm happy for you. For real. Congratulations." I thought of a useful question. "Um. When's the wedding?"

"That's the fun part. In two weeks!"

I coughed my surprise. "Wait, what?"

"Yeah. That's the real reason I called. You have to get to Ketchikan for the wedding."

"Uh. I have work."

"Take it off. I'm your sister and I'm getting married."

"I can't afford a plane ticket."

"I'll buy you one."

"No, no," I muttered. "I'll figure it out."

She sighed. "Torie, for real. We'll fly you up. Please let me."

"Would you accept that, if it was the other way around?"

Her silence was telling. "No."

"All right, then. I'll find my own way to Alaska." I laughed. "Why Alaska?"

She giggled. "Ask Mom. She was the one to move up here. But once you're up here, you never want to leave."

"Great. I'll get stuck in B-F-E, Alaska, and have no future in the middle of nowhere."

"God, Torie, you're such a downer," she griped.

"Leighton calls me Tor-Eeyore."

"Oh—my—*god*, that's perfect. Tor-Eeyore." She cackled. "I'm calling you that, now."

"No, you're not." I huffed. "Shouldn't have told you."

"But ya did!" She sing-songed. "Anyway. Two weeks from today, that's the date. Be here. If you get stuck in like Kansas, call me. I'll have Myles send his jet down to pick you up."

"He has a private jet?"

"Yep."

"You bitch." I laughed. "You had to snag a rich and famous dude?"

She laughed with me. "Right? Luckiest girl in the world, right here." A serious pause, then. "I love you, Tor. Get here. And ask for help if you need it. I know the feeling, but ask. Okay? Don't just be stuck."

"Yeah, yeah. Love you too." I picked at a scab on my knee. "Is Poppy coming?"

"Yeah, she's driving. She met some guy apparently, and they're making it a road trip."

"Poppy has a boyfriend?" I asked. "No fucking way. I thought she swore off men forever after the last guy. I was half convinced she'd turn lesbian."

"I know, right? But yeah, I guess. I don't know, she's cagey about it. I guess we'll meet him at the wedding, though." A pause, and I knew what was coming. "Are you gonna bring Max?"

I sputtered. "Max? Hell no. He's a friend. But not the kind of friend you bring to a wedding. It's never been like that."

"Didn't you lose your virginity to him?"

I blushed, swallowed hard. "To Max?" I scoffed. "No."

Leave it at that, Lexie—please leave it at that.

"Tor?"

"Lex?"

"Are you still a virgin?"

"Shut up."

"You are!" she squealed. "Oh my god! I thought for sure you'd done it with Max."

"He wants to," I muttered, hating this conversation with all my soul. "But I'm not in love with him. I don't even really *like* him—not like that. He's just a friend. And it's fun messing around. But if and when I give a man my virginity, I want it to mean something. I've waited this long, I mean god, I'm almost twenty. Practically an old maid. If it happens now, it's going to be meaningful."

"Your first time probably won't be this magical thing, Tor. I'm not trying to ruin any dreams here, but—"

My face was on fire. "I know, okay? I'm not some little girl daydreaming of Prince Charming, here."

"Tor, we gotta talk when you get up here."

"Not about this we don't."

"Fine, fine. I'll drop it. I can see you blushing from here. But...promise me you won't change your mind on this?" She sounded oddly serious. "Promise me, swear to me, you won't just give it away to the first hot, charming guy who kisses you just right. Make it worthwhile. *Promise* me."

I was baffled. "You sound like you're about to cry, Lex."

"Shut the fuck up and swear." She was crying, softly, and choking it back, but I could tell she was emotional. And Lex *NEVER* cried.

Weird.

"Yeah, yeah—I promise."

"*Victoria.*"

"I swear on Dad's grave it'll mean something, okay?" I was shaken by her sudden intensity on this. "Lex, what's—?"

"Another time. You just keep that promise, sis. That's what matters, here." And now she was bright and chipper again. "And...that you get your cute little butt up here for my wedding."

"My butt is neither small nor cute, I'm afraid," I said. "So don't go buying any size zero bridesmaid dress for me, because I done gained a few, Lex."

"Oh shut up, I saw you six months ago and you're

smaller than me. And no bridesmaid dresses. We're going informal."

"Thank fuck."

She laughed. "I gotta go."

"Me too. I need breakfast, and to process that my sister is getting married to a famous country singer with his own jet—and figure out how I'm getting to Alaska."

"Tor—"

"I'm not taking your money, so shut up. I love you. I'll see you in two weeks."

"Okay, okay. Love you. Bye."

I hung up, left the phone on the charger, and went in search of breakfast…and ideas.

Could I ride a bicycle to Alaska?

That was looking like my best option from here.

Oh lordy.

Alaska, for a wedding.

And me too stubborn to ask for help. Could I get a bus ride with twenty-four bucks?

Why, Lexie? Why now?

But, one way or another, I'd be there for my sister.

If only to find out why the hell she was so worked up about my virginity. That story alone would be worth the trip.

Alaska, here I come.

Somehow.

The Black Room
(With Jade London):
Door One

Door Two

Door Three

Door Four

Door Five

Door Six

Door Seven

Door Eight

The One Series
The Long Way Home

Where the Heart Is

There's No Place Like Home

Badd Brothers:
Badd Motherf*cker

Badd Ass

Badd to the Bone

Good Girl Gone Badd

Badd Luck

Badd Mojo

Big Badd Wolf

Badd Boy

Badd Kitty

Badd Business

Badd Medicine

Badd Daddy

The world of *Wounded:*
Wounded
Captured

The world of *Stripped:*
Stripped
Trashed

The world of *Alpha:*
Alpha
Beta
Omega
Harris: Alpha One Security Book 1
Thresh: Alpha One Security Book 2
Duke Alpha One Security Book 3
Puck: Alpha One Security Book 4
Lear: Alpha One Security Book 5
Anselm: Alpha One Security Book 6

The Houri Legends:
Jack and Djinn
Djinn and Tonic

The Madame X Series:
Madame X
Exposed
Exiled

Dad Bod Contracting:
Hammered
Drilled
Nailed
Screwed

Fifty States of Love:
Pregnant in Pennsylvania
Cowboy in Colorado
Married in Michigan

Goode Girls
For a Goode Time Call…
Not So Goode

Standalone titles:
Yours

Non-Fiction titles:
You Can Do It
You Can Do It: Strength
You Can Do It: Fasting

Jack Wilder Titles:
The Missionary

JJ Wilder Titles:
Ark

To be informed of new releases, special offers, and other Jasinda news, sign up for Jasinda's email newsletter.